THE DEMON'S DUE

Bedevilled AF, #5

DEBORAH WILDE

te da media inc.
vancouver

Issued in print and electronic formats.
ISBN: 978-1-998888-54-2 (paperback)
ISBN: 978-1-998888-55-9 (epub)

Chapter 1

The Brink tasted like ozone and fear, but I swallowed both as Alastair's fingers dug into my arm. While I might be done hiding my shedim side, I wasn't done being hunted.

I picked my way over patches of ice that bloomed into carpets of tiny flowers with sharp crystalline petals, a lifetime of running over uneven terrain saving me a twisted ankle on the slick ground. Crunching a lopsided carnation —Mother Nature's gas station flower—under my boot, I wondered whether Alastair's head would make that same satisfying noise when I killed him for good.

Operative Fleischer, champion of justice, had vanished the second the bloodsucking parasite blackmailed me into leaving—

I dropped my gaze from the mud-brown sky to the fortress looming ahead of us. The weathered gray stone walls were lined with crenellations and guard towers, while bushes with oversized thorns grew wild in the dry moat. Their barbs coiled like hungry serpents, waiting for unwary flesh to pierce.

Annoyingly, my eyes stung from the stench of pine cleaner that had followed us for the past half hour. The reek made as much sense as the floating reefs of bone-white coral resembling teeth we'd navigated in eerie silence.

Usually, trips to the Brink were anything but quick. Count on Alastair to have some dumb artifact that could whisk us from the rift through the Brink to the fortress like an overeager puppy with a full bladder bounding to its favorite tree.

Though even one second spent in his charming presence was an eternity too long. He'd forsaken any pretense of civility, exposing a man-shaped reservoir of spite and brutishness.

The handcuffs bit painfully into my wrists as he hauled me forward by the chain, his casual flick sending me lurching behind him. My stomach churned with revulsion at being reduced to a prisoner, a possession, while the weight of his control over me made me want to scream with rage, but I refused to give him the satisfaction.

Alastair didn't know it, but the restraints were overkill, given that the very sentience he was frog-marching me toward had already stripped me of my Eishei Kodesh abilities and left my connection to Cherry Bomb on the fritz.

Yes, I'd forfeited my blue flame magic for an hour, but I'd expected the pay up to happen either when I first wagered it days ago or at some random innocuous time. Not that some asshole magic guardian would stalk me and find the exact worst moment to snatch my abilities away.

My captor pounded on the fortress's metal-reinforced wooden gate with an expression of savage triumph, and that old adage about not counting chickens flitted through my head.

I still had a shot. One requiring extraordinary luck, insanely perfect timing, and possibly a minor miracle, but technically, still a shot.

But with my shedim side fading in and out, my Eishei Kodesh magic in absentia, and the nulling cuffs squashing the hope that I'd be able to do anything even if I got my powers back, I was swimming in a catastrophe cocktail. My brain had locked up completely, like a computer with too many fatal errors. No reboot and no strategic thinking.

Sensing my distress, the Brimstone Baroness tore through the staticky barrier separating us. Our link clicked into place like a dislocated joint popping back to where it belonged.

Cherry itched to tear that British bastard limb from limb for orchestrating horrors from his comfortable shadows. I forced the sudden toxic green of my eyes back to their regular light brown and ordered her to shove her hate down, because my jaw still throbbed from Alastair's backhanded blow when I'd attempted to bond over deadbeat supernatural parents.

Who could have guessed that while Calista had hidden her dhampir son, she'd also protected him, visiting as often as she could to not only train him with valuable survival skills, but simply spend time with him.

Alastair had stoked his hatred for the parties he believed responsible for his mother's death like precious glowing coals. To be fair, he had plenty of that emotion to go around, along with a list of every vampire who'd ever dissed or underestimated him.

"They'll get theirs when I have the power of a Prime and they don't," he'd said darkly.

Alastair's hand now flitted to a green camo canteen worn on a canvas shoulder strap, the uncharacteristic accessory first revealed when he lost his wool coat back in the bone reefs. BYOB? Supplies for a tailgate party? Picky about his food? In any case, he hadn't touched it yet, so perchance it was a boutique hemoglobin to be savored in celebration.

So long as he didn't try snacking on me.

With a shuddery creak, the gate opened into a courtyard. There was no one to greet us, which meant that either Daphne was out on sentience-related business or unavailable. Small things like being polite didn't bother Alastair anymore, so he walked right in.

I barely had one last glimpse of the giant bone wall stretching out in the distance before the gate slammed shut with a thud that made me jump. How was Shiny Jimmy doing? If I got the chance to see him on this visit from hell, I'd have to tell—

I swallowed. Ezra was a Prime. Even infected by whatever weird magic had spread from Rukhsana into him, he'd be healed by now.

"Move it." Alastair's broad British accent had a bladed edge. He pushed me past a clump of cacti and over a small arched bridge whose reflecting pool boasted lazily floating lotuses.

It was sunny in the courtyard, but I couldn't even enjoy a moment of warmth because while the sky was blue, it throbbed with malevolent mud-brown threads that sent shivers down my spine.

The sound of snipping grew louder, rhythmic and hungry like the clicking of a predator's teeth, its source revealed when we rounded a massive tangled rosebush.

Daphne, gatekeeper and arbiter of magic-seekers' fates, tipped up the brim of her straw gardener's hat with her gloved hand to coolly survey us. "How dumpster-chic," she said in her Brooklyn drawl and cut away some dead branches.

I didn't care about my disheveled, sweaty self. What did cleanliness matter when I planned to add bloodstains to the mix?

Alastair ran a hand over his once-beautifully tailored shirt that was now dirty and crumpled. A smear of grease marred his black stubbled jaw, but his undead fashionista self was visible in the quality of the torn cotton and the remaining misaligned pearl buttons.

He pushed me forward. "We're here for the test."

A muscle ticked in Daphne's jaw, but she yanked off her gloves, dropped the pruning shears, and stood up. Her ivory V-neck sweater and tailored slacks were spotless. Now, that was a magic feat. "Are you now?"

"After he removes these nulling cuffs," I said. There. Step one of a strategy.

Alastair hesitated.

The smile Daphne unfurled was venom wrapped in spun sugar. "I've never had someone bring a hostage cheerleader, but then again, there's a first time for everything." She shook her fists like pom-poms. "Do you require her to spell out your name letter by letter or will general encouragements suffice?"

The dhampir yanked the key out of his pocket.

My wrists burned even more as the metal fell away, though the numbness in my hands was a pleasant counterpart to that.

Better still, my Eishei Kodesh magic came flooding back.

A smile tugged at the corner of my mouth despite everything. My hour forfeit was up, and the gameboard had just shifted. I stepped through the doorway with renewed purpose.

"Shoes off," our hostess commanded.

I toed out of my ankle boots and settled myself on a comfy sofa under a bright tapestry of a hunting scene, letting my magic settle itself. Books overflowed their shelves, a fire crackled cheerily, and lush plants and wildflowers gave the air an earthy, humid tinge.

Daphne switched her gardening clogs for marabou feather slippers with satin-covered kitten heels. The hostess with the mostess.

Alastair positioned himself next to a tall rubber plant, wrapping the scrap of grimy fabric that had once been his tie around his knuckles and then sliding it off again. As if trying to reclaim some dignity after being reduced to socked feet.

White filmy curtains billowed out the open glass door behind him.

I longed to probe the dhampir with my synesthete vision in case I could see his weaknesses or any previous injuries that would give me an advantage, but I didn't dare.

Not because I didn't have his consent, but because I got the sense that fairness was important to the magic guardian, and as I was the supplicant, I would do nothing to cause offense and risk my shot at passing the test—i.e. the aforementioned minor miracle.

I pushed away the memory of the wriggling maggot that had been the last supplicant's name.

Daphne leaned against a long wooden table. When I'd been here last, it held a tea set, but it was currently covered with a soil-splattered plastic tarp, a preposterously sharp trowel that Sachie would demand buying info for, and seedling pots. "You can leave if you want, Aviva."

I rubbed my fingers, waking the numbness into such a searing pins-and-needles sensation that my breath hitched. "I wish to try for the power word."

Daphne blinked at me. "Really."

"Yup," I said.

"When you're still recovering from your forfeited Eishei Kodesh magic."

She knew that, huh?

"No time like the present." I swept a lank strand of hair out of my eyes.

"You were forcibly brought here." Daphne shook her head. "As outlined in Statute 7.B of the Threshold Protocols, 'No supplicant may petition for a power word under duress or constraint, physical or magical. The seeking must stem from genuine desire, freely formed and freely acted upon. Violation renders the test void and the petitioner subject to immediate expulsion—or, in cases of willful deception, permanent dissolution.'"

Dissolution? I swallowed. How omnipotent was the sentience? Because those cuffs had been the least of my problems. If Alastair missed the check-in with his vampire minions, they'd execute Secretary Pederson and frame my mother for it, along with her ordering Ezra to murder the operative Roman Whittaker.

All lies, but the photo Alastair had of my infernal form would convince Dmitri Kozlov that Michael would do anything to protect her own half-shedim abomination. She'd end up in Sector A, the top-secret maximum-security jail where people who colluded with demons or rogue vamps were sent.

Ezra would be hunted down, the investigation spreading to Silas's escape and potentially dragging Sachie, Darsh, and the entire Vancouver Maccabee chapter into that terrifying prison alongside the director.

Meantime, I'd be left breathing just long enough to watch it all unfold.

I weighed all that against what could be done to me now for lying about my situation. I had to come clean. "There's no cell service in the Brink, but is there some way for Alastair to contact his people and give the order that Secretary Pederson is not to be touched? That my mother is safe? I'll exercise my true free will if he does that."

"After I have the Luce." Alastair pronounced the word "lou-chay" like the Italian word for "light."

I frowned. "Is that the power word?"

"It's the name of the healing magic contained in it." Daphne placed her palm flat against the nearest wall, and a low, hungry rumble echoed through the room. "When you arrived," she said to Alastair, "you said 'We're here for the test.' That makes *both* of you the petitioners and *both* of you subject to the Threshold Protocol." She patted the scary wall like it was a favored pet. "But it's up to you."

He made the call, which amazingly connected, even putting it on speaker so we could ascertain for ourselves that he'd called off the hit.

One terrifying situation mitigated, but I still had to stop Alastair once and for all.

"I'm exercising my free will," I said, fighting to keep my voice steady. "I want to take this test."

Daphne crossed her arms and narrowed her eyes. "You swore the last time you showed up that you didn't want the power word." The charge, delivered in her Beastie Boys accent, would have been amusing if it didn't also come with a menacing glower that made both me and Cherry flinch.

"It's a woman's prerogative…" I smiled with false bravado.

My hostess toyed with the trowel. Why was I surrounded by people with violent urges?

My inner demoness admired how the sharp edge caught the light. Never mind.

"You can't refuse her." Alastair snapped a leaf off the rubber plant.

"Touch my plant again and I'll dig a hole where your dick should be and grow seedlings there instead," Daphne said conversationally.

The dhampir dropped the leaf and glared at me.

I sent up a silent plea for Daphne to not make this harder on me.

No one had successfully acquired the power word since the early twentieth century. Failure meant joining the vibrant bone wall community with no sense of myself, and no purpose but a cautionary tale.

But not to be given a shot at all to change this incredibly shitty day and take power back for myself? To rescue people important to me? I pumped a fist. "Goooo test!"

"We're wasting time." Alastair busted out his fangs. The manic hostile energy rolling off him didn't so much deter his commanding air as twist it into something feral.

Daphne pushed up her sleeve. Runes carved into her flesh glowed copper against her tanned skin. "You began this petition under murky conditions, so I'll let you know what my boss and I decide when we decide it. Now shut up."

I studied my abductor through slitted lids.

Alastair was the right-hand man in the most powerful vampire Mafia in existence, and no one, not even its leader, Natán Cardoso, had figured out he was only a halfie. Any uptick in the Brit's abilities, like siring an undead army, would convince everyone he *was* a Prime and confer scary levels of power upon him. He might even be able to steal the Kosher Nostra's command away from Natán.

I clenched my fists. The upheaval and damage he'd cause wouldn't just affect vampires.

Not only that, but should Alastair discover my sister orchestrated events leading to his mother's murder (with the killing blow dealt by Ezra, who would be absolutely healthy enough to defend himself when Alastair found out), then he'd target my sister and draw out her death, which would enrage Delacroix. Supernatural war would break out.

I gritted my teeth against the tingly feeling presaging my toxic green eyes. *Not* yet, *Baroness.*

Should Alastair be killed before the ritual happened, his minions would continue this mad quest to sire children, endlessly killing infernals to fuel a broken ritual.

Let the magic sentience that protected the power word dismantle every single vampire supplicant. I didn't give a shit. The thing is, Alastair murdered six half shedim to get the blood necessary for this.

It had taken years to find his perfect victims, including a thirteen-year-old boy, Aleksander, Secretary Pederson's nephew. Sadly, the one thing Alastair's undead followers had plenty of was time.

My gaze shot to the canteen, and a muscle ticked in my jaw. Fuck me.

How did Alastair fit six bodies' worth of blood into that? Was it TARDIS brand or had he magically concentrated the fluid down? I better not be expected to drink it or even touch it.

But what if that was my role as speaker of the power word? I could tell myself that I was giving those people's brutal murders purpose, but the idea of literally having their blood on my hands—or worse—made me gag.

You'll do this because you have to, mi cielo. Ezra's voice filled my head.

For a brief, wonderful second, I thought he was somehow psychically communicating with me, but the continued silence bounced off the walls, mocking me.

Daphne was still communing with the magic sentience, her lids closed and a shivery dark aura surrounding her like a force field, while Alastair remained fixated on her, awaiting the decision.

For the safety of half shedim, I had to murder all hope that this ritual worked.

Think it through, Fleischer. My understanding of the order of events was: get the power word, speak it during a dark magic ritual that Alastair performed in conjunction with the blood, and watch him reap the rewards.

That word was the delivery system of the healing magic, while the ritual defined the parameters of what specifically was to be healed.

Well, one did not simply bounce out of a dark magic blood ritual ready to rock and roll.

I blinked. Was that the solution? Strike once the ritual

was performed, but while Alastair still adjusted to his new super-vamp abilities?

I suspected I had a very small window of opportunity. Possibly seconds.

I'd have to phrase his murder afterward in such a way that the logical inference was the magic power word didn't work as advertised and killed him.

His followers bought their leader's bullshit that this ritual would work on *all* vampires versus one lucky recipient. Because they were desperate to believe. It sucked for them that they couldn't differentiate between faith born of desperation and utter self-delusion.

Regardless, that faith would not be extended to me. My claim had to be irrefutable, and for that, I had to be able to beat him.

Alastair did the ritual and died. Stick me in front of a top Yellow Flame lie detector or a vampire, and neither would claim I lied.

All I had to do was get an impossible power word.

Daphne leveled a long, dubious look from me to Alastair and opened her mouth.

I stood up abruptly, every muscle tensed like a cornered animal. "I'm here of my own free will," I repeated, my voice steadier than the rest of me. "Let me do this. Please."

The word hung between us—"please"—a desperate prayer more than a polite request. Cherry rumbled in agreement, her presence coiling through me like smoke. We were in this together, the Baroness and I, about to face a test no one had survived in a century.

Daphne studied me, her eyes ancient and knowing beneath that ridiculous gardener's hat. She must have seen something in my face—determination, resignation, or perhaps the perfect blend of fear and fury—because she finally nodded.

"As you wish," she said. The words fell like a death sentence.

The air around us charged with electricity. The fortress walls seemed to breathe inward, the space contracting as the test prepared to consume another supplicant. Alastair's fanged smile gleamed in my peripheral vision, but I thanked Daphne.

This was it. My shot. My last extraordinary chance to fix this doomed trajectory.

Too bad I was all out of miracles.

Chapter 2

Daphne proceeded to inform us that supplicants had to perform certain steps before undertaking the test: a cleansing bath (pre-death spa day), a hearty meal (noshes before nothingness), and a sound rest (dreams for the doomed).

A muscle twitched violently in Alastair's cheek as he swallowed whatever protests had risen to his lips, his eyes fixed on Daphne with barely contained hatred.

"Get comfortable. We'll be a while." She arched an eyebrow at him, letting the silence draw out until he sat down, his jaw tight.

"Is this really standard operating procedure?" I said, following her through the courtyard.

"It's not *not* standard." She sniffed primly. "Some people need to cool their jets and recognize they aren't in charge."

We stepped inside a small hut, which was taken up by a hot spring. Electric tealights were set around the edge, and the air smelled of cedar and eucalyptus, not sulphur. It was soothing, but so was the last spa I'd visited. Had I never known a staked Prime was fished out of the bathwater, I would have booked a deluxe treatment.

Honestly, it wasn't off the table.

I peered through the steam into the dark pool with a grimace. "Is this where you keep your name maggots?"

"Please, doll. That skin exfoliation treatment is for VIP supplicants only."

I couldn't tell if she was kidding.

"Ditch the dirty duds." She laid a folded cloth bundle on a low bench. "And soak as long as you want. When you've changed, ring this…" She removed a small silver bell from her pocket and set it on the clean clothing. "I'll come get you. Don't leave this room without me."

I waved a hand in thanks, turning from the slash of daylight as she exited. Once disrobed, I stepped into the steaming water with a medley of swears and wince-breaths but was finally submerged up to my shoulders.

Cherry settled in for a nap. Being patient had worn her out. I promised her that she'd shortly have the best treat ever.

I scrubbed my face and hair clean, then lay back against the cedar planking, stretching out my arms and legs, but I was restless, my thoughts consumed with the test. I got out of the water and threw on the homespun pullover shirt and cropped pants. There were no socks, just slippers. My ruined pedicure would have to stand. I rang the bell.

Daphne led me down corridors lined with vibrant art and past rooms with glass-covered exhibits of weapons. There were cabinets of curiosities and mismatched arrangements of furniture, like the Queen Anne chair cozied up to the 1950s chrome diner table and the wardrobe that the Narnia kids might still be inside grouped with an IKEA dresser.

However, the fortress experience wasn't all awe and a childlike sense of wonder.

There was a room of ice, its crystalline walls glowing with an inner blue light that cast fractured reflections across the floor. Something moved in the depths of that frozen chamber—something large and patient that left no footprints on the gleaming surface.

I sped up, past a doorway that opened into a room of shadows so dense they absorbed all surrounding light. Occasional flickers of movement disrupted the perfect blackness, like creatures swimming through ink. The darkness reached toward me, tendrils of shadow stretching beyond the threshold before reluctantly retreating.

Some of the doors were padlocked with heavy rusted locks or warded with writhing runes. I didn't ask what was behind them.

Then there was a small chamber with no door—just an opening in the wall barely wider than my shoulders. No light illuminated its interior, yet I could see every detail with unnatural clarity. The walls pulsed gently, like the inside of something living, and whispers emanated from within, overlapping voices speaking in languages I both recognized and didn't. Some sounded like pleas, others like threats, all of them somehow directed at me specifically.

I hurried past it, eyes averted, but not before catching a glimpse of handprints pressed into the fleshy walls.

Daphne flung open a pair of French doors. A mahogany dining table dominated the room, its polished surface reflecting crystal chandeliers above. High-backed chairs upholstered in burgundy silk lined both sides, and the deep emerald fabric of heavy damask curtains pooled on marble floors. A sideboard displayed delicate cut-glass decanters under carved cherubs peering down from ceiling medallions.

The sheer amount of dinnerware made my head spin.

I sighed, my shoulders sagging, and followed her to my seat at the far end, my slippers making soft slapping noises.

My dinners generally involved a fork, knife, and plate. Not even that on taco night. There'd be two glasses if I was being fancy. I glanced at a plate setting. What meal needed four spoons?

I scraped the floor when I pulled my chair out and grimaced. "This isn't part of the test, is it? Pass some *Good Housekeeping* seal of approval?"

Daphne dropped into her chair with fluid grace. "Last chance to back out, Aviva."

"Not going to happen." I looked from one of my three forks down the length of the table. "Is there a butler or will food just—"

She slammed her hand on her placemat. "I liked you."

I made a snarky face. "Not loving the past tense."

She jabbed a fork at me, and I flinched. "You know how many threats I deal with from these shmoes seeking healing magic? The sob stories? My gawd. 'Three years and millions of dollars of tests and my medical start-up has nothing. Help me find the cure for blah blah blah, insert disease of choice.'"

"Medical breakthroughs sound kind of worthy," I said tentatively.

Wine appeared on the table—just out of my reach.

"I'm sure the investors agreed. The test thought otherwise. I had one dude whining about how every time he was about to get intimate, his ex's voice started narrating in his head like a nature documentary." She poured herself a glass.

I tried not to make puppy dog eyes at the booze. "That's oddly specific. What happened?"

"Do I look like a therapist? I told him to tell it to the test."

"The last person who was found worthy, what did they come for?"

"Stop gas poisoning orphans during World War II?"

She scrunched up her face. "Maybe they had gout. It all blends together."

"It's not cause dependent."

"Nope." That was good.

"There are a lot of failed supplicants in that bone wall." I peeled my shoulders off the now-damp chair silk. "How did they all find out about this place? It wasn't advertised. Not even on the dark web."

"Be here since time immemorial and word gets around." She sipped her wine. "But you know how infrequently I get a calm request to take the test without any drama? Without oversharing? Fuhgeddaboudit. You were the only one who didn't want the word. Then you showed up with Sir Bangs-A-Lot, disturbing my plants."

"More like the Mayor of Poundtown—and nope. That's not better."

Daphne waved a hand at my plate, the fight gone out of her. "Eat."

A fat, juicy cheeseburger oozing melted cheddar appeared on my plate. My mouth watered, but I hesitated. "Uh…this is treyf. Bad Jew food," I clarified at her confused expression.

"It was pulled from your brain as your favorite." She daintily cut into her golden-brown puff pastry and a rich gravy spilled out.

"True, but…" I looked around and lowered my voice. "Will that be an issue with…" I jerked my chin to the room at large.

"Nah."

I tucked my napkin onto my lap. "Then can I get bacon? Extra crispy." The strips appeared immediately, both improving my burger and, more importantly, confirming my hypothesis.

This power word test had a single component: prove your worthiness in its specific instance. I'd experienced the memory of the last supplicant, Evelyn. The vampire didn't have to demonstrate strength or intelligence or even a strong moral character.

Because the test was deceptively simple. Emphasis on deceptive.

Here's the trouble: Evelyn lied. The poor woman didn't even realize it. She had a personal and valid reason to believe herself worthy in this particular situation, but she parroted the info Alastair fed her—that the word would be used to restore procreation for *all* vampires.

Error or not, she lied to that magic force when she claimed she'd reignite the spark of life for all vamps.

She probably wasn't read the Threshold Protocol—the silver lining in Alastair's abduction.

As Daphne had told me on my previous visit to this fortress: healing is healing. It wasn't good or bad, simply released in a ritual of the supplicant's choosing. The magic guardian didn't give a shit that six people had died to get Alastair to this point. That cockamamie sentience was as reprehensible as an arms dealer determining who received his weapons then washing his hands of any responsibility.

I licked grease off my fingers and snagged a fry from the crisp pile glistening with salt crystals that I hadn't even made a dent in. Did this feel like the Last Supper? Yup. Was this affecting my hunger at all? Nope. I shoveled two more fries into my mouth.

With every fiber of my being, I wanted the healing magic for Alastair, and I would do anything to achieve that.

I'd also kill him after he enjoyed a single glorious moment of the fruit of his labors. It didn't make me any less worthy; quite the opposite in fact. My argument was laid out and ready for the judge.

After I'd stuffed my face with four different courses, using only a fraction of my allotted cutlery, Daphne poured us both a brandy.

She swirled the amber liquid in the snifter. "Magic comes with a price, Aviva, and it always collects its debt. It doesn't care who pays the cost—or when."

"Yeah, I'm familiar with that last part." It wasn't always losers who paid. Sometimes winners like Quentin Baker ended up losing too. I sipped the strong alcohol slowly. The Copper Hell could rebrand with that idea. *Play Now, Pay Later—Someone Always Does.*

A silvery-blue gaze lit with amusement popped into my head.

I choked on the brandy.

Daphne leaned over and pounded me on the back. "It's a lot to think about."

And here I was trying not to think. At all. *He's okay.* "Trust me, I've examined every angle of this. I'm going to succeed, and when this is all over, I'll return with a bottle of my favorite Merlot."

"You'll raise a glass to me." She sounded not sad exactly, more wistful.

"We'll raise a glass together," I promised her.

I was convinced I'd stay up worrying, but it was meat coma to the rescue. I slept like a baby.

When Daphne shook me awake, the sky was streaked with soft peach and orange. Storm clouds shaped like four-leaf clovers also rolled overhead, which was admittedly a mixed message, but I was in an optimistic mood.

Soon Alastair would be stopped for good, and I would be reunited with my boyfriend.

I shoved my bare feet into my ankle boots and followed Daphne in silence down to the basement, assessing every door for dungeon status.

She halted partway down the corridor in front of a large painting of a forest. "Good luck," she said and hugged me tightly.

I hugged her back, but before I could thank her, she vanished along with all modern electricity.

And the fortress.

Pine trees pressed in from all sides, and weak sunshine filtered down through faraway top branches, barely providing enough light for me to pick my way over the uneven path made of decomposing pine needles.

Cherry sang "Barbie Girl" by Aqua, which put a spring in my step. We were on the same page that unless things went sideways, I'd remain fully human.

I pushed branches out of my way, tensing for the brush of cobwebs or nasty little beasts scuttling over my hand. This subdimension of the fortress was still in the Brink, so anything was possible, but the worst injury I suffered was a feathery branch thwacking me in the back of my head.

I'd been walking for about ten minutes when the stout branches of two trees crisscrossed, blocking the path. I wiped sweat off my forehead with my sleeve and kicked my way through.

A tiny house rose before me, squat and ancient. Built into a hill, its limestone blocks furred with moss where water had seeped through the mortar over centuries. Dead vines clutched at the corners like gnarled fingers, and the entrance gaped, a rough-cut empty doorway that drew in the forest's shadows rather than dispelling them.

It had a certain je ne sais quoi. More so than the stretch of stagnant water reeking of bleach that led directly to it. It wasn't a lake, more a pond with an overinflated sense of self. Stones coated in varying degrees of mud and moss were scattered throughout it.

Let's save the broken ankle option for Plan B.

I tore off a branch and dunked it in the dark water to check the depth. Its needles hissed and bubbled, bouncing off the bark and along the pond's surface. They bleached of all color and dissolved into tiny fragments that sank beneath the ripples.

The water returned to its placidity. Plan B it was.

I paced the shore, analyzing the safest route across. Once I was confident that I'd picked the best contenders, I shook out my shoulders, jumped up and down, and exhaled hard a few times. Arms outstretched, I stepped onto the first chosen rock—and immediately slid. I barely regained my balance in time.

Cherry launched into "Waterfalls" by TLC.

For an inner voice who was actually me, I could show myself more support in this situation.

The Baroness sang the chorus louder.

Sometimes the appropriate next rock was a small step away, sometimes it was a pulse-ratcheting stretch, and in one heart-lurching instance, a jump where my heel hit the water.

A sliver of rubber sizzled and crumbled.

I coasted on adrenaline over the remaining stones and leapt onto the rickety wood porch. It was impossible to see through the shadows to inside, but I didn't want to risk any escalation by letting Cherry free. However, I wasn't about to blithely traipse in, when I had no sense of what waited for me. I hovered my scales under my skin, where they were easily accessible, and cautiously stepped through the doorway.

Sawdust scattered under my boots same as it had in Evelyn's memory, each step a heavy thud on the worn stone.

Torches lit my way, the flames swaying to whispers that swept around me on an icy breeze.

I ignored them. Nothing was getting between me and that power word.

I stepped over a broken channel in the floor lined with gravel, listening to faint burbling from the corner. This was a repurposed spring house, albeit one that was much larger than normal, dug deep into the hillside.

The flames shifted, throwing a rough block of stone at the far end of the room into stark relief. A face was carved into it. My heartbeat stampeded at the mouth hanging open in an O, because interacting with it in Evelyn's memory had been awful enough.

I looked around again. Okay, the place was rustic, but with a little work might prove quaint.

Today on Love It or List It: Occult Edition: "Mark and Susan are looking for a home with character, but this eight-hundred-year-old spring house might have a bit too much. Sure, it's an age-old site of mystical power, but there's no flow. The stone face is giving real estate agent David fits about resale value, and designer Hilary is concerned that whispering shadows in the corner will possess new occupants. Still, they're excited to turn it from an interdimensional void of madness into an open-concept kitchen."

Forcing myself to uncurl my fingers and drop my hands, I strode forward.

The face's dead stone eyes woke, flickering with cold purpose.

I froze, heart hammering against my ribs.

Back away now, and Alastair would unleash a deadly vengeance on people I cared about. More half shedim would die. Proceed, and I might be split between name maggot and bone wall.

"Screw it," I whispered. If I was going down, it wouldn't be cowering in fear.

Drawing a deep breath, I squared my shoulders and met those ancient stone eyes with defiance. My fingers trembled visibly—not from fear, I told myself, but from anticipation—as I deliberately extended my hand toward the gaping maw.

Visions of bloody stumps where my fingers used to be danced in my head.

Grimacing, I plunged my hand between its cold lips. "Bite me."

Phrasing, Cherry cough-laughed.

I already know your taste. The stone's voice filled the room. *Mmmmmm.*

I couldn't help the shiver at its reminder that it had already taken my magic. That said, Evelyn had gotten a raspy tongue lick on her fingers and a lake full of maggots writhing in her head when the sentience spoke.

I got bupkis.

I shoved my hand in deeper. "Then you know that I've spent my life protecting people. I'm half-shedim and still, every single day I choose to fight for the continued safety of humans and for a world where my kind no longer has to hide."

I took a breath, my chest rising and falling and my cheeks flushed, but the stone face didn't jump in with any response.

"The mystic concept of neshamah, that divine spark connecting everything to the source of all life, lives inside me," I said. "Just as it lived inside the six half shedim that Alastair Walker murdered. I ask for this power word not out of pride or vengeance, nor even to give meaning to their deaths. I stand here because of the wisdom and sacrifice of many others who helped me understand what must be done."

The face gave nothing away, like it was waiting for me to finish before it squished me like a wee little bug.

I held my free hand out, the gesture carrying all the weight of my final, desperate hope. "Give me the power word, and I will speak it in a ritual combining its healing magic with their spilled blood. This will purge the stagnant energy within Walker and connect him to that divine spark, allowing him to fulfill his deepest desire: to create new life.

And when he is made whole, when his corruption is cleansed, then I will end him. Find. Me. Worthy."

The mouth's smooth upper edge split into stone fangs that punched through my flesh.

I screamed, blood running off my wrist and onto the sawdust. I couldn't pull free.

Cherry Bomb surged through my pain. Crimson hair burst from my scalp and armored scales exploded along my arms, my muscles swelling with demonic strength as short horns thrust from my temples.

I was trapped. Claws erupted from my fingers. I raked against the face.

Say your name and I shall pronounce judgment.

"I am Aviva Jacqueline Fleischer." I ground the words out through teeth gritted in pain, tears streaming down my cheeks. Some small, terrified part of me wondered if these would be the last words I ever spoke as myself—if my name would soon be forgotten, just another erased identity fed to the fortress.

Yet still, I said my name. Because it was mine to give, mine to risk, mine to lose.

The power word materialized like thorns of jagged ice forming one by one, each syllable a separate barb that lodged at the back of my throat. Tendrils of frost spread through my body as the word crystallized, until the full weight of it was etched into the marrow of my bones, humming with dangerous potential.

"You have been found worthy," the mouth intoned.

The torches blew out, leaving me alone with a word that could heal a monster—or end the world. In the perfect darkness, I savored my triumph where others had failed. They came for a cause. I came for an end.

Chapter 3

That would have been an awesome place for the final credits to roll on this adventure, but alas, I still had the worst task ahead. I had to help Alastair perform the ritual —then kill the son of a bitch at the right moment.

A woman's work…

The lights flicked back on, revealing I was in the fortress basement hallway again. There was no sign of Daphne or Alastair, who had probably blown a gasket waiting all this time.

Heh.

For magic lodged at the back of my throat, it was surprisingly noninvasive. I mean, it pulsed through every inch of me, but it didn't make me gag like Daniel Suarez's dick during my ill-fated first blow job.

"Sorry about the teeth, Dan!" Okay, I could speak normally without the power word being uttered. Good to know.

Back in human form, I was poking my head into rooms on the main floor to find Daphne, when a door blew off its hinges, whistling past me to smash against the wall. I jumped backward, arms up, protecting my face from splintered wood. My skull bounced off a tapestry that did little to soften the impact.

"Did you get it?" Alastair's feverishly intense eyes peered into mine.

"Yes."

His fingers dug into my shoulders. "We're doing the ritual."

"Obvious—"

He grabbed my arm and hauled me into the room he'd just exited.

Oh, you meant this second.

The spartan space contained a perfect circle scratched into the floor. Next to it was a small round table with a half-melted candle, a cheap lighter, and a switchblade.

I sighed. I'd been kidnapped and traumatized, did we really need to throw stabbing into the mix?

Daphne sat in a threadbare brocade chair, the only other piece of furniture. "I'm looking forward to that Merlot," she said, looking up from a tattered Salman Rushdie novel.

"You and me both," I said, allowing myself a moment to imagine life beyond an endless string of dangers. "First round's on me."

Alastair lit the candle. "I called off my people before, now make her swear not to attack me while I'm vulnerable. Neither of us gets an advantage."

I curled my fingers into fists. That was *exactly* when I had to attack him. He had to die before his vampness got cranked to eleven. While he wouldn't be as strong as a Prime, I couldn't say how powerful he'd end up once the Luce settled.

Daphne nodded. "That's fair."

"Well?" Alastair flicked the blade open and sterilized it in the flame.

We can still take him, Cherry insisted. *Trust me.*

"Fine," I said.

Alastair gave a mean little smile like he was looking forward to kicking my ass. Knife in hand, he stepped into the circle and pushed up his sleeve. The blade moved with inhuman precision as he carved, his jaw clenched against pain that he couldn't ignore, yet he didn't bleed.

That wasn't even the strangest part.

His design defied geometry, the rune's angles bending in ways that made my vision blur when I tried to follow them. It wasn't so much carved into his skin as carved through it, as if it continued somewhere beneath reality. It looked less like a symbol and more like a wound in the shape of the world.

Alastair studied the rune with glassy eyes, sweat beading on his forehead. He carved one more flourish, then dropped the blade in favor of drinking from the canteen.

Every drop that slid down his chin made me itch to wrap my hands around his throat. Six lives. Six futures destroyed, and he gulped their blood like a frat boy crushing beer cans for Instagram likes.

I, however, saw the faces of the dead in every splash that hit the ground. My jaw clenched, but I forced myself to bear witness. Someone had to remember the cost.

He closed his eyes.

Guess that was my cue.

I didn't so much speak the power word as envision it freed like a bird from a cage. The noise I made didn't correspond to any language I'd ever heard. It was a combination of thunder trapped underwater and whale song.

All memory of its shape and sound vanished, but its release shattered something inside me. My Eishei Kodesh magic erupted, splitting my skin with cracks of blue light. The world contracted to a pinhole, sound fading to distant snaps like someone trying to wake me from a dream.

A wash of dazzling blue light stormed my vision,

obscuring everything else. I felt disconnected to my body, suddenly unable to tell where my arms and legs were. No sight, no proprioception; my heartbeat spiked.

Cherry's voice in my head was white noise, but she was helping to keep me on my feet. I had to remain upright and not show weakness. I'd sworn not to attack Alastair when he was vulnerable; he'd done no such thing in return.

Was he even still in the grips of the healing ritual? Would his fangs tear through my throat or his hands rip out my heart any moment now?

A light touch penetrated my haze and I jumped.

"My bad." Daphne spoke calmly, but she sounded like she was speaking to me down a staticky phone line. "No need for claws. I've got you."

I calmed somewhat at the feel of a chair under my butt. Synesthete overload—my vision had exploded with so many layers of blue auras that I couldn't distinguish one object from another. The world had become a kaleidoscope of azure, cerulean, and cobalt, all of them crashing together in a blinding tidal wave of information that my brain couldn't process.

Every Eishei Kodesh was susceptible to overload, and it manifested differently for every type of flame, but I'd never experienced it before.

Slowly, my vision cleared, sound resumed normally, and my sense of self centered in my body once more. I sucked in a shaky breath and pried my fingers off the armrest.

The air crackled with an electric bite, making the hairs on the back of my neck stand up. I could feel Alastair's molecules rearranging, his athletic build swelling into something that would make peak Arnold Schwarzenegger look wimpy.

His shirt shredded as muscles surged beneath skin mapped with dark veins, his flesh taking on an unnatural luminescence. He laughed with pure joy, fangs flashing, and his head thrown back in triumph like a god accepting worship.

I wasn't about to check out his junk with my magic sight to see if he could procreate, but it was pretty fucking safe to say that the ritual worked. Looking at the raw power radiating from him, I felt dread pool in my stomach. How could I possibly defeat that?

What had I done? I could almost hear a doomsday clock ticking down, the faces of everyone who'd suffer flashing before my eyes as nausea rose in my throat. I'd given a monster exactly what he wanted and now everyone would pay the price.

Daphne watched him with the impassiveness of one who'd seen it all.

The room stilled into the unnatural silence of the eye of a hurricane. A single perfect moment of calm, marred only by the disquieting certainty that even if I survived, I had to ride out the other side of the storm.

Alastair cracked his neck, rolled his shoulders, and shot me an ugly leer.

I dropped into a fighter stance.

He stepped forward, then stumbled, his foot suddenly grotesquely distorted.

It was like the first domino falling in a chain that would bring down an empire.

The ground bucked, and a roar built like a thousand angry hornets trapped in steel drums.

Run, Cherry said.

Alastair slapped at a pulpy lump swimming through his veins, his muscles growing bigger and ropier and bulging out as if trying to escape his body. "Stop this!"

I grabbed for the table as the overhead light exploded, raining glass and plaster. The fortress walls shuddered with the sound of ancient stone giving up its fight against time, tremors rolling underfoot.

Alastair pleaded with whatever god or devil would listen. The thing in his veins puffed up, tearing his skin with wet, meaty pops.

We both screamed.

All his teeth elongated into fangs too large for his mouth, his face distorting and stretching until he began to vibrate, his form becoming the blur of a bad video effect.

"Help!" he begged.

Massive chunks of the ceiling crashed around me, my heart trying to punch through my ribs.

Get out! The Baroness clawed at the inside of my skull to get me to move.

"Daphne!" I spun around, and the sound that left me was pure animal fear.

She was collapsing in on herself, withering like time-lapse footage of decay. The runes etched in her flesh dimmed and faded.

I scrambled across the broken stones to reach her. "Stop this! Help yourself!"

"I can't." Her expression held the peace of the already dead, but her voice was the rasp of sandpaper on bone.

The power word was supposed to heal Alastair. How had things gone so wrong? Was it because the ritual was performed here in the fortress? Had Alastair lost control of whatever magic was in his rune?

I shook Daphne, as if I could shake sense into this nightmare. "Why didn't you stop us from doing the ritual here?"

"Not my place." She patted my arm with a hand missing most of its fingers, her reassuring smile revealing a mouth full of dust. "He actually set me free." Her voice quivered with wonder.

The rapturous light in her eyes turned blank, and her skin crumbled away. Suddenly she collapsed, her yellowed bones clattering to the ground.

Daphne—the seemingly immortal gatekeeper—was gone in seconds. Yet somehow, impossibly, I was still standing. The unfairness of her end struck me with unexpected force, a hollowness opening in my chest for someone I barely knew but had grown to respect, perhaps even admire, in our brief, fraught encounters.

A violent rumble beneath my feet pulled me back to my immediate predicament. The fortress was tearing itself apart and Alastair...

I caught one last glimpse of terror in his eyes before his body shattered into a storm of ash.

Aviva! Cherry's scream jolted me into motion. I was the only one left alive, and I intended to stay that way. I ran for the door, dodging falling stones, choking on centuries of disturbed dust, my ears ringing from the fortress's death rattle.

I made it as far as the courtyard before the world turned white. The light engulfed me, and I was blasted backward. Then there was nothing but the sensation of falling, tumbling through empty space.

The Brink, that impossible realm of chaos magic, was collapsing like a house of cards—and I was caught in its freefall.

Chapter 4

I came to, face down on cracked asphalt, my ears ringing. The smell of burnt coffee that tinged the air was mixed with dust and smoke. My hands scraped against broken concrete as I shakily pushed myself up, looking at the world through a hazy film.

I was back in Vancouver, outside the ruined laundromat that housed the rift to the Brink. Where the building had stood was now a half-collapsed mess of brick and twisted metal, its old sign stuck up like a pirate's flag on the skeleton of a ship against a dark sky.

The rubble buried the rift so completely that not a scrap of portal light escaped.

That blast in the fortress was strong enough to reverberate into our world? Were more aftershocks to come? Bile climbed up my throat.

Sirens wailed but they sounded like I was hearing them through a tunnel, same as the car alarms blaring.

The surrounding buildings bore fresh cracks running up their facades. People emerged onto the street, gathering in distressed little groups.

My head throbbed and every muscle ached. Something

warm trickled down the side of my face. I touched it and my fingers came away crimson, mixed with freezing rain-water pelting down.

I was alive and home. Cold and bleeding didn't matter and I couldn't do anything about this destruction. I'd help however I could *after* I got back to the Lions Gallery—and Ezra.

A dark figure loomed over me, speaking and gesturing angrily from me to the laundromat, but his words were a white noise soup. His fangs were nice and clear, though, and he was helpfully attired in the black suits favored by many a vamp goon.

Cherry pulsed under my skin, driving me forward. She'd stayed in check when it mattered, but now that we were back on home turf, her wild desire to find our mate was almost tangible.

My legs shook as I stumbled to my feet, using a busted sign pole to stand. The world tilted sickeningly, and my limbs felt heavy and unwieldy.

The vamp grabbed me.

I punched him in the throat and hobbled to the side-walk, where I blanked. I didn't have my phone, and I couldn't remember Sachie's number or even my mom's, but HQ—that one had been drilled into me.

The vamp grabbed me again. "Did you come out of the rift? What happened?"

I could hear him properly now, but his grip was too strong, and that one attack was all I'd had left in me. Plus, I wasn't on sharing terms with this asshole.

"Operative Fleischer!"

I turned to see a vaguely familiar man jogging toward me.

"You're a Maccabee? Aw, fuck." The vampire reluc-tantly released me. "You're not wearing your ring."

I glanced down at my right hand. Had I lost the ring in

the Brink? A pang twinged in my chest, but that didn't matter either. Rings were replaceable. Ezra was not.

Vamp goon melted back into the shadows before the other operative reached me.

The man's eyes widened as he got closer, taking in my battered appearance, but it was only for a second.

"Was Ezra Cardoso found?" My voice came out raw and cracked.

The operative didn't react negatively to Ezra's name, though he knew who he was and what had happened with the Authority. Everyone at the Vancouver chapter did. "Is he missing?"

"Call the director," I insisted. "Please."

"Let's get you out of the rain first. You're going to get hypothermia."

"I don't have time for that." If he wouldn't call Michael, he definitely wouldn't drive me to the Lions Gallery. No problem, I'd get hold of a phone myself. That woman over there, she'd have a phone. I tried to sidestep the operative, but he caught my sleeve.

"You're in no condition to—"

A furious haze settled around me, like a barbed wire blanket. I tore his hand off me, snarling.

"You're injured and your eyes are crossing," he said in a low and steady voice. "There's blood coming down your head, and by the way you're walking, your ankle is badly sprained. Let me help you first. We're on the same side."

At the sight of my puffy ankle, the pain I'd held off through sheer adrenaline and grit broke through. I breathed shallowly, transferring my weight to my good leg with a winced hiss.

"Please come with me," he said. "I'll call Director Fleischer on the way."

"Fine." The word tasted like defeat, but I could barely walk. "Operative…?"

"Nelson."

I narrowed my eyes at his ring. Why didn't I have mine? *Corrupted shedim magic, undercover disguise...* Right. "Thank you."

Operative Nelson guided me to the nondescript black SUV parked half on the curb, each step sending spikes of pain through my ankle. He kept a steadying hand near my elbow but was careful not to touch me after my earlier reaction.

The back seat was mercifully dim. I slumped against the leather, shaking as the adrenaline began to fade, even though he cranked the heat to sauna-like temperatures for me.

For the first time since this horror began, I allowed myself a moment to simply breathe. No imminent threats. No life-or-death decisions. Just the rhythmic sound of tires on pavement and the gradual loosening of muscles that had been battle-ready for what felt like years. The relief was so intense it was almost painful—a momentary sanctuary that wouldn't last, but one I desperately needed.

Cherry was a caged tiger prowling beneath my skin. Her agitation made the pain sharper, more immediate.

Ezra, she snarled.

We'll find him, I promised. *But we're no good to anyone if we pass out in the street.*

Operative Nelson spoke quietly into his Bluetooth headset as he drove, reporting my condition and requesting medical prep. His words filtered through my fog in fragments: trauma, possible concussion.

The SUV's gentle swaying made my stomach roll. I pressed my forehead against the cool window, watching the city blur past through half-closed eyes.

Cherry's anxiety bled into mine with each passing minute. *Why isn't anyone telling me what had happened to Ezra?*

My thoughts scattered as we hit a pothole. A hot blaze shot through my ribs and ankle, drawing a sharp gasp.

"Director Fleischer is being notified that you've been located, but HQ is requesting more information. When's the last time you saw Mr. Cardoso?"

Sunset was around 4PM here in Vancouver in January. Given the sky right now, it might be late afternoon, early evening, or dead of night. No. The people who came out of the nearby buildings weren't in pajamas.

It couldn't still be Tuesday though. The test and ritual had taken a while, and even if the time conversion wasn't quite the same, it should be similar enough.

Damn it. Ezra wouldn't be at the gallery anymore. Where should I start looking? "I saw him late afternoon yesterday."

"Wednesday afternoon," he reported back to the phone call.

"*Yesterday*. Tuesday."

"It's 20:17 Thursday."

A pained howl punched out of me.

Operative Nelson gave the corrected information to whomever he was speaking with. "Five minutes to HQ. Try to stay conscious."

I nodded, immediately regretting the movement. The world was starting to blur at the edges. Cherry's presence was the only thing keeping me upright, her supernatural stamina fighting my body's desire to shut down.

Michael was waiting when we arrived, her face drawn and gray with exhaustion. She looked like she'd slept in her cream suit and—I narrowed my eyes. Was that a coffee stain on the lapel of her blouse? Had the apocalypse hit?

Was this because of the fortress blast damage here in Vancouver?

Before I could speak, she crushed me in a hug that made my ribs scream in protest.

"Mom," I squeaked, but didn't let go. "Ezra—"

"He's safe," she cut me off, her voice rough. She released me from the hug but kept hold of my hands, her green eyes searching my face as if to make sure I was real. "Go let Chaim fix you."

"I have to see Ezra first."

"Your hair is matted with blood." She gestured to her own head. "There are gashes all over you, you're protecting your left ribs, and paler than those ugly sheets you had back in residence."

"The Brink chewed me up and spat me out. Teeth marks were inevitable."

Are you Daniel Suarez in this anecdote? Cherry said, amused.

No blow job memories in front of Mom!

My mother arched an eyebrow and fixed me with the look that had left teen me quaking. Adult me didn't love it either. She snapped her fingers and suddenly another operative was there with a wheelchair for me. "The faster you get checked out, the faster you see him."

I dropped into the wheelchair like a sack of wet concrete.

The treatment room struck a careful balance between medical necessity and soothing comfort. Warm cream-colored walls and soft recessed lighting helped ease the clinical edge of the vital signs monitors and IV stands positioned near the adjustable bed. The temperature stayed perfectly regulated, warm enough to relax tense muscles but cool enough to prevent overheating during healing sessions.

While one wall held the expected array of medical supplies and emergency equipment, the overall effect was calming: from a bushy potted philodendron to soft knit blankets stacked neatly on top of a cushioned bench, to the ergonomic chair where the healer could work in comfort. Even the air held a subtle freshness, thanks to a top-of-the-line filtration system that kept the space pristine without the harsh bite of antiseptic.

It was a soothing space, which was good because being healed magically was like being stabbed with white-hot acupuncture needles. I blacked out three times. Each time I surfaced back to consciousness, the pain hit fresh and new.

When I finally came to properly, exhausted but no longer hurting, Sach, Silas, and Darsh were arguing in low voices by my bedside.

It was a bright, sunny Friday morning, but with no sign of Ezra, the world felt overcast and gloomy.

Sach's pink hair looked dull and lank, Silas's shirt reminded me of aluminum foil that had been balled up and flattened out, and Darsh wasn't wearing a lick of eyeliner.

My skin prickled.

Sach was talking. "She doesn't need to know yet about—"

"She's awake," Darsh cut in, already moving to smooth my tangled hair back from my face. His hands were gentle, but I could feel them trembling.

I grabbed them. "Ezra?"

"Will want to see you," Darsh finished.

I relaxed. Whatever was wrong, they weren't discussing him. Of course, that left only one other thing they could be discussing. I balled up the blanket in my fists, trying to order all the pieces to explain what happened in the Brink.

"Quite the scare there, Avi," Silas said in a hearty, booming voice that didn't quite reach his eyes and shoved a tray at me.

There was enough food for three: cut strawberries and slices of pineapple, a take-out cup of coffee from my favorite café, and an entire carton of orange juice. Warm muffins stacked like a mini pyramid on a plate rounded out the meal.

My stomach churned at the sight, but the hollow ache

in my core meant I should eat. "Are those your mom's zucchini chocolate chip muffins?" I said.

"Yeah," Sachie said. "She was stress baking for when you showed up again."

While fights between my best friend and her parents over her joining the Spook Squad had ended after her dad's heart attack, her relationship with them remained strained and tense. Now wasn't the time to ask if that had changed.

"Start your day with a good breakfast," Silas said, briefly touching Darsh's shoulder before withdrawing his hand when Darsh stiffened. "Yup, that's what I always say."

"Not even once," Darsh muttered, shifting away slightly.

Silas shot him a frustrated look, jaw tightening. "Could we not?"

Sach glanced wearily between the boyfriends. *Were* they still boyfriends?

"Look at all those treats." I poked at one of the paper muffin holders, pretending not to notice the crackling tension. "What a lucky girl I am."

"You had extensive internal injuries," Sachie said. "What happened?"

Silas shoved a muffin in my hand. "We'll talk after she eats."

"Let me see Ezra." I tried to sit up, but the room spun.

"Start carbo-loading already," Sachie said, "or I'll find new and inventive ways to murder you with this plastic butter knife."

"Or," Darsh said gently, putting a hand on Sachie's plastic weapon and lowering it, "you can have some food first, so you don't black out in front of him. Fainting as flirting stopped being cute in the 1800s. Everything else can wait."

My friends exchanged glances loaded with meaning. This was about more than the damage from the blast, but I was too exhausted to decipher it, and Darsh had made it clear I'd get no answers until I ate.

I bit into the muffin, which was delicious, same as all of Reina's baking. I swallowed and motioned to my hospital gown, now dusted with crumbs. "Clothes?"

"Got you covered." Sachie gestured to my carry-on suitcase in the corner. "Clean clothes, toiletries, everything you need. Found your coat and phone in your car and brought those too." She placed my phone on the bedside table.

"My hero." A flutter of genuine relief broke through at the sight of my cell, that small rectangle suddenly representing everything normal that I'd left behind.

"Your hero to whom you owe a hundred and eighty bucks in parking and impound lot fines."

Hadn't I paid enough? I took a deep breath. Michael could gather a team to track down Alastair's followers, but everyone I cared about was safe, and hopefully, the murdered half shedim would rest easy now.

My appetite came back—somewhat. Every yummy bite still felt like it took forever.

Yet unlike my last meal, amazeball burger aside, this one assured me I was truly home. The hint of cinnamon Reina used, the coffee doctored to my specific tastes, even my bickering friends—they made my homecoming feel more real.

"You're smiling," Sachie said, her voice warm with surprise.

"It's just…nice. To be back." I reached for another piece of fruit with renewed determination to build up my strength.

Darsh's eyes softened, the hardness he'd been directing at Silas momentarily forgotten. "We're glad you're back too, Avi."

My friends stood over me until they decided I'd eaten

enough to be allowed to shower, at which point I forced them to leave. There was caring and then there was stalking.

I washed quickly, the hot water cleansing away the last traces of the Brink. Sach had brought me my TV-watching leggings and the crimson sweater that Ezra knit for me. Ordinarily I would never have worn them while at work, but it wasn't every day I destroyed a super-evil vampire and nearly died. Comfort clothes were appreciated.

Sach was getting a dozen cookies from her favorite bakery for being the bestest best friend in the world. Speaking of my friend, or rather her mother, I phoned Reina to thank her, getting teary approximately four seconds into the call.

Michael appeared in the doorway in a fresh change of clothes, her makeup reapplied and her silver hair back to its ruthless blunt line. "Ready?"

"I have to go, Reina," I said.

The weight of the past few days—my abduction, the desperate fight to survive—all of it had been endured with one thought burning through me: get back to Ezra. I thanked her for the muffins again and ended the call.

My mind was already elsewhere—picturing Ezra as I'd last seen him, his body contorted by Rukhsana's demon magic and all awareness gone as the darkness crawled beneath his skin.

Michael had said Ezra was safe, but after everything I'd seen, everything I'd endured to return home, I wouldn't believe it until I saw him with my own eyes.

Chapter 5

It was hard to tell if Darsh was right and Ezra wanted to see me because my boyfriend's closed lids didn't convey a ton of emotion. Much easier to decipher? The sickly gray undertone to his brown skin that matched the long-sleeved sweatshirt with a Maccabee logo he'd been put in. But hey, his sunken eye sockets and a third less muscle mass really popped against that neutral palette.

My heart clenched, then soared with a fierce joy. He was alive, and I could finally reach out and touch him. I smiled but my fingertips trembled as they hovered over his cheek, afraid that even the gentlest contact might cause him pain. This powerful man, this Prime who had always seemed indestructible, now looked so fragile I was afraid he might shatter. Still, he was here. We both had made it out alive.

I tucked his foot back under a blanket that I'd last seen on my bed. He had my pillow as well. I could almost be convinced that my Prime was tuckered out and had settled in for a catnap on the sofa.

In the director's office.

While hooked to an IV slowly dropping blood into him.

"How is this 'Ezra is safe'?" I said. "If you wanted me to believe that bullshit, you shouldn't have healed my concussion."

Michael felt his forehead. "His fever is gone. I pulled strings and brought in the best healer the Maccabees have."

"There's *paperwork* that Ezra is compromised?" I dragged a chair up to his bedside on legs gone rubbery from a burst of fear. The Authority was coming for him. They'd never miss a chance like this.

Michael actually glared at me. "I obviously lied. I said it was for Sachie and made Magdalena sign an NDA when she got here. The point is, Ezra stabilized in a magic coma is the best she could do. Silas told us shedim magic was responsible. I could have asked Delacroix—"

"No way!" I moved the IV tube so it didn't kink when I took Ezra's hand.

"Which is why I waited until you returned to brainstorm how to get Ezra's innate healing magic to kick in."

Returned. Like I'd been at the grocery store for milk. It was probably easier for Michael to think of it that way. It would be for me if our positions had been reversed.

I bowed my head and stroked my boyfriend's hand. I'd had a power word with healing magic beyond comprehension. And I'd spoken it into the air like it was nothing. Just another breath.

Then I remembered what it did to Alastair. Which might have been because of the ritual, but still. There was no point regretting or second-guessing now.

"I appreciate you bringing my blanket and pillow for him," I said.

"He'd want to come back to you. It was worth a try enveloping him in your scent."

Ezra spoke in a rasped whisper.

I jumped, leaning close. "I'm sorry it took so long, but I'm here now."

Michael laid her hand on my shoulder. "He does that sometimes. His vitals don't change when it happens."

Ezra spoke again.

"It's Spanish," I said. "Has anyone translated? I think Silas speaks it."

"He does, but it's fragments. Ezra's quoted books, even described a rock-climbing hold and several knitting stitches. But now you can talk to him."

"How did you find him?"

"When I couldn't get hold of you, I called Ezra, but it went to voice mail."

"Our phones were in my car."

"I gave it an hour, but when neither of you checked in, I sent Silas back to the gallery. You weren't…" She cleared her throat. "You're back now, and we *will* find a way to wake Ezra up. Stay as long as you like. Louis has orders not to let anyone in. He won't share that Ezra is here, and other than your friends and Magdalena, no one else knows. I've got my laptop in Conference Room C and am working from there. It's my new effort to be 'more accessible' to my staff." She gave a wry smile.

"Thank you," I said, but the door was already closing behind her.

The first thing I did was kiss Ezra on the lips. It didn't work because he wasn't Prince Charming, much less Sleeping Beauty, but I had to try.

"You need to wake up, Zee, because this is going to put a real crimp in our sex life."

Nothing. Not even an eyelid flutter.

I watched blood droplets roll down the tube. This nourishment wasn't helping him. Because it wasn't *my* blood? I'd tried to get him to feed from me when this first happened at the gallery, but he hadn't manifested fangs. Or even reacted to my presence.

Would it work if I put my blood in an IV bag? I plumped the pillow behind his head and forced myself to be realistic. He was my boyfriend, but we didn't have some magical connection where my blood would…

I blinked. Ezra and I didn't have a magical connection yet, but we could.

A blood bond.

I had no idea how to create one, but I'd bet anything that Darsh or Silas would.

I phoned them to come to Michael's office, then told them my idea in a hushed voice, the three of us grouped over by the window.

"Blood bonds are sacred," Darsh said. "This gives it the emotional weight of an aspirin."

"Look at him," I said, my voice quivering. "He's clearly not well! I have to do something!"

Darsh glanced at Ezra then sat on Michael's desk, touching each of the pens in her fancy cup holder in turn. "You have three options. One: jumpstart him with a blood bond." He grimaced. "Setting aside how precious they are and how one should never be performed without both parties really desiring it—"

I groaned and buried my face in my hands.

"Those bonds are permanent." He wandered over to the sofa and crossed Ezra's arms over his chest, like a cartoon vamp's. "You sure it's worth the risk?"

Silas hip-checked him out of the way and placed Ezra's arms back at his sides. "You want to rephrase that insultin' question about my best friend and our darling Aviva?"

"She heard me."

The ongoing level of bite in their communication confused me. Silas had played a role, albeit unknowingly, in the death of Darsh's brother years ago, but I'd seen them make up.

It's only been a few days, Cherry pointed out.

True. Even though I swear I'd aged years. It was naïve to believe their road to happiness would be easy.

That didn't mean Darsh could insult my relationship.

I planted my hands on my hips. "Ezra is worth the risk."

"I didn't mean to *you*, puiul meu."

"Because I'm an infernal?" I huffed.

Silas glared at Darsh.

He ran a hand through his hair with a dramatic sigh. "Let a girl speak. Ezra is in this condition because of shedim magic. Is adding more, i.e. *yours*, going to help?"

I sat down hard.

"Well, damn," Silas said.

Darsh flipped his hair off his shoulders. "I'm more than a pretty face."

"Aw. Bless your heart."

Darsh blinked at Silas then a surprised laugh burst out of him.

Silas gave a small smile.

I snapped my fingers. "Back to me. What do I do? The only one with any possible answers is Delacroix and—"

"Absolutely not," Silas said at the same time that Darsh said, "Hard pass."

I stroked Ezra's forehead. "I can't leave him like this and just chance he'll get better."

"Right? Michael'll want her couch back." Darsh tapped the IV bag to get the last few drops of blood down the tube. "Then where do we store him?"

"He's not a box of Christmas decorations, you ass," I said.

"No," he said sadly. "Ever since you got sucked into the

hostage dimension, there's been a distinct lack of sparkle with that boy."

"Go back to being a pretty face, Darsh." Silas brought his hands together, pleading.

"What are my other options?" I said.

"You wait for his innate healing magic to kick in," Darsh said. "Which could take hours to never. Three, let healers keep working on him. Same disclaimer as option two."

"Plus, who's to say that the magic coma will hold?" I scrubbed a hand over my face.

Silas cleared his throat. "There's a fourth option. A thrall."

"That sounds sexy." I waggled my eyebrows.

"It's not," Darsh said flatly.

"It boosts Ezra in a similar way as a blood bond, but it's not permanent," Silas said. "He has to keep feeding from you to maintain it."

"It's a terrible option," Darsh said. "He's only suggesting it because he wants his best friend to get better. I understand that, but—"

"I'm suggesting it," Silas said in a voice of steel, "because Aviva deserves to know all the options and make decisions for herself."

"How long would this thrall last?" I said.

"Two to three days? Tops?" Silas looked at Darsh, who reluctantly nodded.

"Then if adding my magic to Ezra's makes his condition worse, at least it's only a short-term thing."

"A thrall is also a risk for you, Avi," Silas continued. "You'd be a giant battery for him."

"That's the entire point. For me to boost his ability to wake up."

"Any sense of equality in your relationship?" Darsh snapped his fingers. "Gone."

Silas's jaw hardened.

"But I initiate it," I said.

"Yes," Darsh said, "but creating a thrall doesn't give you control. You're putting yourself in the position of being *enthralled*. Being reduced to an object or a resource versus being an equal partner to Ezra."

Put like that, it sounded less than ideal.

Ezra whimpered something in Spanish.

His pained voice was the cue for my treacherous brain to replay Daphne's last horrific moments, but with Ezra in the starring role.

I laid my hand on his forehead, murmuring that I was here. I couldn't stand seeing him like this, a half-life version of himself, trapped and suffering.

The worst part was knowing exactly what he'd say about this idea. Something insufferably noble about how my magic was too precious to waste on him. That there was as much of a risk to me with being enthralled to a Prime as there was to him with my shedim magic. And if I insisted on being stubborn and going ahead despite that, then I should take a moment and think about what it would mean for my career if it got out that I was feeding him on the regular.

All excellent points, but I couldn't leave him imprisoned in his own mind. Not with all the darkness that lived in there.

Not when I was determined to illuminate every shadowy sad corner with happiness.

I crossed my arms. "Ezra is one of the most vital people I know, and now he's out cold. Rukshana's magic is frying his engine or clogging his oil tank—"

Darsh heaved an exaggerated sigh. "That man is not a race car and you're definitely not a mechanic."

"Continuing with my brilliant metaphor, if me being a battery jump-starts him and he opens his eyes?" I stroked my boyfriend's hand. "Then yes, it's worth it. I'm going to thrall with Ezra."

"It's not a verb," Darsh growled.

I arched an eyebrow. "I won a power word that eluded supplicants for a century and survived the Brink imploding. Pretty sure I can turn 'thrall' into whatever the hell part of speech I feel like. Now, which of you is going to tell me how to do it?"

Chapter 6

Silas bound the back of my hand with Ezra's, securing our wrists. The Prime's arm had atrophied to be almost as slender as mine, his muscles a haunting testament to his rapid decline.

"Elastic band?" Darsh sniffed. He curled up the IV tube and hooked it over the stand. "How uninspired."

I pointed at the door. "Heckling is not a required component."

"Just a marvelous extra service I provide."

I couldn't be mad at him. I mean, I could, but while Silas was off finding a silver needle, Darsh had fixed my hair and done my makeup, so I'd look my best when Ezra awoke.

My friend also taught me the four words I'd have to speak for the thrall to set, correcting my pronunciation of some dead language until he was satisfied.

Apparently, the slightest deviation in syllabic stress could result in a very different outcome. Darsh refused to elaborate on what that was.

"The thrall requires the use of something that belongs to one of them," Silas said, breaking me out of my thoughts. "And neither is wearing a bracelet, so elastic band it is. Avi, are you ready?"

"Yes." My pulse fluttered in my throat, but Cherry vibrated with excitement.

Silas handed me the needle. "You've got this." He headed for the door, followed by Darsh. Both had felt awkward about being in the room while I undertook this private process.

Darsh paused in the doorway. "Whatever happens, I've got your back."

There was an authority to the door's click, and even the building's usual creaks and gentle hum of the heating vents quieted in reverence of this moment.

I found Ezra's jugular vein, lightly scratching the image of two interlocking blood drops on his skin before mimicking the drawing on my own throat.

This was the moment of truth. The moment Ezra and I were either thralled together and he woke up or… I wiped my free hand off on my leggings. In that heartbeat, every possibility stretched before me like light through a prism. Power. Connection. Shared magic. Or darkness.

But I'd made my choice.

Whispering the unfamiliar words, I jammed the needle's sharp tip into my jugular with a hiss. Unlike with the power word, there was no sense of release, simply a rote recital.

There I was, kneeling by my comatose boyfriend, with a needle sticking out of my neck like a nervous voodoo doll.

Nothing happened. Had I not found the jugular? Should I call Darsh and Silas back? I grimaced. One look at me like this and they'd make fun of me forever.

I removed the needle.

Ezra's fangs extended and, still unconscious, he surged up, finding my neck with one hand. The rush of his fangs piercing my skin hit my system like lightning—a burst that made my teeth ache and my breath catch.

A tangle of fear and desire jolted through me, though he held me loosely, his drinking weak.

Warmth burgeoned through my chest.

His grip tightened, and the pull of his drinking intensified to a razor-thin wire of pain.

Steady there, Cherry calmly directed. *We're not done yet.*

Ezra's sickly gray tone melted like morning frost, rich brown skin blooming. The hollows around his eyes smoothed away, while his limbs swelled with renewed strength.

His magic reached for mine. When they finally touched, the resonance shivered through me like a struck gong, setting every nerve alight.

I opened my eyes in time to see the elastic hair band magically burn away into dancing motes.

Ezra slipped his fangs free of my flesh. His lids fluttered open, revealing a clear silver blue gaze that immediately found me.

"Well," he said hoarsely. "That was something."

I laughed, happiness making me dizzy. "Welcome back."

His hands settled on my sleeves. "Nice sweater."

"Thanks. This hot guy I know made it for me."

His expression turned serious. "You shouldn't have—"

I kissed him, tasting the lingering copper.

Almost immediately, my boyfriend gently pulled away.

I glared at him, arms crossed.

He peered into my eyes. "How do you feel? Are you really happy?"

"I was. Less so now."

"Seriously, are you feeling all glowy?"

"Glowy?" I checked his forehead for a fever. "Since when do you talk that way?"

"You're enthralled by me," he said.

"I thralled you," I corrected him.

He scrunched up his face. "Can it be used as a verb?"

I crossed my arms. "Yes."

"It's making you happy when you're around me."

"Trust me when I say I'm really not. I'm half-shedim. Maybe I'm exempt from glowyness."

"You think?" His eyes lit up and he tugged me closer.

Champagne bubbles fizzed in my belly. I wanted to dance and sing at finally being reunited with him, but he wasn't getting off the hook that fast. Besides, this bantery argument was fun. "Get real."

He mock pouted at me. "You don't want to kiss your boyfriend who was on the verge of death?"

I rolled my eyes. "Fine." But when our lips brushed, I poured all my relief and joy into that kiss, then I hugged him tightly.

He hissed sharply and I pulled away, my eyebrows raised. "Just a bit sore," he said.

A purplish-black bruise peeked up along the collar.

I rolled up his sleeve. His arms were covered in them, as was his torso when I pushed his shirt up. "Rukhsana's magic isn't flushed out of your system."

"Not yet," he said. "But soon. You won't be enthralled for long." He bundled me back into his arms and buried his face in the crook of my neck.

Careful to keep my grip loose, I breathed in his natural scent of a windswept summer breeze that was mixed with the faint tinge of sweat and closed my eyes, blocking out pointless details like the room. I snuggled closer to his broad chest.

"Are *you* happy about our situation?" I said. "I forced it onto you, but waiting for you to wake up didn't seem like a good option."

"You did the right thing." He glanced at a bruise on the underside of his wrist. "Thank you."

"Thank Silas for telling me about this. My solution was to blood bond us."

Ezra flinched.

"I won't ever consider it again." I stood up, looking off to the side and blinking rapidly. It's not like I schemed a blood bond to trap him. I'd only come up with the idea in the first place to heal him.

"Aviva, I—"

I didn't need to be gently let down. Not right now. "How are you feeling other than the bruising?" I said briskly.

He threw back the blanket to stand and test his weight. "Steady."

"Let's talk logistics. What if one of us is injured during this thralldom? Do we both feel it?"

"Nope. See?" He pinched himself hard.

"What if one of us dies?"

"The other one figures out a way to keep living without them."

Enough with the emo. In my head, Cherry grinned. *We're going to live a very long time and have a lot of fun.*

I'd drink to that.

"In other news," I said, "guess what happened to Alastair?"

Ezra arched an eyebrow. "I don't suppose he conveniently fell on a stake while I was out?"

"Not exactly." I sat down next to my boyfriend. "But he's dead."

Ezra rubbed his chest. "I feel your unease. What happened?" His eyes flashed red. "*Did he do something to you?*"

"Not in any way that you're thinking," I hurriedly reassured him.

Was that the thrall or simply a normal Ezra reaction? Would I be able to tell the difference?

His eyes morphed back to their regular silver blue, so I wrapped his hand between mine and gave him the rundown.

Ezra fist bumped me in triumph at passing the test for the power word, but frowned at the description of Alastair's freaky rune, and wrapped an arm around my shoulders when I got to Daphne's death.

Alastair encountering a fatal bout of body-building didn't faze Ezra, though his fingers dug into the blanket at the fortress's implosion and me being blown out of the Brink.

I wrapped up my tale with the earthquake here in Vancouver and that something else was worrying our friends. I hoped it wasn't anything more than the blast.

Ezra remained still for a long moment. "Alastair is lucky he's dead."

I appreciated the sentiment, but the dhampir had been Zee's friend, and though Alastair betrayed that, he was still gone.

I was glad I couldn't feel his emotions, the way he could mine.

A knock at the door interrupted whatever else Ezra might have said.

Michael poked her head in. "Ezra, I thought I heard you. The shedim magic—" Her voice caught. "Good to see you recovered."

"Thanks to your daughter." Ezra's smile was soft.

Michael turned a puzzled look on me. "How so?"

I shifted uneasily. "I thralled him."

She blinked oddly. It may have been Morse code for "God help me," but she didn't comment on my verb tense.

My stomach lurched. What else was she so worried about? Aftershocks?

"Well, you're up and around," she said, "which frees up my sofa."

Ezra nodded somberly, though his eyes danced in amusement. "The use of a good couch is unparalleled." He folded the blanket. "Thank you, Michael, for letting me recover here and watching over me."

She waved away his gratitude, but I could see how pleased she was. It was strange seeing them like this, my mother and my boyfriend getting along. Strange, but nice. Really nice.

"Aviva, if you're up for it," she said, back in director mode, "Spook Squad's called an emergency meeting. There's quite a bit to discuss, and your debrief is vital."

"Of course." I stood up but gave Ezra an uncertain glance.

"Go. I can't attend anyway, since I'm not a Maccabee."

I could have made the case that taking Rukhsana down almost cost him his life. Michael didn't look like she'd object if I did, but Ezra spoke out against it.

"We need to test the range of this thrall, see how distance affects it. Better to do that now, in controlled circumstances."

I hesitated. "Are you sure? You just woke up."

"I'm not going anywhere except to raid the Spook Squad's fridge for something else to drink." He pressed a kiss to my temple. "Just…try not to blow anything else up without me."

"No promises," I said with a wink.

Michael shook her head. "This is going to be quite the debrief."

THE ATMOSPHERE in the small conference room was subdued.

I took a seat at the round table between Sachie and Darsh, with Michael and Silas completing the group.

Sach was drawing in a dog-eared notebook. She'd done this her entire life as a way of better absorbing information, but not in the past few months. She'd confessed she didn't require it anymore.

How bad were things that she'd reverted back?

She mustered up a ghost of a smirk. "I've started a thrall playlist. Screamin' Jay Hawkins's version of 'I Put a Spell on You.'"

"Technically incorrect."

Sachie shrugged. "I've also got 'Abracadabra' by the Steve Miller Band, Lady Gaga's 'Teeth,' and 'Blood' by My Chemical Romance."

"Is this playlist about thralls or taxidermy?"

"Nice one." She sketched the head of a shaggy monster. "Just know that should I have to add 'Poor Unfortunate Souls' from Disney's *The Little Mermaid*, there will be consequences."

"Noted. Where's—" I caught myself from asking where Cécile, the former leader of the squad, was. "Nasir?"

"He took some of his vacation time to visit family in Babel," Michael said.

Darsh cleared his throat. "I've been given the rundown of events at the gallery up to the point of Rukhsana being killed and Jordy Green and the two love lock cells returned to our custody. What happened next?"

"Alastair showed up," I said.

None of their faces registered surprise.

"How could—why did you leave Ez when he was wounded?" The words burst out of Silas like he'd been trying to suppress them all this time.

"Let her speak." Darsh placed his hand over the other vamp's clenched fist but didn't let it linger there. It was as if they were playing boyfriends in a shitty community theater production and not getting the dynamics right.

It made me almost as angry as Silas's question.

"You think I would have abandoned him if I had any other fucking option?" I wrestled my claws back to fingers and took a deep breath. "That's not true. I had a choice. Go with Alastair or he'd call his minion to kill Secretary Pederson then frame Michael for it. He also planned to prove Michael orchestrated Roman Whittaker's death to protect me. Ezra was conveniently at London HQ at the time, remember?"

My mother compressed her lips into a flat line.

"For his finale, Alastair would expose me as an infernal thanks to a damning photo." I spread my hands wide. "The dominos would fall. Michael to Sector A, my friends under investigation or worse, and Ezra hunted down."

"I see," Michael said tightly. "I imagine that the threat to the secretary is gone?"

"Yes. Alastair called everything off before he died."

"Why didn't he kill Ezra at the gallery?" Sachie erased part of her drawing. "Natán was hunting Alastair. What a blow that would have been to take out his enemy's son, the only Prime, and claim that title in his stead." She blew eraser shavings off her paper.

"He couldn't sense Ezra," I said. "The one good thing Rukhsana's magic did was mask his presence."

"And you left before that changed," Silas said slowly. "I shouldn't have doubted you."

Sach shot Silas an unreadable glance from under her lashes before adding fangs to her monster.

"No," I said evenly to the vampire. "You shouldn't have. But I don't blame you."

"Where did you go next?" Darsh said.

I gave them the whole sordid story. It was easier to

recount this time around. Or easier to disassociate and tell it.

Silas whistled softly while Sachie drew dark thunderclouds.

"That's our culprit," Darsh said.

"Culprit for what?" I said, scratching my arms. My skin wasn't itchy, but my bones felt like they were.

"All the cities where rifts are located suffered minor localized earthquakes at the same moment," Darsh said. "Even in areas that normally aren't prone to them."

"So it was the Luce." I slumped back against my chair.

Michael nodded. "It blew through the Brink and out the rifts like air vents." She paused. "It's gone."

I frowned. "What is?"

"The Brink," Sachie said.

"That's impossible. The Brink is as old as time. It can't just vanish." I looked between their grim faces, searching for any sign they were mistaken.

"Avi." My friend tapped my hand with her pencil. I was scratching my skin hard enough to draw blood.

I stopped immediately and threw Darsh and Silas a stricken look. "Sorry."

"Not a problem." Silas pulled a clean but crumpled red and white bandana from his pocket and tossed it to me.

I blotted the blood and wrapped the bandana around the gash, my heart banging against my ribs. "I'm going to be blamed."

"For what?" Michael clicked a pen with titanium plating and a navy leather wrap on the grip. It was one of the most expensive writing implements she owned. "A psychopath kidnapped the operative tracking him, forcing her to watch a ritual involving the blood of victims he'd ordered murdered."

"Then the ritual backfired and killed him," Silas said. "No great loss."

"Too bad the dhampir's not around to face justice," Darsh said with a tsk.

Sachie snorted. "Too bad we can't kill him again."

I gave them all a grateful smile, though I felt like my blood had been replaced with static electricity.

"Silas," Michael said, "can you put it out on the dark web that the ritual killed Alastair? Meantime, I'll speak with the other directors to round up his followers."

"Will do," Silas said.

"Have the rifts vanished as well?" Cold sweat beaded the back of my neck. When I wriggled my hand, I saw claws and fingers at the same time, along with an increasing pressure in my chest, as if invisible threads were being pulled taut.

Silas shook his head. "No, but they now lead directly to Babel instead of going through the Brink."

Sharp needlelike pains darted through my body at random intervals. I hunched over, my hand on my belly.

"There was no way to anticipate these other effects of the ritual," Silas said insistently. "You did what you thought was best for all of us."

My gut churned, but his words jolted me into sitting up straight. "What other effects?"

"Ever since the rift disturbance, Nippers in those cities have gotten really thirsty," Sachie said. The perspective from the canyon cliff she was drawing was realistic enough to induce vertigo. "Their hunger comes on suddenly," she continued, "and they're unable to control their feeds."

"Is it all newbies or is this skewing to whether the vamp was a Trad in life or an Eishei Kodesh?" I said.

Former Trads slept through the day. Even one lick of sun on their skin fried them. Vamps who'd had flame magic had more ability to stay awake and endure the sun, based on age.

"It doesn't seem to matter," Silas said.

"Have there been human casualties?"

Sachie nodded. "Some."

"The Luce is attempting to 'heal' all vampires." I closed my eyes with a pained exhale.

Then immediately opened them as the door was torn off its hinges.

Ezra burst in, his fangs bared like daggers.

He looked wildly around with eyes that were solid pools of toxic green. Why the hell did he have my eyes?

And what was with his behavior? Had he lost his mind? I jumped to my feet, placing myself between my boyfriend and the others.

Silas shoved Michael—still in her chair—behind him.

Sach's pencil was gone, replaced by a stake.

Darsh narrowed his eyes but didn't move. Should he determine that Ezra was a threat, he'd move as quickly as the Prime could.

"Danger?" Ezra managed to grind out, his body a solid wall of tension.

"No, Zee. Calm down."

Other operatives should have been gawking at us, gossip mode engaged, but the entire floor was deserted. I could almost see cartoon puffs of smoke still lingering in the air.

Ezra slowly closed his fist on a broken hinge, crushing it, then he wrestled his fangs away and dropped his shoulders down. "Houston," he said, "we have a problem."

Chapter 7

Not only was Ezra manifesting my shedim eye color, he'd suffered the same thread-in-chest pulling and sharp darting pain that I had.

"Worse than any of that," he said, "was feeling Aviva's distress so deep in my bones that I couldn't concentrate on anything other than getting to her. I dropped my phone partway through a call with my casino manager."

Ezra had changed from those sweats into his regular clothes while I'd been in the meeting, and he now checked the underside of his leather shoe. "I may have trampled my cell in my rush from the basement," he said.

We moved to a different conference room. One with a door.

I pulled Ezra aside before we entered.

His sleeves were rolled down, the cuffs were buttoned, and his collar was snug against his neck. None of the bruises were visible, but I forced him to roll up his sleeve. The injuries hadn't worsened, but they didn't look any better either.

"Until all traces of Rukhsana's magic disappear," I said,

"plus a decent 'just in case' period longer, we should keep up this thrall."

"You're smiling at the thought of prolonging it." He swore. "These side effects are untenable."

I caught myself rubbing my cheek against his chest and grimaced. "They're not just untenable. They suck. Not knowing whether I'm happy to be with you or it's the thrall talking?"

"I mean, I'm generally a delight," he teased.

"Keep telling yourself that, Cardoso." I shook my head. "It's worse than that for me though. I felt seriously destabilized back there, like two people at once. That's not something I've experienced with Cherry before. And things are tense enough right now without you activating Hulk mode whenever you think I'm in danger."

"Especially considering how that's become a full-time occurrence these days. Plus, the two of us getting itchy if we spend too long apart or are too far away isn't ideal."

"Let's figure out our range of separation." I entered the new conference room, telling Sach that I had a math problem for her.

Louis showed up with two operatives to deal with the busted door and give the all-clear for the level threes who worked on this floor to return.

Michael ordered Louis to spread the word that should the slightest whisper about Ezra's outburst get back to her, every single level three would be on night shift foot patrol for the next month.

Even I blanched at that. It was *January*. Wet and cold and awful. Operatives were gossipy, but we did so at our own risk, well aware that Michael always managed to hear what we were repeating.

However, I was relieved that any rumors would be kiboshed fast.

Sachie looked up from her phone. "Average height of a

single story is fourteen feet. We're on the fifth floor with Spook Squad in the second level basement, so roughly one hundred feet."

"Nice old round number for a separation range," Silas said.

"Great," I said waspishly. "I'll carry a measuring tape with me at all times, shall I?"

"What? Don't tell me you regret this raw deal," Darsh said with a small gasp, eyes theatrically wide. "No one saw that coming."

"Is that you having my back?"

"I always have your back," he said sincerely. "But I tooooooold you sooooo."

"Singing it doesn't make it less bitchy," I snapped.

"The thrall will settle," Ezra said, "giving us more breathing room."

"Since Count von Cardoso is now Avi's shadow," Darsh said, earning a glare from Ezra, "I'm going to fill him in."

He wasn't asking Michael for permission, but she nodded just the same.

Sachie's scritches were a soothing background noise.

Darsh succinctly recapped the earthquake and the baby vamp problems. "It's not only hunger. There's been reports of their speed stuttering and their strength surging and ebbing."

"What can you tell us about the Luce?" Michael said.

"Just that it's the healing magic that was released by the power word," I said. "Don't ask what that was because I forgot it as soon as I spoke it. The magic itself isn't good or bad. It comes down to how it's deployed. In this case, it was mixed with half-shedim blood, giving the dhampir the same level of power as a regular vampire along with a Prime's ability to have kids."

"Aviva and I didn't believe this ritual would work on full vampires," Michael said. "Not that Alastair ever intended that. We just didn't foresee it adversely affecting newly turned vampires." She clicked her pen at Ezra. "Any news from the Copper Hell?"

"We don't get many young vampires, but my manager didn't report any issues."

"Your magic is a main component of the security system," Silas said. "It might be making the Hell secure from this too."

"Hard to say. It works in tandem with Delacroix's," Ezra pointed out.

"Still." The other vampire pursed his lips thoughtfully. "Prime magic may provide a buffer against the Luce."

I clutched my boyfriend's sleeve. "Is Maud safe?"

"She's not at the Hell anymore," Michael said. "I contacted her when you were first discovered missing because I had no idea whether Delacroix was behind it. She's back home. Maccabees from the Hong Kong chapter are guarding her."

"Delacroix wouldn't hurt Maud," I said. "She's safer at the Hell…which is a yacht full of vamps who could go off at any moment. Fuck. Right call."

"I can't take credit for that," Michael said, "because the Luce hadn't hit when I pulled her. However, Maud's godmother was a Maccabee in Hong Kong. They take care of their own and that includes Maud."

"I agree with Michael," Ezra said. "Delacroix probably wouldn't hurt her, but he's still a demon. And there are no issues on the yacht yet, but if my magic doesn't hold against the Luce, she's safer in predominantly human territory."

I fished a random elastic band out of my pocket and tied my hair back in a low ponytail. "I wasn't affected by Alastair's ritual, and given that the yacht's security system with Delacroix's magic has held up, I think anyone or anything with shedim magic is impervious to the Luce."

"Babel won't be affected, then, since it was built in an abandoned demon realm," Ezra said.

Silas shook his head. "That doesn't preclude weaker vampires over there being hit."

"Communications with Babel are spotty." Darsh frowned. "We think we got a message to Nasir but there's been no response."

"So far none of Babel's residents have shown up here in a panic," Michael said. "Let's hope that reinforces the theory that the city is exempt from the effects of the Luce."

"I don't mean to sound uncaring," Sachie said, "but we've got enough on our plate to worry about without Babel. The Brink is gone. Young vampires are freaking out and attacking humans. Let the other realms take care of themselves for a hot minute."

Michael wrote some notes on a pad. "I'll update the Authority and the other chapters. Helping these young vamps stay safe also helps humans."

"Ah, but will the Authority share that view?" Darsh said wryly. "There's only one solution that helps humans truly stay safe."

"No more vamps." Silas crossed his arms.

Of all the times for them to be on the same page.

I swallowed, assuring myself that this enormous displeased vampire did not want to hurt us mortals. Well, not the ones in this room.

"They'll use us to 'help' the injured now," Darsh said. "It might not involve staking them but there'll be a tipping point. And should their own operatives show signs of this infection, you'll be ordered to help *us*."

Silas snorted. "Help us right off this mortal coil."

Michael flinched, dropping the pen. "I'll never let it come to that."

Darsh's gentle smile was more damning than any retort.

"Maybe if the ritual had been conducted here on

earth," I said, steering us away from that charged topic, "no one else would have been affected. But the Brink has always been a wild card."

"I don't think that's it," Darsh said. "There must have been other successful supplicants for the power word who wanted the Luce for themselves. All of them waited until they got back to use it?" He shook his head. "Doubtful. There's a more likely cause. Alastair's rune." He slid a pad from the middle of the table toward me. "Can you draw it?"

"No." I huffed a laugh.

"That's okay," Ezra immediately said. "You can't be expected to remember it."

"It's not that." I frowned, trying to explain it. "I don't think I'll ever forget it. I just can't draw it. It bent and twisted, and looking at it was like looking through reality. Everything about it was wrong, and there's no way to recount it."

"I've never heard of anything like that," Michael said. "Darsh?"

He shook his head. None of the others were familiar with such a thing either.

Sachie rubbed her index finger and thumb together to wipe off some smudged pencil. "The rune's magic has to be shedim-based, right?"

Darsh nodded. "That makes sense with the description and that it was used in conjunction with demon magic in those victims' blood."

"Give me a team to learn everything about the Luce so we can stop it from spreading further," I said.

Michael laughed incredulously. "You're taking time off."

"But—"

"But nothing, Operative Fleischer."

"Uh-oh," Sachie said in a low voice, putting the

finishing touches on a raven.

Michael clicked her pen. "You just survived a traumatic ordeal and are negotiating the effects of your enthrallment."

"Sure, but that's just background noise."

"Ouch." Ezra placed a hand on his heart.

I rolled my eyes. "You know what I mean."

"Let me go see Burning Eddie." Sachie closed her notebook and slid the pencil in through the spiral binding. "He's got a library of rare books about magic. There might be something on that rune that gives us insights. And he's fun to talk to if nothing else."

"I need you here," Darsh said.

"I'll be gone less than two days."

"Fine," he said reluctantly, "but I'm holding you to that timeframe."

Sachie kicked me under the table.

I was about to kick her back when I clued in. "Sachie formed a connection with Burning Eddie, but she shouldn't go alone, and it's not like Darsh or Silas can leave."

Darsh shot me "the look" at the same time as Michael did. Good for him for learning it.

"Both of you stop it right now." I shook my head. "I say that respectfully but face facts. I'm the only eyewitness to the ritual, and I might spot something in one of Eddie's books that no one else would pick up on. This is me taking time off from active duty and recovering. How bad could it possibly be when I have one of the most deadly people I know around me?"

The director tightened the top part of her pen. "You're assuming this demon is going to cooperate."

"He did give me a hat," Sachie said. "And signed my cast. We're summer camp besties."

"That's irrelevant, Saito," Michael admonished her.

She fixed the pen. "What if he senses that Aviva is a half shedim and isn't happy about it?"

"Then I'll dazzle him with my winning personality." I met her glower with a grin. "And throw a Prime at him."

Silas laughed out loud.

Ezra blinked. "Oh. No. He and I didn't exactly start off on the right foot."

Michael smirked and spread her hands wide. "Then it's settled. Aviva stays. The other directors and I will put our best minds on the Luce and—"

"It's because Eddie's horses hate Ezra," Silas said. "They go out of their way to kick him."

Darsh's shoulders shook.

"Thank you for clarifying that," Ezra said tightly.

"Charm his horses and he'll love you," Silas said.

Ezra looked doubtful, and my heart sank. He wouldn't agree if his presence put me or Sachie in danger, but I couldn't sit back when I'd helped kick all of this into motion.

Michael and the other directors could assign every Maccabee in existence to the Luce problem, but I was investigating as well.

"I'm going to follow your advice, Director, and take some time off to recover," I said.

She threw her pen at me.

I caught it. "Handing over hostages? You know better than that."

"Give it back, you horrible child."

"I suck as a daughter but as an operative…?"

She drummed her fingers on the table, her lips pursed. "You and Ezra may accompany Sachie," she said at last.

I tossed the pen back.

The Prime looked faintly ill. "Giddy up."

Things moved quickly after that.

Darsh got word that some human residents were fleeing

their formerly desirable vamp-controlled neighborhoods. Trad officers had shown up to assist with the panicked families, but things were beginning to get out of control.

"Continue the stepped-up patrolling, especially in the neighborhood around the rift," the director said.

I bit the inside of my cheek. With Cécile dead, Darsh was now the senior member of the squad. I hoped Rukhsana was rotting in the worst circle of demon hell.

Well, most of you does, Cherry said. *You still feel sorry for her, but keep telling yourself she deserves what she got. Maybe you'll eventually believe it.*

Michael sailed out the door, already on the phone to Chief Constable Keira Davis, head of the Trad police force, arranging for officers who'd been trained to stake vamps to team up with Maccabees.

Darsh and Silas were right behind her.

"You get to visit a demon lair. You're welcome," Sachie said to me.

"Yeah, that was pretty smooth of you." I frowned. "I didn't know Trad officers were taught to stake vamps. How do they practice?"

"Mannequins. Very few of them have actual experience." She paused, looking grim. "And are still around to tell the tale."

"Olivier?"

"He trained. I trained him more."

"He'll volunteer for this duty, then."

"Not just volunteer," Sachie said. "Olivier told me yesterday that he'd offer to head up a squad if it came to this. He was excited." She spoke in a grumpy, disgusted tone, but it was followed by this faraway, almost dreamy look.

I snorted at her expression, doing my damnedest not to imagine their training sessions.

No wonder Sach was torn about his participation.

It was hard enough for Maccabees to stake vampires and come away uninjured, and we had magic of our own. That said, Detective Olivier Desmond was smart, experienced, and capable.

I didn't offer a platitude that Olivier would be okay, but I did squeeze Sachie's hand. "Stay here. Help him. Ezra and I will visit Burning Eddie on our own."

She stood up. "No. I have the strongest relationship with that shedim and the best shot at accessing his library." She scooped up her notebook and pencil. "Ezra, can you charter a jet for tonight? Regular flights will take too long."

"Sure, but it would be faster to portal through the Hell." Ezra could create portals only because he drew on the shedim magic infused in the yacht. Since it wasn't a Prime ability, he had to use the Hell as a transit point.

"I'm not sure we should," I said. "I'm not particularly excited about running into Delacroix and a ton of potentially freaked-out vamps."

"I'll leave it up to the two of you." He headed for the door. "I have to go downstairs and see if my phone still works."

Sach and I debated the pros and cons of going through the Copper Hell. Ezra would be swarmed by his staff, though that would still be faster than a plane. But what if we encountered a baby vamp infected by the Luce?

Or worse, what if I was wrong about shedim magic being exempt from the Luce and the portals went sideways while we were using them?

Besides, my gut was telling me not to give Delacroix the heads-up about this journey, so how could we get to Burning Eddie quickly and discreetly?

Once Sachie and I made our decision, I casually changed the subject. "Is Silas still staying with Darsh?"

"As far as I know, but I'm betting he's still in the guest

room." Sachie shook her head. "Another thing that sucks right now."

My chest tightened. The twisted connection between Fintan (aka the Ashbishop, aka Silas's best friend before he turned him into that vampire) and Patrin threatened to derail my friends' happiness before it had a chance to take root. After everything life had thrown at them, if two people deserved to find joy in each other's arms, it was them.

Ezra returned. "I cracked my phone's screen, but it works. Am I chartering a plane or opening a portal?"

"Are you sure we have to go via the yacht?" I said. "You may not need to anymore now that you're powered up."

He raised his eyebrows. "You want me to draw on you again?"

"Your portal-making happens because you draw on Delacroix's magic in the Hell's security system. It's why you can't go from point A to point B unless you travel through the yacht. Well, the thrall is tied to my blood. Does it use my shedim magic?" I spread my hands wide. "If it does, maybe you can create portals without the Hell as a transit point. It's worth a shot, right?"

Anything to delay my reunion with Daddy Dearest.

Chapter 8

Opening portals here in HQ or inside Sach's and my apartment wouldn't work because of the mezuzah wards, so Ezra traipsed downstairs to the bottom of the underground parking lot, which wasn't warded.

It was a more private place for him to practice than in the alley behind our home, which was where we'd ultimately depart from, since Sach had to get the cowboy hat that Burning Eddie had gifted her.

Sachie and I intended to follow, but the garage was outside the calculated safe zone of the thrall, and I had to discover the effects of Ezra breaching that.

Ezra stayed on the phone with Sachie, slowly making his way down each level.

The tightness in my chest grew stronger, sweat running between my shoulder blades, and my head throbbing to the point of my teeth hurting.

By level P2, my vision was a blurry pinprick, but I insisted on pushing the limit a bit more. Halfway to P3, pain shot up my left arm, my breathing shallow.

Sachie called it and Ezra blurred back up to P1.

Weirdly, the second he was back in range, all my symptoms vanished. I didn't have any lingering effects, not even fatigue.

According to my boyfriend, he hadn't even sensed he'd breached the safety zone until I'd freaked out.

Sach glared at me.

Ezra was now two stairwells ahead of us, going back to the lower level of the parking garage.

"I still don't regret thralling him," I said. "And this valuable data will help keep me safe."

P4 smelled like trapped exhaust and mildew, but there weren't many cars. No operatives willingly parked down here, and visitor parking was up on P1.

Ezra was stationed in a far corner, practicing the portal.

I unzipped my coat. "It occurred to me that while I didn't feed off Ezra when we thralled, I did feel his magic inside me. Surely I've gained some new ability from that."

Sachie's stare grew flatter. Impressive.

She shook her head and wandered over to Ezra.

I tried to tear the elevator sign off the wall, but I didn't suddenly possess superstrength, nor could I hear conversations on other levels.

Lowering my expectations, I attempted to illuminate Ezra's weaknesses with my blue flame sight. After all, that was possible when I was in Babel. Was it so unreasonable that I'd be granted that one power?

Apparently, yes, it was. I still couldn't illuminate vampire weaknesses, not even when I tried in Cherry Bomb form.

"Avi." Sachie waved me over.

The air thickened and hummed, resisting Ezra's magic as if he was trying to part honey rather than empty space, but a portal slowly materialized. It was made of the same dark light woven into a mesh net as all the portals from the Hell.

I leaned forward on the balls of my feet.

Its edges wavered, threatening to unravel.

"Come on," Sachie whispered.

For a heart-stopping moment, the black netting grew so thin I could barely see it, leaving only the faintest web of shadows. Then the portal pulled taut and held, its center crystallizing into a stable, though delicate, gateway.

A heaviness settled behind my eyes, and I suppressed a sudden yawn. "Got a protein bar?" I murmured.

Sach dug one out of her coat pocket and slapped it in my hand.

Ezra busted out a pleased smile. "I only crossed the city with it, but not bad for a first attempt." He waved a hand and the portal disappeared.

While he practiced, I dealt with the increasingly panicked texts from my mom, my friends, and even Maud, from my time in the Brink.

Even with the ordeals I'd recently faced, in some ways I'd been lucky. Most of the time I'd been too busy trying to survive and able to keep my fears about Ezra to a dull roar. That hadn't been the case for the others. The vamp problems hadn't started until after the Brink blew up, which meant they'd worried about me for two days.

I swallowed the last third of the peanut buttery lump and texted Maud, relieved when she immediately replied back. I promised we'd have a longer catch-up soon. As I scrolled through the rest of the messages, I found a few from Orly. The first one asked where Ezra was, since he always messaged her back quickly, with follow-ups demanding I check in with her as well.

"Call your cousin," I told Ezra. "She's worried sick. Also, she wants you to know that yarn is on sale at the place in Toronto you like."

"We already spoke before I joined your meeting, but check this out," he said with a huge grin. He moved his fingers like he was playing chords on a piano, moving the dark strands of varying thickness that were woven into the mesh netting.

"Pretty."

"It's not a party trick, Aviva," he said with much more hauteur than the moment warranted. "I'm manipulating magical forces in an entirely new way."

Sach looked up from her phone and elbowed me. "Bad girlfriend."

"Think of it as bandwidth in a network," Ezra said. "When I create thicker strands, larger objects or more entities can pass through my portal, while thinner ones limit the flow." He practically bounced up and down. "Magic knitting."

I smiled at the giant nerd. "Very cool. Should we find ourselves on a speeding bus needing a magic exit, you've got our backs."

"Or"—he glared at me—"I can cast off the thread, so to speak, and prevent others from following."

"Yeah, that's more useful," Sachie agreed. "How far have you gotten?"

"I've made a portal as far as the Gander airport in Newfoundland. It's tricky because I have to have been where I'm going. I tried creating one to Notre-Dame Basilica in Montreal, but I'd only seen photos, so it didn't work."

She waved her phone at us. "I've got something to take care of upstairs, so let me know when you've nailed this, and I'll drive us home to portal."

"Copy that," I said. "Can you grab the bag you brought me earlier?"

"Will do." Sach left.

I sat down on someone's trunk with another yawn.

Ezra hovered nervously around me. "Could we top up the thrall?"

I tried to keep the surprise off my face that he required

it this soon. But he had been exerting himself and those bruises—the remnants of Rukhsana's magic—were still present. Some of the purply black might have faded into yellow but that also might have been the lighting down here.

Was my battery power flushing her magic out of his system or simply keeping it at bay?

"It's a lot to ask," he said, "but I can't portal all three of us directly to Burning Eddie's and expect to have any strength left over. I'd rather not be vulnerable."

Would this add another two or three more days to our current thrall effect timeframe?

"Yeah, of course." No point risking Ezra powering down mid-portal, and it hadn't been too harsh a process for me. A couple more protein bars wouldn't hurt though.

I glanced around the parking garage one more time to ensure no one was around, then he fed.

The first time I'd thralled him, at least I'd blissed out a bit from it. Not now. There was a mild enjoyable pull on my end, and I felt his magic for a moment, but that was about it.

Yet the gentle brush of his shoulder against mine sent electricity dancing across my skin like summer lightning, leaving me breathless and wondering if it was this amazing for him—and fuck, that was the thrall, wasn't it?

I scowled.

"Thank you for rethralling me." He smiled.

I pressed my hands to my heart. "Is that active verb usage I hear? Half a point for the Prime."

"Tough judge," he joked.

My gash healed almost as quickly as his. "Do you mind avoiding the Hell a little longer?"

For all that I disparaged Ezra playing Lord of the Copper Hell, he took pride in how he ran the casino and had turned it into a well-oiled machine.

"No." He shook out his hands. "Let me get back to work."

There were a few misfires, including a splash of Atlantic Ocean seawater from the portal that sent me searching same-day delivery lifejackets, and Ezra stopped at one point while the parkade got busy, but it wasn't long before he announced he'd stabilized a portal directly from here to the foot of Burning Eddie's driveway. No Copper Hell transit point required.

I texted Sach we were ready to go, then sprinted up a few levels to where her car was parked. Sadly, I was no faster, I couldn't leapfrog an SUV, and I almost crashed into someone's car door because I didn't hear it opening over the electrical hum in the parkade.

This was the second time I'd sensed his magic inside me while he fed, yet I still had bupkis in the way of enhancements. Was the thrall really just the one-way street that Darsh and Silas had warned me about?

"To be fair," Ezra said after beating me in less than a second in the arm-wrestling contest I'd demanded, "it's not like I'm feeling any bump in my powers."

I shook out my hand. "Boo-hoo. You're already a Prime. And you're opening portals outside of the Hell, you big liar."

"I'm sure something will kick in for you," he said.

"No, you aren't."

"I hope something will?"

"I know you do. Hey, Sach." I waved at my friend's approach.

We spent the drive home discussing strategies over the rhythmic swipe of the windshield wipers. Sachie and Ezra sketched out Eddie's property, including any known booby-traps, so we weren't blindsided by flaming arrows or something.

The safest route was via the front door. Sach and I

proposed that Ezra stay out of sight but within thrall range until Eddie allowed us in.

My boyfriend presented a reasonable counterargument to that strategy (i.e. pitched a fit about insane ideas) but our logic convinced him. (We wore him down until he gave in.)

The plan was to dump our stuff in the condo and then head down to the alley for Ezra to portal us, but in the elevator, Sach and I got a text from Darsh telling us to tune into a local news broadcast.

We raced into our place and turned on the TV.

Jared Casey, the Vancouver-based politician with an anti–Eishei Kodesh agenda, was giving a fire and brimstone oration on the steps of City Hall, standing under the over-hang at the grand Art Deco front entrance to protect himself from the rain.

His words resonated through the downpour like thunder, each pronouncement drawing frenzied cheers from the crowd that had gathered despite the deluge. The polls showed him gaining ground every day with his fellow politicians as well, getting perilously close to turning his anti–Eishei Kodesh rhetoric into devastating federal legislation.

He'd replaced his smarmy smile with a look of such manufactured sincerity that I itched to introduce his face to the nearest hard surface. The noticeably fake tan he'd acquired to go with his blond combover made my eye twitch.

Casey played up how vampires were swarming earth looking for their next meal and how Maccabees couldn't be trusted to keep people safe because they were getting kickbacks from the vampire Mafias to look the other way. Luckily, his magic oversight proposal was closer to becoming reality through emergency measures, at which point, he assured everyone, real humans would be put in charge.

"Impressive," Sachie said disgustedly. "He managed to diss us and do a callback to his 'real humans don't need magic' bullshit. Riled-up fools can do a lot of damage, and there's always a black market for anyone determined to get illegal firearms."

The footage changed from Casey to people swarming local vampire neighborhoods—along with some mobs outside Maccabee HQ. There were no reported incidents of gunfire yet, which was a blessing, especially around vampires, but Casey had knowingly lit the match on an already volatile situation.

"Rukhsana should have killed him when she had the chance," Sachie said and went into her bedroom to call Darsh.

"Leaving in five," Ezra called out.

"Back in a sec." I hurried into my bedroom, took my Maccabee ring out of my jewelry box, and slid it on.

When I first learned that the magic cocktail in our Maccabee rings didn't kill shedim, only imprisoned them in the love lock cells, I wrestled with whether to continue hunting demons to satiate the Baroness. This wasn't out of any humanitarian concern for their prison conditions, but because I didn't want to add to the battery power that the shedim owners drew off these cells.

It was the same issue the Authority struggled with. They considered making us drain the magic entirely but let us keep it. In the event of a shedim run-in, it was better to send the demons into prisons than lose our lives.

I held out my hand, the tiny gems representing each of the flame types catching in the light. There was a familiar comfort in wearing it, but no deeper connection or feeling like this was a talisman anymore. I put that sorrow away to deal with at a later date, since it was go time.

Ezra swore loudly in Spanish.

I grabbed my passport (just in case), and raced back into the living room, heart thudding in dread that someone had died, mildly surprised to find Ezra still staring at the television.

A handsome gentleman who looked disturbingly like my boyfriend was holding a press conference.

Natán Cardoso was back on earth.

The fact that Ezra's vampire father looked the same age as him never failed to creep me out. It was worse because while Ezra inherited his brown skin from his Mizrahi Jewish mom, his features were almost identical to his Sephardic dad's.

Natán's hair was lighter and straighter and his corn-flower-blue eyes lacked my boyfriend's warmth, though most wouldn't see that, fooled by the charming smile he had at the ready. Light winked off the gold embroidery in his kippah. So pious.

He spoke Spanish while standing on a covered balcony with salmon-pink arches. It was tiled in a pale stone, and spotlights glinted off the crisp white railing running under a series of Italianate arches.

The footage cut to a wide shot. A grand plaza in a wash of colored lights stretched out like a vast canvas. It teemed with people gathered around the pyramid monument at its heart to watch the speech.

With that backdrop against the night sky, the balcony appeared both intimate and a place of significance.

I squinted at the screen. "Where is he?"

"Caracas," Ezra said. "That's Plaza de Mayo behind him. He's at Casa Rosada, the seat of our national government."

"Is he on Evita's balcony?" I would have laughed if this wasn't so troubling.

Natán had switched to English. Ezra took the remote from me and turned up the volume.

"…spent years as a Maccabee operative, caring for humanity. It's true that I am a vampire now, but I still have that protective drive, extended to all beings. Until we understand what is happening, we must work together. It's our only way forward to keep this beautiful planet safe." He looked off wistfully. "It's what my late wife, Eva, would have wished. May her memory be a blessing."

Shards of plastic from my mangled remote control fell to the carpet from Ezra's fist.

"To that end, I have purchased the Seaside group," Natán said, "which owns rehabilitation in-patient treatment facilities around the world. I'm sinking my money and resources into retrofitting these clinics as quickly as possible to become secure sites for the afflicted. I, myself, will be based at the one here in my hometown of Caracas."

He smiled and extended a hand at the older man to his left, who beamed at the cameras.

"Thanks to President Lara," Natán said, "Venezuela will be the birthplace of the Vampire Care Initiative. Not only will this benefit vampires and humans, this enterprise will go down in the history books for starting a new chapter of vampire-human collaboration and the good work we can do when we join forces."

In my head, Cherry made a raspberry sound.

"I'll work with all of earth's vampire communities to get my infected brethren off the streets and into treatment to address the magic ravaging them." Natán leaned forward into the camera and placed his hand on his heart. "Let me assure people that the oath I took to do good in this world as a Maccabee burns as strongly within me today as when I first spoke it."

Ezra snorted.

"I invite Maccabees and Trad authorities to work with me. Gracias."

The assembled reporters broke out in a flurry of questions, but I found the power button on the side of the TV and shut it off.

"You trust this sudden benevolence?" I said.

Ezra shook his head. "Not for a second. We'll find out what he's really up to."

"Add it to the list." I tapped his fist.

He blinked at the twisted remains of my remote control on the ground. "Sorry."

"No worries." I dumped them in the garbage. Rest in peace, plastic.

A hate-filled politician, a vampire mob boss—this nest of vipers was already too crowded for my liking. Couldn't wait to see which snake struck next.

Chapter 9

Ezra's portal to England worked like a mesh dream. He created it perfectly on his first try, we stepped through, and wham, instant time change and zero sticky hug sensation.

Props for the thrall working in Ezra's favor. Well, on his magic. He hadn't fully healed from Rukhsana's attack yet. Would I have to thrall him a third time?

An owl hooted, bringing me back to my surroundings.

Hedgerows and ancient stone walls divided the fields into a patchwork that stretched toward the lights of the nearest village, while bare oak trees stood sentinel against the winter night sky.

Cold starlight speared through gaps in the drifting clouds. They softened the appearance of the weathered stone of the old farmhouse that was our destination.

Ezra melted into the shadows with a whispered "Good luck."

Sachie and I hopscotched between the dirt driveway and a scrubby faint trail in the grass, my friend navigating the landmarks such as a gnarled tree or rusted-out pickup as safe passage through the boobytraps.

Correction. I hopscotched, Sach swaggered, her

thumbs hooked into her belt loops and her cowboy hat worn at a jaunty angle. The cream Stetson looked incongruent on my willowy friend with her pink-tipped hair, but she'd insisted it would be rude to leave it at home.

Frost had begun to crystallize on the paddock gates, and somewhere in the darkness, the wind carried the distant sound of hooves shifting against stable bedding.

There was no sense of being watched. Was Burning Eddie tucked in for the night?

"Hello, the house!" Sach broadly waved her arms, stopping well before we reached the front door. She turned in a slow circle, peering into the darkness.

I resisted the urge to do the same, convinced I'd give away Ezra's presence. He was keeping pace within thrall-approved range because my awareness of him over to my right hummed under my skin, but not in an unpleasant way.

Sachie's fingers twitched but she didn't unearth a weapon. "The door should have creaked open by now."

"He just lets people in?"

"Sure, if they've made it this far." She trotted toward the house. "Why should he have to come outside to kill them?"

"The fact that you find that logical scares me."

She grinned, her teeth flashing white in the darkness, and tipped the hat back. "Ready?"

I drew the Zen Zapper from my holster belt. The prototype, which combined electroshock technology with white flame calming magic, had been destroyed, but over the past couple months, R&D pushed through production of this weapon. It wouldn't kill a shedim, but could it help chill one the fuck out? I'd know soon enough. "Ready."

The door was unlocked. I braced myself for rat taxidermy—or people taxidermy—but found hand-knitted blankets in muted greens and browns draped over well-worn leather chairs. The wide windowsills held rosemary, their ceramic pots painted with delicate wildflower patterns that echoed the faded florals of the open linen curtains.

Sachie headed upstairs, making a lot of noise and calling Eddie's name, but we reconvened in the kitchen without finding him.

I poked one of the copper saucepans hanging from a beam above the old Aga stove. This cottagecore vibe was a trap, right? Those small fragrant bundles of herbs were poison? The mismatched teacups lining open wooden shelves hid demon rodents or something?

Nope. Everything was as benign as it appeared.

I looked up—the thing people never did in horror movies—in case Sach had learned her wall-climbing gecko moves from Eddie, but he wasn't poised and ready to drop down on our heads.

"Was this what it looked like when you were here before?" I said.

Sachie shook her head, jerking a thumb at the jars of homemade preserves. "He hadn't started making jam yet."

Uh-huh. "I didn't see a library."

She fired finger guns at the door set between the fridge and the sink, the metal around the knob grooved with scratches. "We gotta be moseying on down to the dungeons," she drawled in a Southern accent.

I crossed my arms, still clutching the Zen Zapper. "Do you have that out of your system now?"

"I reckon that might be it." She dipped her chin at me. "Ma'am."

Laughing, I pushed her toward the door.

It was thoughtful of Eddie to install modern electricity to illuminate the creaking stairs and dirty walls. Or it was fiendishly clever, as the glare made the bloodstains and unidentifiable glossy smears look like a Tarantino film.

The basement was a windowless labyrinth and there was no cell service down here.

My bones were starting to itch again, but I did my best to keep my anxiety tamped down so Ezra didn't feel it and freak out.

I wish you were here.

Should I come in?

Hearing his voice in my head made me crack my noggin on a low bulkhead. I swore, rubbing the goose egg.

Sachie glanced over her shoulder. "You okay?"

"Yeah."

Ezra and I weren't really psychically linked, were we? That was not… I mean, I didn't want… Did I?

Zee?

No response.

Sachie picked something up off the floor and sighed. "Eddie never took this off."

The bolo tie was torn and filthy, either from a struggle or because he always wore it.

My friend readied a stake and a dagger. She eyed the Zen Zapper. "Non-lethal may not be the best move anymore."

"Yup." I tucked the Zapper into my belt.

The claws on my fingers stuttered before snapping into place, the toxic green scales unfurling across my skin like the slow dissolution of ink-clouded water, rather than a blink-of-the-eye transformation.

Ezra was magically knitting light, and I was working harder to settle into my armor and bulked-up shedim body. Fan-fucking-tastic.

I gagged, assaulted by a stench of death and decay that hadn't been noticeable in my human form. Gee thanks, Cherry. Breathing shallowly through my nose, I marched forward. "Follow me."

I led Sachie through a few more twists and turns, the

basement's shadows seeming to pulse with each rapid beat of my heart, before I stopped in front of an unassuming metal door.

It was cracked open, a slash of light from the hallway falling into the dense shadows inside.

"Eddie?" I mouthed.

Sach shook her head. "Too obvious," she mouthed back.

We did rock, paper, scissors to see who'd traipse into the trap first.

"What's in here?" Sachie said loudly and stepped through the door with me on her heels.

A vampire exploded from the dark corner with the intensity of a starved predator and grabbed Sach, fangs extended.

She staked him before he broke skin.

Two more vamps came at me, all desperation and no technique.

I slid into my blue flame sight.

Their previous injuries were helpfully laid out in blue pulsing dots. Finally! One crumb of coolness for moi!

Now that's more like it. I snapped into a crystalline state of perfect focus, my movements sharp and precise.

I caught the first one with an elbow to the throat, using his own momentum to slam him into the concrete wall. Before he'd dazedly bounced off it, I'd torn his head off, flinging it into a corner by my claws.

I hadn't finished dusting ash off my hands before the second vampire grazed my arm with his fangs. I drove my knee up into his solar plexus, following through with a strike to the temple that dropped him. Then I stomped him into oblivion.

Cherry provided a lively soundtrack with Queen's "Another One Bites the Dust."

More shapes moved in the darkness. These vampires

were weak and uncoordinated in their starvation, but they made up for it with feral abandon.

I fended them off like they were puppies, though one got close enough that his fangs ghosted along my neck before I took him down for good.

Barely winded, I bounced on the balls of my feet, seeking out more opponents, but the vampires were done and dusted.

Ezra and Sachie stood in the doorway with their mouths hanging open and the flashlights on their phones trained on me like spotlights.

"You've got a little…" Ezra stepped toward me with his hand up, then stopped. "May I?" He gestured to my cheek.

I wiped the blood off with the side of my ashy hand. "Why are you acting so weird?"

"Your eyes are red, Crimson Princess," he replied.

His weaknesses were still illumination-proof. Pity.

"And you were cackling like a crazy person while you killed those vampires," Sachie said. "Single-handedly. With no stake."

I held out my hands. Ignore the blood and ash and they didn't look any different from their usual demon form.

Except I could now kill vampires with my bare hands and use my synesthete vision to see injuries on all non-Prime vampires. Sure, I could do the injury-spotting thing in Babel, but Burning Eddie's home was firmly on earth.

"Did the thrall benefits finally kick in or did I unlock a new ability?" I said.

Cherry didn't know, and sadly, neither did Ezra.

Something cold settled in my stomach. I wanted these new powers to be earned through my own strength and struggles, not handed to me as some magical side effect.

Changed your tune, did you, Fleischer?

It was worse, though, if they were suddenly present

because Ezra had somehow boosted my magic so I could play protector.

I couldn't bring myself to ask.

I looked at the other two. "Did I freak you out?"

"It was exhilarating," Sachie said. "Like a good ringside fight."

Ezra grimaced.

I let my features slide back to human. "What?"

"I felt your bloodlust."

"Oh. Okay, well, yes, that's a bit weird."

"You were really into it," he said. "Reeeeaaaally."

"Best birthday present really?" Sachie asked. "Or orgasm really?"

My boyfriend pointed at her. "That one."

Frowning, I picked up the Zen Zapper that had fallen during the fight. "I did not have an orgasm fighting vampires."

"Well, you'd know best," Ezra said with an unconvincing smile.

I tried one more time to illuminate his weaknesses.

"Can we do something useful like find Eddie or the library?" I said.

Sachie shone the flashlight into every corner of the large stone chamber. Metal hooks protruded from the walls, dark stains marked the floor, and ancient manacles hung at intervals, their chains trailing like dead vines.

Scattered across a rusted metal table were implements whose purposes I didn't want to contemplate, while drainage channels were carved into the floor, all leading to a central grate.

"This is where Eddie tortured vampires who came in challenge." Ezra toed at an open handcuff. "Where is he?"

"Dead." Sachie showed him the bolo tie.

"That's not conclusive proof," Ezra said.

"Maybe not. But this is." She kicked a bloody calf with

a mangled foot that had only three toes. "There's more of him over here," she said in a dull voice, turning away from the grisly remains. "The vamps really feasted."

Ezra paced the perimeter of the wall, stopping in front of a small upended bucket. A trail of dried blood led from it to the floor drain. "The vamps got free and swarmed Eddie. Got the jump on him."

"He's a demon," I pointed out. "He didn't sense them?"

Sachie headed back into the hallway. "He'd suffered a lot of concussions fighting vampires for centuries. Hate and rage were the only things holding his mushy brains together."

"Lovely." I added my phone's light to theirs. "And yet you two managed to form the supernatural equivalent of a buddy comedy despite his scrambled neurons."

Sachie snorted.

We searched the basement for the library in silence, splitting up to cover more ground.

Zee? You there? Had his voice in my head been real before or just wishful thinking?

I'm here. Everything okay?

I resorted to poking promising stones in hopes of a secret passage. *Well, we're chatting psychically when we haven't even had a second date, so you tell me.*

His bark of laughter boomed through the basement.

"Found it!" Sachie called out landmarks like "Take a left at the wall of definitely not-cursed jewelry," "Avoid the creepy statue that moves when it thinks you're not looking," and my least favorite, "You'll have to jump the ritual circle with the yellow skid marks."

Gross.

The library was crammed into what might have once been a large storage room, with books stacked in precarious towers.

Ancient tomes shared space with paperback romances,

grimoires were wedged between manga volumes, and scrolls stuck haphazardly out of filing cabinets. Narrow paths wound between the stacks, some dead-ending in cluttered reading nooks where mismatched armchairs nestled under strings of old Moroccan lamps, tangled with charging cables that snaked their way to an overloaded power strip.

Every horizontal surface hosted either more books or half-empty coffee mugs with suspicious growths. A battered desk barely visible under layers of Post-it notes and opened references served as some kind of command center, with a mini fridge humming away beside it. The whole space smelled of old paper, coffee grounds, and something vaguely mystical—possibly incense, possibly just very old carpet.

I pointed at a handful of items scattered around the room: a skull, a stuffed turtle, and an egg bejeweled with leering demon faces that was totally purchased at the Dante's Inferno gift shop. "There's shedim magic on all of those. I can sense them even though I'm wearing my Maccabee ring."

There was no nausea either. I put aside any unease. It didn't matter why this was happening, the timing was fortuitous.

"Can you use your Spidey-sense to find books with demon magic on them?" Sachie said. "We'll check those first for answers."

Ezra followed me, collecting the ones I pointed out, and dumping them in a stack on the desk.

We divvied up the pile and got researching. Somewhere in these yellowed pages lurked our answers. I just hoped they didn't also spell our doom.

Chapter 10

References to the Luce were few and far between, hardly more than waxing rhapsodical about its great healing power. There was nothing about it infecting and harming newly turned vampires.

Having reverted back to human form, I stretched out the kinks in my neck and moved on to another book.

"Does this look familiar?" Ezra pushed a slim volume in front of me, tapping an illustration.

I managed a single brief glance at the rune before turning away and swallowing hard. "As much as my brain can process identifiable details, yes."

Sach grimaced at it then quickly averted her gaze. "Anyone speak Latin?"

Even Ezra had to cover the rune with one hand while he translated the text under the illustration. "It's an ancient shedim rune used to amplify magic."

"Of course it is," Sachie said with a huff. "More equals better. Typical dude thinking."

"The amplification rune blew the Brink apart, letting the Luce flood out," I said.

"Where it started affecting baby vamps," Sach said gravely. "Babel might be okay, or it might take longer to affect it, like the Luce so far only hitting young or infirm vamps."

"You said you didn't have the bandwidth to worry about Babel."

"I honestly thought it was impervious to harm, but an amplification rune changes everything. And if Babel is hit, then infected and freaked-out vampires will stampede to earth." Sachie's voice was tight. "They can't close themselves off because they'll be unable to import synthetic or human blood, and its citizens will turn on each other for sustenance."

"There are humans living there," Ezra said grimly.

"Which will be awful for them, but that's a small and finite supply. At some point the vampires will come our way."

"It'll shift the balance of power in favor of vamps over humans." I shut the book, sending up a cloud of dust that I choke-coughed on. "Even Maccabees don't have the resources to prevent that."

Ezra snapped a photo of the illustration of the rune. He had a particular furrow between his eyebrows, the one that made him look like he was trying to solve differential equations in his head while simultaneously tasting something unpleasant. "Alastair had half-shedim blood in addition to the power word, which were the only necessary components for the ritual."

"As far as we knew," Sachie said.

"Assume we were correct," Ezra said. "Alastair never intended to share these new abilities with his followers, so why bring an amplification rune into it? Was he deluded enough to think he could *truly* become a Prime? Or was something else at play? Think about it. How did Alastair, a dhampir, find a shedim rune, and this one in particular, when neither Darsh, Silas, or I was familiar with it?"

"What are you proposing?" I said.

"If Babel's vamps show up here in a panic, they'll beeline to one place and one place only. Right into the open arms of my father's Vampire Care Initiative." Ezra threw his arms wide. "The great undead savior."

"Natán gave Alastair the rune?" Sach said doubtfully. "Why? He put a bounty on the guy."

"Publicly, sure," Ezra said. "But privately? My father is a master manipulator. Sometimes he would orchestrate feuds with other Mafias in order to solidify his own power base. Both sides always benefitted, even if the Kosher Nostra was the one to come out on top. I don't see why now would be any different."

"To what end?"

"Get all vampires under his thumb here on earth *then* cause a shift in power that neither Maccabees nor armies can prevent. He'd rule the world with the help of a Prime who actually did his bidding."

Sach shot me a look at the bitterness in Ezra's voice.

"Natán claims to want to work with the Maccabees," I pointed out.

Ezra shook his head. "He doesn't think they'll call his bluff."

Sach snapped her fingers. "The handcuffs. Those vampires weren't in them, but Eddie wouldn't have freed his prisoners."

I frowned. "What does that have to do with the rune?"

"The cuffs were open. How?"

"If they weren't opened with a key," Ezra said, "then shedim magic secured them, and when Eddie died, his magic failed."

"But any magic had to fail *before* Eddie was killed," Sach

insisted. "Otherwise, those vampires wouldn't have been free to stage a surprise attack and murder him. Did Eddie's magic fail on those cuffs because of the Luce?"

"Well," Ezra said slowly, "if they opened because the Luce ate away the magic on them, same as it's doing to vampires, that implies that vampire magic is shedim based. Or at least springs from a similar source."

"Vampires don't have shifting shadows like half shedim," I said, "so they're not demon children genetically." The prevalent rumor around vampire creation was that vampires were descended from the human workers who built the Tower of Babel and subsequently cursed by God. "Vamps and shedim could have a similar original story, though that makes both susceptible to the Luce."

I froze mid-gesture as the implications crystalized. Would Ezra and I be hit? What would happen to Maud? I started frantically combing through books for an answer.

I found one—potentially—not in a book, but in a small grimy painting depicting demons experimenting on creatures that weren't exactly human but possessed vampire characteristics.

Sachie stepped closer to the wall, squinting at it. "Is this confirmation of vampires and shedim springing from the same magic source or does it refute that?"

Ezra snapped a photo of the painting. "I've had my fill of this place. I'll send this to Silas and see what he can learn from it."

We hiked up to the ground level.

Sachie headed for the stable to feed and water the horses, arguing on her phone as she left the farmhouse with someone at London HQ to get out here ASAP and rehome them. Whoever she was talking to was going to lose that argument. Sach had been on the Canadian Equestrian Team when she was eighteen; her love of horses ran deep.

I stepped onto the porch and took a deep breath of

fresh air, though it would take another forty million or so to expel the fetidness in my lungs.

It was only late afternoon, but dusk was already falling. I watched the sun sink behind the buildings, leaving a rim of burnt orange on the horizon.

The answer we'd gotten here today—that the rune amplified the ritual and brought about the end of the Brink —was useful, but there were still so many questions.

Not all Nippers had been affected when the Luce flooded out into our world, so how did it choose its victims? How fast was it spreading?

And above all, how the fuck would we wipe it out?

I bowed my head. I'd kickstarted this by winning the power word. Would I have made different choices if I'd known Alastair had an amplification rune? I honestly couldn't say. I'd lived to fight another day. That would have to be enough. Yeah, right.

Ezra eventually joined me, bracing his hands on the crude wooden railing and staring out over the field. "Silas unraveled the mystery of that painting."

I shuffled closer to him. "He's still all right? The Luce hasn't expanded its repertoire to go after older vamps?"

"No," Ezra said. "Darsh is healthy as well. No word from Nasir yet though."

The good-natured vamp was an experienced operative who could take care of himself. We'd lost Cécile; we weren't losing him.

"What's the deal with the painting?" I said.

"Shedim experimented with their magic to create lesser beings they could control. They weren't vampires. Those didn't exist until one of these creatures bit a human, infecting them, but yeah, indirectly, modern vampires have shedim to thank for their existence."

I sat on the railing, my back to a post. "The Luce

perceives shedim magic as unnatural and needing to be healed."

It was a solid answer, and I should have been relieved. It's just that I'd made so many strides in terms of how people in my life viewed half shedim, and to have a primordial force brand it as a flaw really sucked. "We're screwed."

"I think you and I are safe." Ezra perched on the rail next to me. "Our magic is inherent. We were born with it. Think about it, the Luce is targeting shedim magic that was infused into beings or physical items. Magic that invaded them."

"Maybe that's true of vampires or even Eddie's handcuffs, but the Brink?"

Ezra shook his head. "When I'm in Babel, I feel the shedim magic like a foundational faint hum. But in the Brink, it was more of a breeze blowing through it. Not of it, just present."

"That makes sense. It's a transitional space, ever changing. It's volatile. The amplification rune gave the Luce the force necessary to implode it."

"This means my theory about Natán's grand plan has traction," Ezra said quietly.

I tried to read his expression but couldn't. His feelings were likely extremely complicated, like everything regarding his father.

"Using vamps' precarious situation to bring them under his rule for a power shift?" I shrugged. "I guess it does. Depending on who's left standing." I slumped against Ezra's shoulder. My eyes were dry and gritty and any adrenaline from killing the vamps in Eddie's dungeon was long gone. "I feel overwhelmed."

His arm tightened around me, a silent promise of protection. It was a comfort against the crushing weight of everything I'd faced and everything still to come.

But no warmth from his body seeped into mine.

Vampires' skin got cold when they were hungry. Primes didn't have to feed as often and Ezra wasn't ice-cold, yet a coolness emanated from him.

"You need some blood, sweetheart." I tugged his collar away from his throat to check his bruises, which were still sadly present. "Just feed longer off me this time. That will kill two birds with one stone: your hunger and getting rid of the rest of Rukhsana's magic."

He rubbed his eyes. "I'm tapped out, but so are you. Since we'll have to fly home, I'll make sure there's blood on the plane. And plenty of food for you and Sachie. We'll get a healthy nourishment baseline."

I opened my mouth to protest.

He booped me on the nose. "Nothing will happen to me before then. I'm not being stubborn, just practical."

I yawned, nodding. "The only thing that eases my mind in all this is that Maud is safe and so are Eishei Kodesh. Even if what the Luce deems unnatural extends beyond non-inherent shedim magic to *all* non-inherent magic, it won't try and heal Eishei Kodesh. Had all this been going down when humans first gained flame powers, they'd be in danger, but unlike vampires, it's in our DNA now."

"There also would have already been reports of children or the elderly being hit since they're weaker than new vamps." Ezra squeezed my hands. "Humans are safe. Same with our friends, because they're older and stronger and *will* survive."

"I want to believe that, but we can't predict if the Luce will gain strength and affect *any* vampire, no matter what their age." My shoulders sagged as I dwelled on that depressing thought—for all of three seconds when another, so much worse thought hit me so hard that I whimpered. My hands pressed on the sides of my ribs like I'd never get air into them again.

"What's wrong?" Ezra was immediately in front of me.

"If those handcuffs failed because the Luce healed the magic on them, i.e. dissolved it, and that happens to the love locks? All those furious, hungry, escaped shedim?"

"Fantastic," Sachie said, stepping onto the porch. "Demon prison break wasn't on my apocalyptic bingo card, but here we are."

Chapter 11

I snapped my fingers at Ezra, all fatigue gone. "Portal! Wherever you've seen those locks in person. Now!"

A lattice of shadowy light rippled into existence, its strands weaving and unweaving like a spiderweb caught in a breeze. The portal flickered, its mesh-like surface crackling with unstable energy before dissolving into wisps of smoke.

Ezra flexed his hands. "It's not going to happen."

I shoved my wrist at him. "Then thrall!"

He brushed it aside. "We're near an airport. I don't know what the love lock situation in London is, but Paris is famous for them. We can be there relatively quickly."

"There's no time." I slapped my arm into his hand. "*Feed.*"

"I'm not your dancing monkey," he growled. "And you're running on fumes. You want to be even more enthralled to me? *Fuck*, Aviva." His eyes flashed toxic green.

"That's enough," Sach said firmly. She bravely—or stupidly—muscled between the two of us with outstretched arms. "What are you going to do if the magic on the locks *is* failing, Avi? We don't know how to stop the Luce, and even though we can send shedim back into their cells with our rings, we only have four cocktail doses' worth at the best of times. Mine isn't full, is yours?"

"No," I muttered.

"Then take a breath and think logically. Vampire operatives are already in place at all known lock locations. We'd be notified if something had already happened."

Logic prevailed and the fight went out of me. "Sorry, Ezra. My outburst was wrong."

He gave a tight nod and pulled out his phone. "I'll make arrangements to get us to Charles de Gaulle airport."

"I'll stick around here to arrange for the horses to be cared for and the place secured," Sachie said. "Book me a flight out of London for home in a few hours."

"Got it." Ezra headed back into the farmhouse.

Sach leaned against a post. "Well, that was fun."

I rubbed my forehead. "My fear got the better of me."

"Unlike the rest of us who couldn't give a shit."

"The rest of you didn't release the Luce," I said evenly.

Sach smacked me across the top of my head. "I would have made the same play back at the fortress to nip this in the bud. Besides, releasing the Luce wasn't the problem, it was the amplification rune, which you couldn't have predicted. Get that through your fat, stubborn head because we don't have time for your guilt right now."

"Great pep talk."

She grinned, showing both her dimples. "My motivational speaking skills are unparalleled. And since I'm multitalented, I'll even throw in a brilliant piece of advice: let that stupid thrall die already."

"That stupid thrall healed Ezra. Is healing him," I amended.

Sachie pushed off the post. "Relationships can't survive knowing each other's true feelings at every moment. Or having heart attacks because you didn't stick to each other's sides."

"It's not a two-way street," I said.

"Thanks for making my point," she said and headed back to the stables.

ALL THINGS CONSIDERED, the journey from Eddie's farm to the Paris airport was quite short. It only felt interminable because Ezra grunted a grand total of five words to me.

We both ate and then he grudgingly acknowledged that we should rethrall.

I despised every transactional second of it—the dispassionate press of his mouth, the clinical precision of his fangs lowered into my skin.

It appeared that every time Ezra drank from me to re-up, it would feel less and less pleasurable. The short-term nature of this bond had originally been a plus, but then again, I hadn't envisioned having to juice him up multiple times.

I spent the rest of the flight over the Channel visualizing floating in the ocean and taking so many deep breaths that the passport control officer who'd come to us on board the private plane when we landed at Charles de Gaulle asked if I was having an asthma attack.

Ezra finally laughed.

We climbed into a Lincoln town car with tinted windows and began the drive into Paris.

Nondescript industrial warehouses and office parks eventually gave way to stark white residential towers.

We drove past cops and operatives in front of a large gated stone building, keeping small but vocal opposing camps from coming to blows.

I didn't speak much French, but the gruesome illustrations on some signs made their respective positions clear: those who saw the Seaside facility as the way to keep all humans safe versus those who wanted vampires dusted.

Given Natán's name on signs justifying both sides' arguments, I raised the privacy glass in the limo and called Darsh to ask if Cardoso Sr.'s announcement had caused waves back home.

We had a Seaside of our own outside the city.

"Natán's press conference agitated some people, but Casey's response this morning didn't help," Darsh said.

"What did that asshat say now?"

The neighborhood transitioned to the classic French architecture with cream-colored stone buildings and wrought iron balconies. It was still evening, but the streets were depressingly empty. The few pedestrians hurried along the sidewalk past the occasional boarded-up storefront, their heads bent.

The pa-pom sound of wailing sirens was incessant.

"You have to hand it to Casey," Darsh said blithely, "he can find an anti-magic angle in anything. He's furious that the Maccabees, our so-called supernatural police force, is running around barely doing damage control instead of taking decisive action. What's worse is that it fucking feels that way too."

A loud crash from his side made me flinch.

"Darsh?" I said tentatively.

"He needs a moment for an attitude adjustment," Silas said evenly into the phone. A car engine started up, followed by pop music switched off mid-song. "I've put you on speaker while I drive."

"I'll do the same with me and Ezra." I hit a button. "What else did Casey say?"

"The politician is on a tear about having to put our

faith in vampire Mafias to protect us," Darsh said. "Sorry, those bloodsucking law-breaking bottom-feeders."

"Quite the turn of phrase," Silas said.

"To be fair," Ezra said wryly, "those bloodsucking law-breaking bottom-feeders have way more money than the operating budget of any Maccabee chapter."

Darsh laughed without an ounce of humor. "Speaking of flush with cash, you sent Sachie back on a private plane, Cardoso?"

Ezra propped a foot on the limo seat across from him. "It was the most expedient way to get her home."

"I appreciate it." There was a long pause. "She filled us in that only inherent magic is exempt from the Luce," he said neutrally.

"Hell of a thing," Silas added.

"Yeah," I said sadly.

"We're not throwing a pity party," Darsh chided. "I'm infallible to an enviable degree, and Cowpoke is just stubborn."

"Or the other way round," Silas said.

"We're heading into the tunnel." Darsh spoke through a burst of static. "Be safe."

"You guys as well." Slumping back against the seat, I lowered the window to let in some cool night air.

The Seine slipped beneath stone bridges while church spires soared up to meet the bank of clouds pressing down on the city.

Maud messaged me to bitch about her security detail. They'd assigned her some uptight operative who wouldn't let her out of his sight.

I fired back that that was the point and to play nice.

Shortly after, the limo pulled up to the curb.

"The Pont des Arts is a block away," the limo driver said in French-accented English. "This is as close as I can get."

We thanked him and hurried to the pedestrian bridge.

Down the Seine, the Eiffel Tower glittered with thousands of lights, eager tourists capturing photos of the scene.

Streetlights cast a glow over thousands of love locks—some gleaming new, others weathered and dull. If even a fraction of them contained demon prisoners?

"Breathe," Ezra murmured.

I slid into my synesthete vision. Not every silver lock was a cell, but there were still hundreds of them on the railings, each one a harbinger of doom.

Some of the etched runes pulsed in regular strong waves, but on others the red and purple magic flickered like dying embers. Their glow had dulled to barely a twinkle, the protective sigils fading into the metal as if being slowly erased.

I clutched Ezra's hand. "We need to get these locks out right away."

But where would we take them?

I centered myself. The vampire operatives stationed at one end of the bridge could suggest somewhere.

I hurried over to the pair.

Likely level ones if they'd been given this assignment, they maintained perfect stillness. The woman had close-cropped silver hair and aristocratic features. Her brawny male partner gave us the barest glance before returning to scanning the bridge.

I identified myself, showing my Maccabee ring.

The woman gave Ezra a nod of recognition.

"The lock cells on this bridge must be removed at once," I said. "The protective magic on some of them is failing, and they need to be contained."

Kudos to the woman's professionalism, she didn't waste time reacting, already making a call. She spoke in rapid-fire French, her voice and cadence reminding me of Rukhsana.

I curled my fingers into my palms.

"A crew is coming," she said. "We had a contingency plan for just such an occurrence." She put her phone in a pocket. "That explains the new wrinkle of skirmishes with suspected shedim in the past two days. We believe other demons have been lurking at the perimeters of our patrol zones. The lock owners are on standby to capture their escapees."

"The past two days?" Ezra said. "You're sure?"

"Positive," the male vamp chimed in.

Maccabees know about the Luce because you told them about it. Ezra's voice in my head was quiet but insistent. *Even if shedim prison owners connected affected vampires to failing shedim magic, how did they do it the second the Luce hit to already have their demons in place?*

I glanced at the tourists, some of whom might be glamoured shedim. *It's someone else's play. Someone with prior knowledge.*

Whoever gave Alastair that amplification rune, Ezra agreed. *Told you.*

Was Natán really behind it? Was he making deals with demons?

Had he made one with Delacroix? Wouldn't that be rich, our two fathers in bed with each other?

Phrasing. Cherry grimaced.

"What's the situation with the vampires right now?" I said.

The female vampire shrugged. "The Authority sent word about the Luce, but we don't have a rift here in Paris. Few vampires have been affected."

"That will change," her partner said in disgust. "Meantime, the Authority sits with their thumbs up their asses instead of doing whatever it takes to keep their operatives safe."

"They're working on stopping the magical infection," I said.

"How many will die, vampires or humans, while this research is happening?" He scoffed dismissively. "It took them centuries to find the magic cocktail yet the promise that it killed shedim turned out to be a lie. How many more lies will we be fed? The Authority's probably drafting execution orders for any vampire showing symptoms. When that happens…" He let the threat hang in the air.

Demon prisoners, the Luce, human-on-human violence, and now mistrust from vampire operatives—which threat would tear my organization apart first?

The male operative barked something in French at a couple of tourists fiddling with some locks for their photo, and when they didn't comply, he hurried over to them, side-stepping puddles. His steps hitched and jerked, like an old film strip stuttering.

Ezra, I said through our psychic phone line. *Four o'clock. The operative.*

Ezra flicked his gaze over, then back to the female vampire before she noticed and turned to see what he was looking at. *Damn it.*

"Aside from incidents of infection," she said, "more vampires are coming to Paris from surrounding areas. Willing donors are getting less willing, and the vampires wish to be where the synthetic blood is." She nodded at Ezra. "Good thing your father is on that."

Ezra gave her a noncommittal smile.

The male vamp returned with careful, even steps, his cheeks flushed. "We should be partnering with Mr. Cardoso. He has resources." His voice cracked slightly, desperation bleeding through his carefully maintained composure. "Neither of you understand what those of us turned against our will lost. The only thing we gained was immortality, and now we're facing an eternal nightmare."

He slammed his fist into a lamppost, denting the metal. "Can't you make that partnership happen? Before more of uh—them are lost to the Luce?"

My heart twisted at his stumbled change of pronoun.

"I'll see what I can do," Ezra said with a somber nod.

The Eishei Kodesh removal crew arrived, dressed as city workers. They cleared the bridge of tourists, claiming weight and structural issues, then started cutting off locks.

Ezra and I oversaw their work. Our new psychic connection was a godsend because I told him which runes were weakening and he passed it on to the operatives. No one questioned the Prime's ability to sense that.

The thirty or so cells in most imminent danger of opening were placed in a locked box. Since Ezra and I were accompanying a small squad to the secure site, the operatives staying behind opted to err on the side of caution and remove all silver locks on the bridge. They'd follow us to the underground bunker in a wooded area outside the city.

When I stepped out of the van after the short ride, it was hard to believe Paris was nearby.

Bare branches creaked and swayed in the darkness and the wind whispered through the pine needles, carrying the sharp scent of winter-wet bark. Something small darted through the underbrush with a soft crunch.

One of the operatives unbolted blast doors, and we descended narrow metal staircases for ages then wound through passageways to a small room with thick concrete walls.

Mezuzahs were affixed to the doorframe of the space but facing in the opposite direction from usual. Rather than protecting this room against any demon getting in, they ensured that no shedim could bypass the mezuzahs to exit into the hall.

The locks were sunk into blocks of cement and buried in deep holes, which were also filled in.

I felt queasy at the thought of the cell doors opening, only for the shedim to find themselves trapped for eternity in concrete. It was a barbaric, if necessary, solution.

I only hoped it wasn't a delusional one.

Chapter 12

The male vampire from the Pont des Arts showed up as the last shovelful of concrete was smoothed out on top of the buried locks. The rest of the locks that had been removed were being contained in similar rooms in this bunker.

Twice he attempted to light his cigarette, but his thumb moved so fast that it slipped off the button. He gave a forced laugh. "Should have bought matches."

I mustered up a smile.

"Bad habit I can't break, even after two years of being a vampire." He fanned the smoke away from my direction.

"No worries." It wasn't the cigarette troubling me; it was that I could see every injury he'd ever suffered (yes, I looked without his consent), including specific faint ribbons of blue around his kidneys, which meant kidney failure from when he'd been human.

But there was no sign of the Luce. It remained invisible.

"You were turned while an operative?" I said. "Sorry, I never got your name."

"Mathéo. And yes. It happened shortly after I received my ring." His expression became wistful. "Graduating from Maccababy was a great day."

"Yeah, it was."

"Then a few months later…" Mathéo shook his head. "I'm your ride back to town. Whenever you are ready to leave."

"Let me check in with Ezra."

Mathéo dragged deeply on the cigarette. "Take your time."

Ezra was in a tight knot with the Maccabees we'd ridden over with, chatting away in French while they cleaned up. Whether or not his position with the Authority had changed, he'd gone from persona non grata with operatives to a position of friendly neutrality.

Despite whatever Natán was up to, these Maccabees were cordial to his son and had taken directives from him without complaint.

The group announced they were heading out, so I pulled Ezra aside.

"We need to find that shedim brain we stole from the cactus safe," I whispered. "Tear the Copper Hell apart if we have to. I can't sense the brain because it's a full demon part, unlike infernals or cursed artifacts, but Delacroix would keep it close. It's there somewhere, and if he's stashed it in a special warded-up box or something, I could sense that."

Ezra agreed, so we declined the ride, though we let Mathéo lead us back up to the surface.

By the time I got to the top, my thighs were burning. I was rubbing them and waiting for the ache to subside when there was a heavy thud.

Mathéo lay crumpled on the ground, his flesh eerily transparent. His veins glowed like fiber-optic cables, casting a silver light that was beautiful and horrifying.

Ezra crouched next to him. "He's not unconscious or in a coma. He's dead. Actually dead."

"How—how can you tell with no pulse, no heartbeat,

no breath—" My voice was growing pitchier, but what the fuck? Vampires turned to ash. Ezra had to be wrong.

He placed a hand on my shoulder. "We need to let the others working downstairs know."

We headed back down into the bunker.

It took several tries for the operatives to understand us, and it wasn't because Ezra's French had suddenly gotten rusty. The manner of death was unprecedented.

I directed them to Mathéo, then we all stood motionless in the frozen air, our breath forming clouds as we stared at the strange remains. No one spoke. There was nothing to say in the face of a death that defied even vampire nature.

Healing magic. What a crock. It healed Mathéo right out of existence.

Out of respect, Ezra and I rode back to town with his body, parting ways with the other operatives outside HQ.

"Everything is code red urgent," I said helplessly. "We have to stop the Luce, but we also need to locate every last cell and ensure no demons get free. Maccabees have eyes on major cities with love lock traditions, but one escaped shedim in a rural area could devastate an entire community before we responded."

Ezra pulled me into a tight embrace. "We'll figure this out," he murmured against my hair. "I promise."

I wanted to believe him, but the memory of Mathéo's corpse haunted me.

There was one place to find the answers I sought: Delacroix and that shedim brain I'd stolen for him.

Ezra was totally on board with heading directly for the yacht, because he was worried about his Li'l Hellions. All had been well when he spoke to them, but Mathéo's death was an escalation.

Plus, Ezra confided in me that it required more effort now to maintain the security system on the Copper Hell. He hadn't determined whether it was because the Luce was attempting to grind it down, but he wanted to head back and find out.

He found a spot away from CCTV or onlookers and portaled us to the yacht, choosing to bring us into the foyer instead of his private quarters.

I surveyed the packed casino, my stomach clenching at the sheer number of vampires crammed into the space, because even this shoulder-to-shoulder press of bodies was a drop in the bucket compared to all the ones left in Babel.

Most of the vampire patrons didn't bother to hide their fangs, their edgy energy teetering on the brink of losing control.

Equally as troubling, some of Delacroix's Brimstone Breakfast Club were present, when I'd never seen them around before. The Bilge played craps with his one-eyed, four-tusked blue crony, while mopey Eeyore Demon groomed his donkey mane, occasionally gnawing on the nails of his short hooves that sprouted from his throat like a sunburst.

The Li'l Hellions maintained their professional demeanor, but anxiety rippled off them like an electric current. Every accidental brush of shoulders, every too-loud laugh sent tiny shock waves of tension through the crowd.

Predictably, Ezra was rushed by his staff with questions over his safety, the state of things in general, and a litany of on-board issues for him to solve.

Ezra's casino manager and pit boss snarled at lesser staff to back off. The second those vampires scuttled away, the other two were on Ezra, making demands of him.

Generally, the Copper Hell ran like clockwork, the premises immaculate. But there were signs of strain now: dirt on the carpet, empty glasses perched precariously on the roulette table, and gaming machines with smudged screens.

A portly Eishei Kodesh woman in a bright orange blouse hurried past me, portal bound. The last human on the ship, she was guarded by four Li'l Hellions. She clocked my Maccabee ring and slashed a hand across her throat. "Get out while you can."

My fingers twitched, and Cherry vibrated at the possibility of violence.

Ezra shot me a sideways glance. "Give me a minute," he told his staff.

They didn't listen, and when Ezra physically turned away from them, his pit boss grabbed his sleeve.

Ezra whirled on the vampire, fangs bared.

His Hellions took one look at his furious posture, *and oh yeah his toxic green eyes*, and bolted.

I couldn't let him lose face, not here, not now. Maintaining a neutral expression, I slammed him with a psychic scream: *STAND DOWN.* The effort of holding Cherry— and Ezra— in check while projecting calm nearly brought me to my knees. The hunger in me grew savage, demanding.

Ezra touched the small of my back. "We should eat," he said in a normal voice, his eyes once more their normal silvery blue.

"The famous buffet?" I said with a lightness I didn't feel.

"Your wish is my command."

A velvet rope still marked off the bottom of the wide spiral staircase, though no vampire stood guard now.

Ezra unclipped the rope, and we climbed the stairs up to the sprawling atrium crowned by a massive glass dome.

Even though stars winked down on us, their light competing with the honeyed glow from the modern chandeliers, it was unsettling being alone up here. All Eishei Kodesh had fled, and any vampires and shedim on board were herded together downstairs like that would protect them.

Well, all the shedim but one.

The glass doors were locked tight against any ocean breeze, but the dark water was as smooth as glass. The prow cut through the night with only the faintest rolling motion and hum of the engines.

I strolled past angular furniture grouped around cold fire pits, the air almost aggressively fragrant from predatory-looking plants in one of the themed lounges, toward the lavish buffet that dominated the center of the atrium.

Poached salmon had dried around the edges, tiny quiches sat cold and congealed, and the charcuterie board's meats curled at the corners. Even the chocolate mousse I'd heard rave reviews about looked waxy.

Grimacing, I picked through a silver bowl of buns to find one that wasn't hard, added some olives to my plate, and the least bruised fruit I could find.

Ezra helped himself to a chilled bottle of blood, his mouth a thin line. "You have to understand," he said, "they've been doing their best given the circumstances. All deliveries were stopped, and they've been stretched thin running security as well as trying to keep everything else going."

"The Hellions get a pass." I forced down the few bites that were within food safety freshness. Ish. "But we need to search for the brain."

Ezra pushed the plate closer. "Eat."

I opened my mouth to protest, but all that came out was a giant yawn. I'd lost track of how long I'd been up, and jumping time zones didn't help.

"More food and then you'll nap." He shot me a mock scary glower. "No arguing."

I muscled down everything on my plate. Mostly because my boyfriend looked wilted, and if I didn't rest, he wouldn't either, but I was glad when he brought me to his private quarters.

A heavy bookcase anchored to the charcoal wall held novels behind glass doors. Moonlight spilled across polished floorboards, while a neat stack of logs waited in the fireplace.

The room carried Ezra's scent, mixed with lingering notes of clove from cigars.

He dimmed the lights to a single floor lamp's glow. Despite the dark masculine elements, the space felt personal: chess pieces neatly lined up awaiting the next game, bottles in the vintage bar cabinet gleaming, and above the mantel, a sensual watercolor of intertwined lovers.

After a quick shower, I changed into one of Ezra's T-shirts and boxer shorts, headed back into the living room, and sank onto one of the leather sofas flanking the wide coffee table.

Ezra was playing solitaire. How many of these games had he played during his time at the Hell? Was it a holdover from his lonely childhood?

A pang of sadness hit me as I watched his practiced movements—the familiar comfort he took in this solitary pursuit spoke volumes about years spent finding ways to keep himself company. I stepped forward, wanting to hug him and assure him he wasn't alone anymore.

He looked up from the game, his silvery-blue gaze heating at the sight of me in his clothes.

I batted my lashes at him. "I suddenly have a second wind."

His returning smile was rueful. "Let's wait until the thrall has dissolved."

"Smart idea," I said a beat too late and a fraction too brightly. "Where are my clothes?"

"They're being washed."

I weighed the pros of clean clothes without me doing laundry against rando vamps handling my unmentionables and decided that clean clothes won. "Great. Thanks. And my phone?"

"It's charging on the side table."

"I appreciate your thoughtfulness," I said, a warm surge of happiness fluttering in my chest, and called my mother.

Even though it was Saturday afternoon in Vancouver, she was at work. The rain was so loud, I heard it beating against the glass on her end.

I told her she was on speakerphone and Ezra was present. Luckily—if I could call it luck—I didn't have to break the news about Mathéo's death or that some of the locks were perilously close to opening.

The Paris director had already been in contact, and Sachie had filled her in on the amplification rune and our visit to Burning Eddie.

"Not to pile more shitty news on you, but we have to talk about Natán," I said.

"Saint Cardoso," Michael said wryly. "Or should I say our evil overlord? Yes. Sachie told me that too."

Ezra laughed bitterly and shot back two fingers of bourbon.

"I can't believe I'm saying this," I said, "but you've got to convince the Authority to work with him."

Ezra choked on his drink.

"You've got to be kidding," Michael said.

"I'm not. One of our operatives is dead because of the Luce. There's no way Natán has special resources that combat the healing magic, but it seems other vampires do. Including some of our operatives."

Wishful thinking? Perhaps, but it didn't change anything.

"The Authority must show that they're looking out for their own," I said. "And if that doesn't convince them, then use the argument that we'll have better access to what Natán is up to, should Ezra be right about him wanting to consolidate power here on earth."

There was a long pause, then my mother sighed. "That will be difficult."

"They're deciding the fates of all vampires on earth, aren't they?" I said disgustedly.

"Obviously," Ezra said. "I would, too, if I was them."

"But their own operatives? If the Authority doesn't have their backs when it matters most, we'll lose them, and not to the Luce. How does that help anyone? Michael!"

"I'm not on board with that and neither are a lot of directors," she said blandly. "Or half the Authority."

"Fucking Dmitri," I spat.

"Once upon a time, Natán was one of my closest friends," Michael said, "but whoever he is now is a dangerous stranger. He claims to want this partnership, but what will he do if we call his bluff? Ezra, what do you think?"

"He'll find a way to weasel out of it," he said, sitting down next to me, "and blame the Maccabees."

"Maybe that's the reason *to* do it," Michael said. "And have our own strategy in place to discredit him. I'll propose it. When are you coming back?"

"Soon," I said. "After we find the brain."

"Be careful of Delacroix," my mother said in a worried voice.

"I will. And leave the office, okay?"

"I'm meeting Keira for dinner in a bit."

"Good."

"Love you," my mother said.

"Love you too." I think I kept the surprise out of my voice at that sign-off.

I yawned, my lids heavy, and tossed my phone on the coffee table.

Ezra kissed the top of my head.

In that moment between waking and dreaming, I felt safe, the stillness of his immortal body somehow more comforting than any heartbeat could ever be.

Was this feeling—this profound sense of security—another effect of being enthralled? Or was it simply him, simply us, the way we'd always been drawn together.

I quieted my fears. I had everything I desired—and that wasn't the thrall talking. I didn't think.

Chapter 13

I was woken by a text from Orly, wanting insider intel on the vampires, and, most importantly, the chances of Ezra being affected. I assured her that as a Prime, he was immune, and that the Maccabees were working on the rest.

She hearted the message immediately, adding that once all this mayhem was over, she was throwing a huge party. My presence was not optional.

A future where finding something to wear was my biggest problem sounded heavenly. I promised I'd be there.

"Who's that?" Ezra said from his club chair over the clack of knitting needles. A canvas bag holding yarn with pockets for needles of different sizes, scissors, and a bright green measuring tape sat at his feet.

I blinked dumbly, not at the two blankets piled on the arm that he'd created while I slept, but because he was knitting backward. "Orly. She's throwing a party when we're clear of all this mishegoss."

He chuckled, unraveling more stitches onto his needles. "Her bashes are legendary."

I retrieved the pillow that I'd knocked off the sofa while

I slept. "Was that orange sweater convicted of crimes against eyeballs and must now be unraveled into oblivion?"

"I'm tinking."

"You're thinking of how to answer?"

"Tinking. Knitting backward in word and deed. I'm fixing my brioche."

I squinted at him, my face screwed up. "I think I'm having a stroke."

Ezra chuckled. "You're good. It's just knitting stuff."

I leaned forward and poked the garment with a grimace. The synthetic fabric felt like a grocery bag having an identity crisis as a shirt. "You didn't have any dental floss you could stress knit? At least it would have smelled like mint."

"It's for my pit boss. He lives for this weird 1970s-looking shit." He pointed at a neatly folded bundle on the edge of the sofa. "Your clothes, milady."

"It's Princess Aviva, if you want to be technical about it." The clothes were soft to the touch and smelled like a hot summer's day. "The Copper Hell spares no expense on laundry."

"They're putting in the work where it matters," Ezra said.

I pictured Li'l Hellions huffing fabric softener like guilty teenagers, bit back a laugh, and went into the bedroom to change. No point taunting my boyfriend by getting naked in front of him. Or getting annoyed because he wouldn't act on it.

Not that between the thrall and having to face my father this was an appropriate time for sexy shenanigans, but was a quick boob grab or hot kiss too much to ask for? I slammed the door.

"Whoops! Sorry," I called out.

Someone knocked while I was getting dressed. Ezra

thanked them, then the door shut, and the enticing smell of fresh brewed coffee filled the air.

I bounded back into the living room, clapping my hands at the cart holding a white carafe, milk, sugar, and freshly baked cinnamon buns. "My hero." I poured coffee into the oversized mug. "Fess up. What happened while I was asleep to make you grab yarn from the craft store's 'Abandon All Hope' collection?"

He snorted. "I found something at Burning Eddie's." He pulled a large freezer bag out of the canvas holdall. The partially completed sweater was placed inside the plastic with care unbefitting of such a monstrosity, then the bag was tucked inside the larger carrier.

I licked cream cheese frosting off my fingers.

Ezra disappeared into his bedroom and returned with a dog-eared pocket notebook.

I carried my food over to the sofa to sit next to him, almost causing an interspecies incident when I placed my mug on the coffee table without a coaster.

"We don't want rings," Ezra said unrepentantly.

I poked him. "Referring to oneself as 'we' is reserved for those of us with royal bloodlines."

"I meant as in neither of us. Not on our tables in our living space."

Our living space? Had he dreamed of a future where we lived together? A gooey warmth flowed through me. "Table tattoos have never been on my list of concerns but cute of you to assume that."

"Just look at this," he said wearily and handed me the small notebook.

The pages were filled with cramped writing. It was the English alphabet but most of it was in some kind of code or shorthand that I'd never seen before. There were a few recognizable items, including a well-known date.

"That's when the first vampire went public in the 1960s," I said. "Burning Eddie despised vamps. Is this a chronicle of all the ones who challenged him and lost? A book of torture techniques? That's unsettling, but why would that stress you out?"

Ezra flipped to a page about halfway through the notebook. There were only two entries on it, both circled: Natán Cardoso and Birgitte Pederson. "Could my father have made an enemy of that shedim? Sure. But why is Secretary Pederson here?"

I checked the rest of the book in case there was some clue to explain their inclusion, but that was the last page with any writing. "Yeah, that needs to be figured out."

"It's not in any code I recognize. I got frustrated." Ezra toed the canvas bag. "I also sent photos of the journal to Silas and asked him to write software to crack it."

"Will that interfere with him keeping order and dealing with the Luce-infected vampires in Vancouver?" I ate some more of my cinnamon bun.

"No. The software is already done and humming along. I just hate waiting for the results."

"Fair." I brushed crumbs off my lap. "And on that note, where should we start looking for the brain?"

"I reviewed the blueprints of the yacht when I first partnered with Delacroix," Ezra said. "There aren't any secret passageways and I never found any hidey-holes."

I tamped down my grin at how disappointed he appeared by that, imagining him sneaking around and trying to Scooby Doo search the Hell.

"The brain must be in Delacroix's bubble area," I said. "And if it's not, then we should still rule out his home as the most likely location. Let's rethrall first."

Every fiber of my being ached with the desire to be me and Ezra, not a one-way magic connection, but I wasn't going to let my personal wishes get in the way of what was best.

"Yeah. I should be in top form to face Delacroix."

"That plus I'm not sure if I saw vamp injuries because I leveled up on my own or because I'm getting some benefit. Either way, if I sense actual demon parts now? Like the brain?" I shrugged. "It's an advantage worth having."

I handed him my wrist like I was offering a contract to be signed.

He took it with the same brisk professionalism.

I felt hollow—a vessel being emptied according to schedule. The distance between us in these moments made my chest ache far more than the physical exchange ever could.

Each successive re-up involved less blood, which was good, but felt ickier in how cold and businesslike it was.

However, upon inspection, Ezra's bruises were finally gone. Rukhsana's magic was irrevocably flushed out of his system.

"Do you still feel the thrall?" I asked.

Ezra nodded.

Well, at least he was healed and that was the last time. Five—six days tops until the thrall dissolved? I'd manage until then.

We traipsed up to Delacroix's iridescent bubble home on the top deck. Moonlight glinted off whitecaps as icy wind whipped across the deck. I wrapped my arms around myself, ducking salt spray, the ocean vast and endless around our vessel.

Delacroix opened his door and blew a stream of cigarette smoke in my face. His salt-and-pepper hair was reasonably tame today, like he'd been caught in a breeze, not a hurricane.

"I don't have some magic potion to save vampires," he said, "so don't waste your breath. It's bad enough they think this is a homeless shelter. They've scared off my human customers." He jabbed the hand holding the cigarette at Ezra, ash falling on the Prime's Italian leather shoes. "Those EK suckers go a long way to paying the bills, financially and power-wise. Get them back." He closed the door.

I shoved my ankle boot in, wincing when he leaned his weight on the door. "Asshole. Quit it." I stomped on his foot, grinding my heel down for good measure.

The demon stumbled back with a curse.

I stormed past him, Ezra right behind me.

"By all means," Delacroix grumbled, slamming the door. "Make yourself at home."

The cheery roaring fireplace cast dancing shadows across the room. Fire burning contentedly inside what was essentially a massive water droplet was a surreal touch.

Delacroix had granted me entrance—a clear sign he had an agenda—but even with Ezra being his business partner and necessary to keeping the shedim safe, this conversation would last only as long as my father allowed it.

I slid into my synesthete vision.

Delacroix didn't emit any special shedim signature that I could track, but the room lit up like a constellation map.

Every object touched by shedim magic glowed in my awareness: a burst of blue spilled out from the cabinet, there was a ribbon along one of the stunning framed photos of underwater life adorning the walls, and, oddly, an umbrella stand was also affected.

Sadly, I couldn't see or sense the brain. So much for the hope that I'd be capable of sussing it out directly.

Delacroix sat in the chair closest to the fire and rubbed his knee. "Spit it out already. My friends are waiting for me."

I walked around his room in a game of hot hot cold, watching my father for any reaction that I was getting close to the brain. I couldn't read him with my magic, more's the pity, but I had plenty of experience to draw on.

"The Luce, the healing magic in the power word that Alastair Walker was after, is 'healing' vampires, since the shedim magic that makes them vamps isn't inherent to them." I trailed my fingers over the cabinet with the spill of blue light, silently letting Ezra know that we had to check inside.

Psychic conversations were the bomb.

"Eishei Kodesh are also exempt from the Luce," I said. "Is all of that correct?"

"Look at the girl detective go." Delacroix smirked. "Very good, Fleischer."

His sarcasm didn't make a dent in my relief that Maud, Ezra, and I wouldn't be harmed, and neither would Sachie or my mom or any of my human colleagues. Too bad that relief was short-lived in the face of the catastrophic threat of the prisoners getting free.

I rejected any notion that my vampire friends would be hit.

I slowed down by the bench seat under the window, which pulsed blue, but Delacroix just grumbled at me to sit because I was giving him a crick in his neck. He didn't restrain me when I ignored him, so I crossed that spot off as a possibility.

"Did you see Alastair abduct me from the art gallery?" I wouldn't put it past Delacroix to have seen it go down but not bother to help me.

He laughed. "Is that where you've been?"

I clenched my fists. His habit of answering questions with questions was infuriating.

"I hope you killed him," he said. "It'd make me look bad if you showed mercy."

"Your concern for my well-being warms the cockles of my heart. The Luce killed the dhampir."

Delacroix shrugged. "Should I care?"

"Depends." Ezra showed my father the photo he'd

taken of the rune in Burning Eddie's book. "Ever seen this before?"

"You expect me to remember every rune I've ever come across?" Delacroix said.

I froze, his dismissive tone setting off warning bells in my gut. The shedim was in the information-gathering business. His first question should have been "What does it do?" or "Who gave this to you?" He never missed a chance to hoard knowledge, but he didn't bite this time.

A chill shivered down my spine.

Alastair hadn't simply stumbled across the amplification rune. It wasn't scrawled in some text at his local library or hanging in a museum for all to see.

I flashed back to the steady, methodical way Alastair had carved the design into his flesh. He didn't pause, didn't hesitate. There was no way he'd memorized that intricate pattern on his own because like Ezra and me, he couldn't have looked at it long enough to study it.

Yet the dhampir knew exactly where each stroke belonged.

Someone had guided his hand, walked him through every angle and line. It wasn't merely handed over—it was taught. Ingrained. A lesson he couldn't afford to forget.

Natán wasn't the culprit. Sure, he was profiting off the affected vampires now, but he'd put out a reward for Alastair's capture. His lieutenant's treachery had cut deep.

A shedim had taught Alastair. But not the demon owners of the locks. They'd never risk losing their power source.

I flew at the only other player on this game board, my claws out. "You gave Alastair the amplification rune."

Ezra grabbed me around the waist before I reached the demon. "Avi, calm down." He spoke thickly around his fangs.

I stopped struggling in his hold and exhaled hard to

center myself. "My vampire friends might die," I said coldly to my father.

"It had to be done."

What was his angle? Why harm vampires?

Forcing aside pleasant thoughts of dismembering him, I focused on finding the brain and getting information out of the demon.

I resumed pacing. "The magic on the lock cells is failing."

"You don't say."

I narrowed my eyes at him. "You're not surprised. How did you know?"

"Don't insult me." He ground his cigarette out.

Obviously, he had someone reporting back, but why wasn't he angry? He couldn't juice up on that magic if there were no prisoners as fuel.

Was it because he'd had time to process the news? It *had* been a few days since the Luce stormed earth.

Or had he known longer than that? Cherry's assertion made perfect—and horrible—sense.

"You didn't just give Alastair the rune." I took a step back, the revelation striking like a physical blow. "It didn't register at the time because there was so much happening, but there were only a handful of people who knew I'd taken a test for the supplicant's—"

The words died in my throat as fury clawed its way up, burning everything in its path. My hands trembled with the effort not to lash out.

"You told Alastair where to find me at the gallery. Everything that happened, everything I went through, it was all because of you."

Chapter 14

With a bellow of rage, Ezra grabbed Delacroix and dragged him out of his chair halfway across the room. He slammed the shedim so hard into the wall that the plaster cracked, photographs crashing to the ground in a chorus of broken glass.

Delacroix was already changing, deadly curved horns bursting out of his crown, his body thickening to become coils, and his skin turning to silver scales.

Ezra jammed his fingers so hard into the demon's right side that he tore flesh. "Bust out one more scale and I'll end you." My boyfriend's eyes blazed such a bright green that it hurt to look at them, and his fangs were larger than I'd ever seen them.

"You don't know my weak spot," Delacroix charged, but he also held himself as still as death.

"See if I'm bluffing." Ezra gouged his fingers in deeper. "I'd love nothing better than to end you for putting Aviva in Alastair's path."

You really know it? I said through our psychic connection.

Not for certain but I've watched him for a while now.

Tempting, but...

"Ezra." I waved my arms to get his attention. "We need him alive for answers."

I was annoyed for wanting my father's continued existence for personal reasons as well as practical ones. Why couldn't I want him dead without any other emotions weighing in on the matter?

"You screwed over your own kid for nothing, Delacroix," I said. "Alastair took the test, not me. He's the one who got the power word while I was an innocent bystander who almost died in the Brink because of you."

"I don't belie—"

Ezra pressed a finger against the shedim's lips. "I'd be very careful about spreading lies. If Aviva says she had nothing to do with it, then she didn't."

Delacroix shot him a hate-fueled glare. "How would I have known you took some test to learn about the supplicant?" he said to me. "You never tell your own father anything."

"I asked you for their name," I said. "Which meant I'd been to the fortress. What exactly did you do?"

"Back off," he spat at Ezra, "or I'll pull my magic from the yacht. What'll happen to your precious vampire staff then?"

"You're not withdrawing your magic because there's nowhere else safe enough for you to fall back to," Ezra countered.

"Try me."

The Prime flexed his grip, his eyes sparking with a manic glee.

Let him go. Please.

Ezra didn't immediately comply—not until I reminded him through our psychic connection several times that I was safe. That Delacroix would pay for what he'd done, but now wasn't the time.

The demon sagged against the wall when he was released, morphing back to his human glamor.

"Evelyn Rue," I growled.

Delacroix rolled his eyes. "I paid Daphne a visit. We made a deal based on her telling me about when you two met." Delacroix sat down gingerly, protecting his side. "You know, the vamps here have to sign NDAs, but I like the fortress's employment requirements better. It's clear what staff can and can't do, and the immediate consequences for transgressions are astoundingly efficient."

I white-knuckled the top of a chair. "Daphne wasn't talking about Alastair when she said, 'He actually set me free.' She meant you. She knew how this would play out if we did the ritual in the Brink with that rune." My voice cracked. "You killed her."

"It was her choice," Delacroix said. He slid a cigarette out of the crumpled pack on the side table next to him. "I didn't kill her, just like I didn't kill that idiot dhampir. I told him that if he used the rune in his ritual, there was a good chance he'd actually become a Prime."

Ezra snorted.

"The rune amplified the power word with shedim magic," Delacroix said. "It wasn't an impossible outcome."

"Just a fantastically improbable one. You manipulated him," I said.

"It was his choice," the demon reiterated. "People forget magic isn't free. It's not even credit. It's a loan shark with brass knuckles." He lit his cigarette. "I didn't even need to encourage Alastair to do the ritual right away in the Brink. He was more than eager to get 'er done."

"So that it would roll on through to earth," Ezra said in disgust.

"So that he could return as quickly as possible, ready to sire his baby army. He was ready to kill you, too, Cardoso, to get back at your father. You're welcome."

I massaged a temple. "You said you didn't want to free the demon prisoners. You required that magic boost to stage a demon coup. You lied to me."

It shouldn't have hurt that much. After all, he was a demon, and while being my father never stopped him from physically hurting me, there was a strange code of honor that Delacroix followed in his dealings with me. In terms of the truth, at least.

"I need bodies, not more magic." He tapped his cigarette against the edge of the dirty ashtray next to him. "And I didn't say anything about freeing the shedim. You did. You've made a lot of assumptions about my motives."

"Evaded with questions," I said dully. I drummed my fingers on his humidor—a new addition. The glass door showcased two shelves of cigars, and there wasn't anywhere to hide the brain.

Delacroix watched me, betraying his feigned disinterest when I circled the back of the cigar case with a tightening of his lips.

Hel-lo. Was there something special hidden inside?

"Pay better attention next time, girl detective." My father gestured from me to the sofa. "And sit down already or get out."

Did he have an alternate-reality hidey-hole?

I took a seat, where I was greeted with a smoke ring of secondhand death.

"Good thing you had no part in releasing the Luce," he said nastily. "You'd be so broken up over it, if you had."

"How could you sell out your own daughter to that fucker?" Ezra spoke quietly.

I'd been so caught up in my heated exchange with Delacroix and wondering where the brain was that I'd missed the fact my boyfriend had systematically dismantled the doors to the cabinet, reducing the thick wood to slender curls on the floor.

It wasn't exactly the way I'd have ascertained what was inside, but whatever worked. Delacroix had used the cabinet as an oversized junk drawer, tossing in half-opened packs of cigarettes, a hammer, a couple pairs of shoes, and those damned brass scales, the source of the blue synesthete light.

"I got him out of your way," Delacroix said.

"I would have killed Alastair without your help," I snarled. "Go ahead and burn the demon realm to flames in your coup and I'll dance through the ashes, but you've endangered my world. How do we stop the Luce?"

"It's not reversible. That genie is out of the bottle and it's not going back in."

Not reversible didn't equate to couldn't be stopped. My father had been right: I hadn't paid proper attention to what he said. To be fair, his words were more slippery than his serpent's coils, but he had every ounce of my focus now.

However, like the brain's location, he wasn't about to help me solve the problem of the healing magic.

"It's my turn now," Delacroix said. "You blood bonded, didn't you? Sentimental nonsense." He smoothed a hand over his shirt. "I'm hurt you didn't ask for my blessing. Aviva's own father, and I had to find out about it through the surge shoring up the security system." He smirked. "Good to see Cardoso stepped up his game in the face of everything going on."

We'd strengthened Delacroix's position? I bit back a groan. "We didn't blood bond," I countered. "So don't get too comfortable hiding behind this increased security. It's a thrall and could fade away at any moment."

Counterthreat delivered.

Delacroix's eyes darkened and the air around him thickened, charged with palpable malice. His human body remained unchanged, yet his presence expanded, pushing against the walls of reality itself. When he spoke, his voice carried the weight of centuries, soft yet vibrating through bone and soul: "You dare demean me?"

I fought the urge to take a very large step backward against an anger that made no sense. "What's your problem? A second ago you were gloating over how it benefited you."

"I could forgive you tying yourself to Cardoso with a blood bond, but you've reduced yourself to a battery. You're so desperate to turn your shedim heritage into something palatable for those around you," he hissed. "The blood of kings runs through your veins, but you see it as filth to be squandered or transformed through needy human acts of goodness."

His fury chilled me, a winter storm trapped in human shape. The temperature of the room dropped with each syllable he spat.

I clasped my trembling hands behind my back. "I accept what I am."

"Accept?" He gave a low, sarcastic bow. "How generous. And you don't. You keep it at arm's length and call it by some pithy insulting nickname. Cherry Bomb." He sneered. "Your sister is worth a million of you."

"Why?" The whining note in my voice filled me with self-loathing. "Maud's not marching in demon pride parades either."

"She's not hung up on how much humanity she has." My father mimed crying. "She doesn't play games to trick herself into 'accepting' who and what she is. The world will never see you as human, Aviva. Grow up and stop deluding yourself."

I clenched my fists, my jaw just as tight, but Delacroix's words pierced me like shards of ice, each one finding the exact spot where my doubts made me vulnerable. A hollow ache spread through my chest, and for a moment I couldn't breathe—not from anger, but from the terrible suspicion that he might be right.

That everything I'd worked so hard to achieve might be for naught.

Ezra stepped up beside me. "Aviva isn't the one deluding herself. You are if you believe I'll keep my Prime magic in place protecting you while you amass a demon army." The smile he trained on Delacroix was so cold and sharp that I shivered. "The three shedim who came to the Lions Gallery were very interested in where the brain was. Their partners will be delighted to learn you stole it. I'll broadcast your whereabouts and that you have the brain."

"My death is the last thing you want."

"I dunno," I said tightly. "It's sounding better and better all the time."

Delacroix flicked glowing ash at me. "Guess again. My being in charge is the only thing keeping a lid on utter chaos."

I slapped at a spark on my pants, imagining it was my father's head.

Ezra crossed his arms. "Do tell."

"My loyal shedim are in place, ready to gather the locks before their magic fails and remove them to a safe spot." He put out his cigarette. "Take a message back to the Maccabees, daughter. Leave me alone and stay out of my way. That includes hands off the locks. Or I'll sit back and watch those freaked-out escapees tear a swath of death and destruction across the world."

"There's no fucking way they'll agree to that," I said.

Ezra moved to the window, staring out over the dark ocean.

"Make them or I'll turn earth into my personal battle-ground." Delacroix stood up, vibrating with barely contained power. His scales rippled beneath his skin as ancient magic thrummed through the air. "You wanted me to work with the Authority? Well, this is what it looks like."

I swallowed.

Ezra spared the shedim the briefest pensive glance before tracking a drop of condensation snaking down the window with his finger. "Down, boy," he said mildly.

What was going through his head? Right now, it sucked that our thrall wasn't a two-way street in terms of me feeling his emotions.

There was a rap on the door, one of the Li'l Hellions informing Delacroix that there was an issue with the Bilge.

Ezra hastily took a step back as if scared he'd be forced to pump that demon's stomachs again.

"Alas, our visit has come to an end." Delacroix shooed Ezra and me out the door. "I was disappointed that I didn't get to raise you, Aviva, but I'll concede that in this one instance and one instance only, your pathetic do-gooder impulses worked out in my favor." He ruffled my hair, and I flinched. "In the end, you were the spark who made my dreams of reclaiming my throne a blazing reality."

I hungered to tear that smug satisfaction off his face, his pride more devastating than any curse he could have thrown.

He shut the door with a muffled click, the sound of a trap snapping closed.

Ezra motioned me over to the deck railing, waiting until Delacroix and the Hellion were out of sight and earshot before speaking. "Don't listen to him."

I wasn't. Delacroix had knocked me down, but he wasn't keeping me there. I hadn't dedicated my life to protecting humanity as a needy, desperate bid to be accepted.

Well, not entirely, Cherry said.

Whose side are you on?

"All of Delacroix's recent plays have been in pursuit of one goal: a coup in the demon realm," I said.

"True, he gave Alastair the rune, not Natán, but that doesn't change what my father is up to," Ezra insisted. "Or preclude them working together to fuck us both over."

I smacked the metal. "Now's not the time to give a shit about your father!"

A muscle ticked in his jaw. "Says the woman who just got screwed over by not paying attention to hers."

"Don't you dare belittle me," I said. "And I'm paying very close attention to how the second Delacroix launches his coup, and all those legions of demons come after him, the Hell's security system isn't going to keep him safe. They won't stop with him or his buddies. They'll hunt down anyone who's helped him. Like the two of us. Inadvertent or not won't matter to them."

Ezra closed his hand around the railing, leaving finger indentations in the metal. "I'm sorry. You're right about what's most urgent right now."

"For what it's worth, Delacroix is too selfish to team up with your dad. You heard his derision for the vampires seeking sanctuary on the yacht. Whereas I do believe Natán cares what happens to them, but we'll deal with him in due time. Right now, we're going to hit my bastard of a father where it hurts."

"How?"

"We're going to stop his coup before it begins."

Chapter 15

"It all hinges on stealing the brain away from him," I said.

Since my plan required portal opening precision from Ezra, we'd returned to his quarters to hash it out.

"Once I have it, I'll retrieve the plus codes, the locations of all the locks." I tamped down my shudder at the thought of touching it again. "Then Maccabees move in, remove the locks in one fell swoop, and fend off my father's minions. We'll bury the cells like we did with the ones in Paris. No locks mean no soldiers and thus no coup." I unfurled a cold smile. "We finish him, once and for all."

"You know where the brain is?" Ezra said.

"I'm pretty confident, but I want to talk it out with you. It's taking more effort for you to maintain the security system magic, right? Even though the thrall should make it easier?"

"Right." Ezra tore open a pouch of synthetic blood. "That tracks if Delacroix calibrated the system to include wherever he stashed the brain."

"Does this yacht exist within some sliver of the demon realm? It doesn't show up on the most sophisticated radar equipment."

"It's on earth," Ezra said. "The security system cloaks it."

"Okay, you accused Delacroix of staying on the yacht because there wasn't anywhere else safe enough for him to go. But the brain has to be somewhere safe. And close at hand."

Ezra sucked back the last of his drink. "There's no way to break into his home. I've tried."

"We don't have to. Delacroix is bringing the freed prisoners somewhere and they won't fit on the yacht. Plus, a lot of traffic going through the portals to the Hell gives away his plans. He'll position the demons to be in place for the coup."

"The demon realm."

"Well," I said, "one specific part that Delacroix can control because it's beneath anyone's notice. The foyer of the demon realm. The gathering place of a bunch of feeble old shedim."

"Flaming Flapjacks," Ezra said.

My phone pinged with a photo of a handsome Asian man around my age.

"Keeping your options open in case this whole thrall thing doesn't work out?" Ezra joked.

I snorted and read my sister's follow-up message. "This is Maud's Maccabee security detail. Adrian Koo. She wants me to go through his personnel file."

"Because she likes him? Google stalk him like everyone else," Ezra said.

"Exactly what I'm replying." I sent the text.

"Any hard feelings toward Maud after what Delacroix said?" Ezra asked carefully.

Maud replied to my text with a: *you suck.*

Me: *Love you too, junior.*

I shook my head. "It's almost better knowing why she

was his favorite when she tried to kill him—he'd respect that—but I was reduced to his punching bag."

"Which will make it a million times more satisfying when you punch back."

I smiled at him. "Exactly. Back to the brain. I bet he stashed it in a magic pocket accessible from both his place and the restaurant."

Ezra pitched the empty blood pack in the trash. "If the restaurant is his war room, then it makes sense the brain is reachable from that side as well."

"He won't be worried about me accessing it from the Flaming Flapjacks side either," I said.

"It would never occur to him that you'd come up with that angle," Ezra said.

"Not only that." I put my phone away. "We couldn't have tried it before because that would have involved transiting through the Hell which would give him a heads up on our destination. But thanks to that thrall…"

Stealing the brain would make up for every single shitty thing about being a magic battery.

"Delacroix doesn't know I can portal without using the Hell," Ezra mused.

"Can you get to Flaming Flapjacks? You've seen it but it still is in the demon realm."

"I can, but I haven't seen wherever he's hidden the brain."

"You *have* seen his humidor though, and that's where Delacroix reacted to my presence. I'm hoping that when you open a portal from the pancake house to the back of the humidor, it'll go through wherever the brain is hidden. That it's sandwiched between the Hell and Flaming Flapjacks."

Ezra stood up and held out a hand. "No time like the present."

"There's one more thing."

He dropped his hand.

"You're going to open the portals but I'm the only one going through them. If I'm right about Flaming Flapjacks, Delacroix will have some kind of protection in place. Protection that doesn't involve your shared security magic yet does detect any unwanted presence. That said, he's bringing locks through with shedim magic. Therefore..." I busted out my horns.

Ezra was silent.

"What's the hesitation?"

"The thrall's safety zone."

I pursed my lips thinking, then shook my head. "Even though we're jumping realms, the physical distance between you at the Jolly Hellhound and me in the portal will be minimal, so it shouldn't act up."

"You stay in contact with me the entire time. The second you don't respond, I come in and get you."

"Copy that."

Ezra once more held his hand out to me.

I stood up and clasped it. "Really? You capitulate?"

"I'm agreeing, not saying mercy."

"I bet I could make you say mercy," I teased.

His eyes darkened and he squeezed my hand. "I bet you could," he purred.

I sucked in a shivery breath. "Stay on track."

"Thrall, right." He groaned and slowly stepped away.

Honestly, that reminder had been for me because I'd been ready to rip his clothes off and lick my way across his body.

I grabbed my coat and purse. "Is leaving the Hell a problem when it's, uh, somewhat disorganized?"

"We're no longer open for business, so it's not like it matters." He packed a bag. "The Lord of the Copper Hell is no more. Once the Luce has been stopped and my staff is safe, that is."

I wouldn't expect anything less of him. "While we're taking nicknames off the table," I said, "I vote to retire Prime Playboy."

"Aww. Come on. Crimson Prince doesn't exist now either," Ezra replied. "That means I don't get any fun names anymore."

"You'll just have to reinvent yourself."

We left the yacht, going directly to the Jolly Hellhound. Let Delacroix believe we'd scurried back to Vancouver to pass on his message to the Authority.

I was waltzing, uninvited, into a demon realm where my slippery serpent father was gathering troops to stage a coup, and I intended to steal a prized, if disgusting, blueprint.

What could possibly go wrong?

Fun! Cherry enthused.

Very, I agreed and let her out to play, morphing the rest of my human features to ones that would blend in better.

Ezra informed the pub's staff to keep everyone out of the back room, even though it was unlikely any Eishei Kodesh would visit the casino now.

To be safe, I locked the door to the pub first. I jumped through the mesh light Ezra conjured up with a bounce in my step. It felt like passing through a membrane of static electricity, complete with magic giving me a thorough scan —like a bouncer studiously checking ID—before letting me through.

I'd been worried that the parking lot outside the 1950s pancake house would be busy for once, but it was as empty as ever. Even the apocalyptic sky had grown on me, its violent churning above the jagged obsidian cliffs almost charming.

All good, I said through our psychic bond.

Anything happening there?

The dancing pancake sign is turned off. I glanced inside the curved windows under the pastel green awning. *But the place is bustling.*

With who? Ezra said. *Delacroix's minions? Freed prisoners? Regular clientele?*

No way to determine that from here.

Keep going. I've reconfigured the portal to lead to the humidor.

I stepped back into the darkness. *Can you rearrange the mesh light and give me a gap to see through? This is the part we're guessing on, so it's best to know what I'm facing.*

The dark strands quivered, then a hole about the size of my fist appeared.

I pressed my eye to it, sighing in relief at the sight of the brain hovering in a small bubble whose walls gleamed in pearl-like iridescence. Almost all of its strange growths were gone, but having no clue about demon brain anatomy, I couldn't determine whether that was normal or it had curled in on itself in a bout of seasonal depression.

Is it there? Ezra said.

Yes. On the count of three, connect a portal back to you. One. Two.

I grabbed the brain, recoiling at its meaty, pulsing weight, and careful not to touch any of the remaining nodes yet. It was exactly as gross as remembered.

Three.

I jumped into the pub's back room, prize in hand.

The plan was for me to shove my hand in the brain and speak the plus codes. I had to slow the onslaught of information down enough to parse out each and every lock cell location.

Ezra would record them, at which point we'd put our loot back where we'd found it.

I dreaded reconnecting with that grotesque specimen—not some harmless, dried-out relic, but a pulsating mass of flesh. My stomach turned at the memory of its gelatinous texture quivering around my fingertips, but the sacrifice was worth it to fuck Delacroix over.

And get the love lock locations. Which was the primary goal obviously.

I joined Ezra at the table, plunged my fingers into the brain's three final growths, and got a whopping total of four plus codes. One of which was the Pont des Arts in Paris.

Ezra researched the other three. All were well-known locales for love locks and places we already had Maccabees stationed.

I shoved my fingers deeper into the growths. "Come on," I muttered, but instead of a tsunami of information, there was only a hollow silence. "He drained it."

With the removal of my hand came a sad trombone sound.

From the brain.

Then Delacroix's voice floated up out of it. "Girl detective badge denied."

This was followed by unreasonably long cackling before the brain began to smolder from within. Gray matter hissed and bubbled as if doused with acid, then collapsed into a charred mass that crumbled to ash.

Defeat crashed over me like a wave. My father had outmaneuvered me again. I had no way to find the locks and hadn't gotten anything from him on how to stop the Luce.

Instead, we'd been cornered into taking a shedim's word that he'd keep the supernatural chaos contained— keep humans safe—when trusting demons worked out about as well as using a toaster as a life raft in a tsunami. Sure, you might float for a second, but then you'd just be waterlogged, clutching a minor kitchen appliance, and disappointed in your decision-making skills.

I wiped away brain dust along with any sense of failure.

"We're going to report, regroup, and find a way to stop the Luce once and for all," I said.

As it was after midnight in Vancouver, that put a crimp in heading to HQ immediately. Plus, jumping between time zones that were always night was messing with my circadian rhythm. Loath as I was to waste even a minute, I recognized the sense in getting a good night's rest.

I recognized the sense in staying awake long enough to deliver Delacroix's "back off" message to Michael even more.

That went down as well as expected.

"Look on the bright side." I had the call on speakerphone while I towel dried my hair, already in my pj's after my shower.

"The bright side of a shedim blackmailing us into trusting him?" Michael said, driving home for some much-needed sleep. "The same one who facilitated your abduction, set all this suffering in motion, and somehow stole back the locks that were buried in Paris?"

I almost dropped the towel. He what?

Ezra raised his eyebrows and whistled softly. He was in a pair of cashmere leisure pants, the suitcase he'd brought with him from the Hell already neatly unpacked.

There were two long loud honks from Michael's side of the phone.

"Fucker," she muttered.

Oh dear. My mother wasn't an aggressive driver. I had room for only one person with that tendency in my life and the role was filled by my best friend.

I tossed the towel in the hamper and grabbed my face cream. "Even if we had the location of every single lock cell, Eishei Kodesh operatives couldn't fight those prisoners and there aren't enough of our vampires to handle it, especially not when they're dealing with the Luce-infected. The

Maccabees are stretched thin, and this takes one giant problem off our plate."

"Assuming he can be trusted," Michael said. "Which he cannot."

Another loud honk and the squeal of sliding tires made me flinch.

"*Goddamn* this rain," she snarled.

"Mom, pull over. Please."

"Yes." The hum of her motor shut off. "We can't afford to wage a war on this front as well," she said.

"I'm inclined to believe that Delacroix will keep the prisoners from doing harm," Ezra said. "He wants those soldiers."

"For a coup." She laughed bitterly. "My baby daddy aspires to be king of the demons."

I choke-holded the skin cream bottle and sprayed lotion all over my hands. Did my mother really say baby daddy?

Ezra muffled his laughter with a pillow.

"Technically," I said, spreading the cream over my arms, "he aspires to regain his crown. I'm a princess," I added helpfully, trying to add some levity.

"Mazel tov," Michael said dryly. "Well, should my career go tits up, I can always pull the nepotism card."

"That's the spirit," I said, trying to recover from hearing my mom say "tits" in any context whatsoever. "Maybe he'll make you his royal advisor. Or spymaster? How fun would that be?"

Cherry affirmed that sounded pretty great, but Michael sighed.

"I'll speak with the Authority," she said. "In other news, Ha-joon Park, a Blue Flame in Seoul, cracked the pattern of how the Luce spreads."

"That's great news," Ezra said.

"Is it wind belts and air circulation?" I guessed.

"No," Michael said. "Humidity and air pressure. Places

with a higher humidity and therefore a lower air pressure have been hit harder. Temperature doesn't matter."

"What does that mean for Vancouver?" I said. "We're not as cold as other Canadian cities, but we have relatively high humidity because we're a temperate rainforest."

"With the past five days of torrential rainfall, the Luce is tearing faster and more powerfully through our city," Michael said. "It's expected that all high humidity locations will fully succumb—"

"Define 'succumb,'" Ezra said tightly.

"Globally, that's a complicated determination to—"

"*Michael*," Ezra growled.

"Use your imagination," she snapped. She took a deep breath. "Sorry, Ezra. I can't define it because we have no matrix for such a definition. The Luce will be most potent in a week. Assume the worst and that all vampires in these areas will be affected along with any locks in the vicinity releasing their prisoners."

I pressed my lips together against the scream lodged in my throat. Seven days was a blip—the pause between the latest drops of a favorite television show.

How could that timeline apply to the Luce infecting all the vampires?

Or to the wards on the locks failing and those prisons opening like chrysalises of evil releasing the world's most unfortunate butterfly collection?

Ezra went utterly still, the immortal predator in him surfacing as his face emptied of all expression. Only his haunted eyes betrayed him as he absorbed the death sentence for his entire kind, while knowing that he alone on earth would survive it.

"The Luce is targeting noninherent shedim magic and was unleashed on our vampires because of a shedim rune and you two have more experience with demons than any of us," Michael said. "Tomorrow, comb through all our resources. Spot relevant details and get us answers that others don't have the expertise to see. The clock is ticking."

I padded over to the phone. "Copy that."

"There is no time to waste. *None.*"

"I understand how serious this is," I said waspishly. I drew myself up straighter. "We're on it. Unless there's something else you need to fill me in on?"

Michael paused. "I'm just on edge and need to sleep. You get some rest too."

I disconnected the call and crawled into bed. "Come here and hold me."

"Demanding," Ezra groused, but turned off the light and did as I asked.

We lay there in silence for a long time. The countdown had begun, and with each heartbeat, our borrowed time slipped away. Seven days until chaos reigned. Seven days to face a storm that would unmake us.

Chapter 16

I was incredibly groggy on Sunday morning, yawning while I played a voice mail from Darsh.

"He wants us at brunch," I told Ezra. This used to be a monthly tradition with Darsh, Sachie, and me, and I missed it.

My boyfriend had been stress knitting while I slept. The ugly orange sweater was completed and he was working on a new project. (He'd brought his canvas supply bag, with, yes, much nicer yarn.) On the menu today was a very, very long scarf that verged into blanket territory. Or actual territory because another few feet and it would qualify for its own property tax assessment.

"Darsh is well aware of the urgency of the situation," I said. "For him to ask for a time-out means he really needs this break, but Michael was clear about us getting to work."

Darsh didn't answer my return call. Instead, he texted —uncharacteristically—before I could leave my regrets on his voice mail. *You need to eat. Fuel up then hit the library at HQ. Or take it to go. I want to see my friends outside of a code red situation.*

Ezra gently tugged a lock of my hair. "He's not the only

one who needs to fill up on good friends and good conversation."

"True." I leaned against him. "You and I could both use that."

"I barely like any of these people," Ezra said. "I'm only doing it to remind you how incredible I am."

I caressed his cheek. "Trust me, I remember."

He caught my hand and kissed my knuckles.

"Head out in ten?" I said, sliding off the bed.

Ezra rolled up the scarf. "I have to make one quick stop on the way."

Half an hour later, Ezra had run his errand, and I'd picked up a dozen spicy ginger cookies from Sachie's favorite bakery.

Civilians should have been out for brunch or jogging and cycling, but it was like we were in a movie where all the extras were Trad cops and operatives. Storefronts and restaurants were dark.

Posters had gone up calling on Parliament to declare a national emergency and pass Jared Casey's magic oversight bill. They listed the benefits: wresting control away from the Maccabees, forcing Eishei Kodesh to register their magic. We'd also have to pay special taxes to the government to monitor our community and increase security for the Trad population.

I drove over the Cambie Street Bridge. Sunlight glinted off Yaletown's glass towers, while a seaplane skimmed low over the gentle ripples of False Creek. So normal and yet so not.

"This sucks," I said. "Not the weather. That's finally lovely."

"Yeah. I can't believe it's been over a week."

"Of rain?" I braked at a red light. "Or since the Luce hit? Not quite."

"Since I fucked you," Ezra said blandly.

"Oh. Jeez. We were alone in my bed last night and that didn't even occur to me. Cockblocked by a magic virus and my father."

My boyfriend grimaced. "Never say those words in that order ever again."

I laid a hand on Ezra's cheek.

Our eyes met, our breaths mingling in the quiet space between us.

"Avi," he said regretfully.

"You're my boyfriend. Wanting to kiss you is a perfectly normal desire." I waggled my eyebrows at him. "We're at one of the longest red lights in Vancouver, but if you don't want to…"

He laughed harshly. "I want to, mi cielo."

Our lips met like a whisper, soft and warm against each other. The gentle press held all the sweetness of a first snow, or dawn breaking over still waters.

I floated away on waves of bliss, clutching his shirt with a breathless sigh. My lids fluttered half-open.

Ezra pulled back slightly.

I followed him, needing his lips on mine.

"Avi. Aviva," he repeated more sharply and gently slapped my cheek. "You're unfocused and glassy."

"Hmmm?" The sound floated between us like I was underwater. I reached for Ezra again, the world around us hazy except for the magnetic pull toward him.

"Snap out of it!"

HOOONNNNK!

The sound jarred me back to my senses. My reflection in the rearview mirror showed my head tilted toward Ezra and my mouth working like a fish.

Cheeks burning, I hit the gas and sped forward.

"It's not your fault," Ezra said.

"Could we not?" I mumbled.

"It's mine. As the one enthralling you, it's my responsibility to—"

I smashed my hand on my horn, making Ezra jump and the asshole driver in front of me switch lanes. "Have you forgotten why *I* initiated the thrall, Coma Boy? Yeah, it's embarrassing acting like your mindless super groupie, but if that was it, I'd get over it. I may not have fully comprehended how uneven it would be when I initiated it or how it would change our dynamic, but at least respect me enough to not make it worse by taking responsibility—" I did the air quotes with one hand. "Like I'm some brainless puppet. My choices don't always work out, but I've made them freely and I stand by them."

"Okay," he said quietly.

Only a few more days until this thrall was gone forever. The Luce would also be at its most potent and there might not be a future to enjoy, but that was a problem for tomorrow me.

My biggest concern for the next couple hours would be my champagne to orange juice mimosa ratio at brunch.

We drove deeper into the heart of Kitsilano. I turned off the main thoroughfare onto a residential street not far from Darsh's house.

Ezra slammed the dashboard. "Pull over! Now!"

He exploded out the door before I reached the curb, speeding toward a man with a hunting rifle trained on someone's back.

"Real humans don't need magic!" the Trad cried.

His victim's pivot was halting and jerky, and when he finally turned around, the vampire stared at the man with milky-white eyes.

I gasped. That vamp was either seconds away from a Luce-induced death throe or about to unleash a murderous rampage. Possibly both.

Ezra grabbed the barrel of the gun, but he was a fraction of a second too late.

When the blast hit its target in the shoulder, the only one surprised that it enraged rather than killed the vampire was the man.

He enjoyed that emotion for all of two seconds, at which point the bloodsucker tore the Trad's head off with a super speed that caught even Ezra off guard.

Ezra jumped the other vampire, killing him in less than a heartbeat.

I ran up to the broken vampire corpse splayed on the concrete, jumping the puddle of the Trad's blood, and tugged on Ezra's sleeve. "Get back in the car before someone sees you." I phoned the deaths in, but said I'd come upon the crime scene after both were dead.

Jared Casey was up in arms about depending on vampire Mafias. He'd do anything to further his agenda, especially twist Ezra's involvement—Natán Cardoso's son —to implicate him in a Trad's murder.

Standing there, watching dark fluid seep into the concrete while sirens wailed in the distance, I was struck by how easily I'd slipped into this bizarro reality, where covering up supernatural deaths wasn't just necessary but sadly routine.

A soft, bitter laugh escaped me. My lifetime of keeping secrets and fabricating plausible half-truths was really coming in handy.

Ezra remained out of sight while the cleanup crew arrived. Even though they'd heard about vampires leaving corpses with transparent flesh, their veins glowing silver like fiber-optic cables, that didn't stop their shocked expressions.

I gave them the same statement that I'd phoned in and left them to handle the aftermath.

Five minutes later, Ezra and I stood on Darsh's front

stoop in the mist. His character house was a jewel of a home with slanted creaky floors, richly painted rooms, and plenty of light coming in through the vampire-safe windows.

Ezra held two bottles of Golden Blood. The Rh-null liquid was the rarest blood type in the world.

"You really ponied up for people you barely like," I teased.

"These are for me." Ezra cradled the bottles to his chest. "I don't trust the plonk Darsh will serve."

The door opened, Darsh standing there with his hands on his hips. "Hand the good stuff over, Cardoso."

Had Ezra not had lightning-fast reflexes to grab the bottle he'd almost dropped, it would have crashed onto the stairs.

Deep wrinkles carved valleys across Darsh's once-smooth face, his skin now paper-thin and mottled. His brown hair had turned stark white and his eyes were unnaturally bright in their sunken sockets.

I blinked dumbly at him.

His shoulders were hunched forward, though his fangs still gleamed with predatory sharpness when he spoke.

"I'm trying a new look," he said blithely. At least when he tossed his head, the movement was fluid. "Do you love it? I'm a little undecided."

Ezra shoved the Golden Blood at Darsh, then vaulted past him, calling Silas's name.

Instead of hugging my friend, crying, or raging at the universe, I shrugged. "I'd go back to your old skin care regime if I was you."

"Bitch," he whispered, and pulled me into a tight embrace.

I didn't tense up at how cold and therefore how *hungry* he was, though Cherry was vigilant against his slightest movement. The Baroness had protected me from many dangers; one of my best friends was never supposed to be in that category.

It was too sad to be scary, and I reluctantly ended the hug, going to find Sachie.

My bestie was in the blue and white kitchen with Olivier, who'd been put to work making waffles.

His lean, muscular frame filled out his faded jeans and fitted Henley perfectly, his Black skin contrasting handsomely with vibrant green eyes that sparkled with warmth.

"Hey, Avi," he said, wiping batter off the outside of the griddle. His Nova Scotian accent with hints of New York and Irish influences had softened but not disappeared during his time out west.

"Hey yourself." I gave him a one-shouldered hug, tamping down my smirk at the fact that his hair smelled like Sachie's favorite shampoo. "How's the vampire patrolling going? Lots of volunteers?"

"No, but more than I figured would show up for Toothpick Sentry."

I snorted. "Don't let Darsh and Silas hear you call it that."

"I already ordered T-shirts," Sach said brightly. She held up a mug. "Starter caffeine?"

Shaking my head, I beelined for the open bottle of champagne on the counter, dumping three times the accepted amount for a mimosa into a flute—and forgoing the orange juice.

"I used a beer glass for mine," she said.

I sagged back against the counter. "Why didn't you give me a heads-up?"

"It wouldn't have helped," she said flatly. "Trust me."

I opened my mouth to argue otherwise, remembered the stunned Maccabees seeing the dead vamp whose condition they'd been briefed on, and chugged more champagne.

"I told Darsh we'd need more bottles," Silas said.

I choked on the booze.

He seemed to cave in on himself, his normally imposing frame withered like a deflated balloon. The shirt usually strained by his massive shoulders now hung loose, hollows had formed in his cheeks, and his dark copper hair was threaded with gray. Even his freckles had faded, as if the Luce was draining his very essence.

Silas shot me a ghost of a smile that made my heart twist; another larger-than-life part of him reduced to a shadow.

Ezra hovered behind him like a nervous mother hen.

Darsh trotted into the room, saw how Ezra was behaving, and snorted. "Told you," he said to Olivier. "Etransfer me the ten bucks. I don't take cash."

"Pendejo," Ezra said without any heat.

Smirking, Darsh handed out our marching orders of what to carry into the dining room.

Silas was given a heavy platter of misshapen waffles, which Ezra immediately tried to take from him.

"Don't make me stab you." Silas shakily hefted the dish, holding it above Ezra's head.

Was it wrong of me to hope that the Prime would jump for it like a child going for candy?

I picked up the large bowl of freshly whipped cream. "Has anyone heard from Nasir?"

"No word yet," Sachie said, pouring coffee into a carafe.

Sitting around the large round table in the eating-designated room with its royal purple walls, we threw on a playlist of '90s greatest hits and did our damnedest to make this feel like just another Sunday.

Olivier entertained us with a bizarre case involving smuggled surfboards full of contraband dog medication, and Ezra and Darsh debated the best blood bars in

Monaco versus Lisbon, going so far as to throw rock paper scissors over it.

All of it was an amusing avoidance of why our brunch felt like a wake.

Sach shared choice screenshots from the Ezracurricular fan boards and a couple of gossip site items about how Ezra had dumped his rumored ballet dancer girlfriend, Irene, for a mystery woman.

They were accompanied by a photo of when Ezra hugged me on the Pont des Arts surrounded by love locks and looking very sweet. If you didn't know what those locks hid, that was. Though my face wasn't visible, it would only be a matter of time before someone leaked my name.

Like it or not, Ezra and I had gone public. Well, I had a world to save; let people post their comments. I honestly had no fucks to spare for the haters. As for the others? People longed for an escape right now and I didn't mind being part of that—provided it didn't directly impinge on me.

"If their speculation takes their minds off all the other shit going down in the world," I said, squeezing Ezra's hand, "then have at it."

My boyfriend relaxed long enough to give me a small smile, then his attention was back on the other two vampires.

Silas and Darsh barely even tried the Golden Blood, preferring to fire back small unmarked blood packs. Apparently, Maccabee healers were working around the clock to provide vampire operatives with these magically boosted shots.

Silas swallowed with a grimace. "Tastes like a rattler rolled in a tumbleweed and died in my mouth, but it keeps our strength up."

"Yeah, you and the Rock could be twins," Sachie teased, stress-eating her fifth spicy ginger cookie. Her leg bounced so rapidly under the table that she rippled her coffee like a *Jurassic Park* re-creation.

Olivier pushed the plate of cut fruit in front of her before she could polish off an even half dozen cookies. She glared at him, then stabbed a kiwi slice.

"You're better-looking than the Rock, babe," Darsh said, smacking his boyfriend's cheek.

Silas blushed. He was so pale that his blush was like the barest twinge of pink on a white petal.

It was the first moment since I'd returned that they were the fabulous couple they should be, except it felt discordant given their other interactions. Was it real or just a product of mutual imminent death?

My fork scraped against the ceramic with a harsh screech.

"All I want to do is lie down and sleep." Silas poked the empty blood pack, his hand trembling slightly. "I'm not sure how much good this is doing. It's like fighting the pull of an hourglass."

"Hey!" Darsh elbowed him. "I'm the pessimistic one. Your role is sunny-eyed optimist who I tease mercilessly."

"Guess my naiveté only goes so far."

"It's not naiveté," Darsh said viciously. He grabbed his phone and silenced the playlist. "This sad white boy music is getting on my last nerve."

"Did you hear about the Gryphon Gang?" Sach asked me, referring to the Vancouver branch of a US-based vamp mob.

"What about them?"

"Gone," Darsh said. "The Luce got some of them and the others pulled up stakes and moved into a Seaside clinic."

"I heard it was the one in LA," Silas said.

"What's happening at our Seaside?"

"Hard to say." Darsh absently tore open his fifth

boosted blood pack. Nothing said "we're screwed" quite like vampires mainlining boosted blood like college kids chugging caffeine during finals.

Ezra tracked the motion with narrowed eyes.

"Security is insane at the clinics," Darsh continued. "They might be curing vampires, or draining their blood to send back to Babel, or letting them fight to the death in gladiator bouts in bathroom stalls. We have no clue what's happening inside or what Natán's up to."

Ezra didn't pipe up with his theory about his dad consolidating power over vamps in order to force a shift in power away from Maccabees and Trad authorities. His silence spoke volumes about how worried he was about our friends.

"In more hopeful news," Silas said, "my software has almost decoded the notebook you gave me, Ez."

"The one you took from Burning Eddie?" Olivier said. Off Ezra's nod, he leaned closer to Silas. "Well, hurry it up, man. We could all use the good news most definitely found in a demon's secret diary. Was it encrusted with glittering blood crystals?"

"In the shape of a heart?" Sachie said.

Silas chuckled. "Good thing Orly's party planning is already in the works. I told her to go for an end-of-the-world theme." He reached for another blood pack.

Ezra slammed his hands on the table. "That's it."

"I was kidding," Silas said.

"The two of you are going to the Copper Hell right now. We'll get you safely within the security system so that when I heal you, it'll stick."

Darsh nudged Silas. "He lasted longer than you said he would."

"We're not leaving, Ez," Silas said.

"Yes." He stared at them with the full weight of a Prime decree. "You are."

"I'm in charge of the vamp situation here in Vancouver, and I'm not running off the second things get tough," Darsh said.

"No?" Ezra said. "Because you were ready to do that the other day. Given your histories with the Maccabees, neither you nor Silas owe them shit. And with everything else going down, no one would come after you if you left."

"And yet, here I am, sticking around." Darsh took Silas's hand, receiving a sweet smile and a squeeze of his fingers in return. "We can still help. As long as that's true, neither of us are going anywhere."

"Enjoy playing cavalry for the ten minutes you have left," Ezra said, dripping sarcasm.

I dropped my knife on my plate, mid–jam smear. "*Ezra!*"

Sachie crossed her arms; Olivier pressed his lips together.

"Unlike some," Darsh said coldly, "Silas and I choose to stick by our Maccabee oaths."

Silas shot Ezra a disappointed look.

My boyfriend shoved his chair back and strode out without a second look back.

"Daddy's angry," Darsh said with a shiver.

Silas peered at him. "I can't tell if you're scared or turned on by my best friend and Avi's boyfriend."

"Scared of course." Darsh shook his head in an exaggerated motion, mouthing "Totally turned on."

And though my faint smile as the two of them left the room to talk to Ezra was real, the humor didn't mask the cold dread settling in my stomach.

Between my friends falling victim to the Luce and the people I cared about most at each other's throats, I couldn't shake the feeling that we were all coming undone, piece by piece.

Chapter 17

We three humans left behind strained to hear what was going on.

"No angry voices," Olivier said quietly, tossing his napkin on the table.

Sachie tilted her head, listening. "No broken furniture."

The silence from the other room grew more loaded and ominous.

I tried to reach Ezra on our psychic phone line, but the jerk didn't answer.

"Why is your face twitching?" Olivier's eyebrows drew together. "Are muscle spasms a side effect of being enthralled?"

I pressed my hand to my cheek, flustered that I'd been making faces during my communication attempt, and about to clarify that he didn't need to be concerned.

Olivier leaned forward, his eyes wide. "Have you suffered any other symptoms? Brooding majestically? Compulsive cape swishing? Transforming into a bat during sneezing fits?"

Sach buried her face in her boyfriend's shoulder, her shoulders shaking.

There was a burst of annoyed Spanish from the living room, and then Ezra called my name.

Olivier and Sach were on their feet before I was.

"Worried you'll miss the bat transformation?" I said.

"Wouldn't you be?" Sach retorted.

I stomped out, preferring hungry vampires over these two comedians.

Darsh and Silas were crammed on the plush velvet sofa together. Silas had his arms crossed and his chin set at a defiant angle, while Darsh rested his head back, his eyes closed.

Ezra stood stiffly between the mantel and a hideous rubber plant that refused to die. He pointed at me when I entered the room. "Do I have your permission to draw on the thrall to boost my healing magic since they're adamant about not going to the Hell? If they're going to stay put and help, then they better remain in a condition to do so."

I exchanged bewildered glances with Sachie and Olivier. "You can do that?"

"He has no idea if he can," Silas said, "and knowing Ez, he won't stop trying until he's drained himself of all magic. He'll drain you too. No."

Red washed over Ezra's eyes. "I'm not going to jeopardize myself or Aviva. I understand my limits."

"You understand them," Silas countered, "you just ignore them when anyone you care about is involved."

Ezra snarled at him.

I stepped between the two best friends, my arms outstretched. "Everyone take a deep... Aw fuck. Just calm down." I looked from one to the other. "Ezra is fully aware of what's on the line right now. If the thrall facilitates that *and* heals you, then I'm all for it."

Especially if this extra transaction drained the damn thing and Ezra and I could get back to normal faster.

"You say that now," Silas said, "but once may not be

enough. He could heal us and we get reinfected. The Luce is magic; there aren't antibodies built up through exposure."

"I'm sure once will do it," I said with forced cheer.

"If it helps," Olivier said, "remember that the Luce is tied to humidity, and we had a heavy spell of rain. There's dry weather forecast for the next few days. The info was distributed to the Trad officers too," he explained at my confused look.

"That means that even one healing session buys us time to find a proper cure," Darsh said. "I'm selfish enough that I'll risk the Prime's well-being for another chance to fight."

Silas rubbed a hand through his hair, gray strands breaking off and falling from his fingers. "It's what's best as an operative, but it's not right to choose between us or Ezra and Aviva."

"Then go back to the Hell," Ezra growled. "You still have a room there."

"Here we go again," Darsh muttered.

"Absolutely not." Sachie stomped over to Silas and cuffed him across the head. "You self-sacrificing noble bloodsuckers are giving me indigestion. Ezra and Aviva are adults giving informed consent. I respect your decision to stay put, so accept you need this help to remain in the fight. Put on your big-boy pants and let Darsh's selfishness rub off on you."

"Thank you," Darsh said. He screwed up his face. "But rude."

Sachie sighed. "You're allowed to put yourself first, Silas, and I don't mean as an operative."

"I'd listen to her," Olivier said.

"Yes, because I am wise beyond my years," Sach said.

"That and you have that look presaging pointy things in your hands."

She gave him a two-dimple grin. "That too."

Silas threw up his hands in defeat. "I'll agree to it on a one-time basis only."

"But—" Ezra began.

Silas fixed him with a cold stare. "One. Time."

Darsh smirked. "Hot."

Silas rolled his eyes at his boyfriend but also blushed again.

"We don't have the lock locations, Zee," I said. "Much as I loathe going along with Delacroix, we have to abide by his decree for now. A one-time Prime magic infusion to Darsh and Silas shouldn't weaken Delacroix's position, but we can't risk more than that."

"What decree?" Sach said.

I told them everything that had transpired on the yacht.

Silas frowned. "You shouldn't risk anything where that son of a bitch is concerned."

Ezra jabbed a finger at his friend. "Don't even think about backing out because of this. Aviva and I will rethrall—"

I did a double take. Wait. What? *Nonononono.*

Darsh grimaced. "Fancy branding doesn't change what you two are doing."

Ezra mimed for him to zip it. "I'll heal you two in the immediacy of that re-up. Given the boost, siphoning off some of my Prime magic to you two definitely won't affect the Hell enough to piss Delacroix off. Avi, you agree?"

Five pairs of eyes swiveled to me.

Confess that I'd rather have a rectal enema than say yes? Stellar choices: major selfish bitch or major resentful bitch.

The strain of playing multiple chess games without even the release of intimacy with Ezra made me weary down to my bones. Yet, whatever I chose now, I'd stand by what I told Ezra. That I made my decisions freely.

"I'm not redoing this enthrallment."

Darsh smiled.

"Then I decline the offer of Prime magic," Silas said. "I won't chance Delacroix coming after either of you."

"The Luce is growing to potent strength and more and more of those locks are failing," I said. "Delacroix will be focused on getting the prisoners to his turf before their jailers can recapture them. He doesn't have time for either stampeding demons or a hit on me to change the détente with the Maccabees. And as for Ezra, any move against him risks Natán marshaling the vamps. Even if healing you drained all of Ezra's magic on the security system—"

"Which it won't by a long shot," Ezra said.

I pointed at him with a nod. "I truly believe Delacroix won't risk his end goal by coming after us or doing anything to harm other humans."

"All right." Silas crossed his arms. "But push yourself past any sane limit and I'll stake you myself, *pendejo*."

Ezra's lips twitched. "Noted."

Sachie and Olivier said they'd clean up brunch to give us privacy and left.

Ezra crouched down next to the sofa that our friends sat on and bit into his wrist, offering the blood first to Darsh. "Just for the pendejo crack, you can wait your turn," he snarked at Silas.

Darsh latched on to the skin, drinking so deeply that Ezra grimaced.

The thrall tugged hard.

I sat down in the closest chair with wobbly legs. My skin felt like it was being scraped with the blade of a knife, but not in a dangerous cutting way. It was soothing; familiar almost.

Cherry blinked awake, reaching for it.

Suddenly, a change rippled through Darsh; his weathered face grew luminous again. It was like watching ice melt in reverse, smooth and fluid.

Ezra's brown skin tinged an ashy gray, but he didn't pull back. "Avi?"

My heart hammered against my ribs like a trapped bird, electricity flooding my veins.

The winter shadows stretched longer across the hardwood floors, and the fabric grains on the armchair burned against my fingertips.

Silas's concerned face snapped into sharp focus, but his voice sounded like waves crashing onto a shore.

I could count every mote of dust dancing in the pale sunlight streaming through the window, and the creaking floorboards rolled like we were on a ship. I swallowed against the taste of seawater.

Silas put a steadying hand on my shoulder.

I clasped it with clawed fingers, wanting an anchor against feeling vitally, almost overwhelmingly alive.

Darsh's brown hair darkened from white, and his posture straightened proudly. When he leaned back, his mouth was smeared with Ezra's blood. His clear gaze met the Prime's and he nodded.

Ezra nodded back, then touched my leg, his brow wrinkled.

I twirled my hand to indicate he should move on to healing Silas. *Give me more of this rush, baby, stat.*

Ezra hesitated a moment, then shoved his wrist at the other vampire. "Drink."

Silas took a tentative sip, worried eyes trained on his best friend.

Ezra swore under his breath, clasped the back of Silas's head, and forced his wrist against the other vamp's mouth.

The transformation started immediately; Silas's body filled with renewed strength as his freckles emerged like constellations against his skin.

Cherry Bomb reached hungrily for more of the dark note flavoring the thrall with Ezra, and I released a blissed-out sigh. Where had this been all those other times?

Ezra wasn't having a similarly good time. Sweat beaded his ashen forehead, his shoulders sagged lower with each passing second, and his fingers trembled against Silas's head, even as his jaw remained set.

Silas wrenched free, looking like his normal healthy self, save for his crimson lips and the deep furrow between his brows. "What did you do?"

Ezra sat down on the ground at his friend's feet. The ugly gash on his wrist was almost gone, but he was slumped over, drained. "I healed you."

Darsh handed Silas the damp washcloth he'd gotten.

Cherry retreated to sulk at the loss of the incredible magic rush we'd experienced.

I rubbed my arms, feeling the scratchy *titch* of my scales through the fabric. "You drew on the security system of the yacht, didn't you?"

"No," Ezra said. "You did."

Chapter 18

I shook my head. "Impossible."

"Are you sure?" Ezra hauled himself into a chair. "Because one moment I was using my Prime healing, and the next, I was flooded with the security system's magic."

That feeling of being scraped with a blade, but in a soothing, almost familiar way. Cherry waking up and reaching for it...

"Oh fuck!" My hand flew to my mouth.

Olivier and Sach raced into the living room. "What happened?" she said.

Darsh stretched out his hands, eyeing them almost suspiciously. "Apparently, we're not only healed, we're also protected by the Hell's security system."

"Delacroix is going to lose his shit on you two," Silas said.

My father was already furious about me using my own shedim abilities for the thrall and all my "do-gooder instincts"—this would send him freefalling in unbridled wrath.

"Remove it, Ezra," Sachie said.

I looked anxiously at my boyfriend.

"I would if I could," Ezra said. "Think about magic

like strings on a guitar. The thrall, my Prime magic, the security system, all of them are separate. When I started healing you both, I was strumming the thrall and my Prime magic, but because of our connection, Avi joined in this song and added the third string. This chord is vibrating through me," he said through gritted teeth, "and it's not ideal."

Patches of my scales remained on my arms, around my ankles, and on my stomach. When I couldn't will them away, I hurriedly touched my neck and face. There was a small strip on the side of my throat I could cover with a turtleneck but thankfully, none I could find above that.

"Why did I manage this now?" I said.

Ezra shrugged helplessly. "Prime magic mixed with us having rethralled enough times that it was possible?"

I rubbed my hand over the scales again and then dropped it in my lap. "We wait it out."

"I'm not sure it will fade this time," Ezra said. "Like I said, this chord is vibrating through me. As if it's stuck."

"Then cut one of the strings," Olivier said.

"I can't," Ezra said. "Not from within it, but a healer should be able to dissolve the thrall relatively easily." He looked at Darsh and Silas. "Once that happens, you two won't benefit from the security system, but my Prime magic should remain in place."

The "for now" hung in the air.

"I prefer it that way," Darsh said. "The notion of being tethered to Delacroix's magic makes my skin crawl."

Silas nodded. "Same."

"Sorry," I mumbled.

"Your heart was in the right place," Silas said.

I stood up. "We're headed to the library at HQ, so we'll stop by a healer first and get 'er done."

We said our goodbyes. Darsh planned to assess where the vamp neighborhoods were at in person. They'd mapped our city out on a grid, and he, Silas, Sachie, and Olivier with his Trad squad were going to Sector 13.

"I can't guarantee there won't be side effects of undoing the thrall prematurely," Ezra said on the drive. "There might be a recovery period. The healer can tell us for certain."

I changed lanes to pull ahead of a slowpoke driver. Why couldn't anything be simple? I didn't have time to recover. We should have been researching any shedim angle to stop the Luce alrea—

Ezra slammed his hands on the dashboard. "Aviva!"

I hit the brakes before we sailed through the hard red light. "Sorry. Distracted for a second."

Ezra placed the back of his hand on my cheek. "Are you feeling okay?"

"It's nothing like that." I scratched at the patch of scales on my neck. "It's fair to assume that my inability to get rid of these things is tied to being plugged in to Delacroix's demon magic. Could it give me insights into what I find at the library that I would otherwise miss?" The light turned green and I hit the gas pedal. "Library first, healer second."

Ezra crossed his arms. "That's a terrible idea."

"It's an idea born of desperation, but these are desperate times. Six days, Ezra, until every vampire in Vancouver is hit with the Luce. How many will even be left at that point? Will your Prime magic still keep Darsh and Silas healthy? And what if the Luce mutates? We haven't even considered that possibility."

He held up his hands. "Okay. Library first but we're still seeing the healer today."

"Yes. Absolutely."

After I parked, I took a second to arrange my hair and pop my collar like a preppy from the 1980s to hide the scales on my throat, then we raced inside.

The size of a small school cafeteria, our library

contained a surprisingly diverse collection, though it wasn't a showpiece like at some of the other chapters.

We ensconced ourselves at my favorite table by the window with the magnolia tree outside, poring through the stack of books we'd gathered for oblique references to shedim abilities, including anything on shedim creating vamp-like creatures.

Hours later, I closed another book, my eyes dry and gritty, my neck in knots, and pathetically few notes on my laptop. I readjusted my hair and collar because my patchy scales hadn't faded back to skin yet.

The librarian snapped on a small TV set behind the checkout counter, and the handful of us in the room gathered around to watch the Authority's press conference.

Dmitri Koslov was the main speaker, but all of them were there, standing by him in silent solidarity.

He spotlit the terrible, senseless death of the Trad man in Vancouver. Photos of the victim filled the screen, along with Dmitri's grave voice at how the Luce-infected killer was allowed to roam the streets unchecked.

"Where was the Vampire Care Initiative offering him sanctuary and keeping humans safe?" Dmitri said. With his furrowed brow and solicitous lean, he oozed such perfect concern that I almost missed the predatory satisfaction underneath. "The Maccabees are doing everything in our power to find a cure against this magic virus, but sadly, we no longer trust that the vampire leaders have any true desire for a healthy resolution."

Not once did he mention Natán Cardoso by name, but you'd have to be a fool not to get the connection.

I could have throttled Dmitri. Every word that came out of his mouth increased the level of hostility between humans and vampires, making tensions so much worse.

He should have agreed to partner up with Natán and then see what the vampire did next—like whether he reneged on that stated desire. Natán would have looked like the asshole and turned public opinion against him.

Instead, Dmitri's actions almost guaranteed that we'd only learn what Natán's true motives were when he struck back. Cardoso Sr. hadn't experienced a meteoric rise in the Mafia world and kept an iron-clad hold on the Kosher Nostra because he was famed for his mercy.

The operatives in the library glanced nervously at Ezra.

His jaw tightened, muscles jumping beneath his skin as he twisted a heavy book into a mangled mess of paper and bindings. A flash of something murderous darkened his eyes.

Every instinct screamed that we were heading for disaster, and I braced myself for the moment when loyalty to the Maccabees and loyalty to him would tear me apart.

The Maccabees fanned out to give him space—all, that is, except the librarian, who gave him hell for destroying a book.

Ezra relaxed his grip on the tome, though tension still radiated from his rigid spine.

Having spun his narrative, Dmitri decreed that given all these concerns, Maccabees were imposing curfews in all major cities. He ended with a promise made directly to the camera. "Maccabees continue to be stewards of light in the fight against evil. We human soldiers are trained for this battle. Put your faith in us." He shook his head sadly. "Doing otherwise will only get you killed, and anyone who says differently isn't putting your well-being first."

Ezra walked out.

I followed him, not interested in hearing the rest—or hanging around with shocked operatives pointlessly picking over the conference and my boyfriend's behavior.

Besides, it was late, and my stomach was rumbling. Time to remove the thrall, eat, crash, and get an early start tomorrow morning.

Chaim, our most senior healer, was on-site, but he was in a treatment session. The others had gone home for the day, and the operative in charge of scheduling wouldn't call them back. More operatives were getting wounded as the vamp situation declined, and the healers required rest as well.

On top of that, they were trying to keep up with the demand for boosted blood packs. Knowing these operatives, that wouldn't change even should the Authority decree otherwise. If any chapter was going to launch an insurrection, it would be Michael's.

We were told to come back tomorrow.

Ezra looked like his head was going to explode. He was a stompy thundercloud back to my car.

We barely spoke on the drive home. His brusque "good night" was the extent of our quality time before falling asleep.

Sadly, Monday didn't start off with a jaunty "new week, new opportunities" vibe.

Ezra was up, dressed, and sitting in the corner of my room scowling at his phone. "Silas emailed a summary of Burning Eddie's decoded notebook."

I headed for my closet, every steady footfall feeling like a plummet into the abyss. "And?"

"After shedim created those things that bit a human and gave us vampires as we know them, they left vamps to their own devices. Vampires hunted humans, spreading chaos and fear, which suited the demons." He stared off with a small frown.

I wriggled out of my pj's. "Don't keep me in suspense."

"Demons didn't expect vampires to evolve and eventually come out to humans in the 1960s in order to assimilate. Once that happened…" He blinked at the screen of his phone like the next part might have changed, then turned to me with a look of dismay.

I smoothed the turtleneck fabric down, a pit opening in my stomach. "Just tell me."

"Some shedim started a breeding program so they'd have controllable weapons. At first, they tried it with Trads, but those women didn't survive, so the demons switched to using Eishei Kodesh. They called it Operation Inferno, a perverse callback to the magic derived from the Hanukkah flame."

I pressed my hand against my breastbone, trying not to puke. Delacroix had sworn that there weren't demon-breeding programs—hadn't he? Had he evaded my assumption with a question that I'd taken as proof? I couldn't remember anymore.

The only thing preventing my sanity from imploding was Mom's insistence that she hadn't been coerced the night I was conceived. She would never have lied to me about that. And to be fair, Delacroix sounded pissed that he hadn't been able to raise and shape Maud and me.

I let out a breath. He wasn't—*we* weren't—a part of that.

Ezra met my eyes. "I don't believe you were—"

"Me neither. Some shedim-human relations were nothing more than a fun time. But for some half shedim?" I pulled on my trousers. "Demonic lab rat. The least romantic origin story since radioactive spiders."

I threw my hair in a ponytail and tossed on some makeup, waiting for my boyfriend to continue. "There's more or you wouldn't be this upset. Was Burning Eddie one of those shedim?"

"No. He opposed it. Vehemently so, hunting down any demon involved. The program was eventually shut down."

"By Eddie?"

"By the Maccabees, many years later. Though he probably helped."

I motioned for him to follow me out of the bedroom. "Like your dad and Pederson?"

"I'd like to believe that's why their names were included, but Eddie didn't give an explanation in the notebook." Ezra put his phone away. "I have to get to the bottom of their connection once and for all."

"If it isn't because they stopped the breeding program, what do you think it was?"

He shrugged tightly. "The only reason I was accepted into the Maccabees was because I thwarted Natán's attempted hit on the secretary. I'm going to Caracas to confront my father."

I poured my coffee into a large travel mug and snagged a bagel from the fridge. "After that press conference the Authority gave? Natán must be livid. You won't be safe."

"He won't do anything to me. I'm his prized possession."

"You were, but…" I motioned at myself. "You're in too deep with the enemy. The fiction of you working for him doesn't help him anymore, not if healthy vamp mafioso are joining his cause like the Gryphon Gang from Vancouver. And it's futile to press Natán directly for his agenda."

Ezra made a frustrated sound. "Point taken. I'll visit Secretary Pederson in Copenhagen right after we undo the thrall and get answers from her about their connection."

"That's a better plan."

I'd scarfed down most of the bagel before we reached my car. The coffee lasted for half of the drive to HQ. I used the jittery rush for a wave of positive thinking.

Yesterday's research session had been an exercise in frustration. I scratched absently at those damn scales on my neck. It would have been nice if my connection to Delacroix's magic had inspired a grand epiphany, but my father never made it easy to get answers. Why start now?

I still wanted to punch the smug bastard for calling me the spark that made his dreams a blazing reality.

I merged into the left lane with a sharp inhale.

Ezra turned his head to look at me. "What?"

"The Luce is blazing its way across the globe, leaving a trail of devastation," I said.

"Yeah."

"I'm thinking this through out loud so bear with me. Had the foundational strain in our Maccabee rings not been corrupted, then the combination of all the flame types working in tandem would have killed shedim. Could the same idea apply to the Luce?"

Ezra narrowed his eyes. "How so?"

"Eishei Kodesh are the Holy Fire People, so is there anything to the saying 'Fight fire with fire'? All the flame types against the Luce. Is that too crazy?"

Ezra scratched his jaw. "It might just be crazy enough. This has legs, Avi."

"It's uncharted territory, because if something like this was ever tried before, we'd have learned about it. There won't be records or a blueprint we can follow, but operatives are experts in all kinds of areas. We need a think tank."

My phone rang.

"Jared Casey has scheduled his own press conference in two hours." Darsh's voice was strained over distant shouts. "The last thing I need is him taking that Trad's murder as permission to incite vigilantism against all vampires."

"What do you need from me?" I said.

"Can you go see Roger Henderson and get me dirt on Casey? Something to shut him up, for now if not for good?"

"Right after we see the healer," Ezra said.

"You haven't done that yet? Get on it. No. Fuck. Abort.

Henderson first. There's no time to waste," Darsh said. He gave me Roger's address and hung up.

"Zee…"

Ezra's expression turned to granite. "We agreed on this, Aviva. This is important. Healer first! I have to go to Copenhagen, and I can't do that when you'll end up in cardiac arrest."

"I'm sorry," I said quietly.

He snorted in derision.

I didn't have the heart to admonish Ezra for wearing holes into the seat belt with his fingers on the drive to Roger Henderson's place. He'd spent his life searching for the truth about his mother's death and the news he'd gotten about the breeding program was heartbreaking.

Unfortunately, the visit to Roger was a bust.

He'd been officially briefed that his ex, Rukhsana, had been a demon and was now dead. To say he was still shaken up was an understatement. He slumped on his sofa with dark circles under his haunted eyes, his hands trembling as he mechanically squeezed a stress ball.

Bringing up Jared only made things worse. Roger was terrified of where his former boss's power trip would lead. He mumbled it was too much, and to leave him alone.

It's not like this visit was some bucket list item for me either. Time was running out to stop the Luce before it killed all vampires, and Ezra was about to go nuclear, but my gut insisted that Roger possessed dirt on Jared that could put the brakes on his momentum and stop the hate mongering the politician was sowing.

I brought up the Trad going after a vampire with a rifle. "That death was because of Jared. Be the moral arbiter you used to be," I said. "The soldier who fought on the side of good."

He refused to meet my eyes. "I'm not that man anymore."

"You are." There was no point traumatizing him further, so I stood up, and placed my hand on his shoulder. "When you believe it again, call me."

With that, I went to break a thrall—and save my relationship.

<hr>

A HIGHLY FRAZZLED Louis found us within seconds of our arrival at HQ, demanding that I go see the director immediately.

Barely anyone was around, most of the operatives already deployed around town in anticipation of Casey's press conference.

I informed Louis I'd see Michael after a quick stop to the healers. I'd like to think it was my firm tone, or the memory of Cherry Bomb, that made my mother's assistant bob his head nervously, but it was likely Ezra's fangs flashing on a snarl, his now-red eyes narrowed to slits, and his fingers curled into claws.

"After we see Chaim," I promised Louis and beelined for the healers' corridor.

The bags under the healer's eyes had smaller carry-on bags, his handlebar mustache was unkempt, and he crammed a protein bar into his mouth with jittery movements. He was reluctant to spare us the time for this non-life-threatening session.

Ezra physically blocked Chaim, but he kept his body language relaxed and his tone gentle while he convinced the other man that we were here about a simple matter that would take only a few minutes.

I added assurances of immunity from either the Maccabees or the two of us should anything go wrong. When all that still failed to get Chaim on board, I stooped to guilt and mild blackmail, reminding him of the time I found him moonlighting at a health center. Sure, he was donating his services after a fire had ravaged a low-income neighborhood, but Maccabee contracts strictly forbade outside work.

The organization regularly engaged in community outreach and put healers in place a day later to help victims of that tragedy, but paperwork and proper channels had to be followed, and Chaim hadn't.

I'd kept silent about his presence.

"We're even after this?" Chaim asked.

I nodded. "What kind of recovery time am I looking at?"

Chaim asked us for permission to place his hands on our chests to see how complicated a treatment it would be.

I held myself still while he probed us. There was no other way to describe it.

"Okay. It's a simple dissolution that I'll only have to perform on Cardoso," Chaim said. "Aviva, you'll feel flushed, but it won't hurt." He swiped the mag stripe with the card attached to a chain on his waist and opened the treatment door.

Ezra caught my arm before I entered the treatment room. "Thank you," he said sincerely.

I caressed his cheek. "Thrall or not, we're in this together."

"I know, and that means everything to me."

His words wrapped around me like a soft blanket in the gentle silence.

Until the sirens shattered everything.

Chapter 19

"Code Black," a calm voice said over the speakers. "Code Black."

Chaim and I raced down the hallway after Ezra. My fingers tingled with numbness. I clenched and unclenched my fists, trying to force feeling back into them as we ran. The familiar corridors felt alien and threatening—as if the walls themselves had betrayed us by allowing the catastrophe that triggered this impossible alert.

"Code Black." The voice repeated the classification that shouldn't exist within this fortress we called HQ.

Two shedim ripped around the second floor. One was a sinuous mass of patchy scales, the other a spindly tangle of bone and shadow, but both demons possessed eyes like burning coals.

Someone knocked sharply into my shoulder in passing.

"How?" It was all my brain could manage to produce.

"The locks from the Lions Gallery," Gemma said, sprinting in high heels to add her white flame abilities to the mix, battling the scale demon.

It moved like an oil slick, muscles rippling beneath skin that shifted between obsidian scales and raw flesh. Where magic should have crackled around its form, only feral rage remained.

Their pain of being on the wrong side of a mezuzah ward didn't help matters. This should have debilitated them. Were they resistant due to their demon type or simply fury? Both options sucked.

A couple of Orange Flames were attempting to trap it in ice but had frozen the sprinkler systems in the process. Meantime, the blaze created by Red Flames was spreading. Being closest to the fire extinguisher, I sprinted for it. Magic created the physical flames, but our special formula in these contraptions doused them.

The demons' hunger manifested in different ways: one's tongue lolled out as if to taste fear in the air, the other's body constantly shifted as though trying to consume space itself.

Scale Demon elongated its jaws and bit into the chest of the Red Flame attempting to torch it. Its teeth clicked like shattered glass in time to the operative's screams, its breath blowing the fire away as the woman's body crumpled.

Chaim was immediately at her side, working feverishly to save her, while the others kept the demon away from the two of them.

I doused the flames, preventing an inferno. Operation Inferno. I gave a grim snort, frustrated that even though I was tapped into Delacroix's magic, I still couldn't illuminate shedim weaknesses to help my colleagues.

Hopefully, a lifetime of secretly hunting demons to feed Cherry paid off now. I was best positioned to seek patterns in the demons' movements to indicate injury and determine their weak spots.

We still had our rings, and the second those areas were revealed, we'd deploy our magic cocktails into them and send the shedim to new prison cells. Seeing these creatures' torment hammered home how barbaric this decision to imprison them again was, but it was them or us.

Ezra, who, like all vampires, could actually kill shedim, fought the second one single-handedly.

The demon whirled around him, its bones stretching and contracting into needlelike spears to slash out. Its vertebrae jutted through translucent skin like hooks, joints bending backward as it scrambled across walls and ceiling to drop down on Ezra without warning.

Even with his enhanced Prime senses he'd been injured more than once, his hands bleeding from multiple gashes from attempting to grab the demon.

Michael raced out of the elevator with Louis, their arms full of weapons. Zen Zappers, daggers, and—*was that a broadsword*—would only enrage the demons further, but most of our operatives were out of the building and the director was desperate.

Who could blame her? We were down to a skeleton crew, facing an enemy too broken and savage to feel pain.

Chaim rushed the wounded Red Flame out of the room on a gurney that another operative had brought in.

Operatives grabbed the weapons, but our maneuvers against these creatures were as effective as applying a Band-Aid to a severed artery.

My mother shot me a frantic questioning glance, but I shook my head. I couldn't get any bead on their weak spots.

Even though my blue flame power was useless, *I* wasn't.

I had something special precisely for this occasion.

The surprise detonation of one Cherry Bomb.

While my colleagues had seen me fight, they'd never seen my true form. I could keep hiding it and hope we eventually found the demons' weak points or I could expedite matters and hope that my coworkers trusted me.

We were facing down two rampaging demons. If I

didn't do this, I risked people dying. The choice felt inevitable.

Except…

Outing myself had serious repercussions for others. Well, one other. I looked at my mother, my eyebrows raised in question.

She nodded without hesitation.

My skin erupted into toxic-green scales, armoring every inch. Twin horns throbbed through my skull, as needle-sharp as the claws on my left hand. My body had transformed too. Bulky muscle replaced my runner's build, my biceps and thighs straining against fabric.

I shook out my crimson hair. Strange. I'd imagined this moment would feel like exposure. Instead, it felt like freedom.

It also felt like freedom to slam into the demon coming at Gemma, my shoulder catching its weirdly rectangular throat.

Scales scraped scales as we crashed to the floor, the demon thrashing beneath me, predator against predator and—ew! Its tongue flicked against my cheek while it writhed. I almost lost my hold on it, but I readjusted like the boss I was.

Gemma scrambled back as I grappled with the creature.

It unhinged its jaw like a snake, exhaling putrid breaths that made my eyes water.

I drove my claws deep into its flesh where patches of raw copper skin showed between obsidian glints.

The demon's shriek echoed through the room.

It bucked violently, nearly throwing me off, but I locked my thighs around its torso, horns lowered, and slammed my full weight down. There was a wet crack as its spine shattered against the floor.

Its movements grew frantic, no longer calculated

attacks, just violent flailing. I seized its head between my hands, shuddering at the clicking of its glass-sharp teeth.

One savage twist. The crack of bone. The demon went limp. It was so weak I hadn't even required its specific kill spot.

I slammed its head once more against the floor for good measure, nodded in satisfaction at its lifeless stare, and stood up, wiping dark ichor off my hands.

The room was silent; both demons were dead.

But that wasn't the only reason for the preternatural stillness.

My colleagues stared at me with wide eyes while my boyfriend kicked the other demon's corpse aside with a "hurry up" twirl of his fingers.

There was a whispered comment between two operatives, a snide laugh, and a suspicious look from a third.

Gemma's face was a careful mask.

Here it was, the moment of truth that I'd dreaded and dreamed of in equal measure. If I'd learned anything from Michael or my demon daddy, it was the importance of controlling the narrative.

Let the gossip begin—on my terms.

"My human form is not a glamor," I said, "but yes, I am half-shedim."

The Maccabees whipped their heads to Michael.

"Director Fleischer is not a demon," Louis said icily. "Nor will there be any further speculation around Operative Fleischer's birth."

Ooh, the guard dog had shown his teeth—backed by a cold smile from their director that made the operatives hurriedly nod in agreement.

I could have changed back to my human self, but that would only put them at ease temporarily. I had to get them fully on board with this true version of me.

"I've dedicated my life to being the perfect Maccabee in

hopes that when this day came, you'd accept me as you always have. Another flame in this fight. Well, the Luce's blaze is devouring us. It's lit fires on too many fronts to fight indefinitely, and we cannot afford *any* of its casualties." I flexed my claws. "I *am* different, but having a variety of weapons at our disposal means we can handle anything that gets thrown at us, as you just saw. I, Aviva Fleischer, am standing before you, not as a flame, but as a spark."

In my head, Cherry Bomb shot Delacroix the finger. *I'll show you what being a spark means, you demon asshole.*

I calmly met each and every one of my colleagues' stares. "I think I know how to stop the Luce, but I need your fire. Anyone who wants to join me can come to Conference Room A."

Inside the elevator, I relaxed back to my human form. Other than those stupid scaley patches from when I'd tangled myself up with the security system magic during Ezra's healing of Darsh and Silas, that was. I didn't bother to hide the one on my throat peeking out through my torn turtleneck.

Ezra slipped into the car with me while the doors were closing. "The healer," he said. "For my sake and because every second we keep Delacroix's magic in place on Darsh and Silas will stoke your father's rage. You heard Chaim earlier. It won't take long."

"I just came out as a demon to a bunch of colleagues," I hissed. "I can't take a time-out."

I watched the numbers on the panel rise, my stomach in knots. No one else had followed. They'd come, right? They were in the other elevator to give Ezra and me some privacy. Or taking the stairs.

Ezra punched the emergency button, and the car shuttered to a stop. "Natán hasn't refuted the Authority's charges that he doesn't have humans' best interests at heart."

"Hey!" I tried to reach past him, but he put his back against the buttons. I crossed my arms. "He's probably still formulating his response."

"He doesn't sit around and react to things. He's a strategist with dozens of plans in motion at any given time. Why do you think he was able to move so quickly to put the Vampire Care Initiative into place?"

"He had a mole?" I teased out the thought. "Only Alastair and Delacroix knew about the ritual, and my father wouldn't trust someone like Natán with his plans. Maybe Alastair—"

"Despised Natán and wouldn't give him a heads-up."

"Even if the information bought Alastair his life?"

"He wouldn't have lived long enough to plead his case. Natán works on the one-strike-and-you're-dead rule. And he was betrayed by someone he trusted. A dhampir of all things."

"How quickly you discarded the idea of Natán being the one to give Alastair that amplification rune." I managed to knock Ezra aside to get at the buttons. Or he let me, but either way, I got the elevator moving again.

"I was letting emotion rule my thinking," Ezra said. "I wanted to blame him for all of it, but when Delacroix confessed to handing over the rune, I was forced to accept that Natán wasn't part of this business with the Luce. That said, he did know Alastair was after a procreation ritual. My father would have puzzled out every conceivable outcome while Alastair was still on the run and put pieces into place to ensure everyone knew who the most powerful vampire still was."

"He would have anticipated an outcome where the ritual's effects went this badly, even if he didn't know what that would look like?" I said doubtfully.

The doors opened.

"As one of many? Yes," Ezra insisted. "And he'd have

planned accordingly. I need this thrall undone so I can leave you and investigate why my father and Secretary Pederson were in Burning Eddie's notebook. That will give us answers to all of this."

"Okay." I exited the elevator. "Give me two hours. I promise—"

"Aviva, no!" He slammed his hand against the door to prop it open. "This is the final thread between him and my mother's death. I'm sure of it. You know how much I need this answer, and this is my one chance to get it, to finally understand."

"I'm not trying to be a bitch, but you've waited this long, and two more hours won't make a difference. Whereas I've called this meeting, and I can't—I *won't*—tell everyone to wait," I said.

"You're scared they won't listen to you after seeing Cherry."

I crossed my arms. "It's not fear. Severing the thrall and speaking to Secretary Pederson is incredibly important and urgent, but *two shedim were loose in HQ.* I have to prioritize survival, and my idea of fighting fire with fire is the best chance we have. I'm sure of it."

"Fear *and* ego, then."

I took a deep breath so I didn't say something I regretted. "I have to lead this meeting."

"Ah yes." My boyfriend looked up and down the empty hallway. "The meeting."

"They'll come," I insisted. "They need a moment, but they'll show up. Please don't fuck this up for me."

The thrall between us pulled taut like a chain.

"I give you my word that you'll be free of it soon and you can go to Copenhagen. I'll come find you. Meantime, don't leave the building, okay?"

Ezra dropped his hand, his expression inscrutable.

The elevator doors closed on his silence.

"Fleischer."

I jumped and spun around.

Gemma stood behind me with her arms crossed. "I will never like you," she said, "but I do respect you."

"Same," I said tersely.

We shared a moment of utter revulsion over this fact.

Unwounded operatives I'd revealed myself to were filing into the largest conference room.

Gemma headed down the hallway to join them, then stopped and turned back. "Aviva?"

I froze in my tracks, waiting for the other shoe to fall. "Yes?"

She smoothed down her dirt-streaked trousers. "Thank you for saving me," she said, and slipped inside.

Somewhere in Hell, a snowball was melting. I threw my shoulders back, strode into the meeting, and shut the door.

Not everyone who'd seen me had chosen to attend.

Michael took the floor first, her demeanor grim. "Two lock cells containing shedim prisoners were in storage here. I'd arranged for them to be transported before the Brink collapsed, but in the ensuing chaos of the past few days, I didn't personally confirm that happened, and the Luce dissolved the protective runes." The strain of responsibility was etched in the tight lines around her mouth. "Operative Alan Greenberg, who was on duty in the evidence room, was killed."

There were no gasps or cries or recriminations. Each Maccabee simply absorbed the news of their fallen comrade, letting it fuel the cold fire of determination that burned within us all. Alan's death would be answered for, not with dramatic displays of grief, but with the ruthless efficiency that defined us.

"Aviva is going to take over now," Michael said. "Phones on silent, focus on the topic." She motioned that the meeting was mine.

"Eishei Kodesh magic stems from the Hanukkah fire, and the Luce's healing magic is spreading like wildfire." My voice was steady, betraying none of my anxiety. What if I said something that made them leave or second-guess supporting me? "Can we fight magic fire with magic fire?"

Ezra wouldn't head off to Copenhagen and induce a heart attack in me, right? Was it fair of me to ask him to wait after he'd waited this long?

The director took a seat in front of a legal pad that Louis had set out for her and clicked her titanium-plated pen.

He was currently making himself useful bringing in bottles of water and a coffee dispenser that he set up at the back.

"I did some quick research," I said, "and there's a technique in firefighting called backfires or back burning."

"I've read about that." Joe, a level three, and one of our only Métis operatives, slipped into the room, followed by a few more level twos and threes. "It's when firefighters light counterfires."

Build it and they will come, Cherry said wryly.

"Yes." I obsessively checked for the faintest sense of the thrall going off the rails, but all was well.

Ezra really had understood how important this was to me. My shoulders relaxed. I was so grateful I had a partner who got me.

"Backfires are deliberately set in front of an active fire front," I said. "It's a controlled prescribed burn that starves the fire of the fuel it needs to spread by consuming some of the combustible material."

"It also creates a fire belt that the wildfire has trouble crossing, right?" Joe said.

I nodded. "At best, a backburn can totally prevent the fire from spreading."

"What's the risk?" Gemma said. "I don't love something called backfire."

Everyone chuckled.

"Fair," I said with a smile. "There's a risk of the counterfire spreading or even worsening the wildfire."

"There's something to this idea." Marilyn, an older level three who had assigned Sachie and me the Toussaint art fraud case a million years ago, played with a paperclip. "But how do we mitigate that risk and create a backburn strong enough to circle the globe like the Luce has?"

"We use the model of our Maccabee rings and all the flame types working together. I'm not sure exactly how yet, but that's what we're here to figure out." I uncapped a marker and moved over to a stand containing a chart with large sheets of paper.

"With the Luce releasing shedim prisoners on top of everything?" a level two cried out. "We'd be in the center of a death trap!"

The room broke into angry chatter.

Michael stood up with an ear-piercing whistle. "What happened here with the locks will not happen on a global scale. The Authority has measures in place which absolutely ensure that."

I tamped down my snort, wishing Delacroix could hear himself referred to as "measures."

"It's above your clearance levels," Michael continued, "so don't bother asking. Yet that's only part of why the Luce must be stopped in its tracks as quickly as possible."

"Darsh, Silas, and Nasir," Gemma said resolutely.

The level two piped up once more. "If Nasir is still—"

"He is." A bunch of us growled variations of that sentiment at the same time.

"We stop the Luce to help *all* vampire operatives," Marilyn said.

Someone declared that it wasn't enough to stop the Luce; we had to reverse its effects on infected vampires

"Exactly," I said, "And we have to do it in a matter of days." I waved my marker. "Bearing in mind that the Luce spreads faster in high humidity, and it will be most potent here in Vancouver on Saturday, throw out your ideas for a magic backfire."

Using how our magic kicked in one type at a time in our ring's cocktail as a template, we vigorously discussed the order in which it should be deployed now.

Did it make more sense for Blue Flames to go first to identify the current direction and flow of the Luce magic wildfire, determining where it was spreading the fastest and where it was weakest?

I was getting hand cramps from how fast I was writing, all while checking in psychically with Ezra—and never receiving a response. It wasn't as if he didn't hear me.

I'd been left on "read" in my own head.

I ground off enough tooth enamel that a visit to the dentist was mandatory, though he hadn't left HQ. Yet.

The conference room had been growing more crowded, with everyone Darsh could spare given the option of joining this meeting.

Yet, there were plenty of operatives who hadn't shown up. I couldn't say whether it was because they'd stayed in the field to keep the peace or now regarded me with contempt, but I'd find out soon enough.

Our discussions intensified. Should step one *not* involve the Blue Flames but rather let Orange Flames create the right "conditions" for this backfire by banding together to lower humidity? How else could we create optimal spread conditions for our magic counter burn?

Eduardo, a level three with yellow flame powers, posited that Yellow Flames could create magic channels to ensure the fire devoured only the Luce and not physical structures.

Louis slipped in and whispered something to Michael. Her eyes widened for a split second, then she murmured, "Excuse me," and left the room.

Olivier called, but I ignored the buzzing, pointedly staring at a couple of operatives who were checking their phones. It was like once Michael left, certain people no longer felt the need to obey her "phones on silent" directive.

Whatever. This was more important. They'd see that.

Whispering broke out in the back, along with glances my way.

Yeah, a half shedim was leading strategy talks and helping to save everyone. They could get over it. I was tapped out, crashing from the demon fight and my boyfriend's angst, and yet, here I was, still giving my all.

"Order!" I snapped. "Red Flames use physical fire, but while devouring power could be launched into the path of the Luce with more energy concentrated on the high humidity spots globally, we don't want to literally set the world ablaze."

That set off another round of frenzied brainstorming. I shook my head. They were like kindergartners requiring their teacher to keep them focused and in line.

I blotted my forehead. The room was oppressively hot with all the operatives crowded in here.

Gemma said something, but her words filtered through to me slowly, like sound underwater.

My nodded response was several beats too late.

The whispering was growing; more operatives shot me hooded looks before leaving without even an "Excuse me" or "Sorry, Aviva, gotta run."

My stomach sank as I registered their expressions, a mixture of doubt and something worse. Disappointment? Suspicion? What had I done to make them leave? Were they questioning my abilities? Had I lost their respect? My throat tightened.

I was roasting, my pits were damp, and sweat trickled between my shoulder blades. Was I having a visceral reaction to all this talk of flames? Great. Add looking like a dumpster fire in front of my colleagues to my résumé.

I gripped the edge of the table, my vision flickering.

Olivier phoned again, followed immediately by Sachie. This wasn't because she was dead, so modeling professional behavior, I again ignored it. Plus, I felt guilty for even glancing at the screen when I'd mentally reamed out others for doing the same.

The fluorescent lights overhead pulsed and writhed, each flash a needle in my eyes, like I was living misaligned with everyone else.

I blinked dumbly at my notes about how White Flames had to amplify the spread of the backfire without any memory of writing them down.

Hanging on by my fingernails, I placed an operative in charge of each flame type. I was obviously the Blue Flame rep, but I made Gemma White Flame chief, relishing her look of surprise. She was the only level two given that responsibility. Joe was tasked with Orange, and Marilyn the Reds. Eduardo rounded out the team for the Yellows.

We'd work in conjunction with the Maccabees around the world who were already on the Luce problem—like Hajoon in Seoul—to help refine our backfire process.

Olivier called yet again, the buzz grating like steel wool against my brain.

A knot of operatives huddled together, ignoring me and no longer bothering to whisper.

Fuck them. I'd done it. I'd come out as a half shedim and I was being the goddamn spark to usher us out of the darkness. It would have been nice if Michael had bothered to stick around to see this victory, but she was always dropping out at the last second and missing the most important moments of my life to focus on her own work. This was nothing new.

The room spun and distorted, faces stretching like melting wax and mouths moving in slow motion.

A searing headache threaded through my temples like a hot wire, my skull throbbing with each heartbeat, and my ribs squeezing like they were constricting inward.

We'd gotten a lot of good ideas, and I was exhausted. Everyone else had to be as well.

I rapped my fist on the conference table. "Meeting adjorn—"

Pain exploded behind my eyes like a supernova. Every nerve ending screamed in protest as the room dissolved into white fire. The cold floor rushed up to meet me, then everything went black.

Chapter 20

I woke to a comfortable mattress, dim lights, and Michael tearing a strip off Chaim.

It was the same treatment room I'd been put in after coming back from the Brink. If I was going to spend time here on a regular basis, I was putting in for a new paint color, maybe some more plants.

"She'd already consented," the healer protested, nervously running his hand over his bushy mustache. "I've never worked with a thrall before, but I didn't think there'd be any side effects. Especially not this significant."

"Well," my mother said snidely, toying with her fiendishly sharp earrings, "if you didn't *think* there'd be side effects, there was obviously no point in checking with the other party on whether this was a good time or not."

"Hey," he snapped. "I didn't have all the information. How was I supposed to know she was an infer—" He coughed. "A half shedim?"

Snatches of what sounded like a news broadcast filtered in from the hallway, along with distressed conversations, but while I could hear tone, I couldn't discern the words.

"You unraveled the thrall?" When I tried to push

myself upright, a bout of nausea knocked me onto my back once more. For all I'd bemoaned our one-way connection, its absence hit me hard, but that was quickly swamped by rage that Ezra had done this after I'd begged him to wait.

"Exactly like you pleaded with me to do," Chaim said in exasperation.

My fists bunched in the heated blanket I'd been given while unconscious. "Where is he?" I said in a low voice.

"Cardoso?" Chaim glanced at the door. "He left the moment it was done."

A muscle in my jaw ticked.

My boyfriend had sliced himself away from me with surgical precision and, once free, slunk off to do precisely what he wanted—with zero word to me.

I lay there seething while Chaim checked my vitals and performed a few tests on my vision and motor skills, all under Michael's baleful eye.

Thankfully, the strips of scales on my arm and neck were gone, proof I was also disconnected from Delacroix's magic.

The second the healer announced I was fine, Michael ordered him out of his own treatment room.

Chaim was thrilled to give us the use of it.

"A demon reveal with a blackout encore." I buried my face in my hands. "I am nothing if not memorable."

My mother sat down on the edge of the bed. "Louis put the word out that it was low blood sugar." She smoothed hair off my forehead, her cool hand comforting against my clammy skin. "How are you really feeling?"

"Hollow." I pulled the blanket up to my chin.

Michael sighed. "Not that I'm condoning what Ezra did, but it might be helpful to hear more facts. It may not have felt like it, but that meeting lasted hours. Every half hour or so Ezra asked Louis how things were going, if maybe there was a moment where you could take a break.

There never seemed to be. While there are many less than complimentary things I'll say about Ezra, him deliberately placing you in harm's way is not on that list."

That was an understatement. Especially since my gut was telling me that severing the thrall hadn't laid me low. Not entirely. It was helped by my father's magic.

Of course, Ezra hadn't assumed that would be an issue, because when I first drew on it during the Darsh and Silas healing session, *Ezra* was adversely affected, not me. I'd gotten the rush of all rushes.

"Are Darsh and Silas okay?" I said.

"Ezra's healing magic is holding. I'm relieved and grateful. Officially, though, the pair were always free of any Luce effects."

Happy as I was about my friends, I dragged the blanket over my head, my rage toward Ezra swept away by an avalanche of well-deserved guilt. I'd been a shitty partner, putting him off again and again. It didn't matter if it was for the greater good, that didn't make my behavior less selfish.

"Do you know if he's still with Secretary Pederson?" I said.

"They met," Michael said, "but he's no longer in Copenhagen."

Ezra had spent years searching for answers about his mother's death. I closed my eyes. How brutal must that have been, Ezra remaining calm enough to use the leverage about Operation Inferno—shedim breeding Eishei Kodesh —to pry the truth out of Secretary Pederson about her connection to Natán and Ezra's tragic family history. He could have forced it out of her, but Michael would be aware were that the case.

Just like he could have forced me to abandon the meeting before it began.

My boyfriend had followed me around for days, doing

everything I asked of him. Why didn't I announce a half-hour break before convening everyone? That way, I'd have been present to tell Chaim what was happening and avoided this mess. No one would have questioned taking some processing time in the wake of the demon attack.

Delacroix was right about my do-gooder instincts being a spark—too bad this time it threatened to burn my relationship to the ground.

I flung the covers off. "I have to talk to Ezra."

"Before you head out, there's something you need to know." Michael looked up at the ceiling, then shook her head. "There's no good way to say this, so here it is. Detective Desmond arrested Roger Henderson for the murder of Jared Casey."

I froze, shaking my head against the impossible words as if they might rattle free and make more sense. "I saw Roger. He didn't even want to discuss his boss."

"He called the police from Casey's home and confessed." Michael fiddled with the rod for the blinds. "Olivier passed on a message from Roger to you."

My gut twisted. "What?"

"'Thank you for helping me find the man inside I'd lost.'"

I sunk my head in my hands with a broken moan. I wasn't a spark; I was a detonator. The whispering in the meeting hadn't been disgust with me being an infernal. It was everyone finding out about Casey's murder. "What's the emotional temperature here in Vancouver?"

"Simmering but not yet boiling over," Michael said. "Other things have come to light, such as Jared Casey's abuse of his staff. Between Keira and me, we've managed to spin it that Henderson, a Trad, snapped under the constant poor treatment and, sadly, took Jared's own words that real humans don't need magic to heart."

"I sense a 'but.'"

Michael pulled up video freezeframed on Natán seated behind a large desk against a darkly paneled wall with moody lighting. At this rate, he'd have to buy a news franchise to keep up with all his on-air appearances. My mother hit play.

"I'm ashamed of the people I once fought so valiantly for and cared so deeply about." Natán held up a Maccabee ring that may have been his or just a prop and set it on the table with a soft *clink*.

I bunched the blanket tightly in my fists.

"Maccabees insist on pointing fingers at the lack of care from vampires," he said. "Yet they fail to mention the many safety and infrastructure improvements vampires have made in local communities. How we've turned neighborhoods around, making them the most sought-after places with the highest quality of life. Our actions show how we treat humans."

The footage cut to Casey's memorial photo. They'd doctored his face, making him slightly younger, leaner, and handsomer than in person.

"Maccabees are pointing the finger at good Trad men and women," Natán said, "but where was their accountability for the murder of Jared Casey, one of Canada's most respected politicians?"

"Of course he becomes one of Canada's great politicians after he gets assassinated," I scoffed.

It cut back to the vampire. "They even covered up a previous attack on this poor man," Natán said. "One which came from within the local Eishei Kodesh community. One that his own Trad head of security, his eventual killer, helped Maccabees to cover up."

I threw double middle fingers at the screen. "That other attack was a demon and that's not what happened at all."

Michael hushed me.

"…didn't even realize he had a pro-magic fanatic

among his inner circle until it was tragically too late." Natán steepled his fingers together, assuming a thoughtful expression. "The ruling powers of the Maccabees say to trust them. And I do. I trust them to destabilize Eishei Kodesh and Trad relations by radicalizing good people. I trust them to cause chaos and bury the truth with lies. But do I trust them to put others first when disaster falls?" He spread his hands wide.

I made a strangled sound.

"His speechwriter deserves a raise," Michael said. "People are buying into this."

"Here's the truth." Natán sighed heavily, a wonderful piece of theater as he didn't breathe. "Vampires don't want to hurt humans. If I'm being blunt, we can't survive without your goodwill. There are far more of you than there are of us. What you have to remember is that before we were vampires, we were human too. We hold humanity in high esteem, appreciating both its fragility and incredible resilience." His expression turned wistful. "Perhaps even more than all of you."

God help me, I actually believed him. Which made me see red. I kept telling people that I valued my humanity because I was part demon, and yet they had a harder time believing my appreciation of it than a known criminal's.

"Here's another truth," he said. "I agree with the restrictions that humans place on vampires. We must have consent to feed or to turn someone. The penalties for vampires who commit crimes are immediate and deadly. We do not get a trial or a jail sentence, and we accept that. Vampires are faster and stronger, and in the interests of the greater good, different measures are in place."

He looked away from the camera for a dramatic pause. "Eishei Kodesh possess magic, which most humans do not, but most are held to no different standard than their Trad neighbors. They are doctors, and nurses, and teachers, valued members of our community, whereas Maccabees wield their magic behind a badge."

I ground my teeth together.

"Perhaps those who wish to place restrictions on Eishei Kodesh should reevaluate their stance on where the real menace lies," he said. "But I don't need to tell any of you what to believe. It's already in your hearts." Natán placed his own hand on his chest. "Just like my vow to do good in this world is always in mine."

I hit stop on Michael's phone. "Jeez, Mom, how long was I unconscious? Six months? Because the amount of shit you're hitting me with could fill that."

"It was only one night, but we're counting it in dog years," she said wryly. "It's about 3:30AM Tuesday."

I tamped down my annoyance at losing valuable time.

"Natán's response has redirected public dialogue away from turning Casey into a martyr and temporarily shut up politicians of Casey's ilk." She pulled a wry face. "Everyone's focused on whether Maccabees should be allowed to exist."

"Wow," I said saltily. "Guess we should let the demons and vampires eat everyone, then."

"It's not all bad. Alastair's minions are no longer of concern. We got them all." She snapped her fingers. "Oh, and I lambasted the mayor for shutting down the investigation into that first magic attack on Jared Casey. Said he was culpable for a dangerous vampire Mafioso spinning lies about the Maccabees not doing their part to keep a prominent Trad politician safe in the mayor's city. That it put the global spotlight on him and not in a good way. That was *very* satisfying."

"I'm glad you had fun," I said,

"There's something else," Michael said.

I braced my hands on the mattress to steady myself

against news I was certain would land like aftershocks. "Another death? The locks?"

"No. Well, the runes on them are failing in some locations, but the Authority is allowing Delacroix to remove the freed prisoners, and thus far he's done so without causing any harm or even awareness among humans. But you've been publicly identified as Ezra's girlfriend. The photo that was taken of you two now has your name attached. There is some level of online…fuss."

How bad was it? General shitposting from the Ezracurriculars or "let's find her and dox her" bad?

Note to self. Don't check phone. Also, don't hold breath for a "may you live happily-ever-after" card. From the Authority *or* Ezra's fans.

Gee, how fortunate I had Casey's murder—which I'd inadvertently inspired—to busy myself with.

"Let me guess," I said, "the Authority ordered you to make me break up with him."

"I wish."

My eyebrows shot into my hairline. "Excuse me?"

"I expected them to, as overreaching as that is, but they didn't. Because they know you're a half shedim."

I'd accepted that as a matter of course when I outed myself. I'd weighed the repercussions against being an effective weapon fighting the two shedim here in HQ, and decided my assistance was worth that risk.

Yet the fact that they didn't protest my relationship, given the animosity with Ezra's dad, underscored how angry they were about my demon heritage.

I stared at the floor. "What actions are they taking?"

"It's being discussed."

I'd killed a shedim, saved an operative, and come up with a plan to stop the Luce, but sure, don't see me as a hero. Was I even a Maccabee in their eyes or was I simply a monster they'd tolerate until they didn't need me anymore? Just like their vampire operatives.

Everything Delacroix had accused me of was coming true. There was no way for me to do enough worthy deeds to make the Maccabees see me as a good person.

A thousand dark scenarios unfolded, each one dropping into my head like stones in a frozen pond, while my heartbeat echoed in my ears like a doomsday countdown clock.

We have to protect Mom. Cherry sounded fierce.

"Sector A?" I said in a croaked voice. "Mom? Can they send us—"

"No." Her firm tone cut through my anxiety.

"I won't let them…" I wrapped my arms around myself.

Who was I kidding? The Authority got what it wanted. We were all just pieces in their game.

And I'd never felt so powerless.

Chapter 21

"You've done far too much to benefit this organization and the world," Michael said. "Without you, we'd still believe we killed shedim. Alastair would have gotten the power word one way or another, but without you seeing that amplification rune, we'd have no idea why vampires were suffering. You saved operatives from demons, and you came up with our first viable idea to stop the Luce. You're a valuable asset, Operative Fleischer, and I made damn sure they knew that."

"I appreciate it, but someone doesn't agree because they ratted me out." Seriously, could this mystery colleague have run blabbing any faster?

She flashed a coy smile. "*I* told them how we'd been rolling out this reveal on a need-to-know basis, not trusting it to any lines of communication, including those with Authority members. We had grave concerns that the dhampir stalking you would get wind of your heritage and use it to his own advantage. Which, we've ascertained, is exactly what happened and the reason behind the abduction."

Control the narrative. Of course she had.

I teased out her story. "Alastair used half-shedim blood in the ritual and made the leap that a half shedim was key to obtaining the power word."

"So deluded," Michael said sadly. "I'm currently hard at work plugging that leak so no other personal information about my operatives can ever be wielded against them."

Only time would tell if that mitigated my punishment, but I wasn't going to sit around worrying.

I had a magic fire management strategy to nail down.

"What about your transgressions?" I clasped her hand. "Having me, hiding me?"

"I made it extremely clear that *they* created those conditions and I would not go down for them." She paused. "We are not powerless, Aviva. I only wish we'd understood that sooner."

Should the Authority come after me—after my mother —we wouldn't go down without a fight. This time, we'd stand as one.

A weight I'd carried since birth began to crack and crumble. I let out a slow breath and straightened up.

"There she is," Michael said with a smile. "Here's something else to cheer you up." She shared how excited other Maccabees were to be part of the task force, how every single one was running with my proposed idea, using the most advanced tech with the help of Eishei Kodesh climate scientists to run simulations and brainstorm solutions.

They'd even broken into subgroups based on flame type to come up with specific strategies.

"Did you replace me?"

"The backfire was your idea," she said, "and everyone wants you on the task force, but with the speed the Luce is advancing, you've simply missed too much to have a leadership role. Ha-joon is overseeing all Blue Flames."

My life had been a long-term campaign to be accepted,

and it had led me to feel like I had to do everything on my own. I'd shed that belief. I was firmly part of a group, part of a team, and wouldn't have it any other way.

"Good choice, but I still need to find Ezra."

After I texted him to reply stat, I tapped my finger against the phone. *Put it away, Fleischer. No good will come of checking—* My jaw dropped. Twenty-five thousand new followers? I'd had only one hundred and four to begin with.

I checked the comments on a photo of me and a s'mores mishap while camping last summer.

OMG, love that treat!

Team Burned Marshmallow all the way.

There's no way Ezra would want to wake up to this gold-digging hag.

I made my profile private.

Ezra had uncoupled himself from me and bolted. Intellectually, I understood why, and strangers' opinions of us shouldn't matter, but the totality of it left me feeling scraped raw.

I'd spent my life presenting myself in a favorable light, and the idea of a groundswell of hate against me—not even because of Cherry but because I was someone's girlfriend—made our reconnection vital.

Still radio silence from my boyfriend. "Permission to track him down."

Michael agreed, provided I was back by 4PM for the next task force meeting with operatives from around the world.

That gave me plenty of time.

Sachie waited for me outside the treatment room with crossed arms. "There's no rewards card. This isn't a 'visit ten times and get a free coffee on the eleventh.'"

I smacked my forehead. "Shit. I got it mixed up with the café across the street."

"Well, get it right next time because I almost had to tell Mom to bust out the muffins again."

"We don't want that," I said somberly.

She snorted. "Did you have fun killing the shedim?"

"Yes, actually." I considered it. "That was probably the least stressful part of the last I don't know how many hours."

"And the super-special cameo appearance went well?" She mimed horns. Her tone was flippant, but she intensely scrutinized my expression.

"So far so good. Time will tell if there is any fallout from that particular bomb. Everything okay with you?"

"Just tired."

I squeezed her shoulder, grabbed some food and a coffee to go from HQ kitchen, and drove to the Jolly Hellhound.

I'd been braced to enter the foyer of the megayacht—and cut a swath through vampires to get to Ezra's private quarters if I had to—but I stepped into his living room.

He may have broken our thrall, but he hadn't changed the portal settings on me.

The Prime-sized knot in my chest unraveled like a fist slowly unclenching after being held tight for too long.

A crystal glass with crimson dregs sat next to an open bottle wafting blood and alcohol fumes on the coffee table.

Ezra was in his bedroom, leaning against his headboard with his legs splayed on the mattress. His shoulders slumped like a marionette with cut strings, his red-rimmed eyes staring at nothing. He hadn't even bothered to take off his shoes, the blankets twisted around his legs like he'd lost the will to move halfway through getting comfortable.

I'd seen broken bottles that looked less shattered than he did.

I crawled onto the bed next to him and tugged his hand into my lap, willing to ride this hollow silence.

"The women in Operation Inferno," he said gruffly.

"What about them?" I kept my voice and grip on his hand steady, a buffer against the dread rising inside me.

"Very few of them made it to term. The shedim would have shut down the program even if Maccabees hadn't busted them, but…" He cleared his throat. "They kept the sperm."

I furrowed my brow. "The demons kept their own sperm? That's kind of weird. They could always, you know, make more of it."

"Not the demons."

"Fuuuuuck."

"No," Ezra said, his expression bleak, "but you could achieve the same result with artificial insemination if you wished. If you were someone hoping to have a child. At a fertility clinic."

Bile burned at the back of my throat. "No…they…no."

We were the good guys. We wouldn't betray our own values. Yet as my claws shredded the bedding, I confronted the uncomfortable truth that wearing the Maccabee ring meant inheriting their legacy, with the blood, moral morass, and outright violations of those who came before me.

Ezra placed a hand against my cheek, but dropped it immediately into his lap, the effort beyond him. "The Maccabees didn't want half-demon babies. The plan was to implant Eishei Kodesh women to study the effects of shedim magic in human hosts. To find a more efficient way to fight what they were effectively treating as demon parasites," he added bitterly. "If the pregnancies progressed beyond the first term, Maccabees could always arrange a medical miscarriage."

"They'd use us to make better weapons and then they'd abort us." Toxic green scales striped across my skin, Cherry's roar thundering inside my skull.

I pressed my hands against my ribs, hoping to guide air

back into my lungs. I'd dedicated my life to proving myself to this organization. I'd swallowed their disgust like bitter medicine—after all, we were the children of evil creatures. But this wasn't just revulsion; it was seeing us as raw material to be exploited and discarded.

Next to me, the man I was falling in love with didn't move to comfort me.

My heart stuttered as the implications of that silence sank in, because for Ezra to hold himself back now meant there was worse to come.

I twisted to face him. "Your mom."

Ezra's mouth worked but no sound came out.

"Zee," I pleaded. "Tell me, sweetheart." I could put most of it together, but he had to say it aloud to lance this wound.

"Mamá wanted a baby so badly." His voice wavered but he notched his chin up, even if he couldn't look at me during this tale. "The rabbi approved the IVF treatments and the facility was under the aegis of Seaside, which had a solid reputation. Her miscarriage devastated her, but she'd had the best care. It was just a horrible tragedy." His lips twisted into a bitter sneer as he drawled those last words. "Except it wasn't. My father," he spat the term, "wasn't seeking power. He wasn't even part of the Authority, simply the leader of the team that stopped Operation Inferno. What a mensch." His expression twisted. "So passionate about fighting for humanity that he was willing to sacrifice his own wife on the battlefield."

I rested my hand on his leg, my stomach in knots. "Was it really a miscarriage?"

Ezra slowly nodded. "When Mamá got to her second trimester, Natán convinced them to let it go a bit longer. Then it was her third, and the fetus was still thriving. If she carried to term, they intended to take the baby away to study it, but she didn't." He sounded robotic. "She almost died. Natán got spooked so badly by the idea of losing her that he threatened to go public unless they shut the program down for good.”

“Did they?”

“Yes. Pederson, who wasn’t on the Authority yet, was the most resentful about it because she’d been in charge of my mother’s care. She was a doctor and giddy about all the breakthroughs this could lead to. Apparently, she was the sole survivor of a shedim ambush early in her career and wanted stronger weapons than the magic cocktail.”

“So much for do no harm.” A surge of hatred welled up inside me, despite the woman’s tragic past. “How soon after that was she promoted?”

“A couple years. My mother was pregnant again with me. It had happened naturally, and both my parents considered it a miracle, so when Natán learned Pederson intended to start the program up again—and silence any protests from him—he had to protect his family. He… He…” Ezra swayed forward as if to give himself momentum to continue. “He left a vamp alive on some job in exchange for turning him and my mother.” For the first time, he met my eyes, his gaze broken and haunted. “Then he promised Pederson that if I was born a Prime, she could study me.”

“But she didn’t.”

“He went back on his word after I was born,” Ezra said dully. “I was a tool.”

“He wanted his son,” I insisted.

Ezra picked at the hole I’d made in his covers. “Pederson’s hands were tied because my family was too high profile among the Maccabee community. Too many operatives had rallied around them.” He drew his knees to his chest. “Five years later, Mamá got a call from someone telling her everything.”

“From Pederson?”

"The secretary wouldn't admit to that," Ezra said. "But my father believed it. Why he waited years to send an assassin, I have no idea. Maybe he meant to be set up in Babel first, powerful and untouchable from any repercussions. Maybe I was supposed to turn out differently and be the hand of his eventual revenge. Whatever it was, he didn't trust me to kill a Maccabee. The Crimson Prince had a pesky moral line." He dropped his head back against the headboard with a soft thud.

Was this fight worth the cost to all the innocents? It was one thing for operatives to pay with our blood, even our lives, but we chose this.

Did you? Cherry whispered. *Hiding in plain sight, remember?*

That was part of it, but my mother was a Maccabee, and I'd gone down this road because I admired her. I had agency and choice.

Something that Eva, who was also an operative, had been denied.

I wanted to judge her because even if she couldn't live with the knowledge of what her husband did, what *she'd* been used to do, how could she still walk into the sun, right in front of her only living child?

But I wouldn't.

It was easy to say she should have left her marriage or reached out for help when I'd never been a mother. There was no way possible for me to understand the staggering depths of the hell she'd endured.

Whether the truth shattered her mind or her guilt at failing two children crushed her spirit, the end result was the same.

A woman so broken she chose to burn.

I hugged Ezra, holding him tight until his resistance crumbled like a dam breaking, his sobs tearing through him with the force of floodwater, each ragged breath carrying decades of buried grief.

He stayed in my arms long past that dam being emptied, leaning into me like I was his only source of strength. Finally, he pulled away, roughly rubbing a hand over his disheveled curls. "It was a lot for one day."

"I know the feeling," I said wryly. "Honestly, I'm surprised Pederson came clean."

"It was because of her nephew, Aleksander," Ezra said. Alastair's youngest half-shedim victim. "I don't know if her much younger sister got pregnant on her own or..." He waved a hand. "Pederson documented Aleksander's magic as he grew up, but she also loved him. She confessed, claiming it was a relief, then she resigned from the Authority, and is now under house arrest."

"Were any of the rest of them complicit in this?"

"No. She and my father were the only ones left of that original team. Thank Burning Eddie for that." Ezra's mouth hardened into a line. "I know what Natán is after. His endgame isn't consolidating power, that's just a means to his true goal." He paused. "Revenge."

Chapter 22

"Natán seeks revenge against the Maccabees?" I got off the bed and walked into the living room, Ezra behind me.

We settled ourselves on the sofa.

"I told you before," he said, "that my father operates on a one-strike-and-you're-dead rule. You're right that he cares about his people. He bought those Seaside clinics to if not help vampires, at least give them dignity in dying."

I'd believed Natán about that. And when he spoke about vampires holding humanity in high esteem. I still did. He wasn't going to unleash whichever vamps were left on us.

"But that's secondary to destroying the Maccabees," Ezra said. "He was denied vengeance for his wife's death because I thwarted the hit on Pederson."

"You're the one person exempt from his rule."

"Lucky me," Ezra said. "But Secretary Pederson is still alive. Why? It's not like Natán forgave and forgot."

"The current Authority knows what happened and has been protecting her. Shit."

It explained why Burning Eddie couldn't get to her either.

"In Natán's last press conference," I said slowly, "he urged people wanting to restrict Eishei Kodesh to think about where the real menace lay. Revenge is a dish best served cold, but that's still assuming he was sure this would all go down with Alastair and the Luce."

"It always bothered me that Natán couldn't find Alastair," Ezra said. "He had his entire Kosher Nostra hunting a dhampir, along with all the other vamps currying favor with him, and Alastair evaded all of them?"

"He wasn't looking for Alastair, he was watching him."

Ezra nodded. "My father knew about the rune, he knew about the ritual, and he made his move, using all his wealth and power to put the pieces into place. But he's never taken responsibility for his role in that insemination program. His role in Mamá's—" He cleared his throat. "Natán has a lot of strikes to his name, but he's never been out. I'm going to rectify that," he said darkly.

"Not the way you're thinking," I said urgently. "This is your opportunity to reinvent yourself. To put the Crimson Prince behind you forever."

"Or it's time for me to show him what it really means to be the Crimson Prince."

"You severed the thrall," I said, switching tactics. "There were side effects. In the middle of my meeting."

I caught the flicker in his expression, a momentary downturn of his eyes and the way his shoulders pulled in slightly before he forced them back.

Guilt serve to Aviva.

Ezra nodded tightly, the only acknowledgment or apology I received. "You promised me two hours," he said. "I waited far longer. And in all the times you reached out to me psychically, not once did you say you were coming to honor that or even explain the delay. You only wanted to make sure I hadn't done anything to compromise your position."

I winced. Tied score and a pull ahead from the Prime. "We hurt each other."

"Yeah." He took my hand. "We'll do better from now on."

"Absolutely. We need to be kind to each other because a lot of people aren't." I shifted, tucking my leg under me. "How do you handle it? Everyone and their dog feeling free to post their opinions about you? Some that are really horrible. And that's from people claiming to be your fans."

"Mostly I ignore it and remind myself whose opinions matter. But I've had years to build up a tolerance and you've been thrown into the storm. I wish I could protect you from that, but I can't. And once your half-shedim status is out there to the public, it's going to complicate every goal you've ever had for yourself."

"You're right, I should leave you."

He wrapped an arm around my shoulder and tucked me into his side. "You can try, but I'll follow."

"Guess I'm stuck with you, then." I looked at him with a grimace. "Unless, of course, you get yourself killed."

He gave me a flat stare. "Aviva—"

"No. We're hashing this out. Say you're successful and stake Natán."

"As I will be."

"You need to make it out alive from wherever he's holed up."

"I can portal, you know." He yawned. "In case you've forgotten that's still a thing."

"Ezra, I'm serious. It's one thing to waltz in there and quite another to leave in one piece. Murder him and you paint a giant target on your back. Both with the Kosher Nostra and the Authority since you'll leave a power vacuum they won't be happy about."

He was silent but I could practically hear his brain

whirring to come up with a strategy to mitigate all the fallout.

Like father like son.

"In the end though," I said, "none of that matters because even though you despise him and want him dead, you won't do it. I understand wanting to murder your father; I also understand what mark that bloodshed will leave on your soul. And more importantly, you do too."

A muscle ticked in his jaw. Then his posture changed, not softening exactly, but shifting, like a weapon being lowered. "Damn it, Aviva," he growled.

I smirked. "Glad you see reason. Besides, our relationship is already on thin ice with the Authority. Do we want to throw conjugal visits in Sector A into the mix?" I teased.

"I mean, you're no longer enthralled by me, so…" He tapped a finger against his lip.

I laughed and he unfurled a wicked smile that sent heat pooling in my belly. Man, I could really use an orgasm or seven to take the edge off. I mean, connect intimately with my chosen life partner.

I trailed a finger along my décolletage. "In thanks for not killing your father, tonight I'll be your willing victim. That's vampire sexy talk, right?" I waggled my eyebrows suggestively. "Did I nail it?"

Ezra shook his head, his eyes dancing in amusement. "You're ridiculous."

"That's a no, then?" I turned away with a pout and was hauled back against his chest.

"Not so fast." He kissed his way up the side of my throat.

"No deal, no touching." I shivered.

"Yeah," he chuckled, his lips vibrating against my skin, "you're really selling that."

I was on the verge of saying to hell with it and letting him take me here and now, hot and hard, but I didn't—not because I exhibited stellar self-control. I didn't. I was exhausted and wanted nothing more than to be held and cherished.

But I didn't because vampires were suddenly phasing through the damn wall.

Ezra and I shot to our feet.

Eight of them moved like an assassination team, sliding into position around Ezra with precision and lethal grace.

They didn't touch him. They didn't have to. Even the Prime couldn't take them all—not with me in the crossfire.

None of them were Li'l Hellions. They weren't common thugs either. Their elegant clothes didn't soften their ancient eyes, the kind evolved from hunting prey across millennia.

Delacroix joined us via wall-transport. "You fucked up."

"And now you intend to kill me for whatever this transgression was," Ezra said, voice flat with boredom.

"I'm not going to kill *you*." The shedim stopped in front of me, his eyes colder than I'd ever seen.

I swallowed down a metallic, slightly sour taste. "Drawing on your magic to protect Darsh and Silas was a mistake. We've undone the thrall and it won't happen again." My voice quivered. "I didn't even know I was doing it. Your magic felt familiar and right."

Delacroix sneered at me. "You sniveling pathetic waste. That was the first thing you'd done that I respected. You showed balls defying me." He leaned in close, red threads flickering in his eyes and his fangs extended. "But you went too far."

"How?"

"Touch Aviva and you die. So, on second thought"— Ezra motioned at my father—"go ahead."

"Shut up, Cardoso. You might have had a shot when you were leeching off her magic but not now." My father pulled a cigarette out from behind his ear and patted his pocket for his matches.

"You sure about that?" Ezra skimmed a hand along his right side, a reminder of the demon's weak spot.

Delacroix hesitated.

One of the vampires hurried forward with a gold lighter.

What a suck-up. I'd have rolled my eyes, but I was too busy trying to keep my legs from shaking. "What are you accusing me of?"

"Figure it out, girl detective," the demon mocked. As he flicked the lighter closed, crimson spikes erupted from his neck.

The helpful vampire was impaled. Ash scattered across the floorboards.

Delacroix dropped the cigarette, putting it out.

Goose bumps broke out over my body, my mind frozen.

"I hate kiss asses." My father stepped through the remains, grinding ash under his heel. "Got an answer for me yet?"

I shook my head, helpless.

None of the strike force vampires even glanced at me, which was a million times more terrifying than if they'd drooled with fangs out. What inhuman control kept them unaffected by both their comrade's murder and my fear?

Delacroix grabbed my shirtfront and lifted me off the ground. "You killed a freed shedim."

Ezra shot forward, but the strike force matched his speed. They held him in place—the seven of them barely enough.

"I killed the other demon," Ezra said. "Take it up with me, not her."

Delacroix spared him a brief contemptuous glance, then shook me hard.

"I've killed them before," I said, through rattling teeth. "To satiate Cher— This isn't news to you."

Delacroix slammed me back onto the ground, and pain lanced up through my left ankle. "I explicitly told you not to touch the prisoners. You chose the Maccabees over me."

"It wasn't like that," I insisted. "I wasn't even thinking of you or your coup. These shedim were trying to slaughter everyone at HQ!"

The shedim roared and shoved me halfway across the room. "*I am a king!* You are a nothing I let live. This is what disobedience earns you."

I shifted my weight off my injured leg and hunched over, staring through a curtain of tangled hair.

"Since you despise this part of yourself so much," Delacroix said, "I'm going to rip it out of you."

Cherry clawed against my skull with a wail, the force of which made me dizzy.

Ice ran down my veins and my ears rang with his words. "I'll die."

Ezra tore out the throat of one vamp, but the others reaffirmed their hold.

"Oh, you'll live," Delacroix said, his fury gone now that he'd dropped his bombshell. "You just may not like it very much."

"Impossible," Ezra said, still struggling. "You can't remove magic from someone."

The shedim arched an eyebrow. "Pederson didn't tell you that part of Operation Inferno?"

I was too busy trying to wrestle Cherry into a semblance of calm to care that he knew who Ezra had visited and why.

"Those shedim didn't need some experiment to make half-demon babies." Delacroix dusted his knuckles against his shirt. "Our natural charm worked well enough. They wanted a way to remove the magic." He paused. "The

Maccabees hated that. They figured that any half human should work for them. It wasn't to their advantage if some deadbeat dad could show up and take that magic away. It's why they never liked infernals. They couldn't control you."

Cherry was numb; I was too. I'd had a lifetime to get used to how humans—including the Powers that Be in my own organization—saw me, but I was frozen by the realization that I'd been nothing more than a container that my father could empty at will.

"It won't be fun, and there'll be a lengthy recovery period," Delacroix said, "but you'll get used to living like"—his lip curled—"a human."

Stop hiding and be a regular Eishei Kodesh. Would I have taken him up on this offer, pain or not, six months ago? Three?

Would I now?

I'd finally be able to be myself without constantly making amends for my shedim side. I'd have to walk back some of my rallying speech to the Maccabees, but I could have a normal life.

"If I may," my boyfriend said.

His mild tone startled both my father and me.

"Thank you for describing your villainous plan, Delacroix." With barely a shrug, Ezra threw off the strike force.

They regrouped quickly.

"Enough." The Prime's command rippled through the room. Raw power emanated from him, freezing the other vampires where they stood. I'd seen Ezra in action, but this was different. He'd come away from our thrall with some new tricks.

The strike force had mistaken a bonfire for a match. They dropped their gazes to the floor, shoulders hunched.

"While you were plotting and using the Hell as your personal buffet of misery, I was running it." Ezra strode forward. "Making connections with staff you never noticed. Who Calista never noticed. The two of you fostered an abusive atmosphere, and when I treated them with respect, they fell over backward to help me out."

"What are you talking about?" Delacroix's voice grated with annoyance.

"They fed me information about you, which I gave to foot soldiers in Dad's Mafia who were eager to impress the Crimson Prince. I didn't go to Copenhagen empty-handed. I gave Secretary Pederson the location of all the locks as a bargaining chip with the Authority."

"You didn't think to mention this?" I snapped.

"I was still pissed off," he said mildly. He released the strike force vampires from his hold with a cocky smile, but fatigue tightened the corners of his mouth.

Delacroix gestured for them to remain still. "You showed your hand too soon, Cardoso. I can take Aviva's magic and still have my followers get to the locks before you can alert the Authority."

I'd spent my life placating and tolerating my Brimstone Baroness, while I remained focused on one goal: acceptance for being a half shedim.

Thirty years of making silent apologies for her existence —making them for *mine*.

What a tragic waste.

"I'll die before I let you take my magic," I said. "That's not some testament to you, Father."

"The Authority is happy to let you take demons away from earth for good. But touch anyone Aviva and I care about, or either of us, and that changes." Ezra unleashed a glacial smile.

"My magic or your coup?" I said. "You can only bet the house on one of them." I held his gaze for three very fast heartbeats.

"Even the house doesn't always win." Delacroix inclined his head. "My coup, it is."

I motioned for him to run along and take his vampires with him.

The strike force fell into formation behind Delacroix, headed for the elevator.

I took the first full breath since they'd appeared.

Delacroix hit the call button, then turned back. "Enjoy your magic while it lasts, daughter." His smile never reached his eyes.

While it lasts? My brief moment of triumph dissolved, replaced by a knot tightening between my shoulder blades.

"Kill them and everyone they care about, or I'll turn you into fish food," my father ordered and vanished through the wall.

Six vampires turned as one to Ezra and me.

The Prime eyed them and cracked his knuckles. "Eh."

Cherry nudged me to slide into my synesthete vision. What I found there shocked me. All of the vampires' previous injuries—save for Ezra's—were laid out in a beautiful blue map for me to exploit.

I wasn't even in my shedim form.

All thanks to drawing on Delacroix's magic to place Darsh and Silas within the boundaries of the security system. My father would be furious.

I almost laughed, but my amusement turned wistful at the one unassailable truth of my existence: I was Cherry and she was me.

I'd gotten halfway to where I needed to be. I'd grown to love all of her.

No, I'd grown to love all of *me.*

Now I took the final step—and released the last threads of pretense.

Thank you, my darling Cherry Bomb, my Brimstone Baroness.

I'll always love you, and I never would have made it this far without you, but I can take it from here.

Cherry's presence swirled through me, not fighting, not struggling, but like water finding its natural course.

Finally. In my head, she smiled and closed her eyes for the last time, merging and settling firmly into the marrow of my bones.

Cherry Bomb was no more.

A quiet ache bloomed in the space she'd occupied, like vast emptiness where a star once burned, yet it would always hum with the memory of her light.

This wasn't loss; it was completion. The divide between Aviva and Cherry had always been artificial, a coping mechanism I no longer needed.

I cracked my knuckles and burst into my full shedim glory.

The fight was bloody and vicious but mercifully brief. Ezra moved like death itself, while I tore their bodies apart with startling ease, as if their flesh knew it was already beaten.

They were good old-fashioned deaths with no trace of the Luce. That was comforting.

I picked up my final victim's shirt, snapped ash off it, and used it to clean myself up.

"I'm going to Toronto to get Orly somewhere safe," Ezra said as the last scream was brutally cut short.

I pitched the shirt into the corner. "I'll tell Darsh and Silas to be on high alert."

Ezra surveyed the detritus of his living room. "I'm not coming back here."

"Then we should say a proper goodbye."

Moments later the words "Fuck you, Delacroix" were written in ash across the floor.

Mic drop and out.

Chapter 23

Ezra and I split up at the Hell's portal, him to Toronto and me back to Vancouver.

The mid-morning sun shone brightly, which buoyed my mood a bit, except this was Vancouver in January. Rain would return and soon.

I sat on my bed, furiously typing a message to Darsh and Silas that Delacroix was on the warpath so be on guard for any attack.

Next, I fired off a text to Maud about outing myself to the Maccabees. I assured her it was just an FYI, and no one other than my inner circle knew we were siblings, but she should give a heads-up to her bodyguard.

Junior: *Got it. Adrian says not to worry.*

Adrian was answering her that quickly? Hold on. I calculated the time difference between Vancouver and Hong Kong. Oooh.

Me: *That's so dedicated of him to be on night shift. Unless he's off the clock? Doing a little moonlighting?*

Junior: *Just for that, I'm going to request new chapters of the fanfic shipping you and Silas that is blowing up in the Ezracurricular forums. It's called Calamity Demon and the Sundance Vampire. I think it's supposed to be enemies to lovers, but I regret to say you didn't last long as sheriff. You abandoned the law to chase a certain lawless Southern vampire.*

Darsh was going to kill me.

Me: *Don't you dare. And don't send me passages about Ezra and me either.*

Junior: *I'd have to read them to do that.* 🤮

Once upon a time, I'd asked Ezra to keep us on the down low. Those days were over, and if part of us being together was people writing fanfic about us—nope, it was still weird.

What was weirder was how our relationship was being used as currency for others to gain popularity online via their own creative outlets.

It didn't feel designed to catch Ezra's or my attention, but the eye of Stasia, the president of his fan club, who held great sway in his fandom.

She hadn't come out for or against us yet and was mostly advocating for everyone remaining respectful toward Ezra. The same stance she generally took whenever he was reported to be with someone new.

The end result, however, was that I was both an active target and a commodity, and I struggled to reconcile myself with either one.

Sachie rapped on my bedroom door, spatula in hand. "Food's up."

The pink had faded from her hair, leaving a disconcerting orangey-bleach color that clashed with the dark circles under her eyes and blood splattered on her wrinkled clothing.

She dropped her head onto my shoulder with a yawn.

I took the spatula out of her hand. "Let's feed you and tuck you in."

She shuffled behind me like a zombie, taking a seat at the dining room table next to Olivier without further chatter. Her boyfriend favored his left side, and a nasty gash peeked out from his torn sleeve.

I dished up the scrambled eggs she'd made, filling them in on everything that had happened since I'd seen them last while we ate.

Ezra texted when I was partway through my story to let me know that Orly was safe and out of Delacroix's reach.

I sent a thumbs-up back, and had almost finished filling my friends in when Sachie's eyes slipped closed, and she pitched forward.

I caught her before she face-planted into her toast. "I'm not that boring," I teased. "A prominent cosplayer posted a photo of herself as me. Her fire hands aren't canon, but the Maccabee uniform she came up with had some pluses."

Sachie quietly huffed a laugh and an "Ew."

Olivier had finished his food, but was completely zoned out, hunched over, fork in hand, rocking slightly.

"Hey." Sachie put her hand on his arm.

Olivier lurched upright, using his utensil like a stake to slam into her eyes. She disarmed her boyfriend before any harm was done, but he gaped at her in horror.

"You're exhausted and in pure reaction mode," she said. "It's okay."

"It's not." He scrubbed a hand over his face, leaving a streak of gray ash on his jaw. "It's really not," he repeated, voice cracking.

Jared's murder was insanely high profile, and even with Roger's confession, Olivier had to be meticulous in his handling of it. Not to mention, he was coming to it from the stress of staking vamps along with every other emergency facing Vancouver.

Olivier needed to rest up in a big way.

My task force *would* solve the mystery of how to stop the Luce, but throw in the damage already caused, plus power plays closing in from all sides, and even we Maccabees were struggling.

The Trad officers fighting alongside us had to feel like they were bobbing in storm-level swells. Forget justice—did they even see a way to survive?

Sachie helped Olivier to his feet.

"Are you going to tell me things will seem better in the morning?" he said.

"No, since it's already morning and we'll be waking up tonight." She punched him in the shoulder in a pep-talk way. "But killing things in the shadows is fun."

He waited for more, but when it didn't come, he glanced at me.

I shrugged. "That's really it. Sach is very simple in her life philosophy."

"You people live a strange reality," he muttered, heading for Sach's bedroom.

"Get used to it, meatsack," she said, padding along behind him.

"We discussed that name." He tossed her over his shoulder in a fireman's carry.

Sachie protested the manhandling with a number of creatively violent threats, but she was laughing and pounding on his back.

Smiling, I watched them until her bedroom door shut with a click. I picked up my phone, running my thumb over the screen and wishing Ezra was here. I didn't contact him though. Orly deserved uninterrupted time with him, and I needed a quick nap before meeting the task force.

Sadly, sleep only made things worse. I'm not sure if the triple-shot latte after I woke up helped, but it kept my eyes open on the drive to work, even if my hands shook when I crammed a muffin in my mouth at red lights.

Once I got to HQ, I snagged some chocolate and

headed to the conference room, uncomfortably aware of all the whispered comments and sideways looks I was getting.

Stay calm. The last time the hubbub was about Casey's murder, not me. Except that just meant that something else terrible had happened.

I picked up my pace, almost colliding with Gemma, who'd stepped into my path.

"You bitch." She multitasked insults and deep squats.

I froze and looked around. The whispers *were* about me?

Had portal at the Hell had returned me to some alternate Vancouver? One that looked the same, but was instead the darkest timeline where all my recent victories were nothing but a dream?

Gemma wagged a finger at me, bobbing up and down in small squat pulses. "You kept him for yourself when I told you I wanted to ride that boy."

I opened my mouth. Closed it. Frowned. "Ezra?"

"Yes, Ezra. Your boyfriend. Who I have been seeing fan art of with you all over my social media." She shuddered, then waved at a nearby group who were failing miserably at pretending not to eavesdrop. "They want you to dish about what he's like. Well, not the ones who asked for transfers to another city so they don't have to work with a half shedim, but the rest of them."

"Who *what*?!"

"Fuck them. The trash is taking itself out. Let it. As for the rest of them…" She stared pointedly at the not-eaves-droppers until they turned away, then snorted. "They're dying for an introduction to the Crimson Prince, which, as we've established, I'm first in line for. Set me up with one of his friends."

She grabbed my elbow, hauling me to the conference room.

"Uh, okay," I said, still shell-shocked by, well, all of it.

The task force greeted me normally, which was reassuring.

Spreadsheets color-coded by flame type had been pinned to the walls. They were broken into three columns: Possible, No Go, and Yes.

Unfortunately, the middle one was the longest, but it was incredible how many ideas about the backfire had been greenlit.

I tore open the peanut butter cup I'd grabbed and received a snarked "Thanks for thinking of the team's chocolate needs" from Gemma.

Her familiar bite rolled through me like aloe across a sunburn.

I got down to work with Gemma, Eduardo, Joe, and Marilyn, swapping notes and jumping onto video calls.

Ha-joon, our Blue Flame in Seoul who'd cracked the humidity and air pressure factors as keys to how fast the Luce spread, walked me through the animated maps he'd created. The Blue Flame subgroup had broken the world down into zones to narrow in on the Luce's most active hotspots, factoring in upcoming weather conditions.

Orange Flames were using these maps to create optimal conditions for the backburn.

Louis interrupted our meeting, making us come watch the Authority's televised response to Natán's press conference. I almost didn't go, unable to handle more of this finger pointing, schoolyard bitching.

It would have been laughable if the ones doing it didn't have a global reach and the ability to plunge not only vampires and humans, but Trads and Eishei Kodesh into war.

I pushed through the crowd gathered in front of the large screen Louis had wheeled onto the third floor.

Dmitri Koslov, my least favorite human—well, now that Jared Casey was dead—once more took center stage. He wasn't flanked by other Authority members this time. He stood on the steps of some imposing official-looking building in front of a bevy of reporter mics.

Operatives three rows deep wearing black jumpsuits stood at attention behind him.

"They better not try and put me in that ninja onesie." Gemma scowled at the screen.

I laughed but also massaged my throbbing temples.

Dmitri shared intelligence reports that healthy vampires had moved into the Seaside facilities and suggested that they were being used as training grounds for planned assaults on humans.

My headache worsened.

"The ones in charge will dispute our claims of what is happening," Dmitri said, "so we're giving them an opportunity to stand by their offer to work with us. Shut down all Seaside clinics and evacuate any vampires currently residing there back to Babel in the next forty-eight hours."

Many vampires preferred Babel, but plenty of them barely ever visited, much less lived there. Earth was their home. It was *humans* who regarded Babel as the vampire homeland.

Now, it was to be their prison.

"Should they refuse or the deadline passes," Dmitri said, "we'll take that as proof that Seasides are being used for nefarious purposes."

"Nefarious?" Gemma rolled her eyes. "Okay, supervillain."

That chick was really growing on me.

"In that event," Dmitri continued, "Maccabees will take the evacuation into our own hands."

Was "evacuation" code for "mass murder"?

Those operatives on the screen nodding along to Dmitri's ultimatum made me sick. How could the rest of the Authority approve this? Had Koslov staged his own coup?

Michael snapped off the television before the flurry of flashes from reporters on-screen had ended.

Fyodor, a competent level two I'd worked with before, tentatively raised his hand. "Director Fleischer? What is being asked of us?"

The entire room leaned forward as one.

"Regular procedure vis-à-vis vampire criminal activity stands," the director said. "I will get clarification around any 'evacuation' policy, but it will not involve the wide-scale extermination of innocent vampires. Not by my chapter."

"But the Authority…" Another man spoke, looking to the operatives around him who nodded nervously.

Michael held up a hand. "I guarantee no operative will suffer repercussions from the Authority for following my orders." She dropped her hand with a sudden sharp motion. "Abuse that directive to play vigilante or let personal prejudices around vampires dictate your behavior and you will be dealt with in the most punitive fashion." She met the gaze of every operative. "Trust me, I will find out. If you have a problem with that or don't believe I can protect you, leave now and I'll arrange your transfer to a different branch."

We exchanged uneasy glances, the silence tense. Then, with a rustle of movement, two men and a woman hurried to the stairwell, eyes to the floor.

"More scared of the Authority than the director." Gemma shook her head. "Idiots."

Michael tracked their departure, then sent the rest of us back to work.

The task force put in another couple hours, nailing down the final details of our backburn.

Suddenly, alarms screeched.

My first thought was that more shedim were roaming

the building, and given how fast the others snatched up their phones for any alert, I wasn't alone.

But no, the crisis wasn't demons. Oh, for the days of that straightforward threat and not another grim milestone in my rapidly deteriorating definition of "normal day."

Dmitri's orders to shut down all Seaside Rehabilitation facilities had been complied with.

The vampires weren't evacuated though, because the rifts to Babel were closed, stranding them earthside.

No one could say if the rift shutdowns were because of the Luce or because residents on that side took preventative measures and sealed themselves off from us.

In the end though, it didn't matter. Only one thing did.

Infected vampires were flooding the streets.

Chapter 24

Not only were infected vampires rampaging, healthy ones were also panicking, which put humans at stratospheric levels of freaked the fuck out.

It was all boots to the ground, each of us assigned a squad and a quadrant in Metro Vancouver.

My task force was in the same unit, deployed to our local Seaside to help our colleagues already on-site deal with the vampires refusing to leave.

I reassured myself that Darsh was in charge out there, and he wouldn't let this become a bloodbath.

Unless he had no choice.

I quickly traded my heels and suit for runners and sweats, then sprinted through the rapidly emptying out building, bound for the bus idling in the underground garage.

Power was out in large swaths of the city, but we sped through the clear night with front-row seats to fleeing citizens, smashed car windows, and pockets of fighting where Trad officers and operatives attempted to regain control of the human population.

Injured people littered the sidewalks, some raging, some crying, and others eerily silent, their shell-shocked faces pale in the moonlight.

Vampire corpses glowed against the concrete like horrible nightlights. A few had stakes protruding from their chests, others looked like they'd been savaged by wild animals, i.e. other crazed vamps, but most were unfortunate victims of the Luce.

I was too numb to worry every time the speeding bus leaned too hard to one side or the other. I had no idea how Sachie, Olivier, Darsh, and Silas were faring, and given the footage Gemma couldn't stop doomscrolling through, it wasn't only Vancouver that had fallen into a dystopian nightmare.

The entire world was burning.

Our bus zoomed into the neighborhood where Seaside was located, passing the smoldering remains of a building and a bashed-in fire hydrant.

I stared out the window at what should have been dark silhouettes of a far-off group of office towers but now had flames licking out of several stories.

Sirens wailed in the distance, punctuated by what sounded like bursting fireworks.

Next to me, Gemma flinched.

"I'm not used to hearing gunfire," she said. "It's Canada, you know?"

"Yeah." I handed her the Zen Zapper I'd grabbed on my way out of HQ.

"You won't need it?"

I flexed my hand, letting scales ripple across my skin.

Gemma gave me a wan smile. "You and your party tricks, Fleischer."

"Step up your game, Huang," I teased back just as half-heartedly.

The driver had barely finished his tire-squealing drive through the high front gates before we were jumping out. He told us that he'd been redeployed to pick up casualties, his taillights disappearing into the night the second the final operative hit the ground.

Toxic green scales burst across my body like living armor and my left hand extended into razor-sharp claws. The transformation sent familiar waves of power through me, my more muscular physical form stretching my shoulder seams.

My crimson hair whipped in the icy wind, which carried dancing sparks from a burning car. I assessed the battlefield, the scene before us something from a medieval painting of Hell.

The wide front lawn had become a killing field, with vampires turning on each other. Pine resin from the trees on the property mixed with the sickly sweet smell of blood and decay.

There shouldn't have been this many undead here. Not if Seaside was only being used as a treatment or hospice facility, yet it seemed like most of southern British Columbia's vamp population was present.

Had their close proximity made it easier for the Luce to tear through them? How many remained strong and uninfected?

Which were more dangerous?

All of the three dozen or so Maccabees on our bus partnered up. Joe with Marilyn, Eduardo with Fyodor.

I wasn't sure how many Vancouver operatives were already on the premises, and thus, our total numbers handling this situation.

Gemma fell into step beside me, her stake in one hand and the Zen Zapper in the other.

The operative who'd laughed snidely when first seeing my shedim side at HQ now looked from the chaos to me and gave a thumbs-up.

Two vampires were locked in combat near the fountain. It took me a second to recognize them as foot soldiers from the same local Mafia. Their grimy clothes hung on withered frames, their mottled skin loose like ancient parchment as they tore at each other with desiccated hands.

One's fangs slashed viciously at his former ally's throat, trying desperately to feed from the other, to heal—not understanding he was beyond repair.

His victim fought back with failing strength. Neither noticed us, they were too far gone, driven mad by the combination of bloodlust and the Luce.

To our left, another vampire crawled across the ground, her legs having given out as her supernatural strength flickered and died. She pursued a vamp who stumbled away from her, his own movements jerky and desperate.

Gemma had deployed the Zen Zapper on the jerkily moving one, but he kept coming. "Fuck!"

"Right femur!" I mimed slashing it.

A fraction of a second later, her dagger glinted through the moonlight. Flesh tore and viscous liquid arced.

The vampire crashed to its knees, where Gemma immediately staked him. She left the Zen Zapper on the ground, its prongs still buried in the vamp's skin.

"Tone down the glow." She squinted and pointed at my eyes. "If I want a flashlight, I'll punch you in the shoulder to power on."

I didn't have that kind of control—yet. Plus, she wasn't funny. I threw her the finger.

We ran across the lawn, almost ploughing into an enormous healthy-looking vamp.

He cracked his knuckles, fangs out and blood running down his chin.

I prayed it was from feeding on one of his own kind and

not any of the human staff who'd chosen to remain when Seaside was repurposed to treat infected vampires.

The vamp blurred forward with the speed of a cobra striking.

I barely managed to thrust myself in his path, his fangs striking my scales and not Gemma's throat. A tingly reverberation ran down to my toes. It was almost ticklish, unlike his grip crushing my windpipe as he lifted me off my feet.

Lungs seizing and toes scrabbling against the concrete, I jammed my claws into his eyes. The second he dropped me, I snapped his neck.

He crumpled to the ground, where Gemma staked him.

"Over here!" One of our younger operatives, Rupinder, was supporting a wounded male Trad officer. Rupinder hadn't been with us on the bus or around for my shedim reveal, but word had traveled fast, the gossip working to my advantage since I didn't have to offer explanations or deal with her attacking *me* in terror.

The Trad officer, however, took one look at me and fainted in Rupinder's hold.

"Better that way," Gemma muttered.

True, but the pair were caught in the crossfire of vampire-on-vampire violence, and now the cop was dead weight in our operative's arms.

"Yoo hoo! Bloodsuckers!" I waggled my claws in a flirtatious wave.

The vamps charged Gemma and me. One moved with terrifying speed, another stumbling but determined, the third dragging a clearly broken leg. The fast one reached us first.

I spun sideways, calling, "Left kidney!"

The vamp's momentum carried him forward—right into Gemma's one-two combo of stab and stake.

Luckily, the other two were also quickly vanquished, their compromised abilities making them easy targets despite their enhanced strength. Sadly, we had no time to celebrate because more bodies were emerging from the shadows.

Inside the facility, someone screamed.

Gemma called out to Joe and Marilyn, our closest team members.

They fought their way to us, ending vampires with practiced efficiency.

We gave Rupinder and the Trad officer's care over to them and ran for Seaside's door.

Just before we reached it, another vamp dropped from the roof—or tried to. Her supernatural abilities stuttered mid-leap, turning catlike reflexes into a catastrophic fall. She hit the ground hard, bones snapping. When she looked up, her eyes were wild with pain and hunger, yet they flicked between Gemma and me, the vampire having enough presence of mind to assess which of us was the greater threat.

She reached out psychically, attempting to control my mind, but the infection had corrupted that power too. Her compulsion whispered across my skull, barely an itch.

Her scream of pure anguish when her psychic assault rebounded, however, shivered through me, ringing in my ears.

I was on her before she could recover, my clawed hand tearing through her chest.

Her lifeless body fell to the grass with a sound like dry leaves in autumn.

Gemma and I hopped over her corpse and ran inside. Glass crinkled underfoot from the blown-out lights, fixtures torn out of the ceiling and discarded on the tiles under dangling live wires.

Photos of past staff and founders that once hung neatly on the wall had been strewn around like a child flinging toys in a temper tantrum.

We edged around a corner.

A vampire slumped against the wall. His healing powers had turned against him and a small cut on his arm was spreading, flesh decaying faster than vampire regeneration could handle. He struggled to stay on his feet, but seeing us, he gave one last burst of speed.

My claws found his heart before the infection could finish its work. Mercy, of a sort.

A crash from above drew our attention. Through a huge hole in the second-floor ceiling, a vampire fell, couldn't catch himself with his supernatural reflexes on the fritz, and shattered like ancient pottery against the marble floor. The sound drew more of them, some still graceful, others moving like broken puppets.

We cleared assailant after assailant, slashing, staking, breaking bones, gaining inch by precious inch of territory, all while bathed in the red glow of the emergency lights.

"Behind you!" Sachie emerged from the cafeteria, her stake whipping past my head to take down a vampire attempting to flank us.

"Coming through!" Darsh was right behind her, herding three terrified human staff into the hallway.

I pressed a hand to my sternum, trying to contain the wild beating of my heart at seeing him and Sachie safe.

Ezra's Prime magic and the lack of rain were on Darsh's side, because the Luce hadn't harmed him beyond a couple white streaks in his hair. It was a good look on him, though Darsh tended to rock most vibes.

"The Authority blindsided us with that fucking announcement!" The raw pain in Darsh's voice yanked me back to our desperate situation. A woman leaned on him for support, and while he kept his solicitous attention on her, one of his fists was clenched and a muscle ticked in his jaw.

A howl shook the walls.

Silas.

Incredibly, Darsh didn't abandon his flock. He told Gemma to help him get everyone outside to safety. He didn't need to ask Sach and me to check on his boyfriend because we were already halfway down the corridor.

Silas was upstairs in one of the activity rooms, his massive frame gone utterly still as he stood over a crumpled form on the floor.

I said a quick thank-you to the universe that Silas looked uninjured, but my heart clenched at the corpse with its thinning yellow hair.

Green eyes, once so alert and alive, now stared sightlessly upward, the man's prosthetic legs splayed at awkward angles. Rylan Quinn was one of the Ashbishop's many victims. He'd spent his life paying forward the kindness he'd received from Silas, his unknown benefactor who'd cared for him from afar.

What a testament to this man that he'd remained here to help the same kind of beings who destroyed his village, killed his mother, and took his legs. I wasn't sure I'd find that same compassion were our situations reversed.

"This isn't how we were supposed to meet." Silas spoke softly, his voice heavy with a weight I'd never heard before. Not even when he admitted to creating the Ashbishop. "I was going to introduce myself properly once the madness with the Luce was over. I'd finally forgiven myself, you see, and I wanted to say hello."

He knelt beside Rylan, gently closing those unseeing eyes with one massive hand. The tenderness of the gesture stood in stark contrast to the sounds of violence raging around us.

Sachie placed her hand on his shoulder, and he gripped it without turning around.

The three of us held this awful tableau, glued together

by senseless loss, until the screams of the infected forced us to move again.

Over a century of carefully preserved humanity crumbled in my friend's boyish face, Silas now stripped down to nothing but teeth and hunger and ancient animal grief.

"Let's end this and get the survivors to safety," he said in a rough voice, and plunged back into the fray.

Dawn was a long time coming.

Chapter 25

I claimed the seat next to Darsh for the ride back on that somber Wednesday morning.

The bus had super-tinted special filters on the windows, good for both people who wished to sleep and to prevent vamp operatives from being crispified.

Silas sat by himself at the back while Sachie sat across from me talking to Chief Constable Keira Davis to track down Olivier.

Gemma was among the Maccabees who'd been patched up by healers before heading back to Vancouver. She and Joe were asleep on the seats in front of me.

All of my task force was on the bus, but we'd lost four operatives and six Trads who'd been dispatched after the staff's terrified 911 call. Darsh arrived with his crew before them, but he didn't realize for quite some time that those officers had shown up.

One of the non-magic cops who'd died was the young man Rupinder had been helping. Her eyes were fixed on a distant point, but every few seconds she'd blink, slow and mechanical like a doll with dying batteries, all while her face remained a perfect mask of nothing.

Marilyn had taken the young woman under her wing, making her drink water and see the healer for a broken wrist before sticking close to her on the ride back.

I'd driven down this highway a million times, the trees and grass along the side of the road a verdant green backdrop, but in the early morning mist, there was a wrongness to our world.

The characteristic drooping branches of Sitka spruce had been "corrected" upward into rigid right angles, the normally scattered spray of needles locked into precise rows like teeth on a comb.

I blinked at grass that looked painted, every blade the same height and hue of green, exactly like artificial turf.

"Darsh." I pointed out the window.

"Yeah," he said grimly. "I see it."

Running out of vampires or magically infused artifacts to "heal," the Luce was turning its sights on earth herself, like an immune system gone out of whack.

How long until it remade humans? Vancouver had only until Saturday for the predicted apex of the Luce. Would people suffer painful aberrations or simply crumble away, their very humanity now deemed an imperfection?

I couldn't shake the image of streets filled with nothing but abandoned clothes and the echo of screams.

My phone vibrated, a band around my chest loosening at Maud's message that she was okay. Adrian had stashed her at Maccabee HQ behind mezuzah wards when the madness broke out, and they were currently headed back to his place.

I replied with a heart and told her to stay in touch.

"Spook Squad operatives in other cities walked off the job to support the Vampire Care Initiative." Darsh secured his hair with an elastic, the gesture quick and fluid despite his exhaustion. "I wonder how many of them survived.

They should have gone to Babel." He snapped his fingers. "Oh, wait. They couldn't because the rifts were closed."

"By the Luce or shut down?"

"Oh, I'm sure it was the Luce and the timing for Natán being unable to get evac'd vamps to Babel after all the clinics were closed was completely coincidental," Darsh drawled sarcastically.

"How do you feel about Babel being cut off?"

He half twisted to watch Silas, who was slumped against the window with a blank expression. "I never had much of an emotional attachment to it. I just wish Nasir had made contact."

News of what was happening around the globe must have filtered back to the megacity. Was the situation so critical there that he couldn't come back to stand alongside his fellow Maccabees before the rifts closed? Or had he simply chosen not to?

I nudged Darsh's shoulder. "You're still here."

It was a statement and a question.

He laughed bitterly, but his gaze lingered on Silas a moment longer before he turned back to me. "I'm still serving time with the Maccabees in exchange for them sparing Patrin's life. Ezra was right. Now would be my shot at freedom without the Authority coming after me, but I'm choosing to remain in their faces."

What a bitter decision they put on my friend: finally free to bolt but staying put to prove he mattered.

He shook his head. "I'm lying to myself again. It's not just about forcing them to acknowledge my value or upholding the tikkun olam vow. I could have cut and run days ago." He got a cross look on his face. "Silas makes me want to be a better man. One worthy of him."

The raw honesty in his voice surprised me. This wasn't the defiant Darsh who'd declared his loyalty to his job at

Ezra like a taunt. My friend had found something worth staying for beyond principle or spite.

Darsh nudged me. "Don't you dare tell Cowpoke I said that though."

I mimed zipping my lips, processing this new side of him as we fell into a tired silence.

Luce hit or not, our attackers at Seaside had left no room for verbal negotiations. It had been us or them.

Michael would, of course, back that call, but I understood with blinding clarity why she'd ordered us to refrain from executing all vampires.

It wasn't because it played into the Authority's desire to rid itself of vamps on earth; it was because it played into Natán's hands.

He'd masterfully spun Authority orders, able to claim that the doors to Babel were locked and that he'd complied in the only way possible: by closing all Seasides.

Natán could now hold up the slaughter of his people as proof the Maccabees were power-hungry murderers who had to be stopped.

In fact, I found his broadcast of that very response.

"Today they came for vampires," he said. "But should anyone, those with magic or without, get in the way of the Maccabee agenda, their lives will also be forfeit." His voice dripped with sorrow when he added, "I'm a proud man. A powerful man. I do not like to admit to vulnerability. But the lesson of how little Maccabees regard the lives of those they profess to value was branded into me years ago at a cost I still pay today."

Fury blazed through me. Natán hadn't paid; Ezra had. He carried the weight of a broken childhood, his mother's absence a void that Natán forged into a weapon. The Maccabees and Natán played their power games—against shedim and each other—while Ezra survived on fragments of a childhood that should have been whole.

I texted Ezra that I loved him and was thinking about him.

Natán wrapped up by urging people to write their government representatives to not only cut off all Maccabee funding but dismantle the organization entirely.

Sometimes the most devastating revenge required nothing more than the truth mixed with time. In this case, a carefully curated truth, with the glaring omission of his own role.

Natán had played a long game with masterful patience and perfect timing. Each calculated statement since the Luce hit was designed to plant seeds of doubt that had, judging by comments online, bloomed into public outrage.

He knew when to strike and when to let others do the work for him.

As if that wasn't bad enough, in finding his broadcast, I had the dubious pleasure of seeing posts about Ezra and me. People were *so* considerate about tagging me and making sure I was aware of their opinions.

Even the well-wishers' comments were invasive, transforming my private relationship into public entertainment, while the worst comments left me feeling nauseous and vulnerable.

Sachie ended her call and rested her head against the seat, her eyes closed.

I leaned across the aisle. "Did you find Olivier?"

"He's in emergency vascular surgery to repair a torn carotid artery in his neck he got while patrolling downtown. He was overworked and was unable to defend himself like I'd trained him to." She recited it without a trace of emotion, but her grip on her phone was so tight that her knuckles had gone white.

"What?!" *A torn carotid? With that kind of blood loss, he should be dead. Please don't let there be complications, he's suffered enough.* "Do they know how much longer he'll be in surgery for?" I moderated my voice to sound like this was no bigger of a deal than Olivier having his tonsils out.

"No."

While she didn't need my fear and wouldn't want my sympathy, the dread in her eyes had me moving before I could think twice.

I leaned across the aisle, grabbed her hand, and didn't let go for the rest of the ride.

She didn't either.

Once we got off the bus at HQ, I asked if she wanted me to come to the hospital.

Sachie shook her head. "I want some time alone with him."

I hugged her. "I'm here if you need me. Any time."

"I know." She pulled free, endured a hug from Darsh, then hurried to her car.

"Where are you off to now, missy?" Darsh playfully tugged a lock of my hair, but half his attention was on Silas.

Silas dug his nails into his palms, drawing blood, though he didn't seem to notice, his gaze distant and sad.

"I have to get hold of Ezra," I said.

"Good. Do that." Silas's voice was raspy.

Darsh and I both waited for something more, but he'd relapsed into silence.

"We'll catch you later, puiul meu," Darsh said and led Silas away.

Some of the operatives I'd fought with last night still gathered around the bus in small groups bathed by the gloomy overcast morning.

Our phones buzzed simultaneously with texts from Monserrat, a vivacious Orange Flame in Madrid. Her flame cohort had analyzed global weather patterns in consultation with meteorologists and Blue Flames' information on humidity and air pressure.

There were some fronts moving in with high humidity conditions she wanted to avoid in a number of rift locations, so we were to meet at 1PM Vancouver time to shut the Luce down for good.

We'd launch our magical backfire from all the rift sites simultaneously, letting it spread out and meet the healing magic head-on.

Ha-joon chimed in with the next message. Given some cities were still in the thick of battle, anyone in the clear was to get some sleep.

The Luce attacking anything it perceived as imperfect in nature put even more pressure on the global task force to stop it, but we couldn't afford to make mistakes.

I started leaving but caught Gemma's eye and threw her a small salute.

A smile tugged at her lips as she returned it.

I hurried into HQ, took a fast shower so I didn't have to drive home in battle-gucked clothing, and changed back into the suit I'd worn to the office.

Pulling my towel-dried hair into a ponytail, I jogged down the stairs to the parking garage, phone in hand and Ezra's number already ringing.

He asked if I was okay instead of saying hello, and when I assured him that I was, he muttered a quiet "Thank fuck."

The air was faintly tinged with a musty warmth that grew stronger the deeper I headed into the parkade.

"How are you?" I said.

"Good. I helped out here in Toronto. King-Spadina was a mess, and the Maccabees were short on vamp operatives."

"You didn't need to put yourself out, after everything they did to you."

"It wasn't about them. Canada is your country and

Orly's adopted one, and it's special to me, too. I had to protect it."

"You're a mensch."

"Does that mean no more Count von Cardoso?"

"Since you were so mopey about all your nicknames disappearing, we'll keep that one for a while longer until you reinvent yourself." I pressed closer to the wall as a couple of cars drove past me. "But speaking of Orly, where is she now?"

"My dumb cousin refused to stay in a safehouse. She's volunteering at a soup kitchen that was set up." His gruff tone gave way to pride.

I beeped my fob at my car. "I really want to be with you right now."

"Same."

Ezra had been clear about not returning to the Hell, and quite frankly, I didn't want him to either.

Since we were no longer thralled, hopefully he wouldn't mind hopping on a plane for four and half hours from Toronto to Vancouver so we could celebrate after our backfire worked as planned.

"Come home with me," Ezra said, "even for a few hours."

I frowned. "Aren't you done with the Copper Hell?"

"The Hell was never my home."

"Babel? The rifts are closed," I said. "How—"

The air around me grew heavy and charged, vibrating as strands of dark light wove into a mesh net a scant five feet away.

Ezra stepped out of the center of the portal, immaculately dressed in a gray suit that flowed over his warrior's frame like smoke given structure and intent. But his silvery-blue eyes under thick arched eyebrows were dull with fatigue, and he carried the faint acrid scent of a bonfire.

I ran into his arms, hugging him tightly.

My boyfriend kissed the top of my head.

"You're still opening portals without the Hell as a way-stop?" I said.

"Yeah." His voice rumbled against my cheek which I pressed to his chest.

"I'm still illuminating vamp weaknesses." I released him from the hug. "The Delacroix shit show was almost worth the trade-off of retaining that ability. So, uh, how do we get to Babel?"

"I can't get there directly, because whatever happened sealed them off for good from this side. But remember, anywhere I've been, I can portal to. That includes Flaming Flapjacks."

"Use a demon realm to get to a demon realm. You're more than just a pretty face."

He dusted his knuckles against his chest then blew on them.

"Don't be too smug." I wagged a finger at him. "The security system that Delacroix set up around Flaming Flapjacks may not be friendly to me anymore, and who knows what it'll do to you? Not to mention whatever shit might be exploding in Babel."

"If you don't want to go, that's okay."

Did I want to insert myself into another potential war zone? One that was populated entirely by desperate vampires who wouldn't look kindly on a Maccabee?

On the other hand, this was a huge step forward in our relationship, and honestly, I was super curious to see his place.

Curiosity killed the cat, Fleischer. Yeah, well, there was that.

Going to my boyfriend's home aside, it would be good to have an eyewitness account of what state the megacity was in right now. Plus, Nasir was still there.

I swooned into Ezra's arms. "Just protect me, my Prime one."

"You're not even in my thrall right now and you're in submissive mode. I like it."

"Aaaaand that's over." I winked at him.

To blend in while we transited through Flaming Flapjacks, I morphed into shedim features, though I didn't bulk up to protect my clothing. With the divide between Cherry and me gone, I'd gained more control over what aspects of my form I shifted.

Hand in hand, Ezra and I stepped into the portal.

I didn't feel that same thorough assessment that I had before. It was more of an absent scan, like the magic's attention was busy elsewhere.

It spit us onto steaming concrete.

A seething mass of shedim was packed wing to arm to tentacle in the parking lot. Their hunger pressed against me like a physical force, stronger than the hot acrid wind. It was a living, writhing thing that tasted of ancient rage and endless malice.

The pancake house was lost somewhere in the crush of bodies, and even the roiling clouds were blotted out by flying demons.

My hand slipped free of Ezra's, and I stumbled back, my feet grinding against a liquid silver lake frozen mid-ripple. I did a double take: the "water" was twisted and discarded lock cells.

The demon closest to us had too many faces. Not in a way I could count, but one that made my mind skitter away from trying.

A creature to our left was essentially a void shaped like broken glass, its edges drinking in light and sanity alike, while another was made entirely of burning wings and watching eyes, its form constantly shifting between states of matter I had no words for.

Something warm trickled down my face. I wiped the tears away, expecting salt or even blood, but this was something darker, like liquid shadows leaking from my eyes and nose.

Mere seconds in their presence felt like an eternity of drowning in pure dread.

I shrank back against Ezra, my claws clutching his sleeve.

My father commanded these legions, this vast army of horror. If he ever decided to unleash them on earth, we wouldn't just lose, we'd be erased from existence itself.

One more fun scenario in this week from Hell.

Chapter 26

A couple shedim turned our way with ferocious shrieks, but Ezra was already pulling me through a second portal.

We stumbled into Babel, Ezra ripping off the arm of some demon who was trying to follow us in order to slam the rift closed. He tossed the limb onto the grass.

I morphed back to my human form, relieved I had a choice about how I presented myself. That hadn't been the case for me before in Babel.

Okay, it wasn't just about choice. Sex in my shedim body was nowhere near as fun, since sensation in very important places was dulled. Mama needed an orgasm stat.

The city hung suspended in perpetual dusk, the sky a bruised canvas of indigo stained with one defiant streak of peach.

On my previous visit, the air's velvet touch held a predatory bite, the sharp tang of an eternally promised but never delivered storm. Yet now, after the horrors I'd seen at Flaming Flapjacks, all I felt was a gentle breeze along my skin.

The lakeside district thronged with vampires, chatting or having a drink. Floating orbs of light drifted between the buildings like lazy fireflies, casting ever-shifting shadows across the faces of the revelers.

It was normal here, as if the end of the world was a movie playing at a different theater.

To my left, a lake stretched out like obsidian glass, disturbed only by ripples that glowed from within, as if something luminescent swam in its depths. I flashed back on shedim trapped in the Crypt's waters and shuddered. Maybe one did.

The lake smelled like brine with an underlying current of ozone that made my teeth ache. Though that might have been the cloying perfume of the female vamp who tottered past, eyes bright, sucking on a boozy blood concoction in an overly large glass.

A sound nearby made me flinch, not from its volume, but its nature.

Laughter.

"Do they know what's happening on earth?" I asked.

"No clue." Ezra took my arm.

The waterfront promenade was paved with iridescent tiles that shifted color with each step, from deep purple to midnight blue to blood red.

A passing couple smiled at the Prime, and a shopkeeper from across the street called out with a wave.

Ezra greeted them all by name. Years and tension melted off him. The grin on his face grew larger, and he had a joking comment or friendly hello for what felt like half the population here.

Some of the vampires shot me a curious glance, and a few threw me hateful glares for being the woman on the Prime's arm, but most smiled back and continued on their way.

The banality of it all was surreal.

We passed Art Deco buildings that curved along the shoreline, their facades adorned with delicate metalwork that moved of their own accord: copper serpents and bronze vines writhing slowly.

"Ez! Welcome home!" A Byronesque vamp in a ruffled shirt and a stunning blue velvet blazer saluted the Prime with a glass of champagne held by manicured fingers. He lounged on a chaise, his legs lazily crossed.

"Don't tell me you still have some of that Bollinger left," Ezra said.

"I'm finally down to the last two bottles," the other vampire replied. "I am nothing if not dedicated."

"Or a functioning alcoholic," Ezra teased with a wink.

"That's highly functioning to you, sir," his friend said haughtily.

Ezra introduced us, and we made small talk before continuing on our way.

"You have friends?" I said.

"What's that supposed to mean? Of course I have friends."

"I figured you grew up in a lonely tower until Silas took you in."

"Unbelievable." Ezra steered me around a street vendor pushing a cart that hovered inches above the ground. Tiny pastries steamed with jewel-colored vapors that dissipated into the twilight air.

Two vamps passed us, tasting each other's blood-infused gelato with childlike glee. "Nope," one of them said, licking her lips. "Guilty Pleasure over First Kiss. The O negative pairs better with raspberry."

Music drifted on the breeze from various establishments, mingling with dozens of languages.

Ezra was about to turn us into an arched alleyway between two fashionable bars when I heard my name called.

"Nasir!" I ran over to the van with a blood bank logo

on it that had pulled up to the curb. "We were so worried when we didn't hear back."

He'd accepted my shedim heritage without hesitation and healed me on our last mission together. Seeing my friend sitting in the driver's seat in good health took a weight off my mind.

"I got Darsh's first text but then there was nothing," he said, "and I couldn't reach anyone. I tried to return, but the rifts were unstable and I decided I'd be better off helping out here on the advisory board overseeing blood bank inventory."

"You made the right decision."

Nasir rolled up the window, motioning for me to follow him when he hopped out of the van. He led me into the back, keeping the door open until Ezra had joined us.

"We can speak freely in here," Nasir said, firmly shutting the door. The empty space was cut off from the front seats by a wall. "It's soundproofed against vampire hearing. Are the rumors true? Is earth as bad as they say?"

"The Luce tore through much of the vampire population," I said. "It got violent."

"I see," he said softly.

"It's better that you remain here until we've eradicated it."

His eyes went wide. "Silas and Darsh?"

"They're okay, but they're also much older than you." I didn't share what Ezra had done to keep them safe. He couldn't help everyone, and besides, the effects of his Prime boost were slowly fading.

Three and a half days…

"How are blood supplies?" Ezra asked.

"Babel can sustain itself for another month," Nasir answered. "We don't want that information getting out, so please don't share it. Aviva, how did you get here?"

"I brought her," Ezra said.

Nasir regarded him thoughtfully. "I'll stay here for now, but once the Luce is gone, will you come back and get me too? I'm not sure who ordered the rifts closed, but we don't know whether they can be restored or just reopened and be dangerously unstable like before."

Damn. The rift closure *was* an order, and there was only one vampire with the pull to make that happen.

"Once we stop the Luce," I said, "the rifts should be in good working order again." Even if the Brink was gone for good, passage to Babel would resume.

"If not," Ezra said, "we'll explore alternatives."

"Like the way we came?" Icy dread pooled through my limbs; I'd have to cross through the sea of shedim once more.

Ezra shook his head. "I'm fairly confident I can open a portal from here to the Hell. Not ideal, but not as bad as the alternative. Babel won't be cut off, and you won't be stranded, Nasir, I give you my word."

Nasir nodded, but didn't look hopeful.

I hugged him, then we all got out of the van.

After the press of people and sound, the secluded courtyard at Ezra's condo tower was a leafy haven.

Ezra led me through an Art Nouveau arch nestled between two wrought iron panels depicting intertwined dragons that were so delicately crafted, they seemed to breathe.

His building's door was hand-forged steel, treated to achieve a deep blue-black patina, as if the dragons' scales were rippling onto it. Inside, the foyer's ceiling soared high enough overhead that the tops of the olive trees in steel planters didn't brush the plaster. Their gnarled trunks were illuminated by ground lights that cast complex shadows on marble walls weathered to a soft patina.

I whistled slowly.

"You ain't seen nothin' yet," he drawled.

The elevator was just an elevator. I humphed, unimpressed, but secretly gave it props for its silent warp speed ascent to the penthouse on the sixteenth floor.

Not wanting to make Ezra too smug about his fancy apartment, I was prepared to show restraint when the elevator opened directly into his place, but I couldn't help the soft "oh" that fell from my lips.

A weathered Persian carpet with stories of its own to tell led into the main living area, where floor-to-ceiling windows showcased the city.

Ezra flicked on lights.

It was decorated exactly as expected by a powerful globe-trotting vampire with money and taste: a leather chesterfield sofa that looked super comfortable sat near a fireplace crafted from volcanic stone. On the mantel, a small bronze statue of a willowy goddess shared space with a delicate blown glass bowl, its surface still bearing the fingerprints of its maker.

Doors led off to other rooms; I'd be exploring those in due time.

In the meantime, I wandered over to the mantel and picked up the statue. I squinted at it. *Are those pointy ears?*

Taking a closer look revealed more tells of geekdom. D&D character sheets that grew more detailed and sophisticated were lovingly preserved in slender frames on the wall, and a huge collection of mint-condition *Star Wars* figurines was locked behind glass that was fitted with softly glowing spotlights.

"Are those original to the..." I scratched my head. "Third film? You know, the one with Han and the Wookiee?"

Ezra practically clutched imaginary pearls. "You mean, *A New Hope*? That's episode *four*. Haven't you seen it?"

"Yeah, the big battle scene put me to sleep."

Ezra made a faint noise of distress and swayed on his feet.

"I'm going to go out on a limb," I said, "and guess that you didn't entertain a lot of female visitors here."

"I wasn't bringing gross girls into this haven." He draped his suit jacket on a chair.

Oh, how times had changed. I tamped down a grin and traced a finger along my collar. "Want to fuck me on your Wookiee sheets, Zee?"

Chapter 27

"They were Artoo and Threepio," he said haughtily, "and you should be so lucky. You'll have to settle for my five-hundred-thread-count Egyptian cotton."

"In that case." I batted my lashes at him. "Take me to your bedroom."

My back hit the bedroom wall as Ezra's mouth found mine. He trailed kisses down my neck, his stubbled jaw scraped deliciously against my skin, and the heat of his body pressing against me. I ran my fingers along the muscles of his back, feeling them flex under my touch.

"What's going on in that beautiful mind?" He traced my lower lip with his thumb.

I couldn't help the smile that spread across my face. "Wondering how I got so lucky."

"Funny. I was thinking the same thing."

Twilight cast the room in shades of deep blue and pearl, like being underwater at sunset, a painting framed by windows draped in heavy charcoal silk.

His massive bed dominated the space, the dark wood carved with subtle, intricate patterns that caught shadows.

Crisp Egyptian cotton sheets in deep slate stretched across the mattress.

I slid my hands under his shirt, mapping the planes of his chest, committing every inch to memory.

"Mi cielo." The familiar teasing glint in Ezra's eyes had been replaced by something deeper, more vulnerable.

My heart thundered against my ribs.

"You're not just my sky," he said, "you're my North Star. When I'm lost in the dark, your brightness leads me back." The way he looked at me, like I was some rare astronomical phenomenon he'd discovered, made my stomach flutter.

I'd envisioned myself as different types of fire: a bomb, a spark, but Ezra looked at me and saw a star—a much bigger, more radiant blaze than anything I'd imagined myself as.

"Come here," I murmured, tugging him closer by his belt loops.

His breath hitched when I nipped at his lower lip. "Demanding, aren't we?"

"You love it." I grinned against his mouth.

"I love *you*."

My heartbeat careened, my fingers still hooked in his belt loops, and the taste of him on my lips. Was this simply post-battle feels or had he seized the moment since we couldn't be sure what tomorrow held?

He caught my gaze, his own so tender, but when the silence stretched out, it skipped away.

Say it back. I opened and closed my mouth, trying to get sound past my thick throat. The words were right there for the taking—had been there for so long, pressed against my ribs like a secret.

When Ezra looked back at me, it was with the careful gentleness of someone trying not to startle a wild animal. He unbuttoned his shirt.

Sexy time is a go. At last. My body was on board with that, even if my chest was hollow and I wanted to rewind time.

He shrugged out of his shirt.

I blinked stupidly at the masterpiece of cosmic art sprawled across his chest, an expanse of inky night sky dotted with delicate stars in familiar constellations. Dominating the scene, positioned deliberately over his heart, was a single star whose rays stretched longer, its light pulsing brightly over its celestial neighbors, as if it alone could pierce the deepest dark.

"That must have taken hours," I said. "How did you sit still for so long? Didn't you have to pee?"

Ezra frowned. "I etch my love for you on my skin and that's your takeaway?"

I flailed my hands. "How am I supposed to explain that seeing this makes me feel like I'm made of feathers and one half-hearted gust could blow me away?"

His frown deepened. "That sounds like something I'm doing to you. Like the thrall."

"No! We're not in that dynamic anymore, and what I'm feeling now is nothing like that. That was like a haze that came over me, but this is a mess."

"That bodes well," he said dryly.

"I feel vulnerable and alive. It's scary and wonderful and almost overwhelming but I feel it coming from you, too, and that makes it precious."

"Nope." He screwed up his face. "Still not quite getting what you mean."

I shoved him. "I love you so much, you idiot."

"Okay, I'm going to need to rephrase that grand declaration in the retelling. Maybe throw in some adjectives about my magnificence."

"Ezra?"

He cocked an eyebrow.

I pressed a soft kiss to his lips. "I love you with all my heart and soul."

He grinned and kissed the pulse fluttering under my jaw. "Was that so hard?"

I laughed.

He took his time undressing me, his gaze following each newly revealed inch of skin with such reverence that I had to fight the urge to cover myself.

I'd never felt so exposed, so completely seen by another person. With anyone else, this level of vulnerability would have sent me running. But with Ezra, I wanted to stay forever in this moment, suspended between heartbeats.

When he finally lay me back on the mattress, I couldn't stop touching him, running my hands through his dark curls, tracing the strong line of his jaw, mapping the constellations of those gorgeous stars on his chest. Each touch was like a confession, every kiss a promise.

He made slow, lazy spirals down my body with his lips.

I bunched the cool sheets in my fists.

Ezra sucked on one nipple.

I whimpered, threading my fingers through his soft curls and tugging him up.

His fangs scraped over my neck.

I moaned wantonly and hooked my leg around his waist, rubbing myself against his hard cock.

Ezra made a sound halfway between a hum and a growl. He pinned my legs between his knees, holding my hands in his above my head.

No matter how much I squirmed underneath him, I couldn't get relief, driven higher and hotter by his bruising kisses and the slow grind of his hips.

"Have mercy," I begged in a breathless voice.

"This isn't doing it for you?"

I tried to free my closed legs to get to my clit, but I was trapped. "No," I snarled.

"What about this?" He brushed his nose against mine.

"That was great, baby. I don't plan on replacing you with a battery-operated appliance at all."

He laughed and rolled onto his side. He also nudged my legs apart to stroke my clit, while claiming my mouth with kisses that blurred at the edges, melting into each other like watercolors in the rain.

I canted my hips, desperate to quench the fire burning me up. "Inside me."

Ezra stretched back, reaching for the bedside table, but I stopped him.

"No condom," I said. "I want to feel you. I'm clean if you are, and I'm on the pill."

His lips quirked. "Thank you for that rundown. I, too, am clean and would very much appreciate being inside you with no barriers between us."

"Asshole," I said, laughing. "Stop making my sincere feelings awkward."

He slid inside me, and I let out a breathy sigh. "Oh good," he said. "I was worried you'd keep laughing."

I patted his shoulder. "Your ego may remain intact."

We fell into a slow, perfect rhythm. His hands never stopped moving, stroking my hair, caressing my face, holding me like I might disappear if he let go. His whispered endearments made me shiver.

A bead of sweat trickled down my chest to my stomach, the two of us wrapped in the tangle of our heat.

I scratched my nails across his back.

Ezra thrust hard, and my orgasm tore through me. His body bucked, and with a hoarse cry, he came as well.

We remained intertwined, Ezra's head against my racing heart.

I idly played with his hair. "The earth moved."

"I know." He bucked his hips, cracking a smile. "I'm a sex god. Heap your praises upon me."

"No." I sat up. "The earth really mooo—" I grabbed him as a quake rocked the bed. His moody oil painting of a stormy sea crashed to the ground.

I shrieked, dropped to my knees, and crawled like an Olympic medal was at stake into the office next door, taking shelter under a wide desk. I was a Vancouverite; the safest places in these events had been drilled into us.

"Babel doesn't get earthquakes," Ezra called from the bedroom.

"Beg to differ!" My voice was high and pitchy.

At long last, the tremors stopped.

Ezra crouched down in front of me, holding out his hand. He now wore boxer shorts and slippers.

Damn, I'd never get tired of seeing that night sky inked on his chest, with the place of honor for that single star.

Still, I gave one last look at the nice solid desk before I let him pull me to my feet.

He carried me back to his bedroom, gave me a long T-shirt to sleep in along with my own pair of slippers, then we set his bedroom back to rights.

The room whispered of wealth without shouting it, of power held in careful reserve, and of a man who valued both aesthetics and order. I replaced the oil painting on the wall and straightened a stark black-and-white photograph of ancient ruins.

Ezra was in his custom closet with its cedar interior and smoky glass door, rehanging clothes.

I pushed the antique mahogany bedside tables back against the wall. Luckily the crystal carafe was empty, and neither it nor the sleep lamp had broken when they hit the plush carpet. I nodded in approval at the hardcover mystery book that had been on the bestseller lists last year. It was a good read.

"Almost done," Ezra said.

Minutes later, I was back in his arms. "Well, that was

exciting," I said. "Let's have less natural disasters next time."

"Agreed." He kissed me. When he pulled away, his eyes were mercurial. "I want to bite you."

"Saucy." I turned my head to give him access.

"Not your neck." He tapped his bare chest above his heart. "A more permanent mark. A blood bond." He blurted his words, his blush adorable.

Except…

I sat up and crossed my arms. "You flinched when I mentioned it, remember? Before we first thralled?"

He sat up as well and clasped my hands in his. "They're more precious than a wedding vow. Even if it had worked, it would have been a healing treatment with me unconscious, instead of letting me cherish the moment for the rest of my immortal life."

I met his eyes, my heart beating against my ribs at the seriousness of his voice. "Have you ever wanted to bond with anyone else?"

"Never."

"But you thought about it with me? Before now?"

"You have no idea how many times." His voice was rough. "What you'd taste like when we bonded, how your magic would feel around mine. It's a big decision, so ask me anything."

"Would you feed off me again or…"

"No. We feed off each other. I love you as my equal, and that's how I want to move forward."

I gnawed on my bottom lip. "You once told me blood bonds are a 'stronger together weaker apart' deal for our magic. Even the thrall was…a lot. You felt my emotions, and we couldn't be apart from each other. By the end it was like a noose. What if the blood bond is like that but worse?"

His eyes darted away and he rubbed a hand over his

head. "I may not have explained blood bonds properly back then."

"Excuse me?"

"In my defense, I was trying to get your consent to heal you after your car blew up. I didn't want to waste time on an irrelevant option, so I gave you the broad strokes version. There is zero chance we'll have the same kind of side effects as with a thrall. That was a power source, this is an emotional connection. I can't say whether our magic will be stronger because we aren't both vampires." He motioned between us. "But *we're* stronger together, because I'm yours and you're mine."

"And the weaker part? Specifically?"

"When one dies, it's curtains for both, my dear." His British accent was deliberately woefully bad, but I didn't smile.

I punched him. "I have an extended lifespan but nowhere as long as yours. I'm yours and you're mine is one thing, a suicide pact is quite another."

"Vampires have their own definition of romantic," he said. "Though, I'm not into those pacts either. I hate to thank Delacroix for anything," he grumbled, "but in this case, his genetics are a blessing. As far as I've been able to determine, that condition won't apply to us."

I leaned back against the headboard.

The weight of what he was offering settled over me. This wasn't a one-way magical connection or a suffocating tether. It was a permanent bond between lovers.

A choice made with clear eyes and full hearts between equals in a moment of calm and quiet.

Ezra rested his shoulder against mine. "Like I said, it's a big decision. Can we leave it as an option in the fut—"

"Yes."

"Yes, it's an option?"

I shot him a "don't be daft" look. "Ezra Cardoso, I

would very much like to blood bond with you and have this expression of our love on my skin."

"Way to make it awkward," he teased. "But wait. All kidding aside, I didn't ask properly. That was too clinical." He sat me on the bed then got down on one knee. "Aviva Jacquline Fleischer, will you do me the incredible honor of blood bonding with me?" His eyes gleamed with a mix of vulnerability and reverence that made my breath catch, and his hand trembled slightly as he held it out to me. This immortal vampire of unspeakable power was as nervous as any mortal man awaiting an answer that would change everything.

I squeezed his hand. "Yes, Ezra Aaron Cardoso, I will."

The mattress shifted as he sat down next to me and gently helped me out of my shirt. "Ready?"

I nodded, my feelings of being laid bare having nothing to do with being topless.

His fangs pierced the skin above my heart, and starbursts of pleasure exploded against my closed lids. His magic unfurled inside me like a night-blooming flower opening to moonlight.

Each pull of his mouth made me feel like he was replacing my blood with cosmic fire. All previous bites had been candle flames; this was the sun itself, rewriting me from the inside out and branding me as something gloriously, permanently his.

"Your turn," he said thickly around his fangs.

Resisting the urge to kiss my blood off his lips, I slashed my claws across his left biceps, under the tattoo in Spanish dedicated to me. The blood bond didn't require that we mark Ezra on his heart—and honestly, neither of us wanted to ruin his gorgeous new tattoo.

"Drink," Ezra said, his pupils blown wide.

For one endless moment, I couldn't tell where my powers ended and his began. We were one circuit, one current, one heartbeat. Then our magic separated again, but changed, each carrying an echo of the other that felt like coming home.

Our blood bond crystallized, settling into place with a nearly audible click. It was as delicate as frost but as unbreakable as diamond.

I compared the small purple mark over my heart that resembled a starburst to the identical one on Ezra's arm.

It was still tender to the touch, but he assured me that would be gone in a few minutes.

We curled up together under the covers.

"What are you thinking?" he said.

"Just marveling at how natural this feels. How right. You?"

"That you make me wish I could breathe so I could feel the air stolen from my lungs when I look at your beauty."

"Oh, you're good. For that I'd be willing to wear a gold bikini sometime."

His eyes went wide. "Was that a *Star Wars* reference?"

"Yes, Ezra. I *have* seen a bunch of them."

He did a silly little wiggle. "You're the perfect girlfriend."

"That's right." Yawning, I gingerly stroked the starburst under my T-shirt. "And it's a good thing, given I'm also nonrefundable."

"Honestly, I was making sure there were no takebacks on your part."

My boyfriend promised that he'd wake me with enough time to swing by the hospital to see Olivier before Operation Shut That Fucking Healing Magic Down.

Sleep claimed me with a smile on my face. Whatever came next, this moment was ours. Perfect and infinite as the stars themselves.

<h1 style="text-align:center">Chapter 28</h1>

Sadly, sleep turned into a short nap when the bed started rocking again for all the wrong reasons. Enough was enough. Coasting on adrenaline and a second wind I'd pay for later, I hurriedly dressed and made Ezra return me to Vancouver.

Any concerns about transiting through my father's yacht were immediately put to rest.

The once-vibrant gaming hall was frozen in mid-abandonment. Honey lights still glowed over the prickly moss carpet, but where peacocking patrons had once crowded, now only traces lingered. Dice lay scattered across green felt, a half-finished hand of cards sprawled face up on red velvet, and mah-jongg tiles remained lined up like tiny soldiers, waiting for a play that would never come.

Ezra did a slow circuit of the main room, crouching down to feel spots along the brushed steel wall. "Delacroix's magic is fading. He's pulled his power and I didn't feel it." He smiled at me. "The blood bond prevented any ill effects."

"I'm glad."

"Give me a sec to call my casino manager and make sure the same is true for my staff."

"Sure." I wandered over to the window.

The ship sat motionless in the water. Dawn was breaking over the ocean, the horizon line blurring as indigo darkness gave way to rose-gold light.

The Copper Hell had always offered its games of chance under cover of the night. Those faint rays of sunlight, more than anything, convinced me that its doors had been closed for good.

Ezra rejoined me. "Delacroix gave everyone ten minutes to clear out. My staff went to Babel."

"And my father and his buddies went for a hell of a Brimstone Breakfast Club meeting." I held up a fist. "We brunch at dawn!"

"With a frontal assault dessert," Ezra said. "The quakes? He made his move on the demon realm, and we felt the attack in Babel."

"Is it game over? Did he win?"

"Your guess is as good as mine," Ezra said.

My father would either be the most powerful demon alive—or he was dead. I didn't have the bandwidth to process either possibility.

We headed for the foyer.

"Will the yacht be visible now? Should I have Michael arrange for it to be towed to shore?" I said.

"I don't know, but you have bigger things to handle. I'll speak to her about it." He took in the casino one last time, finally free of a responsibility he never really wanted.

Ezra didn't look back when we left.

I SWUNG by Olivier's hospital bed before going to HQ.

He was asleep under a thin cotton blanket, humming

equipment monitoring his breathing, blood pressure, and heart rate. He looked as good as one could with a fully bandaged neck and scars that wouldn't all be visible to the naked eye.

Sachie was curled in a chair by his bed, her head bent awkwardly on her shoulder. Her sleep was marred by twitches and starts, but she was out of her seat, wild-eyed with a dagger in her hand before I'd made it two steps into the room.

I held up the bag with the world's best chicken soup and a couple of smoked meats on rye from the nearby Jewish deli like a shield. "I come in peace."

"Fuck." She sank back into the chair, rubbing her eyes with the back of her arm. "Sorry."

I placed the takeout on the rolling table and removed containers and aluminum-foil-wrapped sandwiches. "How many nurses have you terrified?"

She glanced around, motioning me to lean in. "None. They don't scare." She sounded intimidated and impressed. "But I'm on probation, so it's good you're the one I almost stabbed."

"Lucky me. How is he?"

"Came through surgery with flying colors, but he's being observed for risk of stroke." Sachie had almost lost her dad to a heart attack; she couldn't lose Olivier.

"He's a fighter." I held up a spoon and a sandwich. "Which first?"

"Is it matzah ball?"

"Chicken noodle." I shook the plastic utensil at her pouting face. "They were out, and this is better for Olivier."

"It'll probably be cold when he wakes up." She snatched the sandwich away from me and viciously tore off the foil.

"Uh-oh." I dragged another chair up to the bedside.

"Does someone need a Disney playlist to sing out all their feels?"

"Stabbing you is still on the table," she snarled. "I'll just do it at home where the nurses won't protest." She bit into the smoked meat with the ferocity of a lion tearing into a gazelle.

"It's easier to stab people than to feel like you're being stabbed when they're hurt, isn't it?"

"Shut up."

"When I was in the Brink facing that sentience for the test, you know what I was most scared of?"

My friend swallowed her bite of sandwich. "Obviously not what it would do to you, since this recollection is all about making a point that is going to annoy the shit out of me."

"Have you admitted how much you like him?" I said.

She glared at me but kept eating, which I took as permission to continue.

"What I was most scared of in the Brink wasn't what would happen to me," I said.

"I know. It was whether Ezra was free of Rukhsana's magic." She made a "get on with it" motion.

"No." I traced a pattern on the arm of the hospital chair. "It was the thought of him facing whatever came next alone."

Sachie stared at Olivier's sleeping form, the steady rise and fall of his chest beneath the thin blanket. "It's stupid," she said finally, her voice quiet enough that I had to lean in. "I didn't even want to like him. Everyone I've ever dated was easy to be with, and for all he's Mr. Chill Surfer, he's got a core of steel."

"Easy to be with, but also easy to walk away from. Not this guy." I nudged her shoulder gently.

She crumpled her sandwich wrapper and tossed it with perfect aim into the trash can. "What's your point? That I should confess my undying love while he's unconscious? Very romantic."

"My point is that being scared for someone else is different than being scared for yourself." I watched her fingers drum nervously against her thigh. "When it's you in danger, there's always something to fight, but when it's someone you care about… And I don't mean someone like me or your parents."

"There's nothing to stab," she finished, a reluctant smile tugging at her lips.

"Exactly." I handed her the container of soup. "Nothing to stab, nothing to punch. Just waiting and feeling all those feels. It's excruciating."

"I should have been there with him."

"You had your hands full. Olivier is in a dangerous profession, even without vamps. You like him because he's a good cop, and you've got to trust him to take care of himself."

She rested the container in her lap. "You're dating a Prime, an invincible vampire. Olivier doesn't even have magic. When he volunteered to be on the Toothpick Sentry? I wanted to tape him into bubble wrap and lock him in our apartment."

"But you didn't. Because it wouldn't be fair to him. And you'd hate him for trying to protect you that way."

"*You* chose to be enthralled to Ezra to wake him up and heal him."

"Yeah, and you saw how well that worked out." I shook my head. "Actually, you didn't see the half of it. It's one thing to have someone's back, but trust me, it's quite another to force your protection on them. For them and you. If I'd known what I know now, well, I would have waited longer before considering it as an option." I shrugged. "And so it comes back to waiting and trusting."

Sachie reached out tentatively, her fingers hovering over

Olivier's hand before she gently covered it with her own. "Tell anyone we discussed feelings," she murmured, "and I really will stab you."

"Your secret's safe with me."

Olivier's fingers twitched slightly beneath Sachie's.

I nodded at the movement. "Something tells me Olivier already knows."

"I'm going to ask my parents to come down." She mustered up a faint smile. "They haven't met him yet."

It sucked so hard that it had taken Olivier being wounded to be what broke that wall between the three of them and restored their loving relationship, but so long as he came out of this with flying colors, it was worth it.

"That's a great idea. Have Reina bake him some muffins. I swear by their healing properties." I stood up, dusting off my lap. "Well, I've fed you and dazzled you with genius advice. My work here is done. I'm off to stop the Luce."

"Take bubble wrap."

I grinned.

She shook a fist at me. "Die at the hands of that fucking magic and your funeral playlist will consist of novelty dances like the Macarena and the Chicken Song. I'll visit your grave every day with it on repeat."

I kissed the top of her head. "Love you too, Sach."

I made it back to HQ on time, catching snatches of conversations from operatives en route to the conference room where my task force was checking equipment.

Apparently, most of the vampire population in the Greater Vancouver area were either dead or had fled for parts unknown. I took mental note of who appeared relieved or outright glad about that.

Everyone, though, was horrified about the Hollow Tree in Stanley Park, one of Vancouver's most famous attractions. The massive ancient red cedar stump had been healed into a mockery of life. The empty core, a cathedral-like space where generations of us had taken photos, had been filled in with perfect, sterile wood, as if the tree was trying to regrow a thousand years in moments. Its weathered exterior with all the furrowed character worn into its bark over centuries had been smoothed out, stripped of every scar and story.

I replied to the text from Ezra telling me he was with Michael and had waved at Joe, Eduardo, and Marilyn through the conference room glass when Orly messaged me.

Trauma Drama Extravaganza! I'm thinking pitchfork-shaped pinatas, thematic cocktails. Dress code formal, mood unhinged. It's all underway. Tell me when the Luce has been stopped.

I laughed and typed *Sounds good.*

She hearted my reply then added: *It feels shallow wanting something frivolous to cling to.*

Orly was a multilingual economist, but even if she was Elle Woods pre-Harvard transformation (*Legally Blonde* was such a good movie), this party was her self-care, and there was no shame in whatever form that took.

It's not frivolous at all. 🤍

I pushed inside the conference room, which was an explosion of equipment we were bringing to the former rift site here in Vancouver.

The crowning glory was a photo of my smirking face projected on the screen we used for video conferencing.

Text on the picture read: *I'm his girlfriend and you're not.*

I curtsied to my team's applause.

"Want to see the rest of the memes I made?" Gemma cackled, rubbing her hands together.

"Let me think about it," I said, scratching my cheek with my middle finger. "Seriously though, what's the deal? This isn't new gossip."

"Google your boyfriend, Fleischer," Gemma said, "but hurry up. We have to save the world in ten minutes."

Chapter 29

Ezra Cardoso had broken the internet with a single photo of him silhouetted against a collapsing condo tower engulfed in flames. He carried a man over each shoulder, and in his arms, he held a curly-haired toddler hugging a beagle puppy.

It was accompanied by such pithy headlines as: "Bloodsucker Turns Lifesaver!" and "Fangs and Flames: Vampire's Epic Rescue Captivates World!"

Then there was the one that made me do a double take and click the link: "Prime Playboy... Crimson Prince... Maccabee?"

The Authority had claimed him as their own.

"I hear his fan club website crashed. They had to close new memberships. Think you can get me in?" Joe teased, packing wound cables into a Rubbermaid. "I want to resell it to the highest bidder."

"I can't believe the Authority claimed him." I joined Eduardo in checking the comms units.

"They had to." Marilyn stacked the monitors on a dolly. "The second that photo hit the airwaves, the mayor of

Toronto was all over the news hailing Ezra as a hero. He was followed by Ontario's premier."

"That was *after* the footage of Ezra on the front lines, personally thanking Trad and Eishei Kodesh firefighters and first responders for their fight against the Luce," Gemma said. "I mean, he was hot before, but now?" She fanned herself.

Ezra's fan club was legion enough, but this had kicked his recognition into the mega-mainstream. I pushed away the sinking feeling at what this might mean for me.

"Even those alt-right wankers have shut up about legislating EKs," Eduardo said. "It was a smart move on Cardoso's part, framing all humans as in this together."

"Not just humans." Joe tossed battery packs into another Rubbermaid. "There are photos of him with the Toronto Spook Squad, gazing sadly at fallen vampires. From what I've read, a lot of people see vampires as victims, with the Luce as the only real villain."

"Not Maccabees?" I said. "Even after Natán's comments?"

"There are definitely some haters," Gemma said, "but the Ezracurricular president jumped into the conversation, getting the club's members to make all kinds of posts and memes about the hero Prime and his Eishei Kodesh girlfriend who also happens to be a Maccabee." She powered down her laptop. "I set them straight about what a cow you are."

I chucked a pen at her.

"Human or vampire, everyone who fought to keep earth safe during the Endless Night is considered a hero," Marilyn said.

"Oh good," I said faintly. "They gave it a catchy name."

She winked at me. "I vote we leverage our heroic service to get raises."

We moved the equipment downstairs into a transport

van, my team debating what kind of pay upgrade would be applicable. I enjoyed a quiet appreciation at how Ezra had managed to unite not only the magic and non-magic human population, but vampires as well.

No wonder the Authority rushed to claim him as one of their own.

The hypocrites.

It took two hours to get every unit wired up and in communication with the others at the rift sites. We were spread out across multiple continents and cell coverage wasn't always consistent on our designated battlefields.

The underwater rift in Turkey was deemed a no go; it was too complicated to navigate water pressure and currents on top of everything.

On top of that, we had only approximate locations of where the rifts had been. The laundromat had been razed and cleared away here in Vancouver, and while we could figure out more or less where the rift once existed in the empty parking lot, we couldn't afford to miss.

At least our rift had been large, which gave us more room for error, but some of them were quite small and called for far more precision in terms of where to direct our magic backburn.

Thanks to my shedim magic, I was able to illuminate traces of them, but it was damned hard to do via a video hookup.

The second the rift coordinates were locked down, other Blue Flames stepped in to act like orchestra conductors, directing Orange Flames to adjust temperature and lower humidity as necessary, but we immediately got bogged down.

Here in Vancouver, unexpected coastal fog rolled in. Mumbai was dealing with unseasonable rain, Singapore was boggy with humidity, and even Adelaide in Australia, generally reliable for low humidity, had unusual weather patterns. It wasn't a rift location, but our backfire had to work in all corners of the globe, so any humid hotspots were of concern.

Our problems dominoed from there.

Yellow Flames had mapped a series of secondary channels. Their job was to connect everything and create a worldwide net for the Reds to pour their magic into.

Except when those linked up, our problems compounded because the channels kept collapsing, dragging the main pathways with them.

Orange Flames attempted to adjust the temperature gradients to help stabilize these pathways, but they dissipated too quickly.

Meantime, Monserrat and her team in Madrid found their temperature modifications dispersing almost as soon as they were established.

In the wake of all that, the physical fire magic of the Red Flames, meant to provide the raw devouring power against the Luce, became dangerously unpredictable.

What should have been controlled bursts of consuming flame contained within magic pathways instead flickered erratically, threatening to spread beyond their intended paths. The Red Flames had to pull back, unable to risk actual fires breaking out across multiple continents.

The fog in Vancouver turned to freezing rain, pelting down on us. We scrambled into the rain gear that Gemma had packed.

I zipped up my jacket with shaking fingers, restraining my immediate urge to call Darsh or Silas and see if with this high humidity, the Luce's effects had gone into overdrive on them again.

My field notebook, despite its waterproof pages, got so wet that the ink ran in places. I'd made copious notes about when and why our magic backburn veered off course and had been chiming in with minute corrections to keep our magic focused, but trying to see them on the monitors, which kept fogging up with condensation was challenging.

We kept morale up by assuring ourselves that some of the rift sites maintained optimal conditions, but with wonky air pressure causing the magic to deviate from our pathways or fizzle out altogether in a number of places, it was hard to remain hopeful.

And these were just the external problems. There were internal ones as well.

"Contact with the Luce feels like being smothered by pure spring water," Joe said with a troubled look.

Marilyn had to stop her red flame attack and sit down, claiming vertigo. "My sense of harmful versus helpful magic is getting distorted," she said. "It's messing up my ability to maintain an offensive push without annihilating our teammates or the environment."

Cue another hour of arguing with everyone over the comms about how to factor this complication in, all against the constant patter of raindrops on buildings now empty of vampire inhabitants. It became white noise, occasionally interrupted by the splash of someone stepping in a puddle or the squeak of wet gear.

Some humans had remained in these once-popular neighborhoods, but we felt their presence as eyes peering out from drawn curtains or the occasional clang of a gate locked tight in front of a store.

We took a break to refuel, those of us in Vancouver huddling in the covered doorway of a locked-up hair salon sucking back strong black coffee and turkey subs.

We weren't beating back the Luce, just wearing ourselves down, burning out into synesthetic overload.

Some Reds suffered self-immolation and had to be doused with the special fire extinguishers. Orange Eishei Kodesh experienced rapid and dangerous levels of hypothermia. We pulled the Yellows before they went into full-on shutdowns of their immune systems.

Luckily, we'd had the foresight to bring a healer along with each unit, but after all that, the Blue Flames monitoring the Luce reported that it barely flickered.

Our frustrations boiled over, the lines of communication devolving into shouting matches.

Even with high-end rain gear, water found its way in, trickling down my neck despite the hood, and seeping through the seams of my jacket. My hands were pruned and trembling inside my wet gloves, and my supposedly waterproof boots had given up hours ago, leaving my socks to squelch with every step.

Ha-joon finally called an end to our misery. Despite our anger and frustration, no one protested too much, and I doubted I was the only one who felt relief, even though we'd failed.

"It's only Thursday," I said to everyone on the comms. "We can try again."

"Provided we have better conditions," one of the operatives stationed at the North Yorkshire Moor rift site said.

"Monserrat? Ha-joon?" I said. "What's it looking like between now and Saturday?"

They moved onto a private back channel to discuss it.

Gemma, Joe, Eduardo, Marilyn, and I kept our comms on but used the time to pack up and scramble back into the van with the heat cranked.

"We have a window to launch the backburn in thirty-two hours," Monserrat finally announced.

Saturday morning. The day the Luce would be at its most potent.

We were all professionals and used to working in adverse conditions. We'd take this as a dress rehearsal—albeit a disastrous one—and learn from the valuable data we collected.

I glanced at the Japanese maples in cedar planter boxes lining the sidewalk whose naturally twisted trunks had been straightened like drawn wire.

We'd been given a second chance.

There wouldn't be a third.

Now, however, we cared about getting warm and fed. Marilyn and Joe almost came to blows over a package of hot chocolate back at HQ, while Gemma's growl when I reached for the last prepackaged ramen noodle bowl was scarier than any sound Cherry had ever made.

I emailed everyone on the global task force a draft of the memo with the request for more operatives to join us when we tried again, then I removed myself to a conference room, so I didn't stab anyone before my hanger was vanquished.

I was stuffing chips in my mouth when Ezra rapped on the door and slipped inside. "Vamps are flammable," I said through a mouthful of crunchy nacho flavoring.

"You saw the photo of the burning building." He reached for a chip, but I slapped his hand away.

"You could have died. Also, you don't even eat, so back off my stash."

"Those people didn't have the luxury of time, Avi, and vampires are fast. Me more than any of them."

"I know." I tipped the plastic bag to my mouth and hoovered up the crumbs. "I'm proud of you. It's just been a shitty day." I sighed. "Did you speak to Silas? How's he handling Rylan's death?"

"Not great, but he threatened to drop a car on me if I phoned him again."

Louis poked his head in the doorway, his expression pinched tight. "Michael wants you in her office."

I shot to my feet. "What's happened?"

It was after midnight, neither of them should have still been here.

"One of the Authority has come to town to talk to you."

He couldn't tell me anything other than it wasn't Dmitri Koslov, but Zhengyu Lin, our Taiwanese representative.

I was tired and my shirt was covered in chip dust. I looked at Ezra in silent entreaty to accompany me.

Louis held up a hand. "Just you."

The elevator ride to Michael's office was endless; each soft chime marked another floor passing, another half-dozen discarded possibilities as to why Zhengyu had come.

My hands were damp against my thighs as I smoothed my trousers down for the third time, fighting the urge to check my collar in the highly polished panel with all the buttons. True, he'd been an ally to me in the past, but I had very little intel on the man other than he was a Real Madrid fan.

When the doors finally opened to the executive level with its sweeping views of the city at night, my heart was pounding so hard I was sure Ezra could hear it, three floors down.

Louis escorted me into Michael's office, then left.

Zhengyu stood up and shook my hand.

My mother gestured for me to take a seat with an almost imperceptible shrug. He hadn't enlightened her on the reason either?

I clenched my teeth, catching myself only when the ache spread down my neck and into my shoulders.

"There's been a lot of suffering," he said, sitting down and rubbing his knee in a gesture reminiscent of Delacroix. "But the Maccabees, no, all Eishei Kodesh, all Holy Fire People, have come out of the darkness stronger than ever. The pressure to rescind legislature against our community is at an all-time high."

"You can thank Ezra for some of that," I said.

"And we will."

Michael clicked her Montblanc pen. "This is all well and good, Zhengyu, but what about moving forward? The threats Maccabees face haven't all been from the outside."

"That's part of why I'm here. We're reaching out personally to our directors to assure them that the crisis affecting our current Authority Council has resolved itself."

Translation: Dmitri wasn't pulling the strings anymore because Eishei Kodesh—and Maccabees—were no longer on the chopping block.

That also didn't explain why I was here. But Michael spoke up before I could ask.

"I'm not talking about whatever power move Dmitri tried to pull," Michael said. "I'm talking about systemic issues. Starting with Operation Inferno."

I clasped my hands tightly in my lap so I didn't throw out a fist pump or seven. Michael's meteoric rise to director was based on her dismantling massive corruption in the Vancouver chapter, but I'd been too young to witness it firsthand.

Seeing her do that exact thing now was thrilling.

Zhengyu, however, didn't miss a beat after her accusation. "A dark chapter that I've only just learned of. With the exception of Birgitte, no council member was part of that operation. And Michael," he rebuked her gently, "you shouldn't be aware of that either. It's above your clearance level."

She leaned forward. "Spare me the bullshit. Did you really expect I wouldn't eventually root this out? It's what I do."

He sighed. "That's the other reason I've come. I think very highly of you and Aviva. You've been instrumental in many positive shifts and strides forward in our organization."

There was a "but" coming if I ever heard it.

"But your unique nature should have been disclosed to us."

"There wasn't a box to tick for being a half shedim on my application form," I said evenly.

"It should have been disclosed much farther back than that," he said. "However, the Authority has forgiven your oversight, Michael, as well as pardoned you for determining for yourself what evacuation would and would not entail for your chapter."

Michael widened her eyes. "You *didn't* want them all killed? Shit. I wish I'd understood that before they attacked us at Seaside."

A muscle ticked in Zhengyu's jaw. "Regardless, we've forgiven all that."

Michael turned her monitor around. "I don't need the Authority's forgiveness when I've secured signatures from every single director to take over Pederson's seat."

I sat back, enjoying the fuck out of this plot twist. This was so much better than how I'd imagined this meeting would go.

"Now," she continued, "my first responsible act as a council member should be to open all the sealed files on Operation Inferno. You know how I love to trace these things back to their source. I intend to find out who knew what and if there's a statute of limitations on these crimes."

Zhengyu sat back with his arms crossed. "The only council member involved was Birgitte."

"So you said." Michael narrowed her eyes like a shark scenting blood. "But are you positive there's nothing countermanding your plausible deniability? No secret minutes years later discussing it? Not even after Birgitte learned Natán had put a hit on her?" She clicked her pen again. "Maccabees impregnated women with shedim sperm." Her voice dripped with ice. "Women like Eva Cardoso. An operative. *My friend.*"

What a baller.

And I was so proud of Ezra for sharing his quest to find answers with the director. Then again, maybe he simply wanted *his* mom's old friend to know the truth.

"What do you want?" Zhengyu said wearily.

"The resignation of the entire current council. I'm still going to bring all this to light, but I'll make sure no one goes to Sector A."

The older man chuckled softly. "I warned them you'd do this. Michael Fleischer, the great corruption crusader, wouldn't let this stand. Should we agree, there will be no consequences whatsoever for any of us, and in addition, Aviva will do something in return."

"Yeah?" I said. "What's that?"

"Kill Natán Cardoso."

Chapter 30

Killing my boyfriend's father was an unacceptable follow-up gesture to *I love you.*

"Absolutely not and you can't force me."

"Does it help to know that Natán has been working with alt-right politicians, providing funding for their campaigns and promising to use his power to install them as heads of government? They'll be his puppets," Zhengyu said contemptuously.

"So stop him. But not with me."

"We can shape the narrative for your shedim reveal to the population at large. For all half shedim moving forward." The smile the other Maccabee gave Michael was the picture of a kindly old gentleman. What a snake. "You did want to discuss moving forward, after all."

I slammed my hand on the armrest. "Infernals were fine to create when you needed lab rats, right? We're just not people to you."

"I think you're a wonderful operative." There wasn't a trace of guile in Zhengyu's expression.

"Then why didn't you protect us? You tripped over yourselves to claim Ezra, *Natán's* son, but me, the operative who *didn't* leave you high and dry? The person who's faithfully served you for years somehow isn't worthy of that same regard?"

"Vampires are liked and accepted by much of the world. Infernals are not. We could have done better in that regard but…" Zhengyu shook his head. "All we can do is make amends now."

"In exchange for murdering my probable father-in-law. That seems reasonable." I shot Michael a "help me" look.

"This is despicable," Michael said. "You want Natán gone for good, no surprise there, but to use Aviva of all people?"

"Security around him is insane. She can get close to him, and with her shedim abilities, he'll never see her coming."

"You know what I am, he does too." I shook my head so hard I got dizzy. Though maybe that was the sheer horror of what they were suggesting. "Do what you want. I always knew I'd be taking my chances when I came out about what I was."

"Maccabees have been quite accepting," Michael said. "Who's to say the public won't be the same?"

"They might." Zhengyu nodded. "Aviva's record speaks for itself, and I'd love to hail her as the hero who found a way to stop the Luce. It would be a shame if it got out that infernals were responsible for the Luce getting loose to wreak such devastation on the world in the first place."

I clenched my fists. "The murder victims who were drained of their blood?!"

He met my eyes. "Not them."

Check and mate.

Michael slammed her hand on the desk. "If you dare spread that dangerous lie—"

Zhengyu waved a hand. "The bottom line is that Aviva *is* an operative, and she's been tasked with an important mission." Not once did he lose his genial demeanor. "It's as you said, Michael. We failed to properly support our vampire operatives during this crisis, and as for Eva Cardoso…"

He looked exhausted but I refused to give in to sympathy.

"We let her down in the worst way possible," he said. "I won't let that happen again. But if Aviva is no longer a Maccabee, well, I don't have that same responsibility toward her." He stood up. "I'm flying back to Taiwan tonight. I expect your answer—or your ring—by then."

I glared at the quiet click of the door. "I have to find Ezra."

"Aviva."

I froze halfway out of the chair because Mom's eyes were blurry.

She stared at her Maccabee ring for a long moment, her brows crinkled together, and her lips pressed in a tight line. "I didn't know about Operation Inferno. Not even with my clearance."

"I never thought you did."

She sighed heavily. "What a tangled web. Eva's death, Birgitte a broken husk, even Natán… He was one of our best."

It reassured me that the shedim-breeding experiments weren't worth commenting on.

Michael shook her head. "Poor Ezra. I hope he's found peace."

"I think he has." But if he hadn't, we had the rest of our lives for me to comfort him and build new, happier memories together, ones that would eventually ease the sting and allow him to remember his mother without pain.

Provided I didn't murder his dad first. Fuck my life.

EZRA LAUGHED for so long and for so hard after we returned to my condo and I told him what I'd been ordered to do and why, that I worried I'd irrevocably broken him.

"I've got a plan," I said, scooping up the last of the pad Thai.

"Kill him and dance on his grave?"

"*No.*"

He nodded. "Right. I should get the honors."

Apparently, my boyfriend was nowhere near finding peace yet.

"Still no." I forked a prawn. "The Maccabees want him out of the picture so he can't pull strings anymore and affect world politics and attitudes toward their power base. Natán doesn't need to actually be dead for that to happen."

"He's not going to quietly retire. Not that the Maccabees would trust it if he did."

"Right. That's why we're going to convince him to fake his death."

Ezra started his unhinged laughter again.

I snapped my Coke can open in front of his face, startling him and sending fizz up his nose. I'd lost track of how long it had been since I had a proper rest and was more caffeine than blood at this point. "It's a fun plan. You get to blackmail him."

The laughter stopped.

Ezra leaned in, his eyes narrowed. "Continue."

"He loved Eva."

"And yet he used her death as a sympathy card."

"Yeah, your father is a manipulative snake, but his reaction to losing her wasn't fake. I spoke to Michael, and she called some old friends. Do you remember him disappearing for a couple of weeks?"

"I was five, so no."

"He'd left you with your grandmother, who was panicking because she couldn't get hold of him. Some of his friends in Caracas tracked him down." I took Ezra's hand. "He was in a hotel, starved of blood, and trying to die because of what he'd done and how he'd lost her. He didn't want to come back and face you."

"We're going to threaten to publicly reveal that weak moment to make him permanently disappear?" Ezra shook his head. "That might have worked at the time, but it's been too many years."

"'Blackmail' may have been the wrong word," I conceded. "It's more of a trade. Your forgiveness for his fake death."

I braced myself for more laughter.

His icy "no" sliced through the air like a blade.

"That's your right," I said. "Luckily, I have a plan B. I'm confident I can appease the Authority so long as Natán cuts all those nutbar politicians loose, steps down as head of his Mafia, and agrees to stay in Babel."

Ezra shot me a dubious look.

"Appease them provided Michael gets the other directors to agree with that course of action. We don't hit optimum conditions for dealing with the Luce for another twenty-five hours, and I have until tonight to tell Zhengyu what I've decided."

I'd notified the task force that I was being sent on a side job and would touch base as soon as possible. Final adjustments would have to be hashed out without me.

"That's plenty of time to fly to Caracas, meet with Natán, and get back." I batted my lashes at Ezra. "Be a doll and charter me a plane?"

Portaling was faster but I had to sleep.

Ezra came with me, explaining once we were onboard that we weren't going to Caracas but the island of Margarita off Venezuela's north coast.

Somebody had been keeping tabs on his father.

Within two minutes of fastening my seat belt, it was

clear my boyfriend had no desire to talk, lost to a broody expression and whatever was going on in his head.

That was fine by me. As soon as we hit altitude, I crashed out on one of the sofas, wearing an eye mask, ear plugs, and with a soft blanket pulled up to my nose.

The flight was almost nine hours long, and I slept for every blessed second of it. I even napped in the limo to the luxury villa that Natán had owned for many years, preferring sleep over the view as we wound along dizzying curves up a mountain.

Okay, yes, I may have cracked an eye open now and again for a glimpse of the passing scenery, but the Luce had hit this island as well, and depressed, I quickly closed them again.

The limo driver let us out at the gate of a high white stone fence.

I clocked several security cameras as Ezra punched in the code. After some back-and-forth we'd agreed that it was best not to give Natán a heads-up about our visit, but no one was on hand to challenge our entry.

"Shouldn't there be guards?" I said.

"Yeah. We should have passed a half dozen on the last approach alone, and I don't sense anyone around."

It was early afternoon, but even if vamps who'd been Eishei Kodesh in life couldn't hack the sun's tropical rays, surely Natán would employ top-notch human security?

I glanced up at one of the cameras. "Are you sure Natán is even here?"

The gate swung open, beckoning us to enter, but without a formal invitation, how we'd be received was anyone's guess.

"I thought he was," Ezra said doubtfully.

Sighing, I followed him up the drive, which swung sharply to the left, preventing any curious passersby from seeing the villa.

The once-tall stately palms lining either side of the road had lost their fronds. Mangos the size of footballs had plummeted off trees, their exploded skins revealing waxy insides swarmed by ants.

The villa was an unremarkable two-level home with red terracotta roof tiles and tinted windows. Then Ezra led me around back, and I gasped.

Tinted windows showcased soaring twenty-foot ceilings and an airy interior with impressive artwork on the walls. Beyond the outdoor kitchen and shaded dining area tiled in lush blue and white was an infinity edge pool overlooking a mountain-to-ocean panorama.

It would have been breathtaking were it not for the effects of the Luce. There was a strained hush over the property, no birdcalls, not even the buzz of mosquitos. Even the breeze limped along like the last strained whisper of a dying patient.

Ezra's jaw hardened. He hurried to the kitchen door and punched in another code. "He's here," he said, stepping inside.

It took a moment for my eyes to adjust to the cool darkness, by which point my boyfriend was gone.

I followed the murmur of Spanish through the living room, up the grand staircase. There were no lights on, and what I'd taken through the windows as an all-white furniture palate was actually draped sheets.

The Spanish was replaced by a hacking cough.

"You find this funny?" Ezra charged.

I backtracked down a different corridor toward his voice.

"It's darkly amusing, yes," Natán rasped in his Spanish-accented English. "To think you fell in love with the same thing that Eva killed herself over."

Oh no he didn't. Natán and I were about to have a reckoning.

Chapter 31

"Aviva is not a *thing*," Ezra snarled from inside the room. "And Mamá killed herself because of you."

"Don't eavesdrop, Aviva," Natán said. "Michael raised you better than that."

I steeled my shoulders and joined them.

The two walls of the cozy sitting room that weren't glass were made of warm honey-colored stone, complementing rich hardwood floors. A pair of deep-seated linen armchairs faced a low-profile sofa in a textured ocean-blue fabric, and a striking teak coffee table sat atop a handwoven rug in muted geometric patterns.

With the vintage rattan bar cart and built-in bookshelves, the room was equally ideal for a cocktail with friends or curling up alone.

The one discordant note was the hospital bed angled for its languishing patient to gaze out the tinted windows.

Natán wasn't a shadow of himself, he was painfully solid. The Luce had made the vampire so hyperreal, it was as if every atom in him had been polished to an unbearable shine.

He lay against silk pillows like a Renaissance painting.

His skin gleamed like burnished metal, each eyelash and pore captured with a vividness that crossed into the grotesque. His eyes had darkened from their cornflower blue to a shifting mercurial color that mirrored the wildness of Ezra's eyes. They stood out like burning coals under his plain black cloth kippah and hair that had also darkened.

The resemblance to Ezra was a physical blow. It was like stumbling across my boyfriend's body laid out for a funereal viewing.

My heart screamed at the sight of those familiar features rendered into this ghastly doppelganger.

I tore my gaze away, seeking Ezra like a lifeline.

He was pouring himself a drink from a bloodred concoction in the decanter. He took the crystal glass to one of the armchairs, angling the seat to stare directly at his father.

"Are you just going to sit here and watch me die?" Natán said.

"Yes," Ezra replied in a gruff voice. "I want to make sure you don't weasel out of it."

His father snorted softly, the corners of his mouth lifting in a brittle smirk.

I took the chair next to Ezra. "When did this happen?"

"Right after my announcement about the Vampire Care Initiative." Natán's blue eyes tracked me with a terrible smoothness, like polished glass spheres rolling in their sockets.

I suppressed a shiver. "You were on TV after that, including yesterday. You looked fine."

"Deepfake technology is a marvelous thing."

"I bet the NDA on that job was deadly," Ezra said wryly.

His father laughed, the sound twisting into a cough. He covered his mouth with his arm, but it fell immediately back to his side, as if his flesh was too heavy to hold up.

I'd spent the Endless Night surrounded by Luce-affected vamps. Hell, I'd witnessed its effects on Darsh and Silas days ago, and yet I struggled with the idea that Natán Cardoso could be so easily felled.

Given how Ezra's hands trembled as he drained his glass and went for round two, he wasn't merely struggling—the reality of his father's mortality was tearing him apart.

Natán jerked his chin at me, then sagged against his pillows like even that tiny gesture was all-consuming. "Did you come to kill me?"

"Is that why you pulled all your guards?" I said. "Hoping I'd put you out of your misery?" I looked around the room. "Is there a final last deepfake message to go out after your death about how if people are viewing it, it means the Maccabees murdered you?"

Natán gave me a lopsided smile. "That one isn't a deep-fake. I made it ages ago as an insurance policy, but no, I haven't deployed it yet."

"You will," Ezra scoffed. "You want your revenge even if it's from beyond the grave."

I sat in the tense silence twisting my hands painfully, darting glances between my boyfriend, who was committed to getting drunk on a Prime's metabolism, and his father watching him impassively.

"You and Ezra met once when you were about two and he was four," Natán said. "You ran after him, chattering nonstop about a stuffed panda you wouldn't let go of."

My face lit up. That toy was my best friend, carried with me and lovingly repaired time and time again by Michael until he was more replacement parts than original toy. "Fangsley."

Ezra almost dropped his glass. "Fangsley was my stuffed lion."

"Sí." Natán nodded. "Aviva called her panda 'Panda' but you told her it was a stupid name."

Ezra sat down next to me.

I nudged his leg. "That tracks."

"Then you presented your lion, and she decided to call her doll Fangsley too. Coño, the fits you both pitched. Ezra screaming it was his name and Aviva screaming back 'Mine!'"

Ezra nudged my leg back. "That tracks."

I leaned forward, my arms braced on my thighs. "What happened?"

"We bribed you both with the *Jungle Book* cartoon, went into the kitchen, and drank heavily."

"I loved that movie," my boyfriend and I said in unison.

"You used to sneak up on me," Ezra said to his dad, "and recite Kaa's lines about finding a delicious man cub."

Maybe between the two of them it was a cherished memory, but to me it just sounded unbelievably creepy.

"You remember." Natán tried to sit up but barely lifted his head off the pillow before falling back against it. "You'd laugh and laugh and then push me away just like Mowgli did."

Ezra wiped the wistful look off his face in favor of a cold mask.

"I appreciate you sharing that memory with us," I told Natán, "but I'm still not going to kill you."

"I'm dead from the waist down," he said conversationally. "No hope of recovery, and I'm not looking forward to the Luce slowly claiming the rest of me as it crawls up my body. How long will I remain aware? Weeks? Days? I want to be put out of my misery."

"We can't always get what we want," Ezra said.

"What do *you* want, papito?"

Ezra blinked, then shook his head. "It's a little late to be asking me that now."

"To lead the Kosher Nostra?" Natán pressed.

"Not in any reality whatsoever," his son answered.

"Good, because I sold it to a colleague, with the main condition that my Maccabee son, that traitor, was to have no part of it."

I narrowed my eyes. All of his antagonism, his every play, was a giant fake out? This wasn't about revenge? It was about atonement?

Natán's laughter at the shock on our faces turned into a hacking cough.

I poured him a glass of water and helped him sip it. "When did you broker those deals with the whack job politicians? Before you fell ill or after? Did you ever intend to follow through with your promises to set up these puppet governments or was all of it a ploy to have the Authority send someone in?"

"You really do remind me of your mother," Natán said. "Sharp as a tack."

"The reasons don't matter," Ezra said. "All the things you've put into motion against the Maccabees won't miraculously disappear when you're dead. When the public and governments turn on them and they're dismantled, the world will be fucked. I have no great love of the Maccabees anymore, but we need them."

"The world will flock to their side as soon as they stop the Luce. And if they don't..." Natán gazed out the window for a long moment. "It won't matter for long."

I flinched at that cold, hard truth.

"You're lying," Ezra said. "This isn't about protecting me for the first time in your life."

"It was about revenge at first, but..." Natán touched his kippah, his hand immediately falling away. "Dying changes you."

"Riiight." Ezra had never sounded so bitter. "In the face of your impending mortality, you sought to better yourself before you met God."

"Before I met your mother again," Natán said quietly.

"*No.*" Ezra slashed his hand through the air, his voice cracking.

Natán studied his son for a moment then turned to me. "Ezra will inherit a lot of money. He'll say he doesn't want it, but you take it. For your children. Education is expensive these days."

"I'm not killing you," I said through gritted teeth.

"Use the stake I commissioned. It's in the desk drawer. Cost me a fortune. You can keep it. Tell your niño or niña that it came from their abuelo."

"What a gift," I scoffed. "The hypothetical half-vamp babies can play with a stake."

"Half-Prime. They'll be fine. It's next to the drive with the final recording on it. Take that too." A corner of Natán's mouth lifted in the ghost of a smile. "Tell Michael that I didn't always have to have the last word."

Natán seemed indomitable—Ezra's personal villain who'd also become mine, much like Delacroix had become Ezra's. Our fathers' actions had set our mothers on courses that irrevocably impacted our lives: Eva and her suicide, and Michael's gross overprotection of what I was.

My wounds from my mother were fading, but I had the luxury of working things out with her.

Ezra didn't.

Eva had been shattered when she made her choice that tragic day. If someone else had been with her after she learned the truth, would they have supported her to work through it? Would Ezra not have been left alone with a man who took his guilt and his grief and twisted it into a blade he wielded at the world?

A man who was trying with what little time he had left to fix the devastation he'd wrought. I sighed. It wasn't for me to say this was a matter of too little, too late.

Suddenly, Ezra threw his glass against the wall. It shattered with a devastating sharpness, a punctuation to the heartbroken look on my boyfriend's face.

I reached for him again, but he stood up without looking at me.

"Leave us, please," he said.

"No way." I stood up and planted myself in his path. "You are not in the right frame of mind to make this decision, and it's not something you can undo."

"Mi cielo." The charming smile he unleashed on me was edged in darkness and desperation.

"This isn't closure and it isn't mercy," I said.

"She's right, mijo. You'll hate yourself for this," Natán said.

I propped my hands on my hips. "But I'll live with it, no problem? Why? Because I'm a half shedim?"

"Because if you don't, I will leak it to the Authority that Natán Cardoso is unprotected, and they will send someone else. Someone who won't show compassion when they end my life."

"You don't *deserve* compassion. And you certainly don't deserve it from me."

"That is true," Natán said. "But Ezra does. Please, Aviva. Do this for him. Help him put the past behind him once and for all. Tikkun olam."

That wasn't—I clenched my fists. Orthodox Judaism prohibited suicide, and for Natán to ask for it when he'd kept up his faith all these years as a vampire?

I closed my eyes. I was a firm believer in a person's right to die on their own terms, and with anyone else, even my own mother, I'd like to think I'd accede to their last wish, but this situation was too fraught with tragedy.

It was inconceivable that Ezra would look at me the same way. He might be grateful now, but one day, the loss would hit him, and he'd remember that I took his father from him.

I opened my eyes with a slow exhale. "I can't."

"Avi."

The stake Ezra held spoke of time and patience, whittled from a pale wood with such care that its natural grain had become part of the artistry. Delicate whorls spiraled up its length, each ring worked into the piece in such a way that it seemed almost liquid. The grip was lovingly worn to a subtle hollow that would nestle against the palm, while the tip sung with deadly precision.

It was beautiful in the way of things that had been reduced to their purest essence. A masterpiece intended for one thing and one thing only: death.

Ezra stepped forward. "We'll do it together."

I gnawed the inside of my cheek, studying every nuance of his expression. Had he displayed cautious hope or steely determination, I'd have refused, but there was only love in its most fundamental form.

His eyes held mine, steady and clear.

This wasn't him asking me to carry his burden or trying to shoulder it alone. We'd carry this weight the same way we carried everything else from now on: together, until the end.

I nodded and followed him to the bed.

Ezra took his dad's hand.

Natán attempted to close his fingers around Ezra's, but they wouldn't take hold. A tear streaked his cheek. "Perdóneme. Te amo, mijo."

"Te amo, Papá." Ezra said in a rough voice, his eyes damp. He kissed his father's forehead.

Natán hooked a shaking index finger around Ezra's pinky. "Thank you, Aviva. There's a bottle of twenty-five-year-old Glenfarclas in the living room. Give it to Michael for me, please?"

"I will." I tasted tears when I spoke.

He closed his eyes. "Then I am ready."

Ezra held the stake out, and I placed my hand above his on the grip. We lowered the tip to Natán's heart.

I managed to lock eyes with my boyfriend, despite him being a blurry lump right now.

We pushed the stake in. It really was exceptional craftsmanship. I'd ripped up pieces of paper with more effort.

The vampire gave a shuddery sigh and fell still.

Natán Cardoso was no more.

Ezra gazed down at his father for a long moment, our hands still on the stake. "Tell the Authority it's done," he said and walked out of the room.

Chapter 32

I didn't want Natán's death to fulfill some Authority mandate or get them on my side to make my shedim coming out easier. Ironic, since I'd spent my professional life being the perfect operative in order to achieve exactly that.

I'd held myself to impossible standards, true, yet they hadn't held themselves to a fraction of the same.

Natán, on the other hand, had been many less-than-complimentary things, but in his final moments, his authenticity earned Ezra's forgiveness.

He'd died on his terms; I would live on mine.

It was time for this Maccabee to go public about being a half shedim.

I retrieved the bottle of scotch whiskey and the drive containing Natán's final message, but before I ran down to meet the limo driver, I sent a text to everyone in my task force.

This was the right moment to undertake what I was about to do, and I'd have been disappointed if they didn't approve, but I'd respect it because it impacted them.

I tapped my foot impatiently, waiting for replies to come in.

Encouraging messages lit up my phone.

Buoyed, I opened my social media app and, taking a deep breath, flipped my profile from private back to public. I stared dully at the notifications number crawling ridiculously high, the incessant pinging battering against me.

Not in my most anxiety-soaked nightmares had I envisioned a scenario where I'd be sharing my truth in a world where so many people already had definite opinions about me for totally other reasons. I was supposed to hold my merit up against a clean slate for all to see and be judged on that, not who I was dating.

And after Ezra's heroics in Toronto, my name wasn't just recognized by Ezracurriculars anymore.

I'd been uneasy with people using my relationship as some kind of cred for their own agenda. Yet more people would see my post because I was suddenly (in)famous. Was it okay to exploit that currency to achieve my own agenda: acceptance?

I held my screen up to my face and hit record.

"Hi." I spoke directly into the camera. "My name is Aviva Fleischer. I'm a level three Maccabee operative. Some of you know me as Ezra Cardoso's girlfriend, and that reality way outstrips any rumor." I winked. "More importantly, I'm also…" I morphed my human facial features to shedim. "A half shedim. I spent my life hiding that side of myself, but I'm really proud of the difference I've made as an operative, and I'm done feeling ashamed."

I boosted the screen up a smidge.

"In eleven hours from now, operatives all around the world are going to defeat the Luce based on a strategy that I came up with. We've worked hard as a team to nail down our approach, but it would mean a lot, whether you are a half shedim, Eishei Kodesh, Trad, or vampire, to come out and support us."

I reverted to my human features.

"I can't promise that everyone will welcome half shedim, but there will be more people than you ever dared dream." I nodded. "Earth is our home, and we all want what's best for it. We came through the Endless Night, now let's usher in a new dawn, one where we are stronger together."

I had a moment of hesitation before I posted it, but when it was done, years of my carefully erected shields crumbled to dust. It was like diving into deep water: an initial shock of vulnerability, followed by a rush of wild freedom.

My hands were trembling slightly as I put away my phone, but my breath came easier than it had in years.

Ezra and I stuck to each other's sides for the entire return flight, curled on the couch (so much better than an economy seat).

He rested his chin on the top of my head. "I lived with this identity for so long and now it's gone."

"The Crimson Prince?"

"His son."

"You're still his son."

He shook his head. "Right now, I can't see beyond his death to whatever else I am."

Ezra's grief had to fade from a raw abscess to a scar whose story he could remember without pain. Thinking about the future wouldn't help him.

"Take whatever time you need. I'll be by your side while you do." I smiled up at him. "Tell me about your parents."

His memories came haltingly at first, but then more freely.

Some of them were incredibly funny, like the time Natán took Ezra along on his first territory negotiation with an Eishei Kodesh Mafia to practice all the classic intimidation techniques he'd been taught.

Except his dad had just gotten his first smartphone and it kept buzzing. Ezra's menacing behavior was getting more and more overt in overcompensation for Natán getting more and more flustered trying to silence the notifications.

"Natán finally smashed the phone in rage, totally blowing any upper hand we had. So, I lapsed into a bad Dracula accent and threatened to suck their blood."

I howled with laughter. "What did Natán do?"

"Shot them."

"Oh my God! Your life was so fucked up. What have I gotten myself into?"

"Okay, demon girl. Settle down." He swatted me with a pillow. "Now that we've killed my father, what should we do for our next date? I'm thinking a couple's pottery class."

"Don't get ahead of yourself. Delacroix might still be roaming free."

"Imagine if he's king of the demon realm now." Ezra made a "yikes" face.

"Too hard to get to him? Need to think of a different third date?" I said.

"No, we're saving that for a special occasion. Our five-year anniversary."

"The birth of our first child. Oh no, wait, we'll celebrate that by engraving their name on the stake that murdered their abuelo."

"Do you want kids?" Ezra asked seriously.

"One day. Do you?"

"So long as our dhampir shedim bundle of joy has my temperament."

I screwed up my face. "Can I change my answer?"

"No." He looked at his phone. "By my calculations there's six hours left on this flight, and you need to sleep."

"Right. When we get back, I'll have to hit the ground running with the backburn."

Ezra snuggled up behind me.

"Are you really okay?" I said.

"More than I could have ever hoped. Thank you, mi cielo."

"Just another handy service provided by blood-bonded mates." I twisted around and kissed him. "I love you."

Once the plane had landed and taxied to a complete stop in Vancouver, I turned on my phone—and nearly dropped it at the explosive flurry of bings.

My post had gone viral. #StrongerTogether and #New-Dawn were trending across all social media platforms. To be fair, so was #NotMyMaccabee along with a few other less complimentary hashtags, but I didn't see any death threats. Yet.

I waded through dozens of texts to the ones that mattered.

Junior: *Go big or go home.* It was accompanied by a screenshot of her in all her shedim glory that she'd posted to her own profiles. Duck face was impressive on a demon.

Sachie, Darsh, and Silas were obviously supportive, though Gemma groused that arranging security to handle the crowds they expected was proving to be a bitch.

The Authority was oddly and troublingly silent. As was Michael. After I'd posted my video, I'd let her and Zhengyu know about Natán, but neither had commented. Not on his "murder" and not about my coming-out video.

I hadn't expected the Powers that Be to publicly embrace me (okay, yes, I absolutely had), but where was my mother's reaction? She'd been so supportive of me coming out to my colleagues when the demons attacked HQ that it hadn't crossed my mind that this would be different.

I rode into town with my stomach in knots.

What struck me most on the drive from the airport

wasn't what the Luce had changed, but what was missing: no weeds pushed through cracks in the sidewalks, no moss softened the edges of drainage ditches, and no lichen roughened the concrete barriers. The Luce had deemed these "imperfect" symbioses unnecessary, leaving behind a landscape stripped of its smallest inhabitants.

In their place, every surface gleamed with an unnatural polish, as if the world had been laminated. Even the seams between pavement slabs had been sealed into perfect, unbroken lines.

"The Ezracurriculars are mobilizing," Ezra said, scrolling on his phone. "They're arranging meet-ups at the rift site and are making special friendship bracelets to welcome half shedim."

I blinked rapidly. Damn it, I had to get hold of my emotions before I went into the final showdown with the Luce. "Did you put them up to it?"

"I'd love to take credit for this, but no. It turns out that Stasia is a half shedim."

"The president of your fan club? Did you know?"

He shook his head. "But she put all the Aviva Fleischer dots together: Maccabee, my girlfriend, half-shedim, and she's freaking out."

When I was growing up, it would have meant the world to me to have a half shedim, especially a female one, show that they were an accepted part of a team.

That they could be loved by the hot guy.

I nudged Ezra. "Arrange for me to meet Stasia when this is all over."

"Absolutely not. She's an excellent fan club president and I'm not losing her to you."

I patted his cheek. "You're totally losing her to me. My club won't have a stupid name."

"Ezracurriculars is exceedingly clever."

I blinked at him. "Wow. You chose it, didn't you?"

"Because it's brilliantly clever," he reiterated haughtily.

"No. The Cherry Bombs is brilliantly clever. Fiendishly clever even." My Brimstone Baroness deserved commemorating. "We'll have T-shirts. Yours don't, but my fans deserve superior merch opportunities."

"I can have T-shirts."

"Don't be desperate. It's unseemly."

The world might end tomorrow, but tonight we were two idiots arguing about fan clubs, and I wouldn't trade this moment for anything. Not even superior merch opportunities.

Chapter 33

The second we got back to HQ, I hit Michael's office to drop off the bottle and the drive with Natán's final message, but she wasn't there. I left them with Louis, who told me she was already at the laundromat, setting up equipment.

Gemma texted to say they were outside waiting to head out. I'd expected others to join us, but not the three-quarters of the Vancouver chapter who were present. The heightened anticipation reminded me of the time I'd done the Polar Bear swim, with everyone chanting and pumping themselves up for the icy plunge to come.

We piled into the buses, where the excited murmurs back at HQ dissolved into a heavy silence, thick with unspoken thoughts.

I stepped off the bus and stared up at the Vancouver sky churning with unnatural clouds, their edges burnished by the winter sun.

Sachie appeared at my shoulder, nodding at the perimeter that had been set up at the edges of the laundromat property. "Impressive turnout."

Thousands of onlookers were gathered behind the barriers. Some waved banners with stylized flames, their faces painted in a rainbow of red, orange, white, yellow, and blue.

Others…weren't so friendly.

"Kill the unholy spawn!"

"Magicians belong in Hell!"

I unclenched my jaw.

Any half shedim in the crowed weren't outing themselves, not that I blamed them. I pressed the heel of my hand against the sting in my chest. I'd promised them a warm welcome.

A commotion drew my attention. Darsh and Silas had arrived.

They looked like corpses caught mid-crumble, their skin shrunken and papery, stretched too thin over jutting bones. Their hair was brittle and their eyes were clouded. Even their clothes sagged on their gaunt frames, as if mourning the men they used to be.

Ezra stood behind them, his fingers twitching, but he gave them space.

Claws burst out on my left hand. *Steady, Fleischer.* I shoved them back to fingers.

"You couldn't stay somewhere warm and comfortable, enjoying about a million boosted blood packs, could you? You had to be on the front lines." A muscle ticked in Sachie's jaw. "Did you at least bring folding chairs for your deteriorating asses?"

"I was going to wish you good luck," Darsh whispered, "but insulting my ass is a step too far. Good day, madam!" He jerkily turned around, but Sach hauled him into a hug.

I crashed it, pulling Silas and Ezra into the tight huddle.

"All units, check in," Joe called to us over the comms.

"That's our cue," I said, reluctantly disengaging.

Darsh's eyes flashed with his former fiery spirit. "Go be brilliant."

Ezra followed me.

"Is this where you tell me how much you love me?" I said.

"Why, do you intend to die?" He smacked me on the butt. "Save the world, Fleischer, and you'll get your 'I love you.'"

I wrinkled my nose. "Can I get that chocolate mousse from the Hell's buffet that everyone raved about?"

He gasped, one hand pressed to his chest.

"Hey, it was pretty mediocre the last time and I want the full experience." I rose up on tiptoe, kissed him hard, and strode off.

Michael fell into step beside me, dressed in uncharacteristic black jeans under a black coat. She glanced back at Silas and Darsh.

"Please don't say anything," I said. "I'll start crying, and I really don't want to do that because I think my fan club is watching."

"Silly girl," she said fondly. "I wanted to tell you how incredibly proud of you I am."

"My backburn idea was pretty inspired but don't jinx us. Hold off till we win."

"Not that. Any regrets about coming out?"

"Ah. None. Has the Authority…?"

She shook her head. "Natán… Are you okay?"

I shrugged. "There's a bottle of Glenfarclas on your desk."

My mother closed her eyes briefly, a flicker of pain tightening her features before she forced it away. When she opened them again, her expression was composed, but the lingering tension in her jaw betrayed the effort it took to mask her sorrow.

One by one, teams reported ready status: New York, London, Seoul, Singapore, and dozens of other locations.

My fellow task force operatives had worked through the past day and half adjusting factors from our failed first attempt, but I still wasn't sure if we'd gotten everything right. The calculations were theoretical at best, apocalyptic at worst. But we were out of options.

Out of time.

Ha-joon's voice crackled through. "Air pressure readings are optimal. We won't get better conditions than this. Monserrat, do you agree?"

"Yes," she said.

I walked over to the multiple monitors displaying the rift sites, making tiny calibrations of where dead center was. "Rift teams are in position and good to go. Secondary locations?"

"Also a go." Damali, an operative in Tanzania, had been coordinating the task force members stationed where there were no rifts yet were crucial to propagating our magic wildfire globally.

"Orange Flames, you're up," Ha-Joon ordered.

Monserrat oversaw the vigilant orchestration to keep conditions steady around the globe, lowering humidity and stabilizing the atmosphere.

The shift in the air as temperature manipulators began their work was immediate.

"B units deploy the net," Eduardo said. He consulted with the other Yellow Flames, including Michael, adjusting the secondary channels and issuing orders to the operatives not at the rift sites. "They're holding. We have our connection with the main pathways."

One small hurdle down.

"Count of three," Marilyn said over the comms. "Red Flames, add your magic gently. We don't want to go scorched earth."

Dozens of streams of fire shot into the Vancouver rift.

The crowd oohed, and I visualized the same scene playing out all around the world.

White Flames coaxed the combined magic to elevated levels.

I tapped my blue flame/shedim senses into the collapsed rift here.

The threads of power aligned perfectly. Every temperature gradient, every subtle shift in air pressure was exactly where we needed it, and with the addition of the White Flames' amplifications, our magic sang. Literally sang, a pure note that made my chest vibrate.

"Keep it up, people!" Sweat beaded on Sachie's temples. She'd been assigned to the Orange Flame unit keeping winds down.

Around us, other operatives were grinning, their faces glowing. Our magic was moving in perfect harmony, each flame supporting and amplifying the others.

That's when the Luce struck back.

It surged forward like a tsunami, but instead of trying to perfect everything in its path, it methodically identified and targeted our weaknesses.

"It's learning!" Sachie shouted through chattering teeth. Frost coated her skin. "Using our own powers against us!"

It wasn't just here in Vancouver either; the monitors showed dozens of operatives succumbing to the attack. Two Yellow Flames in Palo Alto collapsed as magic backlashed through their bodies.

I dove to drag a fallen White Flame to safety.

A wave of Blue Flames, including Ha-Joon, fell clutching their heads as their sensitivity to magic was amplified to unbearable levels. Even the crowd wasn't safe; onlookers screamed as the Luce tried to "perfect" them. Luckily, their bodies rejected the forced change, but the panic was spreading.

Some operatives were redeployed to assist Trad officers with crowd control.

I'd been plugged in when the Luce struck back but I wasn't affected. Musingly, I flexed my fingers.

Our backburn wasn't enough. Could I be? By actively deploying my demon magic instead of just using it to monitor the situation, could I tip things in our favor?

A bunch of Red Flames, including Marilyn, found their own fire turning inward, burning them from the inside out.

Ezra blurred forward and knocked her free, smothering her magic, but the screams over the comms from those not so lucky were seared into my soul.

"Let me add my shedim magic." Wind whipped my hair into my face, and I had to yell to be heard on the comms.

"Do it, Aviva!" Gemma said.

Bursting into full-shedim mode, I laid my hands on the ground where the rift existed and thrust my magic into it.

The Luce immediately surged toward me, eager to correct my demonic heritage. It had warped so much that my inherent genetic makeup was now perceived as a flaw.

My scales started disintegrating; I hurriedly disengaged.

My shedim form isn't my natural state, even though that magic is.

"Let's try this again." Fully human, I pressed my hands against the cool ground and slid into my synesthete vision, careful to maintain a perfect balance of my Eishei Kodesh and shedim powers.

The earth was awash in blue, testament to the hits Mother Nature had taken, but for the first time ever, I saw other colors. Forked black veins snaked through the blue, while our backburn manifested as a fat band made of red, orange, yellow, white, and blue stripes, dancing through the veins and the blue damage, burning them up.

There was no cause for celebration yet because jagged black magic lightning bolts slammed into the colorful band in rhythmic hits, fracturing it. It was like a beautiful song on a piano being drowned out by some obnoxious kid banging on a drum.

I was powerless to stop those lightning bolts, and I couldn't thread my combo of flame/shedim powers into the band, but I cocooned part of the Eishei Kodesh magic in a protective crimson blanket.

The next Luce strike hit my blanket and partially crumbled, but the backburn underneath that spot remained intact, allowing it to dissolve more of earth's damage and the forked veins in that section.

"Whatever you just did," Eduardo said next to me, "do it again. It relieved some of the pressure."

"We didn't feel anything different," a Brazilian operative said.

"I need more blankets."

Eduardo frowned at me. "Huh?"

I sprinted over to Michael, requesting one of her ear-piercing whistles. It took her three times before the crowd here stopped their jostling and cries.

They stared at me with scared eyes.

Jared Casey, Natán, Delacroix, Dmitri: the Four Asshats of the Apocalypse exploited fears and promised strength in their speeches and posturing. They kept us at each other's throats instead of bringing us all together to stand against the darkness.

That wasn't who I was. Or who I aspired to be.

I'd revealed my true nature to everyone: the good, the bad, and the monstrous. Now I was asking them to do the same, to embrace what they'd been taught to fear, to not only save the world, but change everyone's idea of us.

That required enormous trust and courage on all sides.

The fact was that magic had a price, and the world was paying.

But half shedim could end the debt.

It would be costly, but maybe sharing the price as our

half-shedim selves would transform the debt into something else.

Hope.

"If there are any half shedim here, I need you," I yelled. "Right now! I know you're scared, and historically it hasn't gone well to reveal yourself, but without our magic, the Luce will win. Stay in your natural human form, and when you join me, balance your shedim and Eishei Kodesh magic. Everyone spread the word." I instructed task force members on the comms to do the same.

There was a horrible stretched-out moment when the crowd didn't move, then people pulled out phones.

I raced back into position, once more careful to balance my magic when I added it to our backburn.

Lighter crimson threads from other half shedim around the world spooled through my blanket. I wove them into my own magic base, the paler strands darkening once they were pieced with mine.

The Luce struck again and shuddered, but while it faltered, it didn't stop.

Ezra helped an elderly Black woman onto her knees next to me. I added her strands to the blanket.

"Thank you for coming forward," I said. "I'm Aviva."

"It's my great pleasure." The woman smiled calmly at me through a face of wrinkles. "And I know who you are, lovely. Goodness, you've been on the news! I'm Eleanor."

"We need more half shedim," I said into the comms.

"Incoming," a bunch of operatives replied.

The sudden wash of light crimson in my synesthete vision made me sway.

"Steady," Ezra said, grabbing my shoulders.

I was locked into my synesthete sight, but no sunset had ever looked so glorious.

The entire world was laid out for me. Yes, there was the damage and Luce magic, but there was also the majesty of all the flame colors working in tandem, and, most wondrous of all, strands and strands of light crimson yarn.

I burst into a crazed cackling, working outward to connect them as fast as I could into what amounted to a giant sock wrapped around the Eishei Kodesh magic spanning the globe. Every subsequent section I connected to mine darkened in color.

"What's funny?" Michael asked.

"I'm knitting."

Ezra snorted with laughter.

Our cocoon blunted the Luce's strikes, giving the Eishei Kodesh magic a fighting chance.

"I have no clue what's happening," Joe said, "but this is making a difference."

"Operatives!" Ha-joon snapped in our ears. "Give it everything you've got!"

I hit a faraway section where the yarn felt bright and familiar. *Maud.*

The Luce redoubled its assault.

Sachie screamed. I snapped out of my synesthete vision in time to see her crash to her knees, her body contorting as the healing magic tried to force perfection through her.

Two healers, including Chaim, bolted to her side.

Darsh and Silas came closer, swaying like leaves in a breeze, wearing identical fierce expressions like they defied the Luce to come get them—or Sachie.

Ezra shot them a tormented look, but he didn't leave Eleanor's or my side.

I slid back into my synesthete vision. My magic knitting project had strands missing. I reached out, seeking those half shedim whose magic had just been there, but they were gone. Jagged dark light rushed in to fill the holes they'd left behind.

Tense directives flickered over our comms, but I didn't

have time to pay attention. What I was doing had worked. What had gone wrong?

Sweat burned my eyes from the effort of keeping the shedim magic wrapped around the magic flame band while it flowed, changing course with it as necessary.

The Luce was weakening, its forked veins disappearing, but the broken parts of the backburn weren't healing properly even with our operatives pouring everything they had into it.

We shedim could protect the Eishei Kodesh magic from further damage but we couldn't fix it.

Our wildfire was dying, and if we didn't make the blaze a bonfire again, the Luce would triumph.

"Ezra!" I blinked at him, shaking synesthetic afterimages out of my vision. "Pour every ounce of Prime healing magic through our blood bond."

He scanned my face. "Where are you hurt?"

"Not me. The planet. Could using each other as conduits save it?"

"Maybe? But Avi, I—I don't know what that will do to you." The fear in his eyes made my stomach twist.

"Do nothing and it's game over," I said quietly. "I have no intention of dying. Not before I get that chocolate mousse."

His laughter was a broken hollow sound, but he placed his hands over my heart. "Ready?"

I looked around my beloved city at my friends and family and strangers who'd come together. This might be my last glimpse of them.

"Ready," I said.

The moment Ezra's magic surged through our blood bond, my entire body ignited with sensation. It wasn't pain. It was power, raw and electric, racing through every cell. My skin buzzed as if a million tiny lightning bolts danced across it, and the crimson glow that emanated from me was so intense that those nearby shielded their eyes. My hair stood on end.

I gasped as magic cascaded through me and into the earth. Each heartbeat sent another pulse through the crimson threads I'd knitted, transforming them from protective covering to a healing essence that mended the fractured Eishei Kodesh band wherever they touched.

I was everywhere and nowhere, stretched across continents yet anchored by Ezra's hands on my heart.

The Luce couldn't keep up. It was like trying to solve an equation that kept changing its variables.

Weeds sprouted from cracks in the sidewalk and a sparrow's trill broke the unnatural silence, followed by another, then another, as though nature itself was celebrating its return.

An awestruck gasp rippled through the crowd.

Light exploded out of the ground.

"The rift is back!" someone cried.

Its harsh light had mellowed into a soft gold glow, like a sunset, while the unnatural color in the sky faded, returning to a cloudless blue.

My hands were the needles, our shedim and Eishei Kodesh powers the fabric, and Ezra's magic the special sauce pulling it all together.

Together we'd knitted our broken world whole again.

Reports poured in from around the world over the comms. The Luce was gone, vampires had been restored to good health, and the earth was once more perfectly imperfect.

We broke into deafening cheers with lots of high fives and hugs.

Ezra grabbed me. His lips crashed against mine with a fierce joy that stole my breath, his hands steady and strong as they pulled me against him. The kiss deepened, wild and exultant, a celebration of life surging between us as powerful as the magic we'd wielded. "I love you."

"I love you with all my heart, but Zee?"

"Yeah."

"I never want to knit anything again."

He threw back his head and laughed. "I'm happy to take on all the knitting in our relationship forever, mi cielo."

Eleanor broke away from the knot of operatives hugging and cheering her to pat my cheek. "You've made an old woman very happy."

I angled my body to protect her from the spray of champagne.

"Maybe we could have lunch sometime?" I rolled out my neck. "It would be nice to connect with other half shedim."

As we exchanged numbers, a younger Black woman joined us. "Gran, you're a superhero!"

"Aviva, this is my granddaughter, Lisa," Eleanor said. "Seeing as I helped save the world, I deserve to spend the afternoon at the casino."

"Yeah, okay." Lisa smiled fondly at her grandmother. "You card sharp."

"Poker?" I grinned. "You should meet my sister. She's a multiple world champion."

"That sounds fun. Call me soon." Eleanor and Lisa said goodbye and walked off.

"You done good, Avi." Silas one-arm hugged me. He and Darsh were once more the picture of vampiric vitality.

"Look at you two, fresh as a newborn's ass," I said.

Darsh grimaced. "We'll work on your metaphors, but thank heavens I don't have to adjust my skin routine anymore. It was bankrupting me."

We watched Ezra and Silas nattering excitedly to each other about how they should go rock climbing to celebrate.

"Hanging off a cliff by your fingertips doesn't say 'we

just saved the world from magical annihilation,'" Darsh grumbled. "Why can't they do spa days like normal people?"

"We don't want them at our spa days, babe," I said. "That would not be restful."

"Good point."

Gemma accompanied me to Sachie and Michael. "If you'd suggested using shedim magic that way in the original briefing, we would have said it was impossible."

"Sometimes," I said, voice rough with exhaustion, "impossible is exactly what we need."

Chapter 34

I phoned Maud, her squealed "We are so badass" the most beautiful sound in the world.

"We are rather," I laughed. "Now that this is over, what do you think about some quality sister time? I'd love to see Hong Kong."

"We're going to eat our way through the city."

"Does 'we' include Adrian?" I teased.

"Absolutely not."

"Come on. I only have a list of a hundred and seven questions prepared to make sure he's worthy of my little sister."

"Trip canceled."

"This is going to be so much fun." I told her that I'd figure out my vacation time but that it was a date.

"Freak!" The man's taunt was accompanied by a shove. He had a good half foot and sixty pounds of muscle on me. "Go back to whatever demon hole you crawled out of."

Out of the corner of my eye, I saw Ezra tense, but he didn't move.

"It's actually a lovely condo in the west end," I said. "But yes, it's been a long day, and I'd like to get home."

I pushed past him. I was never going to get the entire world on my side and that was okay. I had the ones who mattered.

"Aviva?" Jordy Green timidly stepped into my path, not quite meeting my eyes. He shifted from one foot to the other like he'd been here a while, gathering up the courage to talk to me. His beard was growing back in, but he'd lost weight, and there were circles under his eyes. "I came today to find you and say I'm sorry. I fucked up our friendship. Could we try again?"

He'd been manipulated by Rukhsana, promised by the demon that she could make him an infernal. I hadn't been as close to Rukhsana as he was and yet her betrayal had devastated me.

Luckily for him, today was a day of resets.

"You're buying the first donut," I said. "And it better be the good stuff."

He crossed his heart. "Scout's honor."

"Are you doing okay?"

He shrugged. "Some days are better, some worse, but your mom found me a good therapist and that's helping."

Sachie called my name, and with the promise of being in touch soon, I hurried over to one of the buses to go back to HQ.

Champagne flowed on the ride, both celebratory toasts and for our dead and wounded operatives around the world. Vancouver hadn't lost anyone, thankfully, but a couple Red Flames were in critical condition.

Marilyn raised a glass to me, which was heartily supported by everyone except for Gemma, who rolled her eyes.

"You're going to be insufferable now," she said.

I grinned. "Only to you."

We may have reset the world, but it was nice to know that some things never changed.

The next few days were a whirlwind. Olivier was released from the hospital and Sachie invited him to recuperate at our place for a few days.

I didn't have a problem with that, but Ezra was staying with us, and I wasn't sure how comfortable Olivier would be around vampires right now.

If it was hard for him, he didn't show it, much to his credit. Especially when Darsh and Silas showed up to have a commemorative drink for Natán.

Michael cracked open the Glenfarclas with Keira, who'd met Natán and Eva a few times way back when. To be clear, my mother had done more than crack it open; she'd actually taken a day off to recover from her hangover, though that gossip didn't circulate, as no level threes wanted street duty in the cold.

The news that did send shock waves through the Maccabees was the resignation of the entire Authority Council. Michael's place on it was assured.

I'd miss having my mom as the director here, but I was thrilled that she'd steward our organization from this point on.

Between the Luce and the Endless Night, earth had lost a lot of its vampire population, though Nasir wasn't the only one who came back once the rifts to Babel were stable once more.

Michael publicly declared she'd be establishing a think tank with leaders and innovators in the Trad, Eishei Kodesh, and vampire communities to forge a bright path forward for us all. It garnered enough curiosity, even with the vamps, that many opened discussions with her about the role they could play.

There was no discussion for my boyfriend. The second Ezra learned about it, he offered his services. Michael made him chairman.

When I told Ezra how proud I was of him, he confided

that I'd inspired him to share more of his true self with the world.

I jokingly suggested launching a yarn line.

His eyes lit up. "Now who'd have superior merch? The Knitting Knight," he mused. "Yarn King? Never mind, I'll come up with something brilliant."

The world would lose its collective mind seeing Hot Prime Vampire with knitting needles in his elegant hands. Social media would implode with thirst posts about tension techniques. God, what had I done?

"You've been weighted down with nicknames for so long," I said insistently. "Do you really need another one?"

"Every nickname I've had was given to me by someone else. It would be fun to choose one for myself." He smiled. "Besides, it's not about that. It's about taking a page from my girlfriend's book and living authentically. I'm a Prime who knits, and I'd like to share that with other vampires or anyone who feels they have to keep their favorite hobbies a secret. And it'll be a fun way to destress from the think tank." His eyes widened. "What do you think about Count Cashmere?"

"I think you need to keep working on the branding, but I love that you want to inspire people to live their passion."

Spook Squad had a long meeting when Nasir got back, after which Silas announced he'd be remaining here as a permanent member of the team.

Surprisingly, even the Brink respawned into all its fucked-up glory, supe-vultures and all.

It would be some time before I was ready to face that wasteland again. Ezra planned to go back and forth between Babel and Vancouver, but I had no plans to visit him in the megacity. I had Hong Kong to explore with my sister and that was quite enough excitement for me.

While the Brink was back, the Copper Hell was gone.

The yacht had vanished, and Ezra couldn't open portals anymore—especially not any to the demon realm.

Maud hadn't heard from our father either.

I sat with my conflicted feelings around his disappearance for a few days. My life would involve much less torture and mind games without him around, but he had his moments with his funny underwater photography and dry sense of humor.

Granted they were few and far between, but still.

I went on a lot of runs during this time.

Ezra purchased running clothes so he could come with me. Generally, we set out along the seawall headed for the forest trails in Stanley Park: the same routes I'd taken to hunt shedim for Cherry.

Tonight, the air was crisp off the water, with a typical January mist hanging over the beaches. Our footsteps echoed on the concrete path until we hit the trails, where the towering cedars sheltered us from the worst of the damp. The forest was quiet except for my breathing and the soft thud of running shoes on dirt.

Finally having a running partner felt good, but having it be Ezra put a bounce in my stride. I couldn't help smiling as I glanced over at him in his new gear, both of us falling into an easy rhythm together.

Every time we rounded a corner and I got to show him another favorite spot, I experienced a little bubble of joy. Even the familiar path was better with him beside me.

Two nights before I was due to leave for Hong Kong, Ezra accompanied me to the lookout on Burnaby Mountain. We found a bench overlooking my beautiful city and poured glasses of excellent Merlot.

"To Daphne." I held the glass up. "I'm sorry that we never got to this drink together and that I didn't come back and visit you after we first met." I looked up at the stars twinkling in the cold night. "It sucks that you had to make a deal with my father to escape your situation and die in such a violent way, but I hope you're resting in peace and happy."

Ezra clinked his glass to mine. "To Daphne."

Finally, I was down to the last thing to cross off my list before my departure: attend Orly's "We Saved the World and All We Got Was This Lousy Party" bash here in Vancouver.

Her good friend, Astriid, the single-monikered vampire singing sensation, was performing in town, and Orly had planned the party so the location worked for her friend's attendance.

Though I was told this in the strictest confidence.

Hilariously, Orly told both Ezra and Darsh separately that the reason for holding the bash here in Vancouver was because that's where they were.

Sachie and I had been running around all day trying to find outfits for the Doomsday Black Tie dress code. She'd gone to pick up a medieval knight's costume with armored shoulder pads while I went home to get dressed in a black ballgown with torn ruffles and tiny crystals sewn into the bodice that I wore with combat boots and a utility belt.

"What jewelry do I accessorize this with?" I said, walking into the living room.

Ezra and Olivier, both dressed in intentionally distressed tuxes, looked up from their game of Scrabble and shrugged.

"Very helpful, boys," I snarked. "Thank you."

"You look like paradise at the end of the world," Ezra said.

I blew a raspberry. "Too little, too late."

Sachie burst through the door. She had a large shopping bag in one hand and a much smaller box in the other. "This came for you."

The return address on the box was burned off.

I grabbed a utility knife from the junk drawer in the kitchen, slit open a cardboard flap, and started laughing.

"What is it?" Ezra entered, followed by Sachie and Olivier.

I shook out the red Flaming Flapjacks T-shirt with the dancing pancake logo on it. "There's something else here." I dug through the tissue paper and pulled out a tiara bejeweled in the finest paste gems. "I guess he really did it. Daddy Dearest is king of the demons again."

Ezra grimaced. "Does that mean he's still in our lives?"

I twisted the tiara to catch the light, sending prisms along the wall. "Maybe this fake crown is his way of saying goodbye."

"Uh, Avi?" Olivier leaned in, eyeing it. "I don't think this is fake. Those diamonds look real. So do the rubies."

Ezra caught it before it hit the ground in my shock. "He's right. These are real."

"What was Delacroix thinking?" I said. "I can't wear a small fortune's worth of jewels on my head."

"Sure you can." Sachie propped it in my hair. "Very pretty."

"I'll need bodyguards."

"Please," she scoffed. "If anyone gets the jump on you, go demon on their asses."

I examined it in my bathroom mirror, turning my head from side to side to make the light catch the gems.

The tiara really was very pretty. And the perfect accessory for tonight's party. I *was* royalty, after all.

I went into the living room to wait with Olivier and Ezra for Sachie to get ready.

"You done yet?" Olivier called out.

A soft clanging preceded Sach into the living room. She'd enhanced her knight costume with a bandolier of daggers.

"Are those real?" Ezra said.

She shot him a contemptuous look. "Are Aviva's jewels real?"

He held up his hands. "I did not mean to doubt you."

"You found the blade with the red handle," I said. "Where was it?"

"The cactus planter."

"That thing needs to die," Olivier said ominously. "I swear it fires needles."

Sach nodded. "You've got to give it a wide berth."

We headed over to Darsh's (and now Silas's) place for some pregaming. The door was unlocked.

Darsh called out for us to assemble in the living room, then he sent Silas out as if down a runway, to the strains of "I'm Too Sexy."

Silas stomped into the room in time to the beat, his cheeks bright red.

The rest of us whistled and cheered at his duster that was more burn marks than leather, chain mail shirt, and bolo tie with a bloodred stone. His Stetson had been stripped down and reconstructed with leather strips and brass tacks, matching the brass toes on his cowboy boots.

Darsh appeared in the doorway, draped against the wood frame like liquid sex. He wore a skintight black tactical jumpsuit adorned with asymmetrical pieces of plastic riot gear. A few panels of the jumpsuit had been cut out and replaced with delicate black lace.

Tossing his hair off his shoulders, he strutted around the room, posing poutily in front of each of us.

Silas got a twerk, which made his cheeks blaze.

Then it was our turns.

Ezra tried to refuse, but he was booed loudly and made to go first. Rolling his eyes, he stood up, immediately found the best light, and threw poses like adjusting his small spiked cuff links and running his fingers through his hair.

Silas peered at him. "Are you going through the moves you were taught for that Spanish *Vogue* cover?"

Ezra glared at him and sat down.

Olivier, as the new guy, was allowed to walk the runway with Sachie. He proved himself an excellent addition to our motley crew, throwing James Bond gun poses while Sachie brandished daggers. They ended by circling each other, then Olivier grabbed Sachie and dipped her in a hot kiss.

When they came up for air, Sachie had to threaten grievous bodily harm to shut us up.

I skipped around the room, holding the folds of my ballgown in one hand while presenting my other hand to be kissed by each person in turn.

"I approve of this version," Darsh said, bowing low to comply. "Now we drink!"

He'd prepared a signature cocktail for the evening (blood optional), like old times when Sach and I would come over before the three of us went clubbing.

They were served in World's Best Dad mugs. "In honor of Avi and Ezra, may I present the Father Issues Fizz?"

Everyone laughed, though I shot Darsh the finger, and Ezra good-naturedly grumbled, "Too soon, man."

Darsh handed out the mugs with the gallantry of a knight presenting sacred chalices to fellow members of the Round Table, each drink bestowed with a flourish that somehow managed to spill not a single drop.

Olivier cautiously sipped his. "What's in it?"

"Glad you asked," Darsh replied. "Bourbon, because that's a dad drink. A splash of bitter amaro for those unre-solved feelings—"

Sachie hooted a laugh.

I patted my tiara. "They'll resolve nicely into cold hard cash."

"And club soda," Darsh said. "For the fizz."

"Naturally," Silas said.

"I still can't believe I'm going to a party with Astriid," Olivier said. "You people move in different circles than I'm used to."

"We're just slumming on Ez's coattails." Silas licked a drop of crimson liquid off his lips. "You get used to it."

Two Father Issue Fizzes later, we decided we were fashionably late enough.

Sach, Darsh, and I gathered the others into a huddle and put our hands into the center. Silas, Ezra, and apparently Olivier had been told what comes next because they did the same.

"We! Are! Fabulous!" we chorused giddily.

Party time.

Chapter 35

A limo waited outside, courtesy of Ezra, along with chilled champagne for the humans and Golden Blood for the vamps.

I leaned against my boyfriend's shoulder, already in a hazy, dreamy state, letting the conversation and laughter wash over me. It was amazing how "normal" could feel revolutionary. How the simple act of being happy, being safe, and being in love could feel like the most rebellious thing I'd ever done.

After a smooth ride through the city, we arrived at the popular nightclub in the Granville entertainment district downtown that Orly had rented out.

We got out of the limo to flashing paparazzi cameras, and screams that made my ears ring.

I clutched Ezra's arm tight as we sailed up the red carpet. "If you take up even half these people on their marriage proposals or their…"

I squinted at a sign with "Your face is my emotional support animal" in fancy script over Ezra's face. That was loads better than the one next to it that said "Step on me with your perfect leather shoes."

"Or whatever that is," I said, "you're going to be very busy."

"They aren't all for me." He pointed out a few women in crimson wigs with short horns.

Wild. I blew them kisses and they screamed.

Ezra tugged me over to a young woman with bright pink ponytails bundled in a down jacket that was better suited to an Arctic expedition who stood at the front of the barricades. "Stasia! Why didn't you tell me you were coming?"

"She's not here for you," I said, and shook her hand. "It's excellent to finally meet you." I dug in my clutch for a friendship bracelet, which I handed to her. I'd cheated and had someone with actual skill bead "The Cherry Bombs" on it (superior merch, after all). "You are officially my first member."

"Stasia," Ezra growled playfully. "You better not be leaving me."

She jutted her chin up. "A Prime can't compare with a half shedim. Plus, I'm starting grad school in the fall and won't have time to manage the Ezracurriculars. The Cherry Bombs are just getting off the ground, so it won't be as much work."

"She means my fan club is premiere league and yours isn't," he mansplained helpfully.

"Give me two weeks," I fired back cheerfully. "Do you want to come in?"

Stasia shook her head. "Go have fun. I have friends to visit."

"Are you sticking around town for a few days?" Ezra said. "Can we have lunch?"

I nudged him. "After Stasia and I have ours. We're going to my favorite Italian restaurant."

Stasia grinned. "I've got time for both. Call me."

Security ushered us safely inside the venue. We headed

up the stairs to the second floor club that was decked out in honor of the theme.

The wall leading to the bar featured newspaper clippings from around the world with increasingly hysterical headlines. Magical Mayhem Martinis and Press Release Punch were available in honor of the night. There was even a photo booth with a table of props like fake pitchforks, fangs, and feather boas.

Darsh already had three draped around his neck while putting devil horns on Silas.

Colored lights pulsed in time to the playlist of songs about vampires, magic, and blood.

At the back was a huge buffet.

"It's catered by the Copper Hell's chefs," Ezra said. "Since you never got to properly try it."

I fisted his shirt. "The chocolate mousse?"

"Damn, I forgot to include that." He pried my hands off him with a wince. "Do I strike you as an idiot with a death wish?"

I was elbowing my way to the table before he finished speaking.

The mousse was whipped into perfect tiny peaks dusted with sea salt. I grabbed a spoon and dug in. The high-quality dark chocolate hit a slightly bitter note before melting into caramel sweetness.

I vacuumed down the dessert but stopped myself from reaching for a second, since I had yet to greet our hostess. "Can you pull strings and set some aside for me?"

"Abuse my power?"

"Absolutely."

He chuckled. "That can be arranged. Oh, I see Orly."

We hadn't had a chance to talk to her since her arrival last night, since she'd been overseeing all the final details of the party. Ezra was going to spend time with her and her family in London when I left for Hong Kong tomorrow.

Orly and I screamed when we saw each other, excitedly comparing outfits. The leather of her motorcycle racing suit was polished to a high shine. Its traditional protective padding was replaced with architectural panels of hammered metal that caught the light as she moved, but instead of racing logos, she'd etched kill counts.

Even her tiny dachshund, Schnitzel, was present and thematically attired in a black knit doggie sweater with a repeating red fang pattern and a hat that was a flat metal disc that tied with black ribbon under Schnitzel's chin.

She held the Daschund up to Ezra. "Kiss Uncle Ezzie for the sweater," she said in her Hebrew-accented English.

The dog lunged at Ezra, tongue out.

My boyfriend stumbled back with a grimace, almost taking out a server carrying a tray of drinks.

Orly planted a hand on her hip. "Are you dissing my baby's thank-you?"

"No?" Ezra said meekly, presenting his cheek to be licked. He almost hid his shudder.

"Beseder." Orly clapped her hands together. "I must greet other guests. Yalla, Ezzie, be ready for your dance."

His eyes bugged out of his head. "My what?"

"The dance."

"No fucking way, Orly. I let your dog touch me but that's too far."

"Chaim shelli, it's my party." She poked him in the chest.

"Chaim shelli," he parroted back to her and crossed his arms. "No."

A sly look crossed her face. "Aviva asked specially for it."

Aviva had no clue what she was talking about but was very much enjoying the direction of this conversation. "Oh yes. I want to see this dance more than anything."

"See if you get more chocolate mousse," Ezra said.

I held up my hands. "Sorry, Orly. I'm out."

"Not sababa," she scolded. "Now I have to go tell Astriid that Ezra won't dance with her, even though she took time out of her busy performing schedule to brush up on the moves."

"Hang on." I nudged my boyfriend. "This is a choreographed number with Astriid?"

"You just want to see me embarrassed," he accused Orly.

"Everyone will love it," she replied.

Hmm. An embarrassing dance with a pop superstar? I could give up dessert for that. I threw Ezra puppy dog eyes and a pout.

"All right, I'll do the stupid thing," he grumbled. "You two aren't spending any more time together."

"You're the best cousin in the world." Orly pecked his cheek.

"And you're a brat. I hate you."

"You'll thank me when it's over." She winked and sashayed off, crooning at Schnitzel.

"I'm going to need to be far less sober," he said.

"Then let's get you a drink. Tell me one thing," I said, leading him to the bar. "Is it anything like the Chicken Dance?"

He refused to give me any details.

We spent the next couple hours having a great time with our friends. Ezra had sworn me to secrecy about the dance, not because it had to be a surprise, but because he couldn't bear the idea of them ragging on him about it all night.

Astriid performed two numbers in her gravelly voice that sent the crowd into a tizzy of singing and frenetic dancing. She'd foregone the apocalypse chic memo for a sparkly silver mini dress with strappy sandals embedded with crystals.

I touched my tiara. Maybe they weren't crystals.

When the applause for the second song died down and she'd taken a bow, she stepped to the mic once more and grinned at Ezra. "Hey, Prime Playboy, get your ass up here."

He sighed theatrically, then took the stairs to the stage two at a time.

Silas cough-gasped. "He's doing the dance?"

"What dance?" Darsh demanded.

"It's that bad?" I fanned myself with a napkin, wondering if it was too late to stop this. Funny embarrassing was one thing, but "this will kill me ever seeing him in a sexy light again" embarrassing was quite another.

"It's something all right," Silas said. "They usually only break it out when they're drunk."

Sachie cackled.

"What's so funny?" Olivier said, joining us with the waters he'd fetched for Sachie and me.

"Ezra is going to do some embarrassing dance," she said, taking a glass.

Olivier handed me the other water. "Like the Macarena?"

"Not exactly," Silas said.

On stage, Ezra took off his tux jacket and draped it over a stool.

The opening notes of Flo Rida's "Low" came on.

Astriid took Ezra's hand, appearing to be counting them in. They did this fast side-to-side step, with Ezra pretty much bobbing up and down while he moved. He was just off the beat, the pop star still counting out loud for him.

People around me had the same "WTF" expression as I did, though Orly was howling with laughter.

I clutched my water glass, wondering if I could help Ezra drown in it. Or drown myself.

On the first chorus, Ezra spun Astriid out, then back in. They collided with a visible *thunk*.

Everyone laughed.

I darted a nervous glance at Silas, who rolled his eyes.

Astriid threw her hands up in annoyance and started to walk off, but Ezra grabbed her wrist.

"Put us out of this misery," Darsh called.

Ezra danced up close to her, rolling his hips in time with the song.

I blinked.

He grooved down her body, getting lower and lower as Astriid writhed against him.

I pressed the cool glass to my forehead.

Orly watched me with a smirk.

Ezra's moves rippled through his whole body, each cant of his hips flowing up through his chest and shoulders like a wave. When Astriid draped herself backward over his arm, his free hand traced a slow path from her throat down to her hip, which was both respectful and absolutely filthy at the same time.

The bass synced with my heartbeat, and I couldn't tear my eyes away from how his body caught every accent in the music.

"You lucky girl," Darsh said.

I made a strangled noise in response.

"Silas…" Darsh purred.

"I'm not dancing like that. Ever. And before you complain, it's not like you'd go square dancing."

"I would totally go square dancing!" Darsh squealed.

Silas blinked at him.

"I'm thinking rhinestone-studded couples' shirts and assless chaps." Darsh arced his hands like a rainbow.

"On second thought," Silas began weakly.

"You're a genius." Darsh kissed his cheek. "Now hush and watch the dance."

Ezra led Astriid through a smooth spin that ended with her pressed against him, his hands splayed across her ribs as they moved perfectly in sync. There was something incredibly hot about watching him dance with someone who knew what they were doing, the way they played off each other's energy, and how every touch looked both calculated and completely natural.

My glass was definitely going to leave a bruise on my forehead, but the cool press of it was the only thing keeping me from dragging him off the stage right now.

Ezra hooked his thumb through one of Astriid's belt loops, using it as an anchor point while they swayed with her back against his chest.

He slid his hand down her thigh as they dropped low together.

"Strong core," Sachie said.

"Yeah," Olivier teased. "That's my takeaway too."

Ezra and Astriid ground upward in this slow, controlled rise that was pure sin. She spun and unknotted his bow tie, pulling him to her by its ends.

I was definitely overheating.

Silas nudged me, reminding me to actually drink some water.

But then Ezra did this thing where he jerked his shoulders while his hips moved in the opposite direction, each motion hitting a different accent in the music, and I forgot how to swallow.

Where had he learned moves like that?

"You don't just break something like that out in public," I said.

Darsh took my glass away and flicked drops of water on himself. "Yes, Daddy should only ever dance that way in front of a private audience."

Silas gagged.

Darsh snaked his arm around his boyfriend's waist. "You know I only love you, right, Cowpoke?"

Sach and I shot gaping stares at the two of them. Had we just witnessed A DECLARATION?!

"Yeah, Rapunzel," Silas said. "I know."

Darsh waved a hand at us. "Faces forward. We are not the show."

All around us, people had broken into their own dirty dancing, eyes still on the performers, but I was rooted to the spot.

The music built to its climax, and Ezra slid his hands down to Astriid's hips, guiding her into a slow body roll that was somehow even more explicit than before. For their finale, they sank into a controlled crouch, bodies pressed together, then snapped up into perfect stillness as the last beat hit.

The room erupted in cheers and wolf whistles. Astriid gave an exaggerated bow while Ezra stood there looking pleased with himself. When he caught my eye, his expression shifted to something darker, more intimate.

I set my glass down on a table with maybe too much force.

Orly's delighted hoot followed me as I crossed to the stage to meet him.

He jogged down the stairs. "Did you like it?"

I hauled him close and kissed him with everything I was worth.

"That's a yes, then?" he said when we broke apart.

Orly walked by and boffed him across the head. "You're both welcome," she trilled.

I laughed and rested my forehead to my boyfriend's chest. "You've been keeping moves from me, Prime Playboy."

"A vampire's got to have some secrets," he said primly.

"Luckily I've got two or three hundred years to worm them out of you," I said.

"Lucky indeed."

Ezra kissed me again, soft and lazy, like we had all the time in the world.

"Conventional" wasn't exactly the word for a half demon and a vampire who'd survived murders, apocalyptic rituals, and enough supernatural smackdowns to fill a highlight reel.

As I'd learned, magic always demanded its price, whether you were ready to pay or not. Sometimes all you could do was hope what you got in return was worth it.

These days, I didn't have to hide what I was or fear what I could do, and through it all, Ezra and I had found our way back to each other.

I smiled against his lips as the bass thrummed through us. Looking back on my journey—the losses, the hard choices—I wouldn't change a thing. Some prices were worth paying, some debts worth owing, if they led you exactly where you needed to be.

And finally, completely, I was.

THANK you for reading THE DEMON'S DUE.

I hope you had a blast with Aviva and the gang. Why not catch up on any of my other completed series you might have missed?

You can buy exclusive discounted bundles of them direct from me at Deborah Wilde Books: https://deborah wildebooks.com/collections/bonus-collections

---

About the Author

Deborah Wilde is a global wanderer and hopeless romantic. After twelve years as a screenwriter, she was also a total cynic with a broken edit button, so, she jumped ship, started writing funny, sexy, urban fantasy and paranormal women's fiction novels, and never looked back.

She loves writing smart, flawed, wisecracking women who can solve a mystery, kick supernatural butt, banter with hot men, and still make time for their best female friend, because those were the women she grew up around and admired. Granted, her grandmother never had to kill a demon at her weekly friend lunches, but Deborah is pretty sure she could have.

Smart (ass) heroines. Epic magic. Red-hot romance.

www.deborahwilde.com

9 781999 888542